To Beth,

Many thanks for a

I really hope

GAWAIN

Best Wishes,

J M [signature]

GAWAIN

A novel
by

JP HARKER

Adelaide Books
New York / Lisbon
2021

GAWAIN

A novel

By JP Harker

Published by Adelaide Books, New York / Lisbon
adelaidebooks.org

Editor-in-Chief
Stevan V. Nikolic

For any information, please address Adelaide Books
at info@adelaidebooks.org

or write to:

Adelaide Books
244 Fifth Ave. Suite D27
New York, NY, 10001

ISBN: 978-1-955196-26-0

Printed in the United States of America

Dedicated to all my beta readers, for putting up with my endless pestering

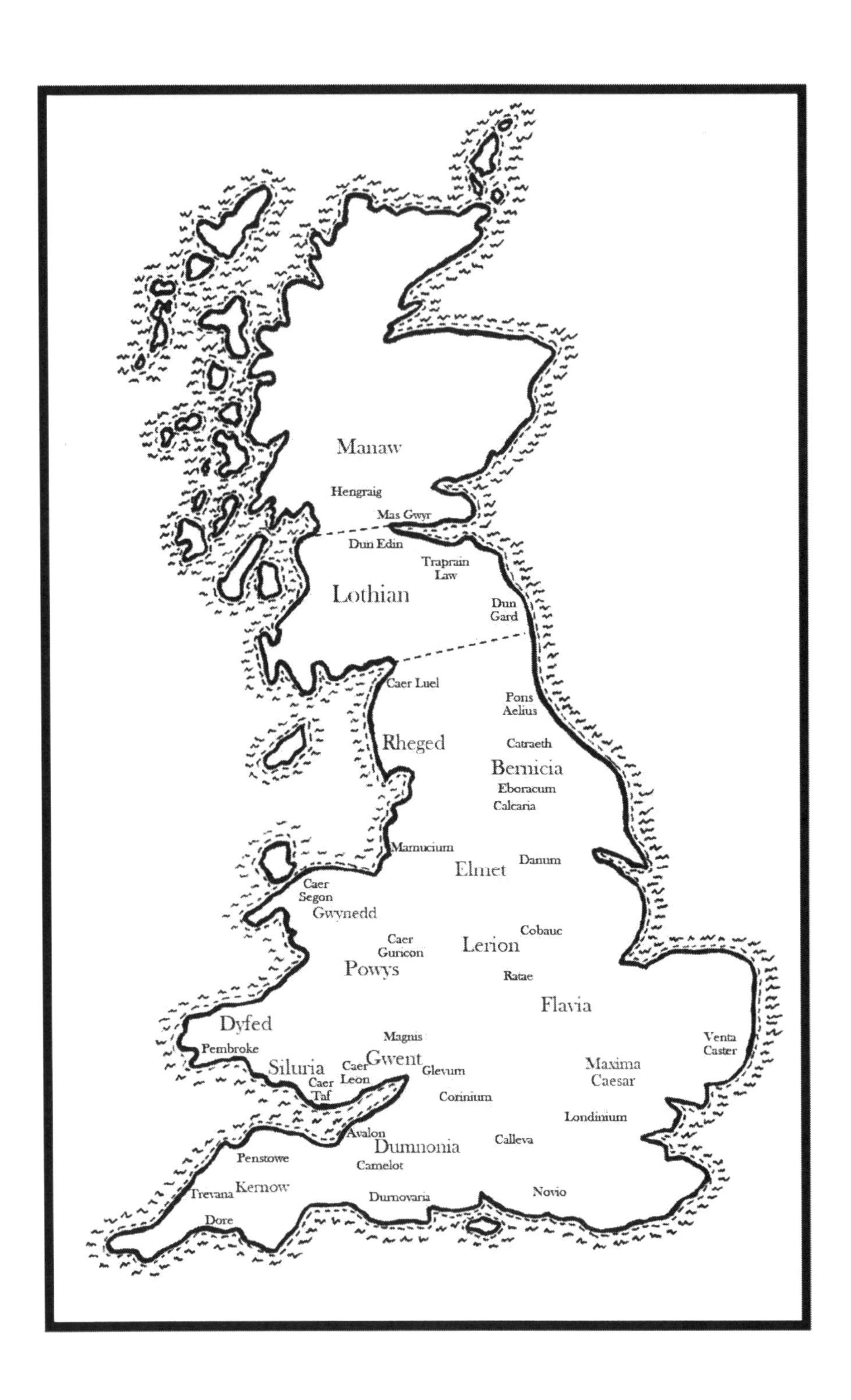
Manaw
Hengraig
Mas Gwyr
Dun Edin
Traprain Law
Lothian
Dun Gard
Caer Luel
Pons Aelius
Rheged
Catraeth
Bernicia
Eboracum
Calcaria
Mamucium
Danum
Elmet
Caer Segon
Gwynedd
Cobauc
Caer Guricon
Lerion
Powys
Ratae
Flavia
Dyfed
Magnis
Venta Caster
Pembroke
Siluria
Caer Leon
Gwent
Glevum
Maxima Caesar
Caer Taf
Corinium
Londinium
Avalon
Dumnonia
Calleva
Penstowe
Camelot
Trevana
Kernow
Durnovaria
Novio
Dore

Prologue

Mhari did not trust the Grey Woman. The others might look at her and see a walking talisman, but Mhari saw her for what she truly was; an opportunist. The druid, or whatever she was, knew that Mhari's warband was the best in all the north and she'd attached herself to them at exactly the right moment, just as things were beginning to look up. Mhari had led her band on a dozen raids since winter's end, and the profits had been lush all the way to the eastern coast. The hard work had paid off, and Mhari had been revelling in the spoils and reputation she had gained from it. Then the Grey Woman had come, and everything had changed. She had persuaded them to target settlements further south, which Mhari would likely have done eventually anyway, and at each raid she would say her spells and throw her charms and predict a great victory for them. All well and good, except now the warriors were convinced that their string of successes were thanks to the Grey Woman's magic, not to their leader's cunning. Mhari frowned at them through the drizzle. Most of her warriors were brave as bears and loyal as hounds, but sometimes they could be such bloody fools.

Mhari pushed a strand of copper hair from her eyes. Both her hair and the black furs about her shoulders were drenched from the steady shower, and even the tunic beneath was growing uncomfortably clammy. She took a slow breath. The air up in the mountains was generally clean and fresh, but today it was thick with smoke as thatch smouldered in the half-hearted rain. The village wouldn't burn down, everything was too wet for that, though brands had been thrown into several of the houses, and flames still licked hungrily at one or two of them. But rain would douse them eventually, and the majority of the wattle huts would survive. *At least the folk we leave behind will have somewhere dry to die.*

The Grey Woman hadn't accompanied the warband on the raid itself, and that alone was enough to make Mhari dislike her. A druid's magic was invaluable to any chief, but a true druid would stay with the warband when they fought, even if he didn't do any actual fighting. Not so the Grey Woman. She'd led them through the mist, weaved enchantments against potential ward-spells, and then skulked away while Mhari and her people did the dirty work. And some of it had been dirty indeed.

The bodies of some fifty Venicones lay strewn about the settlement, most of them cut down trying to flee when the burning brands were thrown into their huts. Mhari had little sympathy for them; the Venicones were a contemptible people. For generations they'd been nothing but lickspittles to the Romans, cheerfully forgetting who they were and abandoning their ancestors' noble ways. She walked slowly between the huts and sneered as she eyed the corpses. *Well, the Romans are gone now. And perhaps if you hadn't spat on who you were, you might have had the strength to fight back when we came.* But they hadn't, as she'd known they wouldn't. The Venicones had sacrificed their strength before Mhari was even born; the Picts were the only true Britons left.

Her sword was still slick with Venicon blood and she paused to wipe it clean on a dead man's cloak. Brathir was Mhari's pride and joy, a quality blade forged from folded steel rods, a rowan-wood handle wrapped in deep red leather, and a pommel and guard that gleamed with polished bronze. Mhari's fine black furs and crimson cloak marked her out as a woman of wealth, and the tattoos on her face marked her out as a warrior, but it was the presence of Brathir at her side that showed the world she was a chief. And with the Grey Woman's influence only growing as time went on, it was important that the weapon be kept bright. *There can only be one leader.* Mhari sighed as she straightened up and saw a gaggle of her more troublesome warriors. Even before the Grey Woman had come, the nature of leadership here had never been as simple as Mhari wished; as usual, Temar was among the troublemakers.

Temar was a big, flat-faced man with beady eyes and lank hair the colour of dirty straw. Like all of them he wore heavy furs over his clothing, but though his tunic and breeches had been well-made they was also stained and poorly kept. So far as battle went he was, despite his size, one of the least valued fighters in the whole warband, being stupid, malicious, and possessed of only the merest scrap of courage. Yet by some cruel jest of the gods, Mhari needed to keep him on her side. Temar might be as much use in battle as a fish in a fistfight, but his mother was the legendary Alva mer Colm, and when Temar had come to Mhari's band he'd brought twenty of her oath-men with him. Mhari had more than thirty warriors who were oath-bound to *her* and so the warband was clearly still hers to command, but if she wished to keep making daring raids then she needed Temar's people as well. And that sometimes meant pandering to the vicious bastard. Mhari walked towards the knot of men and deliberately sheathed Brathir as she went. She didn't want to be tempted to use it.

Temar's warriors had gathered around a water-barrel in front of what passed for a chief's hall in this place. Most of the survivors of the raid had been ancients who'd be left to die in their own time, or young women and children who'd be taken back north as slaves. But one or two men of fighting age had been fool enough to be taken alive, and Temar and his cronies were enjoying themselves with them. Mhari watched as they dragged a half-drowned Venicon from the barrel, laughing as the man retched water onto the mud. Despite the time of year the powdery rain had been constant for days and the barrel was overfull, and when they thrust the man's head back in again, water sloshed out over the sides. Temar laughed the loudest as the man thrashed and kicked helplessly, but two burly Picts were holding him down, and only when his struggling started petering away did they haul the fool out again.

The Venicon sputtered and coughed up more water, and would have collapsed had Temar's man not been holding him up. Mhari frowned. She didn't approve of games like this, but if it kept Temar's warriors from straying to another warband then she could put up with it. Besides, the man had been weak enough to be captured, which meant it was no worse fate than he deserved. The Venicones as a people were generally a wretched lot, living complacent lives in their fertile lands while true northerners were driven to banditry. *Can they really expect us not to hate them for that?*

A cry sounded from the huddle of prisoners and a woman, presumably the man's wife, wrapped her arms tight around a boy who was struggling to break free from her hold. His voice was high with youth and cracked pitifully as he wept.

'Stop it!'

He looked maybe ten years old and was clearly trying to reach his father. He shouted curses, both at his mother and at Temar's men, and Mhari had to give him credit; he was bolder than most of his kind. Maybe he had some Pictish blood in him.

Mhari took a step forward and glared at them, her hand on Brathir's pommel. For all his spirit the lad cowered away, and his mother put a protective arm about his head. It felt shallow to be threatening children, but better he learn now than later; Venicones did *not* give orders to Picts. Naturally, Temar had to make things worse, and he grinned unpleasantly at the boy.

'I bet you thought your da was strong, eh?'

He dragged the coughing man up by his collar and kept his eyes on the child as he rammed his father's head back in the barrel. A few of his cronies laughed and the boy began to sob. Mhari just spat into the mud. Why did Temar have to be such a bastard to everyone? She knew the answer of course; it was because beneath all his bravado he was a coward, and it took a coward's heart to inflict misery on a child. Not for the first time Mhari toyed with the idea of killing him and having done with it, but she needed Alva on her side, and it would hardly endear her to the old warlord if she murdered her eldest son.

Unfortunately, just as Mhari was making peace with having to keep the worthless cur around, Temar decided to press his luck. Mhari had half-turned away, intending to find Conn and see what they'd managed to gain today, when Temar dragged the Venicon out again and winked at his cowering wife.

'Don't worry about him, my lass. You need a stronger man than this.' He tilted his head towards her half-drowned husband. 'I'll be done with him soon, and then I'll come and take care of you.'

He nodded to his warriors and Darr took a step towards the prisoners. Mhari sighed. *Must he make* everything *so difficult?* She interposed herself between Darr and the woman and, without preamble, smashed her right fist into his face. Mhari was both tall and strong for a woman, and with her flaming hair and swirling tattoos, men said she was the image of a warrior queen of old. In thirty years of living she had spent sixteen of them fighting, and all told she was justifiably confident in her skills; but she wasn't fool enough to be cocky. Darr was big, and in a clash between a strong man and a strong woman, the man always had the edge if the fight was fair. This was, of course, why sensible women didn't fight fair. Mhari had trained herself to strike quickly, had attacked Darr without warning, and, as usual, was wearing heavy rings on every finger.

Silver, bronze and gold all cracked into Darr's cheek, tearing the skin cruelly as his head snapped to the side. Mhari was willing to put up with a great deal from Temar, but everyone knew that she didn't hold with rape, even of weak fools like the Venicones. Sometimes Mhari wondered if she was a fool herself; once the women were taken north and either kept by warriors' families or sold on to another, there was every chance their masters would ravage them day and night. Perhaps defending them here was a wasted effort. *But this is* my *warband. And in my warband, the men obey* my *rules.*

Darr staggered but kept his feet, and though he didn't dare say anything he scowled at her with anger in his eyes. Mhari stared back, impassive, watching the blood dribble down his cheek into his beard. Behind him Temar looked furious, and he and his men began squaring up to her, ready for violence. Mhari's eyes made a quick count. There were nine men with him who looked ready for a fight, and only half a dozen of her own warriors were close-by. If it came down to it then more of her people would come running, and Conn and the others would make short work of Temar, but by then she might very well be too dead to care. She cursed in her head. There was no need for this; neither band wanted to be weakened by infighting, but Temar had crossed a boundary and Mhari had no choice but to respond.

Temar himself was keeping back, of course, but Darr and the others came forward and one or two even had the gall to be fingering their weapons. Mhari let a hand rest casually on Brathir's pommel and for a moment, their advance faltered. *They know the first to come at me will die; likely the second and third as well.* None of them wanted to be one of those three. She was wondering what she ought to say to calm them when she felt a presence behind her and, even in the drizzling rain, she recognised Conn's scent. She held back a smile. Her lover was a clever man, and would have signalled to the others to join him. Already she could hear footsteps behind her as her own warriors gathered to stand with their leader. Temar's men hesitated, and Mhari took a step forward, making sure to sound neither too weak nor too derogatory.

'There's no sense wasting our time on a squabble. We have loot to gather and slaves that need binding.' She jerked her head at the prisoners. 'Now let's get to work, we've a long road ahead.'

Some of the tension left the glaring warriors. Mhari hadn't set out to belittle any of them and they could back away now without losing much face. *No more than Darr has lost already, anyhow.* She wanted to sigh with relief but she kept her posture firm, and slowly the warriors began to disperse. But then the Grey Woman appeared among them as if from nowhere, and she raised a pale-skinned hand. Mhari was disgusted at how quickly they all froze in place.

Like Mhari, the Grey Woman's hair was red, though hardly any of it could be seen beneath the hood of her mist-coloured cloak. Beneath it she wore a long, pale robe, like a druid, the garment so baggy it was impossible to see her shape. From the size of her wrists Mhari guessed that she was slim, and from what little she saw of her face she guessed she was around her own age. It looked like a fair face, with no sign of scars or blemishes, and with a pair of dark eyes that always seemed a little wider than was natural.

When she spoke she had the sharp accent of a Pict, but tinged with something that made Mhari think she'd spent a good deal of time down south.

'There will be plunder and glory for all when we move on. There is no sense in fighting amongst ourselves.'

Mhari frowned. She'd made exactly the same point seconds before, but she knew that the Grey Woman would now take credit for having calmed down the warband. The druid began mumbling to herself and reached into the bag she kept slung beneath the cloak. Mhari had seen her pull all sorts of strange objects from there and, sure enough, when her hand emerged it held a dozen tiny bones, along with what looked like a heron's feather. The Grey Woman crouched down and the warriors edged cautiously forward, keen to see what she was doing, but fearful of her magic all the same. Mhari took care to hide her wariness as she moved forward along with the others; she might not *like* the Grey Woman, but only a fool ignored a druid.

The robed woman made nine slow circles with her clasped hands then dropped their contents to the muddy ground. She hunched forward and stared intently at the bones, though Mhari was more interested in the feather. In the old times heron feathers were used for the tufts of spears, and while the tiny bones were a mystery to her, there could be no arguing with what the feather meant; the white tip was pointing directly south. Mhari hadn't been the only one to see it and a murmur went around the group, though it died when the Grey Woman looked up. Her too-wide eyes roamed about the circle of warriors.

'The Thunderer would guide you south, to where greater riches lie, but the path ahead is not an easy one.' She ran a hand over the scattered bones, her palm not quite touching them. 'Six fine men and one shall die before Lughnas.'

The warriors began exchanging looks. Seven of them would die, but since they didn't know *which* seven, that was a risk most of them would take. The Grey Woman was right about the south being a place of riches and if Taranis thought it right for them to go, then seven lives was a small price to pay. Mhari kept looking at her. She was young to be a druid, and Mhari suspected she was really some rejected student of one, half-trained and dangerous. But she'd guided them well on three raids now, taking them to settlements hidden away up in mountains, and if she was right about this then they might all become rich before long. Riches would tempt more warriors, and more warriors meant more glory; Mhari liked being called *chief,* but if she led enough warriors then soon enough she'd be called *lord.* It would be risky, raiding too close to Lothian meant inviting King Lot's wrath and southerner or not, Lot was a tough bastard. *But Lord Mhari does have a pleasant ring to it, and Lothian must fall someday. Maybe even at my hand?* But that was a grand ambition, and Mhari shoved the thought away. For now.

The Grey Woman spoke what so many of them were thinking.

'There is risk, of course, but a month of good raids in the south will keep you all rich for a year and more.'

She hated to agree with her, but Mhari nodded.

'We shall head home with this lot first.' She gestured vaguely at the smouldering village and cowering Venicones. 'Once done, we can head south.'

There were nods of assent all around; they didn't need slaves and livestock slowing them down. Besides, Mhari had to show who was in charge here. The Grey Woman bowed her head, as if acquiescing, but then spoke just as Mhari was turning away.

'You would be wise to make sacrifices to the Thunderer first.'

Mhari wanted to disagree but once again, the druid was right. It was Beltane Eve and they had no time for fires and rituals, and little enough sheep or cattle in any case; far quicker and simpler to appease Taranis here and now. She nodded once, and Temar was naturally the first one to move. He would enjoy this for all the wrong reasons. *Temar is no friend to the Thunderer; Taranis loves only the brave.*

The big man dragged his soaked captive to his knees and jerked back his chin with both hands. Mhari saw that the wife and child had fallen silent, the woman holding the boy's head to her chest while she shook and cried into his hair. *Weakling! At least your man's dying for a purpose now, not just for some fool's amusement.*

The Grey Woman produced a bowl from her bag, and the men's eyes were drawn to it like flies to a corpse; it looked like solid silver. The druid didn't seem to notice their looks, though Mhari was sure she missed nothing, and walked slowly towards the doomed man. She muttered the whole time, but they were either words Mhari didn't recognise or they were spoken too quietly for her to hear. When she reached the kneeling Venicon she leaned close to him and whispered in his ear, stroking his sopping hair almost lovingly as she spoke. The terrified man seemed to calm a little, and if Mhari had blinked at the wrong second she would have missed what happened next.

The druid's one hand left the Venicon's hair and a bronze dagger just seemed to *appear* in it, while with her other hand she smoothly placed the silver bowl against his chest. The cut was so fast Mhari doubted if the kneeling man even felt it. His eyes went wide and bright blood gushed from his throat, but whatever else she was the Grey Woman knew her trade, and the silver bowl caught nearly all of it. A few spatters of red struck her face and robe, but she paid them no mind. Instead she focused on the blood still pouring into the bowl, and Mhari recognised at least one word of her chant, spoken over and over with obvious reverence; *Taranis, Taranis, Taranis.*

All around the druid men were fondling talismans or kissing their weapons to show respect to the war god. Mhari touched her fingers to Brathir's pommel, and beside her she saw Conn put his lips to his spear-blade. As a rule Mhari left spoken prayers to the druids, she honoured the Thunderer by deeds, not words, but she felt the strange need to make an exception, and whispered a prayer under her breath.

'Taranis, be with us.'

She could see that the Grey Woman was watching her, and there was self-satisfaction in those too-wide eyes but Mhari looked past it. This was a time to show reverence to the Thunderer; she could deal with petty rivalries later. She let her hand wrap around Brathir's hilt, and whispered once more to the god closest to her heart.

'Taranis, bless your warriors. Taranis, bring me victory!'

Chapter One

Gareth still seemed nervous, and Gawain gave him a confident smile.

'All will be well! I know what I'm doing.'

His brother looked at him sceptically, and Gawain put a hand to his heart.

'When have I ever let you down?'

Gareth raised an eyebrow.

'There will be a first time, and I wouldn't choose this to be it.'

Gawain clapped his brother's shoulder. Gareth, being so much slighter than he was, bucked a little.

'Do this for me and I swear that when you find a girl you like, I will do *anything* to help you impress her.'

Gareth affected not to be interested but Gawain could tell he was intrigued; his little brother was nearly fourteen now, and impressing girls was becoming a priority. *It is to us all.* The younger boy sighed and shook his head.

'Alright,' he glanced around the corner, 'as soon as he gets here.'

Gawain smiled again and nodded. The two were speaking in whispers, crouched down behind the barrels below the fortress' western rampart. Though the upper part of it was timber palisade the lower part was of earth and stone, and it felt cool as Gawain rested his back against it. Dun Edin's stables were just along the wall from them but Durro hadn't been led in yet, and so the boys waited on the dewy grass. Gawain leaned sideways to look out into the yard. The fortress was always a busy place but today it teemed with activity, as all of Dun Edin prepared itself for Beltane. The festival itself would take place down in the town but everyone would come up to the Dun for the evening feast, and every man, woman, and capable child was working hard on the preparations. Gawain was already counting the hours. With his older brothers away he was sure he would be Summer King this year, and he started grinning to himself as he imagined it.

Gareth's tunic rustled as he shifted in place, and the sound brought Gawain back to the present. He shook his head to clear away the fantasy of what was to come; he had a task in hand that demanded his focus. And it was on the way here even now. From the north gate he saw that a groom was finally leading Durro across the yard, and Gawain forced himself to breathe slowly. It was almost time.

Durro was a truly magnificent animal, a great black stallion sired from the old Sarmatian breeds. He was tall and proud and possessed of a fiery temper, and only the king himself was permitted to ride him. But riding him was not the plan today. Gawain watched as Durro was led towards the stable, careful not to lean too far around the barrels and risk being seen. Beside him Gareth was looking nervous again, and Gawain put a hand back on his shoulder. He hated to say it, and quietly hoped his brother would refuse, but he felt that an offer had to be made:

'You don't have to...'

Gareth swatted at his hand.

'Oh, be quiet.' The younger boy did his best to smile confidently. 'Just be sure to do *your* part properly.'

Gawain looked at his brother. Like Gawain himself he had the red hair and green eyes of the Royal House of Lothian, but where Gawain could at best be called 'pleasant-looking', Gareth was already growing to be a very handsome lad. He was most of three years younger than Gawain and still slender with youth, and when he stood beside his brothers he looked like a half-starved dwarf. But today he also looked determined, and Gawain smiled at him.

'Don't worry, I've been practicing hard.'

Every day for a fortnight Gawain had been going to the stables and talking to Durro, going at different times of day so that the beast would be used to him whether tired or fresh, full or hungry. Whenever he could he'd brought a carrot for him, and Gawain was confident that as long as Durro was merely irritated, not angered, he would trust his voice. The scheme would work perfectly. He leaned out again and looked across to the opposite palisade, where women sat on wooden stools in the shade of the fortress wall. Hundreds of green and yellow ribbons had been made in the lead-up to Beltane, and Dun Edin's womenfolk were patiently braiding them together or tying them to staves. Sitting among those women was Halwen.

Of all the girls of Dun Edin, both fortress and town, Halwen was undoubtedly the loveliest. Her hair hovered somewhere between red and blonde, and whenever she stood in sunlight it would shine like spun gold, and the bronze rings in her braids would glitter. She had a sweet button nose, smooth creamy skin, and a smile that could light up the world. Gawain loved it when he could make her smile. She was sitting on a stool beside her mother, wearing a simple white dress and woven belt, and from where he was Gawain could see a tiny glimpse of her beautiful calves. Halwen was the liveliest girl he'd ever met, and her love of dancing, running and swimming had made those calves both strong and somehow delicate too, not to mention very difficult not to stare at. He'd heard whispers that she was a favourite to be Spring Maiden this year, and he longed more than ever to be Summer King when he thought of it. *And you will be; Agravain and Gaheris are both away, and Agravain would be too old now anyway. It* must *be you.* He imagined how it would feel to hold her hand as they walked through the festival, then started imagining how it would feel to kiss her at the fire…

He snapped himself out of it. *Focus, damn you; horses before carts.* After a few more moments Gareth nudged him in the ribs, nodding his head towards the stables. Gawain took a careful peek. It looked like Durro had been put in his paddock, and that the groom had moved on to other chores. Gawain felt his heart flutter in anticipation. It was now or never.

Gareth gave him a quick nod then picked up the willow branch and got up from his crouch. He held it against his forearm and moved off at a slow walk, trying to stay close to the wall without seeming conspicuous. Gawain had to fight not to hold his breath. This would work! The willow branch wasn't thick enough to hurt or even anger the great stallion, but a thwack on the rump would annoy him, and that was all they needed. Durro would gallop irritably from his paddock, seemingly uncontrolled, and when Gawain stepped in to calm him down he would appear both madly brave and extremely capable. And Halwen would see it all.

It was hard work to sit still as he waited for Gareth to do his part. His brother had to be sure he wasn't seen sneaking in or leaving the paddock gate unhooked, and in a busy fortress that was no easy thing. But it was easier for a slender lad like Gareth than for a lump of a youth like Gawain. He sighed and leaned his head back on the wall. From where he crouched he could see the main gate and the northeast watchtower, and above both fluttered green banners showing the prowling Red Fox of Lothian.

He hoped quietly that his father too would be impressed when he heard of today's little adventure. It wasn't much of an achievement, and he'd be lucky if the king granted him a single nod, but with two brothers who'd already seen combat and glory, Gawain had to take whatever credit he could get.

After what felt like hours he heard the first signs of his plan in action. There came an irritated whinny from the stables, followed by the thudding of hooves and the crack of splintering timber. Then a cry sounded, presumably from one of the grooms, his voice sounding high and shrill.

'He's loose!'

Gawain leaped to his feet and rushed around the barrels, just as Durro came galloping into the fortress yard. He threw a quick glance towards the stables to ensure Gareth was alright, and when he saw him in one corner, half-hidden behind a post, Gawain grinned to himself and dashed after the stallion. Men were shouting out warnings and people were fleeing left and right to get out of the charging beast's way, but Gawain wasn't worried; Durro wasn't truly angered, just spirited. He spotted Halwen as she jumped from her stool and started hurrying the other women towards the hall. *Just stay in the yard long enough to see it.* Now would be his moment in the sun.

He closed in on Durro, who was stamping his hooves in the turf and snorting. There was no bridle on him but Gawain reached a hand towards his mane, the same way he'd done a dozen times, and began speaking to him very softly.

'Come now Durro, there's my boy.'

He could hear people shouting for him to back away but he ignored them; he knew what he was doing.

'Easy now, that's it, easy…'

But apparently Durro was not in a listening mood. As Gawain drew close the black stallion reared up, and only a sideways dive saved him from catching a hoof in the chest. His heart was in his throat as he scrambled back to his feet, and when he tried to approach the beast Durro snorted angrily and lashed out again. Gawain dodged, and cold fear flooded through him as his clever plan unravelled. *Damn it all, why won't he listen?* The great stallion was paying no attention to Gawain's soothing words, and a horrible guilt joined his fear as more cries of alarm came from around the yard. He shoved the feeling away and focused. *You can handle this; just guide him back to the paddock!* The grooms would know what to do with him, if he could just get Durro to them before he trampled someone.

He began circling around him, back towards the west wall and the stables, calling out to the stamping horse and waving his arms to get his attention. Durro eyed him angrily for a moment, and then Gawain's heart almost stopped as the great stallion proceeded to do almost exactly what he'd hoped for. He put his head down and galloped towards the west wall, ears back and nostrils flared, but for some horrible reason he did not come straight for Gawain. Instead he charged towards the stables at an angle, straight towards where Gareth had just emerged from his hiding place. The boy's eyes were wide with panic and he didn't seem to know which way to run, he just stood with his feet frozen in place and stared at the charging horse. Gawain felt himself panic. *Bel and Christ, don't let this happen!*

Durro was only seconds away from running Gareth down, and Gawain sprinted across to him and threw himself onto his brother. He gasped as something clipped his ribs on the way down, but then he and Gareth hit the ground and what little air was left in him was driven from his lungs. He coughed hard and hoped he hadn't crushed the smaller boy beneath him; Gareth was no weakling but Gawain was big for his age, and he'd had no way of controlling the fall.

He could hear Durro above them, snorting and rearing, and he shielded his brother as best he could while praying to every god he could think of that no hooves would come crashing through his back. Years ago Old Ifan had been crippled by a wild horse, and the notion of the same thing happening to him was enough to make Gawain shake. The noise above them was truly awful and Gawain, cursing his stupidity, wondered if this would be the day he died.

Then a voice cut through the wild neighing and trampling. It was deep and strong as mountain roots, yet somehow soft as a mother's lullaby.

'Durro, Durro, easy my lad.'

Gawain couldn't see what was happening, he was face down and with his eyes tight shut, but the tramping sound faded to just a few dull thumps, and the snorting grew calmer as the deep voice went on.

'There's my lad, Durro. Easy now, easy.'

After a few more moments Gawain dared to look up, and he saw Drustan standing over them, one hand gently patting the stallion's mane. Drustan was a tall, broad-nosed man, with dark skin that was testament to his Assyrian grandfather. Though there were grey hairs in his beard he was still a formidable warrior, and had been King Lot's champion since before Gawain was born. Drustan had a heart of oak and a will of steel, and was everything a king could ever want in a warlord; Gawain wanted to squirm under his gaze.

Drustan looked down at the boys, and though his ancestry might be mixed, his accent was unmistakably Lothian.

'What in Bel's name did you think you were doing?'

Gawain didn't have an answer for him. He felt like such a fool. He rolled from Gareth and, with Drustan's help, rose to his feet. His ribs ached horribly but he forced himself not to grimace in front of the champion. Down on the grass Gareth looked shaken but unhurt, and Gawain gave him his hand and hauled him up too. Drustan eyed them both but settled his glare on Gawain.

'Did no-one ever tell you the difference between a bold man and a stupid one?' Before Gawain could answer Drustan cuffed him about the head. 'Oh, now I recall; *I* did!'

Gawain's first instinct was to glare back in defiance, but he couldn't justify it today. Drustan was not only a warlord and a champion, he was also one of the men charged with training the king's sons to fight, and his teachings had been more than just sword-strokes and shieldwalls; he'd also tried to hammer good warrior instincts into them. *Instincts you ignored today to impress a pretty girl. And almost got Gareth trampled for.* He nodded to Drustan and swallowed his pride, his eyes cast down.

'I am sorry. I thought I could handle him.'

When he dared to look up Drustan was still scowling.

'How many men do you think died with the final thought; *"I thought I could handle him."*?'

Gawain nodded again.

'I know, you are right.'

Drustan snorted as he handed Durro over to a groom, the great stallion now completely calmed.

'Of course I am right. I've lived this long because I am *always* right.'

Gawain didn't know what to do except nod again. He looked sideways at Gareth, who seemed just as humbled by Drustan's tirade. Despite his own shame, Gawain couldn't help but glance around the yard to see if Halwen was still around, and whether she was witnessing his scolding. It seemed he had at least a modicum of good luck because she looked to be nowhere in sight, though a moment later Gawain had to suppress a groan. His speck of good fortune was being blotted out as Father Iain, his black robe flapping about him, came hurrying towards them from the king's hall.

A little older than Drustan, Iain's head was so bald he had no need for a priest's tonsure, with only a few wisps of hair clinging stubbornly above his ears. He strode up to the boys and, without preamble, cuffed first Gawain and then Gareth about the head. Drustan, who rarely agreed with Iain about anything, nodded in approval as the priest took his turn at rebuking them.

'Idiot boy!' His grey eyes, normally kindly and intelligent, were filled with nothing but bitter disappointment. 'You'd have been blessed if that beast had stamped on your thick skull; he just might have managed to knock some good sense into you.'

Once again Gawain could do little but look abashed, but then the priest leaned close to his ear and a spike of dread mixed in with his shame.

'You think I do not know what you were doing?'

Gawain felt his guts twist and he tried to speak only with his eyes, imploring Iain not to shame him further in front of Drustan. The champion had begun to walk away, clearly content to leave the rest of this to the priest, but he paused when he heard the whispered words. He turned back to face them.

'What's that, father?'

Iain seemed to debate with himself for a moment before looking up at Drustan.

'The boy needs to learn some responsibility.' He turned his attention back to Gawain and jerked his head towards the hall. 'Follow.'

He began walking that way and Gawain trailed miserably at his heels. He supposed that if he were a nobler man, he'd be feeling glad that he'd apparently not dragged Gareth into trouble with him. But the only thing Gawain felt was trepidation. Iain would be taking him to his father, and compared to Iain and Drustan's scolding, King Lot's reprimand would be a lion stood next to a kitten.

The king had only just come in from the kennels, and he was washing his hands in a shallow brass bowl when Gawain and Iain came to his rooms. Though the hall at Dun Edin was home to more than sixty souls, the royal family had a third of the structure to themselves, and of that third nearly half belonged to the king alone. They met him his in his outer room, the one where he held private council with lords or advisors. It was fairly spacious, as such places went, with half a dozen chairs, a large table in the centre, and multiple smaller ones scattered about to hold the candles which lit the room. There was no fire in the hearth, it was high spring after all, but the rich tapestries that covered the walls always gave the room a warm feeling. Though when the king noted Father Iain's expression, the look he gave his son was *far* from warm.

King Lot of Lothian was tall and broad, with little by way of a paunch despite his years, and was dressed in a dark green tunic beneath a sleeveless leather coat. His red hair was long and tied back with a black ribbon, and his beard clung tightly to a solid jawline. Neither showed more than a sliver of grey. He spoke to Father Iain as he dried his hands, but his eyes were fixed on his son.

'What has he done now?'

As with Drustan, Gawain ignored the instinct to be defiant or argumentative towards his father; this time there was no denying that he was in the wrong. Instead he looked appropriately shamefaced as Iain recounted the morning's disaster, including his guess that it had been started deliberately as a chance for Gawain to show off. The moment he was done, Lot wasted no time in sharing his opinion. He crossed the room in three long strides and slapped Gawain hard across the face, sending his son's head snapping sideways.

'You stupid, arrogant, imbecilic boy!'

The blow stung both body and pride, and Gawain's whole cheek tingled as he straightened up. He hated that he had to take such a thing without fighting back, but he accepted the slap without comment; he'd earned it. Lot glared at him, his eyes flashing.

'You risk your brother's life, and the lives of anyone else in the yard today, for the sake of your own ridiculous vanity?'

He looked like he wanted to hit him again and Gawain wouldn't have blamed him for it, but the king settled for a scowl, his voice lowering from a shout to a menacing rumble.

'As if that were not enough, you have dared to touch the king's prize stallion without leave, something that would cost a common boy his hand.' He let that image sink into his son's head before continuing. 'What did you do, sneak into his paddock and prick his rump?'

At heart Gawain was glad that Gareth hadn't been dragged into this, but a shameful part of him wished there was someone here to share the blame with him. After all, *he'd* shared plenty of blame when Gaheris had done stupid things in his youth. He pushed the resentment away, it was an unworthy thought, and nodded at the glaring king.

'Struck him with a willow rod, lord.'

Lot's hands balled into fists, and Gawain heard the knuckles crack.

'And you thought Durro would meekly submit to your touch? You thought you could antagonise a stallion of his blood, and he would calm down at the cooing of some beardless youth?'

On another day Gawain might have pointed out that his stubble was, albeit slowly, thickening into something almost beard-like, but this was no time for idle cheek. Lot paced while Father Iain stood still, his hands clasped before his belt, and Gawain guessed that the king would soon be asking the priest for counsel. Lot could be short-tempered but he was a man well-aware of his faults, and he surrounded himself with level-headed advisors to balance his judgement. Father Iain, Druid Elgan, and Queen Morgause were all cool-minded, contemplative people, and Lot relied on them when his own temper could not be trusted.

Sure enough, after a little more pacing he turned to face Iain.

'What am I to do with him, father?'

Iain bowed his head and spoke very calmly.

'Lord, this was no harmless lake-dunking or a brawl between boisterous lads. This affair could have ended in serious harm had Drustan not come to calm the horse.' He crossed himself. 'God be thanked that he was there.'

That comment, if nothing else, spoke volumes about how seriously Iain was taking this; it took a great deal to make the priest speak so well of the champion. Drustan was what the priests called a *pagan*, and that meant Iain was as good as oath-bound to dislike him. Most people in Lothian, and indeed, most people in Britain, were willing to give the God of Rome his due respect, and apart from the queen all of Lothian's Royal House had been baptised, but Drustan stubbornly refused to accept Christ in any form. He would be courteous enough to Iain because of his age and station, but he would hear no talk of his god. *Yet what you did today was so damned stupid that a priest has just thanked God for a pagan's help.*

Lot frowned, and made a half-hearted show of crossing himself as well. King Lot was a Christian only in the very loosest sense.

'Yes, indeed, God be thanked.' He turned his eyes back to Gawain. 'By rights I ought to have you whipped for this.'

Gawain fought to keep the shock from his face. Did he mean a belting, like the ones he'd had as a child, or was he to be flogged like a common thief? From the look on Lot's face it might have been either one, but before he could elaborate the far door of the chamber opened and the three of them turned to see who entered. It was the queen.

Morgause mer Gwrlais was a tall and stately woman with black hair and dark eyes, and with her long nose and strong chin she was a handsome woman for her years. Most people agreed it was from her that Gaheris and Anna had inherited their fine features. *And Gareth too grows handsomer each day; it seems only Agravain and I drew short lots for our looks.* Morgause took in the sight of the king, the priest, and the shamefaced boy, then strode over to her husband, her blue gown swishing at her ankles.

'I could hear you shouting three rooms away.'

Her voice was low and melodious, and for a moment Lot's face calmed. Gawain couldn't help thinking of Drustan's effect on Durro, then for a horrible moment he thought he might laugh as he imagined Drustan and Durro sharing a bed. *Which one would play the woman's part?* But that threat of a smile died when Lot's eyes fell on him again.

'Our son has been making a disgrace of himself.'

Queen Morgause might have lacked her husband's quick temper, but her glare was easily a match for his.

'What have you done?'

Gawain really didn't want to repeat the whole tale, and hearing it again would only enrage his father anyway. He decided to simply confess to the worst of it.

'I played a trick to make myself seem impressive. It put Gareth's life in danger.'

Her look was almost enough to make him want to cry. He could have resisted a look of fury from her, but all he saw from his mother was a flash of distress and a hefty measure of disappointment.

'Is Gareth…?'

Father Iain raised a calming hand.

'He is well, my queen. None were harmed in this.'

Gawain thought briefly of his aching ribs but shoved the self-pity away. Some of the worry faded from Morgause's face, and her husband reached out to take her hand. Their fingers intertwined out of long habit.

'I was thinking a few red stripes on his back might be what's needed to set this one right?'

The king didn't even dignify Gawain by naming him. Morgause looked only a little uncertain, and Gawain did his best not to let the fear show; it seemed a real whipping was what he had in store then. He wondered how badly it would hurt. The harsh law of King Lot meant that serious crime was rare, especially at the Dun, but more than once Gawain had seen a thief tied to a whipping post and scourged. Only the very bravest didn't cry out. *Then nor will I!*

Gawain squared his shoulders, determined to take his punishment like a man, but Father Iain spoke before his parents could make their decision.

'My king, my lady, perhaps the rod is not the answer in this case?'

Lot didn't seem so sure about that.

'And what do you suggest, father?'

The priest took half a pace forward, his hands still clasped lightly in front of him.

'Gawain has grown too old for such punishment to serve any good as a teacher, besides which, I do not doubt that

Drustan has taught him how to take a beating. It is his *mind* that requires discipline, not his back.' The priest gave Gawain a stern look. 'The sin of pride is his great folly, and there are cures for that beyond a simple whipping.'

Morgause looked unconvinced by the talk of sin, but that was hardly surprising; she was the daughter of a king of Kernow, and the folk of her homeland had little time for Christianity. All the same she spoke respectfully.

'What did you have in mind, father?'

Iain gave her a little dip of his head.

'Lady, the Lord says there is dignity in toil. I am blessed, by both God and your good selves, my king and queen, with a fine church here at the Dun.'

Gawain really wasn't sure where this was going. It looked like he might be escaping a whipping, but what was Iain getting at? There was indeed a fine church here, a great long building two dozen paces from door to altar, built as a shadow of the great Roman structures of old. Would he be made to stand a vigil there and pray all night for forgiveness? Or would he be given a shirt of hair and told to sit on the church floor for days on end without food or water? It was the sort of thing some priests and monks went in for, and the other stories Gawain had heard of their penances ranged from the ridiculous to the atrocious.

Lot shrugged at the priest.

'What of it?'

Iain gave him a very small smile.

'I do believe that the boy is best served by learning some humility. As you know my church has a fine stone floor, but alas, Lachlan's goats got in there yesterday and for a House of God it is in a truly shameful state.' He turned the smile towards Gawain. 'Tragically, I have only a very small brush with which to clean it.'

Chapter Two

On balance, Gawain would have preferred a whipping. The initial prospect of cleaning the church had seemed like no hardship at all, and he'd even thanked Iain for persuading his father into letting this be an end to his punishment. But that had been six long hours ago, and Gawain had decided within the first three that he'd learned his lesson and would never do anything reckless ever again. He liked to think that he'd come to that conclusion because he was wise and aware of his failings, but he strongly suspected it had more to do with the smarting wound to his pride, and the burning agony in his knees and back. There was no way to clean the floors without putting pressure on one or the other, and his muscles, bones and joints were all screaming at him in turn. *At least a whipping would have been over and done by now.*

Just to put a little iron in the glove, in addition to making him sweep and scrub the floors, Father Iain had encouraged the other boys to come into the church at regular intervals so that they could laugh at Gawain's chastisement, and that had hurt almost as much as the pains that wracked his body. Every one of their insults, whether good-natured or not, had made his cheeks burn with shame, and he'd longed to jump to his feet and shout that he was Gawain ab Lot, the son of a king, and they had best show him some bloody damned respect! Only he wasn't the son of a king right now. Right now he was a barefoot boy in filthy breeches and a rough-spun shirt, on his knees washing stones like a common slave. He knew that he deserved his punishment, but the humiliation was a hard thing to bear.

Gawain leaned forward and scrubbed hard at what felt like the ten-thousandth dirty slab. He'd already gone through three full water-buckets, and must have used up a whole pig's worth of hog's-fat soap, yet still the church looked barely half-cleaned. So many of the marks refused to budge no matter what he did, and his fingers ached from gripping the brush so hard. He paused for a moment and flexed his hands, hoping that Father Iain wouldn't notice.

The priest was sitting not far away, his cane within easy reach, carefully reading from a yellowed scroll. Gawain suspected that Iain wasn't quiet as absorbed in it as he seemed, and would be quick to take the cane to his charge if he saw him shirking. But he couldn't stop himself; his hands, knees and back were all on fire. He dropped the brush, raised himself up and stretched. Iain spoke without looking up.

'Are my floors clean yet?'

They were not. The church was a long, thickly-thatched building of grey stone and dark timber, and was large enough that every soul in the Dun could squeeze into it to hear Mass. Despite the endless sweeping and scrubbing he'd done, Gawain was only a little more than halfway finished, and he completely failed to keep himself from griping.

'They are the bishop's floors, father. And I don't think he minds.'

It was a safe guess; Bishop Dyfan was a drunken fool who was almost certainly asleep in his chambers, and would likely remain so for most of the day. It was well known that he cared only for wine, sleep, and groping Dun Edin's prettier girls whenever he found the energy, which wasn't often. Dyfan probably didn't know or care what day it was, much less whether the church floors were clean. Father Iain, who was generally considered to be the *real* bishop of Dun Edin, peered at Gawain over the top of his scroll.

'They are God's floors, my boy, and He wants them clean. Now get on with it.'

His eyes went back to the paper but Gawain kept on grumbling, arching his body with a groan.

'I thought you said it was my mind that needed discipline, not my back?'

His muscles were horribly tight and his spine clicked unpleasantly as it stretched. Iain shrugged, still barely bothering to look at him.

'Apparently your mind has yet to absorb the salient message and your back is attempting to get it through to you.' He picked up the cane and jabbed it at the floor. 'Get back to work, and think on what you've done.'

Gawain did as he was bid, trying to think suitably repentant thoughts. He was sorry for what he'd done, but it was hard not to let resentment overwhelm the guilt. Fool or not he was still a king's son, and nothing truly bad had happened because of him. *That is not the point. A stray hoof-stamp and you or Gareth might have been crushed or crippled.* He sighed sullenly and scrubbed at the stubborn stains. On top of everything else there was no chance of his being Summer King at Beltane now, and if Halwen became Spring Maiden he'd have to watch some other boy take her hand in the procession. And watch someone else kiss her at the fires.

Three miserable slabs further on, he found his knees could no longer take it. Gawain sat back on the floor and stretched out his legs, groaning as the joints creaked and popped. He saw Father Iain looking at him but he waved a hand in surrender; straightening his legs felt so good that he didn't care what it might cost him.

'Sorry, father, but the respite is worth the thrashing.'

The priest frowned and set down his scroll. He took the cane in one hand and his chair in the other, then walked across the church to where Gawain sat. The priest gave him a sharp whack in the thigh with his stick, and Gawain grimaced as the already sore muscle was stung again; Father Iain was a master of striking the same bruise time after time.

'I'm glad it is worth it.' He sank into the chair and leaned forward, one elbow on his leg. 'Have you learned anything yet, my boy?'

Gawain rubbed at his thigh and nodded.

'It was stupid and selfish of me to endanger Gareth and the others. I won't do such a thing ever again.'

Iain looked down and nodded as if in thought. Then he brought his eyes up to meet Gawain's again.

'Do you wish to tell me why you did it in the first place?

Gawain decidedly did *not* wish to tell him, but Iain made a fairly good guess on his own.

'Would I be right in thinking there is a girl of whom you are fond?'

He avoided the priest's eyes, and Iain shook his head before Gawain could make an excuse.

'Gawain my boy, the sin of lust tempts us all. You should pray for the strength to overcome such base urges. Indulging them at all is bad enough, but to endanger another for the sake of…'

Gawain looked up quickly and interrupted.

'It's not just lust, father, and…'

But Iain raised a hand for silence, frowning down at him.

'Along with pride, I suspect that your next sin is envy, correct? Of your brothers, and their achievements?'

Gawain hated how right Iain could be. *Of course* he envied his brothers. Agravain had fought the Picts a dozen times, earning himself the name Hardhand for his strength, and now he represented their house at the court of High King Uther. Gaheris was fighting Irish raiders on the western coast, a warlord in his own right, and he'd distinguished himself in more than one battle. What did Gawain have to compare with that? Iain voiced his next thought for him, and Gawain blushed to hear it spoken aloud.

'Did you truly think that letting a half-wild stallion loose in the yard would make you a hero? Did you think calming a horse would make you like them?'

Gawain sat up straighter, though he still struggled to meet Iain's gaze.

'No, father.' He looked up and started speaking quickly. 'But I am old enough to be proving myself; Agravain was fighting the Picts at my age. I'm skilled at arms, ask Drustan or any of the others, I…'

But Iain's face became stern and Gawain felt his voice trailing off. The priest's grey eyes bored into his.

'For a boy here to do penance you are being remarkably insolent.'

Gawain wanted to keep arguing but Iain was right. He always was. He cast his eyes down at the half-cleaned floor.

'I'm sorry, father.'

He heard the priest sigh, and then clack the cane on the stones.

'Gawain my boy, true warriors do not endanger others. Even fools who lust after glory risk only themselves, if they are true men.' Iain leaned forward and Gawain looked up to meet his gaze. 'And Drustan would agree with me. For all his pagan follies he is wise in the ways of war, and he will tell you the same truth that I do. What you became today was a braggart, not a hero.'

The words made Gawain feel even more wretched than before, and Iain raised the cane and prodded him in the chest. Gawain almost toppled backwards but he put a hand out and stopped himself. The priest's voice lowered, though if anything his eyes had grown brighter.

'And in *there*, you know I am right.' He prodded him again, right in the same spot. 'If you listened to your heart a little more I do believe you might become a fine man someday, as fine a man as any of your brothers. You are not a wicked soul and you have been raised in the light of God. He has given us all a conscience in our hearts, my boy, if only we would listen to it.'

Yet again Iain had struck the mark. Gawain had known that what he'd done was reckless but he'd done it anyway; he'd let himself be blinded by wanting Halwen and the others to think well of him, the way they all did of Agravain and Gaheris. And Gareth had almost been hurt as a result. He sighed quietly to himself. *Well, even if you can't avoid doing something that stupid again, at least be sure that you do it alone next time!* Gawain nodded obediently.

'Yes, father.'

Without waiting to be told he shifted around on the floor and got back to work on the stones. His knees and back screamed but Iain had been right; he'd been a bragger, not a hero, and if Halwen knew of his plan she'd be ashamed to know him. He'd more than earned his punishment.

Iain waited for him to finish the stone then looked down at him again.

'You have heard all I have said?' Gawain nodded silently, and Iain nodded back. 'Then pray with me.'

The priest slid from his chair to join him on the floor, and he knelt beside Gawain with his arms spread out to his sides, the palms facing up towards heaven. Gawain copied him. He rarely prayed beyond what was required during Mass, and was glad that Iain did the talking for him.

'Father God, bless your son Gawain with wisdom and with Christian humility. Keep him free of sinful pride, of lust and of envy, and lead him always in the light of your holy grace.' He crossed himself. 'Amen.'

Gawain echoed him. He wasn't certain that he wanted rid of *all* his lust and pride, but he would be grateful if the God of Rome could give him some wisdom to temper them with. Iain looked across at him and smiled.

'Go on with you. You will return tomorrow to finish your work.'

Gawain smiled but then felt suddenly awkward. Tomorrow was Beltane, but that would be no excuse to a Christian priest. He cast his eyes about the half-finished floor, trying to work out how much time it would take to clean. He was sure he could get it done before the festival if he got to the church early enough. *Besides, you won't be missed; it's not as if you'll have much of a role to play.* The thought was unpleasant but hardly undeserved, and he nodded to Iain, who was heaving himself to his feet. Gawain leaped up as quickly as his creaking knees would allow and lent the old man his hand.

'I will. Thank you, father.'

He hauled Iain to his feet and the priest immediately sank down onto his chair.

'Very well, gather your things.'

Gawain hurried to take his brush and bucket to the corner and collect his discarded shoes. His stomach was growling and his throat painfully dry, but he decided that he'd only take a short drink for now and then head to the training yard; he had to work his muscles loose somehow or he'd be too crippled to walk in the morning. He limped back to Iain, ignoring his protesting joints, and bowed his head respectfully to the priest.

'I have your leave to go?'

For some reason Iain seemed to ponder the question for a moment, then he gave Gawain's thigh another hard thwack with the cane. The sting was so unexpected that Gawain almost yelped, and when he spoke he sounded like an indignant child.

'What was that for?'

The wise old priest shrugged and gave him a rather mischievous smirk.

'Oh, I don't doubt you will do something to earn it later on; this spares me from having to find out about it.' He waved him away. 'God go with you, Gawain.'

Despite himself Gawain found himself grinning at Iain, and he bowed his head again before hobbling from the church as fast as his screaming knees would let him.

Dun Edin's training yard was an almost grassless patch in the southeast corner, trampled flat by the feet of countless warriors and warriors-to-be, and large enough for two twenty-man shieldwalls to face each other. At one end stood a dozen archery barrels, their butts painted with red marks, while at the other end a group of oak pillars had been sunk into the ground. Half of them were chipped and haggard by countless sword-blows, while the other half were wrapped with old sacks of earth for the boys to practice striking with their fists. Gawain wasn't sure but he guessed it was now a couple of hours after noon, and there were only two other boys at work when he walked into the yard. He had fully expected some mockery when they saw him, and when the boys looked over they did not disappoint him. First to approach was Ulfric, a straw-haired Saxon whose father had fought for King Lot against the Picts. He and Burian had been working at the archers' marks, but the moment Ulfric saw Gawain he dropped his bow and rushed up to him, eyes full of fake concern.

'Gawain! You need to talk to your father; that priest has your sister scrubbing his floors like a common scullion!'

Ulfric was a full year older than he was but the Saxon was also shorter and lighter, and Gawain sent him staggering with a single shove. Ulfric just grinned and Burian piped up as he unstrung the bows. Burian was one of Drustan's nephews and had the same dark hair and Assyrian features, though, like his uncle's, his accent was thickly Lothian.

'It can't have been; Gawain's sister is pretty. I saw that girl scrubbing the floors and she had a face like an angry mule's arse!'

Burian was too far away for Gawain to hit him with anything, so he simply shouted back.

'I thought a mule's arse was what you looked for in a lover?'

The swarthy youth grinned at him.

'Oh, I wasn't *that* drunk this morning. Besides, *this* mule's arse even Ulfric wouldn't touch.'

The Saxon didn't bother rising to his friend's jibe; the pair were enjoying themselves too much at Gawain's expense. Ulfric trotted back up to him and threw an arm around his shoulders.

'Maybe you should go and see this girl. She looked miserable and friendless, as if the whole world was against her.' He patted Gawain's back. 'Someone that wretched might even let *you* touch her!'

Gawain shrugged him off.

'Your ma didn't seem miserable when I was…'

But he never had the chance to finish the insult. Before he could weave a suitably graphic tale of unspeakable acts performed with Ulfric's mother, Drustan strode into the training yard with a gaggle of younger boys in tow. The three friends fell silent at the sight of him; Drustan did not approve of ill-discipline in his yard.

Gawain tried not to let his disappointment show. He was always appreciative of Drustan's instruction but he'd been hoping to have the yard to himself for a while. He just wanted a quiet hour alone to loosen his muscles, then he could bolt down a meal and collapse somewhere. But if the champion was here it meant he would be taking over the yard, and with his creaking knees and aching back, Gawain doubted if he'd give a good account of himself.

Despite the fact that they'd stopped talking the moment they saw him, Drustan still saw the need to bark at the trio.

'Shut your noise lads, time to work.'

His dark eyes rested on Gawain for a moment but he made no comment on his presence. Under one arm he held a bundle of blunt and battered training swords, and he gestured towards the oaken poles. Gawain and the others made their way towards them, though Gawain looked longingly at the woodpile in the opposite corner, where he'd been hoping to work with his preferred weapon; the two-handed war-axe. Huge and heavy, what the war-axe lacked in grace it made up for in raw power, and Gawain practiced with it whenever he could. Not only had it built up his strength in a way that sword-work alone never could have, there was the added boon that he was being productive by splitting wood for the fortress' fires. Naturally, Drustan didn't see it that way, and he frowned when he caught Gawain looking.

'Axes are for lumber-men, not soldiers.'

He began handing out the chipped old swords and Gawain grumbled quietly as he took one.

'Saxons use war-axes.'

He saw Ulfric give him an approving look but then Drustan answered curtly, barely looking at them as he handed out blades to the youngsters.

'Saxons bugger their goats at night, are you going to do that too?'

Ulfric said something indignant in his father's tongue, and for an eyeblink Drustan's teeth flashed white in his dark face.

'Oh, my apologies, Ulfric; sometimes they go in the front way with their goats, else you'd not be here, of course.'

Both Gawain and Burian chortled, and Burian elbowed Ulfric in the ribs.

'I'd only ever go in the front way with your ma.' He grinned and cupped his hands before his chest. 'I would hate to miss the view.'

Ulfric barged a shoulder into his chest, and Gawain put his foot behind him as Burian tried to step back. Burian's arms flailed comically as he realised he was falling, and dust flew when his rump hit the ground, accompanied by a muttered curse. Drustan's voice cut through the laughter.

'Alright, enough of that.'

He hauled his nephew up and pressed a training sword into his hand.

'You, go and take the boys through their sword-strokes.' He turned to Gawain and Ulfric. 'You two, get to work on the poles. I want to see good footwork from the pair of you.'

There was no point arguing with Drustan; in the training yard his word was law. Burian began teaching the youngsters the basic cuts by having them swing at thin air, while Gawain and Ulfric practiced those same strokes against hard targets. The oak pillars barely moved when they were struck, which meant the arm would jar on impact and the steel would either bite into the wood or else rebound, mimicking real combat that much better. Gawain started slowly, placing his feet carefully and letting his arms and shoulders warm up. Every now and then, mainly when Drustan wasn't looking his way, he switched the sword to his left hand to loosen the muscles on that side as well, and though his knees and back still ached, the more he moved the less pain he felt.

Drustan alternated between keeping an eye on Burian and the youngsters and criticising Ulfric and Gawain. When they struck with power he would berate them for a lack of control, and when they aimed their strikes more carefully he would reprimand them for not fully committing. Either their footwork was too lazy or their recovery wasn't smooth enough, or the blow was ill-timed or the follow-up was clumsy. Always there was something wrong with that they did, no matter how hard they worked or how much they improved, but he'd been teaching them that way for years now, and it was a method that worked.

By the time Gawain had found his stride even Drustan was struggling to find fault with him, and he followed the champion's lessons as he struck and moved. The guilt that had been weighing him down began to ease away as Gawain lost himself in the simple joy of doing something he was good at. The aches and pains wracking his body began to melt away too as he struck and dodged and struck again, revelling in the moment. It was hard not to grin as he felt years' worth of strength and skill flowing right to the tips of his fingers, and he attacked the pole with a speed that belied his bulky size. Gawain could still remember Drustan's reaction the first time he had proudly hacked an old training pole in two. '*I don't give a rat's turd how strong you are; if you're too slow to hit the mark, it won't matter to anyone.'* Strength in a fight was important, but more vital than anything was speed. And so Gawain had learned to move fast.

His hair was lank with sweat by the time Drustan called a halt, but though he was hot and breathing hard, Gawain was feeling happier than he had done all day. He leaned his hands against his thighs, the pain in his knees forgotten, as the champion gave out his next instructions.

'Blades down. Gather staves for man-to-man.' He turned and called over his shoulder. 'Burian, pair them up and don't let them kill each other.'

Gawain set his blade against one of the barrels and waited while Ulfric fetched them a pair of sparring staves. Drustan watched them keenly, waiting for some word of protest. Only that winter Gawain, Ulfric and Burian had been permitted to start sparring with blunted steel, but Gawain had clipped the Saxon's shoulder with a poorly-controlled swing, and ever since the trio had been demoted to using wooden staves again. At every other session they'd had, at least one of the boys had tried to talk Drustan into letting them use steel, and he was clearly ready for them to ask again today. But Gawain for one didn't have it in him to argue. He was finally feeling better after a truly dreadful morning, and he wasn't about to spoil his good mood by having Drustan be angry with him.

Apparently Ulfric was contented enough to keep silent as well, and he brought the staves over without comment. Drustan eyed the boys suspiciously for a moment, but then gave them a short nod.

'Take your guard.'

Gawain took a stave, and he and Ulfric held them ready, waiting for Drustan's word. The champion nodded again and took a step back.

'Don't forget your footwork. Get to it.'

The pair grinned at each other, and went to it with a will. The ash staves were heavy enough that they tired the arms, but not so heavy that a blow would cause real harm if it struck anywhere but the head. And they had learned early on to keep their guards high. Ulfric came swinging at Gawain with quick cuts to his left and right, but Gawain dodged the first and parried the second, thrusting forward with his stave and catching the Saxon a glancer across his chest. He grinned but Drustan's voice was unimpressed.

'If he'd been in mail that would be nothing; continue.'

Gawain didn't argue with the correction, and he and Ulfric traded half a dozen more cuts and parries. He'd just scored what must have been a solid killing blow when another voice caused them all to stop and turn.

'Drustan.'

The voice was deep and strong, and belonged to the handsomest man that Gawain, and indeed most of Dun Edin, had ever known. He had a large build but his shoulders tapered down to a slender waist, his blue-green tunic showing no bulge of fat anywhere on his frame. About his neck was a gold torque shaped with twin horses' heads, and gold also winked from the hilt of the dagger sheathed at his belt. His hair was dark red and worn long, so thick and sleek it might make a fox envious, though by far his most striking feature were his eyes. They were such a bright green they might have belonged to one of the fair folk, and as a babe they'd been enough to make men whisper that he was a changeling; a half-fae child left in a human crib. But then he'd grown, and the flaming hair of King Lot and sharp looks of Queen Morgause had made his parentage undeniable. This was Gaheris, and if there was a man anywhere that Gawain envied more, he had yet to encounter him.

Gaheris strode into the yard with careless grace, the barest hint of a swagger in his stride. He was a vain man who did his best to keep people from seeing it, but little things like the sway of his walk, and the fact that he refused to let a beard hide his face, made it plain that Gaheris was extremely fond of himself. *And he's not alone in that.* Gawain, Burian and Ulfric all liked to *talk* about girls but as yet none of them had done more than steal a kiss from one. At only two years Gawain's senior, Gaheris had left a trail of broken hearts a mile long, and since he'd refused more than one marriage offer, it seemed that trail was destined to grow longer before he was settled.

But for all his vanities Gawain and Gareth had grown up worshipping this man. Unlike the dour Agravain, Gaheris had tempered his arrogance with a quick wit and a generous nature, and had always been the first to laugh at a prank, whether he was the mark or the maker. But Gaheris was not laughing now. He didn't even glance at Gawain and the nod he gave to Drustan was short. The champion bowed his head.

'Lord Gaheris, welcome home.' He stepped forward and clapped the younger man on the back. 'So, you saw off the Irish easily enough?'

Gaheris smiled but only a very little.

'We stung them hard, but they'll be back. My father wishes to speak to you; I will be heading west again after Beltane and he wishes to know what new lads are fit to join me. Peleus may want spearmen sent north to him as well.'

Drustan nodded thoughtfully.

'Yes. I have a few who could suit, I think.' He turned to his charges. 'Continue with your practice. Burian; keep a close eye on the youngsters.'

He made as if to leave then hesitated when he saw Gaheris was not following him. The handsome man smiled again.

'I will join you shortly.'

Drustan's eyes flicked between Gaheris and Gawain but he simply nodded and left the yard without a word. Gawain moved towards his brother, hoping quietly that Lot hadn't told him about the escapade with Durro. One glare from those bright green eyes dashed his hopes to pieces, and Gawain felt his stomach lurch.

'Gaheris…'

But his brother interrupted him.

'So, what's this I hear about you turning a horse loose and almost getting Gareth killed?'

Despite the difference in years the two brothers were of similar size, and Gawain didn't have to look up when Gaheris stepped close to him.

'I was stupid, and…'

Before he could finish, Gaheris shoved him with both hands, and he lost his footing and sat down hard on the trampled earth.

'Damned *right* you were stupid!' He wasn't quite shouting, but his voice was full of barely-restrained anger. 'What in Bel's name were you thinking you bloody fool?'

Gawain saw Ulfric approach, looking nervous.

'Lord, he…'

But Gaheris barely even looked at him to slap him down.

'He's *my* brother is what he is.' He turned his shining eyes back on Gawain. 'Did you think taming a horse would make you a big man? Was that it?'

Gawain tried to stand but Gaheris shoved him back down again.

'You thought risking Gareth's life was worth it if you could feel a few inches taller, eh?'

Gawain scrambled to his feet, a spark of anger burning off some of the guilt. When Gaheris tried to push him again he thrust his palm hard into his brother's chest, forcing him to take a step back.

'I was stupid, and I never thought anyone would be in danger. I am sorry.'

Gaheris' bright eyes never left Gawain's.

'Oh, you will be.' His gaze snapped to Ulfric. 'Give me yours.'

By the time the Saxon realised that he was still holding a training stave Gaheris had already snatched it from him. Gawain had let his go when he'd first been pushed down, and Gaheris jerked his chin at it before fixing him with a glare.

'Pick it up, or you can take your beating without it.'

Gawain didn't want to fight his brother. For one thing he would almost certainly lose, and for another, this would be no sparring match between comrades. This would be exactly what Gaheris had called it; a beating, and if Gaheris came in hard then Gawain would have to fight back just as hard, and both of them might easily end up hurt. But reluctant or not, Gawain wasn't fool enough to take a thrashing unarmed, and he took up the stave and faced his brother. The moment he did, Gaheris was on him.

The first three strokes came in so fast Gawain only stopped them by blind luck and instinct, and the fourth caught him completely unawares. The stave thudded dully into the muscle of his left leg, and in the half-second it took him to wince, Gaheris had struck him again. This time the stave caught him low in the ribs, right where they were already tender, and Gawain coughed out in pain. Gaheris didn't relent. He attacked again, and then again, and no matter how many of them Gawain stopped, solid blows kept breaking through his defence. Within moments his limbs and torso were a screaming mass of pain, and still his brother went on.

Gawain's guilt vanished completely as anger took over from it. He was sorry for what he'd done, and he'd taken the punishment Lot and Iain had agreed upon. Gaheris had every right to be angry, and every right to box his ears, even. But enough was enough.

Completely ignoring the rules of the yard, Gawain blocked his brother's stave and then grabbed hold of it by the 'blade'. In their usual training this would have earned him a bellowed reprimand from Drustan, but the champion wasn't here, and Gaheris had gone too far. Gawain yanked back hard and tore the weapon from his brother's grip. He only blinked once, but it was time enough for Gawain to drop the staves and drive a solid punch into Gaheris' midriff. The shock of the blow gave him another momentary opening, and Gawain used it to duck in low and grab hold of Gaheris' legs. He shoved forward hard and drove his elder to the ground, landing with as much weight on him as he could. Gaheris huffed out a breath as the impact jarred him, but he recovered himself in an eyeblink and lashed out with a closed fist. Gawain felt his eyes flood with tears as stinging pain burned through his nose, and a moment later he was being rolled over. Gaheris pinned him with his knees and drew his fist back for another blow, but someone grabbed his arm and hauled him back.

'That's enough!'

Gaheris struggled and swore.

'Let go of me you Saxon bastard!'

Gawain scrabbled to his feet as Ulfric and Burian dragged Gaheris from him. Hurt and angry though he was, Gawain felt a little surge of warmth at the sight; this was their king's second eldest they were manhandling after all, and they were doing it to help *him*. Gaheris spat obscenities and looked like he was about to start fighting all three of them, but then a voice from the oak posts struck him dumb.

'Stop it!'

Gawain turned to see the speaker, and felt his guts twist as Gareth came running towards them; the guilt he'd so easily banished in the heat of the fight came flooding back at the sight of his little brother. Even slender Ulfric looked big compared with the youngest Lothian, but nonetheless the boy's voice brooked no argument.

'Stop it now!'

Gaheris had stopped struggling and he held his hands up, palms open.

'Alright. Alright, enough.'

Ulfric and Burian backed away from him, looking relieved, and Gawain tried to think of something suitable to say. Gareth spoke first.

'He didn't mean any…'

But Gaheris cut him off.

'I said *enough*, and that means enough from all of us.'

Gareth looked like he wanted to say more but a look from Gaheris silenced him. The handsome man, his face flushed and his hair ruffled, looked from one brother to another, and then spoke the word again.

'Enough.'

Before either Gawain or Gareth could say anything he spun around and strode away, and the youngsters at the other end of the yard, who'd been watching all this open-mouthed, scattered at his approach. He was out of sight in ten heartbeats.

Gawain turned to Gareth and tried to ignore the blood dripping from his nose.

'You didn't have to…'

Gareth waved a hand as if swatting away a fly.

'Oh, be quiet.' He cocked his head and looked at him, concerned. 'Are you alright?'

Gawain saw the same question in the faces of his friends, and he wiped the blood away as casually as he could. More trickled down but he ignored it.

'Of course. He was angry, and with good cause.' He tried for a roguish grin and gestured at his nose. 'It's lucky for Gaheris you stopped us when you did. I'd have hated to pay him back for this and spoil his pretty face.'

He ruffled Gareth's hair, which he knew irritated him, and Gareth slapped at his hand.

'Don't make this harder than it has to be.'

Gawain frowned, not sure what he meant. Gareth elaborated, not quite meeting his eyes.

'Halwen came to see me after that business with Durro. She wanted to know I was alright.'

It was understandable, Gawain thought. Gareth wasn't just the darling of the Lothian family, he was the darling of all Dun Edin, and Halwen doted on him as much as anyone. Naturally Gareth hated this, the same as he hated having people ruffle his hair, but Gawain suspected he'd soon grow to appreciate it when girls lavished their attention on him. *But what must Halwen think of* me *after all this?* Gareth would never betray their plan, but had anyone outside Iain and the family suspected the truth of what happened? He swallowed before replying.

'And, what did you say to her?'

Gareth shrugged, looking uncomfortable.

'I told her I was well. Then she asked about you.'

Gawain nodded, wishing his brother would get on with it. 'And what did you tell her then?'

Gareth shuffled his feet.

'I told her you were being blamed for it, and that Father was punishing you. She didn't think that was fair and said I should give you a message if I saw you.'

Gawain's spirits lifted at the news that Halwen was, albeit misguidedly, on his side, but his thoughts were interrupted as Gareth took a step closer and, reaching up, planted a kiss on his cheek. He blinked in surprise, then realisation struck him like a thunderbolt, and even the whooping jeers of his friends couldn't spoil it as his heart soared. *She sent a kiss! She sent* me *a kiss!* Gawain grinned like a fool as the others laughed and joked. For all the guilt and scrubbing and beatings he'd had to take, this might well be the best Beltane Eve he'd ever had.

Chapter Three

With his nose still tender and Gaheris in his current temper, Gawain was in no mood to go into the hall to eat. Instead he bolted down a quick meal by the kennels, where Ulfric had gone to tend the wolfhounds with his father. It was simple enough fare; a small loaf, some cheese, and handful of sausages, but it was filling and welcome. Una's sausages, carefully seasoned with her various herbs, were a particular favourite of Gawain's, though it seemed they were also a favourite of the hounds', and eating them undisturbed had been a challenge. Mabb, the largest of them, had been leaping on him so wildly that Gawain had sacrificed two of his precious sausages just to calm him down. Now he was ruffling the huge dog's ears with one hand as Mabb licked the other one clean.

Mabb was both the fiercest and the friendliest of all the hounds in Ekbert's kennel. The great grey wolfhound was easily three feet tall at the shoulder and must have weighed as much as Gareth did, if not more. He was entirely shameless when it came to food or affection, and Gawain had been forced to take only quick sips from his ale mug, since whenever he moved his hand Mabb would always shove his head back under it. But he seemed content to be still for a while at least, and Gawain sat and scratched the hound's ears, staring absently into the distance.

His guilt over the incident with Durro was fading thanks to the punishments he'd endured, but the fight with Gaheris was troubling him. His brother hadn't been in the wrong exactly, but though Gawain had felt terrible for letting down his idol, at the same time Gaheris had surely taken matters too far. Hadn't he? *But then, what would you have done if he'd endangered Gareth as you did?* Gawain didn't much like the answer. He also thought of Beltane, and how he'd have to start work while it was still dark if he was to clean Iain's floors before the festival. It was hard not to feel resentful but once again he reminded himself that it was a punishment he'd earned.

More than anything, he thought of Halwen. What had she meant by that kiss? Was it merely a sign of friendship or sympathy, or appreciation for his seeming to help Gareth? Kin and comrades exchanged kisses every day, perhaps that had been all she'd meant by it. But what if she'd meant more than that? What if she thought of him the way he thought of her, and had seen this morning as a chance to show her affections? Perhaps it was a fool's hope but he couldn't help holding on to it, and all through his meal he'd wondered if he ought to go and see her. He frowned. *And what will you say?*

He was still absently fussing Mabb and trying to think what Gaheris would do in his place, when Ulfric came strolling up to them.

'If all the help you plan to be is distracting this trouble-maker,' he ruffled Mabb's fur affectionately, 'then the least you can do is say you'll do us all a certain favour?'

Gawain looked up at him.

'What sort of favour?'

The Saxon looked at him as though he was slow-witted.

'Talk to your father of course. If Gaheris is looking for men to send to war then we ought to be the first ones considered fit.'

Gawain pointed to his swollen nose.

'You do remember this? Do you think Gaheris will rush to have us join him after today?'

Ulfric brushed the objection aside.

'I didn't say to speak to *him*, I said speak to the king. Gaheris said they might be sending spearmen north as well, remember. Peleus would be glad to have men like us to fight the Picts.'

It was true enough that he, Ulfric and Burian were some of the best candidates to be sent into battle, but he seriously doubted if Lot or Gaheris would be in any mood to do him favours today. Ulfric persevered.

'Burian will speak to Drustan, you just need to ask your father. Just ask him, that's all.'

Gawain felt torn. On the one hand he'd been longing to see battle since the day Drustan first handed him a stave, but on the other, what if Halwen really did share his feelings? Going north to Peleus would mean being parted from her for months, and who knew who else might try seducing her whilst he was gone? She was the prettiest girl in all Dun Edin, there was no chance at all that she would go un-courted. *But there is duty to consider as well.*

Ulfric saw his thoughts.

'We won't be going for a while anyway, and you'll have Beltane to try to charm your girl.'

His girl. It was a pleasant thought, even if it was a foolish one. In the long term any courtship of Halwen was almost certainly a lost cause; he was a son of the Royal House of Lothian and he had his duty, but that didn't mean he couldn't *hope*. Beltane was a time when the veil between the mortal world and the Otherworld grew thin, if ever there was a time for hope, it was now. He tried not to think of the fact that Beltane also meant the ritual of the fire-walk. He wouldn't be Summer King at the festival now, and if Halwen was to be Spring Maiden then at the fire-walk he'd have to watch someone else take her hand through the procession, and see someone else share a kiss with her at the end. He fumed quietly and did his best not to over-think things. It would only be a ritual anyway, and besides, *he* was the one she'd already sent a kiss to.

Ulfric brought his mind back to the present.

'So? If Burian speaks to Drustan, will you speak to your father?' He half-smiled. 'We Saxons won't have much say in the matter.'

Gawain nodded. The king might be displeased with him but there was no harm in asking, and Lot's temper was like lightning; quick to come, terrible to behold, but gone again soon enough. With luck he might have calmed down by now and be keen to see his son seasoned in war. He stood, ruffling Mabb's floppy ears one last time.

'I will ask him.'

Ulfric grinned and clapped him on the arm. Gawain did his best not to wince. Gaheris had struck him more or less everywhere, and Ulfric had just slapped a blossoming bruise.

'Huntsman's luck!'

Gawain gave a wry smile.

'If the Huntsman was on my side today, he'd have made my sword-arm quicker.'

Ulfric just grinned again.

'Then he owes you some luck!'

Gawain hoped that was true, though he hoped as well that neither Father Iain nor Christ found out about that hope. They both disapproved of the Old Gods, even if the Huntsman took more interest in matters of war than they did.

He sighed, not quite convinced.

'I suppose so.'

He and Ulfric exchanged nods and Gawain turned to make for the hall, practicing in his head what he might say to his father.

As it turned out, his practicing was a wasted effort. He circled the hall to reach one of the side doors, but as he opened it to step in he almost collided with his mother coming out. He bowed his head.

'Forgive me.' He glanced around her. 'Is Father inside?'

Morgause shook her head.

'He went into the town with Drustan and your brother; looking for new boys to fight the Irish.' She tilted her head and took in his swollen nose. 'What clumsy fool did that?'

Gawain assumed that Gaheris hadn't spoken of their quarrel and he decided not to mention it either.

'If anyone was clumsy it was me for dropping my guard.'

Morgause sighed, looking torn between wanting him to learn important lessons and a mother's instinctive need to protect her children.

'Well, hopefully a battered nose has been a good enough tutor. I'll fetch you a cool cloth for it.'

Gawain waited dutifully, and she was gone and back within a few moments. At first even the gentle pressure of the cloth stung his tender nose, but the coolness of it was soothing. The queen dabbed a corner of it above his mouth to clean off the blood.

'Now, since you don't seem fit for anything more strenuous, you can go and find Anna for me. She left her spinning half-done and your father needs his green cloak finished before tomorrow.'

Gawain nodded. Even the children of the king weren't spared from work at festival time, and spinning and weaving was the lot of every woman of the Dun, whether common or noble. Morgause went on, and Gawain could tell there was more to her words than it might seem.

'Anna will be gossiping somewhere I'm sure. She was chatting with Sibeal's girl earlier.'

Despite himself Gawain felt his heart quicken, and his mother's eyes showed the sudden triumph of a suspicion confirmed. Morgause had somehow mastered the technique of looking down her nose at sons who were taller than she was, and Gawain found himself subject to that look now.

'I thought as much. Gawain, I will say this only once; you watch yourself around that girl.' He opened his mouth to say something but his mother ignored him and carried on. 'Do not bother denying it, you're wearing your heart all over your broken face. I know Halwen is a lovely girl, but the fact is she's a smith's daughter and I have already begun negotiating a proper match for you.'

Gawain's face fell, and the heart he apparently wore on it sank down to his guts.

'You have?'

Morgause nodded.

'It is early days but I have exchanged letters with Bors of Bernicia. His daughter Leanor is of marrying age and will make a fine match for us.'

She was right, of course, though it pained Gawain to hear it. Bors of Bernicia was the brother of King Bran, who ruled the kingdom south of Lothian. Gawain had heard whispers that Anna was to be matched with one of Bran's own sons, ideally his heir, Hector. If both marriages went ahead then the Lothians and Bernicians would be doubly tied together. *It all makes good sense, so what does it matter what* we *think of it?* Morgause saw the despair in his face.

'It won't happen just yet, and I won't begrudge you a sweetheart in the meantime if she is fond of you, but I expect you to behave yourself. You understand what I mean?'

Gawain felt himself blushing. He'd imagined *exactly* what she meant on more than one occasion, but the idea of admitting that in front of his mother was enough to make him shuffle his feet. He dropped his eyes to the ground.

'I understand, Mother.'

When he looked up her expression was cynical, but she waved him away nonetheless.

'Alright, be off with you.'

Gawain for grateful for the dismissal; the conversation had managed to be both depressing and embarrassing. He kept the cloth pressed to his nose with one hand and started to make his way around the hall. When he'd last seen Halwen she'd been braiding ribbons under the east wall, and assuming Anna was indeed with her, he decided it was best to start there. The walk took him back through the kennels, where he naturally had to pause to ruffle Mabb's ears again and apologise for having no more sausages, and then onward past the stables. Durro wasn't there, and presumably the king had taken him on the ride into the town. Gawain looked at the empty paddock and felt his guilt threatening to resurface, then he reminded himself that he'd paid enough for that little escapade, and he focused instead on what he would say to Halwen when he saw her.

By the time he reached the main yard he had given up on planning anything clever to say and decided to trust to good fortune. As Ulfric had said, he was owed some luck by now, and given that she'd already sent him a kiss, Gawain felt confident he was building on solid ground.

The grassy yard was bright in the afternoon sun, and still a busy hive of activity as the Dun prepared for Beltane. Fires would be lit here as well as down in the town, and long trenches were being dug in readiness for them. More than a few people took second glances when they saw the king's son walking about with a cloth over his face, but nobody stopped to ask him about it, for which Gawain was very grateful. He was in no great rush to explain his bruises.

Halwen and the others were still sitting where they had been, though Gawain noticed their great pile of green and yellow ribbons had grown much smaller, and the pile of intertwined braids had grown much larger. His breath caught in his throat a little at the sight of Halwen, but he was sure the bronze rings in her hair were winking encouragement at him, and he took that as a good omen. Sitting with her were her mother, Sibeal, a handful of other young girls of the Dun, and, as Morgause had predicted, his sister Anna.

Like Agravain, Anna had inherited their mother's dark hair rather than the usual Lothian red, and though she was a full year younger than Gawain, already she had grown taller than most girls three or four years her senior. She had the same long nose and strong chin as Morgause, and but for a single mole on one cheek her pale face was completely unmarred. Folk often said she was the image of how her mother had looked when she'd first come north, and even her voice was strikingly reminiscent of the queen's. Of course, right now she didn't seem quite so much like their mother. Anna was giggling beneath her breath as she shared some quiet jest with Sibeal, and the older woman chuckled in return. She looked up guiltily as Gawain approached and he hoped the laughter hadn't been at his expense; his pride had suffered enough for one day.

It was Sibeal who greeted him first, though her hands kept braiding as she spoke.

'Gawain, what happened to your nose?'

Very aware of Halwen's eyes on him, Gawain smiled and kept his reply casual.

'Just a knock in the training yard.'

He wanted to speak to Halwen but thought he ought to give his reason for being here first. He looked to his sister.

'Mother says you have work to do.'

Anna, whose lap was full of ribbons, held up a fistful and gave him an impatient look.

'And what would you call this?'

Gawain shrugged.

'What I call it doesn't matter. Mother calls it gossip, and said to fetch you back to the hall.'

Anna sighed and Halwen spoke for her.

'Why do you want to drag her indoors when it's so lovely out here?'

She gestured to the sunny day around them, and Gawain tried not to notice how her dress shifted when she moved.

'I don't want to drag her anywhere, but have you ever tried saying *no* to my mother?'

Halwen rolled her shoulders, and again Gawain did his best not to stare.

'I would certainly try it on a day like today.'

Gawain wondered if it was an idle brag, but then Halwen's grandmother *had* been a Pict, and there was a fierceness in those hazel eyes that spoke of her wilder ancestry; he supposed if anyone in Dun Edin would risk standing up to Morgause, it would be Halwen. Gawain tore his eyes from her and spoke to Anna again.

'Well, fair weather or not, she wants you back at the hall.'

Anna shrugged disinterestedly and changed the subject.

'Have you seen that Gaheris is back?'

A couple of the girls giggled at the mention of the handsomest of the Lothians, but Gawain noted with a glimmer of hope that Halwen wasn't one of them.

'I saw him at the yard, yes.'

Anna smirked.

'Did he watch while one of your stupid friends squashed your face for you?'

Gawain felt himself begin to redden, but before he could comment Halwen put a playful elbow into Anna's ribs.

'You didn't think they were stupid earlier. What was it you said about Burian again? That he had…'

This time it was Anna who reddened and she elbowed Halwen back. Gawain raised an eyebrow at her but Anna glared at him. It wasn't a glare to match their mother's, but he suspected she would master the art in time.

'You can wipe that look from your cracked face.'

Gawain raised his free hand.

'It's none of my concern. But you need to get back to the hall, now.'

He'd tried to sound authoritative, as a big brother should, but Anna's glare quickly became a smirk.

'It's hard to take you seriously when you're talking through a soggy rag.' The smile widened. 'It improves your looks though.'

Gawain half-hoped that Halwen would say something to that, but it was a foolish thing to hope and so he ignored the insult.

'Listen, we all have…'

But Anna interrupted him.

'Work, yes. And what vital work are *you* doing today, besides getting your nose smashed in the training yard?'

He was about to say that he was going to volunteer to help with the digging, or sneakily get some practice with the war-axe by chopping wood, but this time Halwen *did* come to his rescue.

'Go easy on him, Anna. He's had a hard morning already.' She kept working as she spoke, her delicate fingers quick and nimble on the ribbons. 'You weren't there when Durro got loose.'

Anna didn't seem to sympathise.

'Father said it was stupid of you to approach him. Durro's a Sarmatian warhorse for Bel's sake; you should have left it to the grooms to calm him down.'

Gawain let a little sarcasm creep into his voice, though he knew his attitude was hardly justified; it *had* been his fault after all.

'I suppose I should have just let him run wild until someone else caught him, is that it?'

He felt a warm tingle in his chest when Halwen agreed with him.

'He had no choice. Gareth might have been trampled if he hadn't come to help him.'

Gawain struggled not to beam as she spoke of him so glowingly. Her eyes met his for a moment and he was sure something passed between them, something that said the kiss she'd sent had been more than a friendly gesture. The look only lasted a heartbeat but Gawain guessed that Anna at least had noticed it, because she suddenly picked up the ribbons from her lap and put them down on the bench.

'Well, as you say, I am needed at the hall. Are you coming too?'

Gawain wanted to scowl at her; he was finally sharing a tender moment with Halwen and she was deliberately ruining it for him. She made things worse when she stood up.

'Oh, and you've probably not heard yet; Elgan has been around and it looks like Halwen will be our Spring Maiden this year.'

Halwen smiled humbly and Gawain's irritation doubled. If the old druid had chosen the maiden then he would certainly have chosen the kings by now, and tomorrow he would have to watch some other smug swine walking Halwen through the fires. He did his best to hide his frustration and bowed his head to her.

'Danu's blessings for the morrow.'

She bowed back.

'Thank you, Gawain.'

Her voice was soft and smooth, and he cursed his stupidity for the hundredth time. If he hadn't been such a damned glory-seeking fool, he'd have been chosen as Summer King and would be at her side for the fire-walk. But, there was nothing he could do about that now. He looked at Halwen's eyes and dearly wished they could speak alone, but then, what would he say to her if they were?

He kept a polite smile on his face but growled inwardly, and he stuck his arm out for Anna to take. His sister looped her arm around his, and he tried not to sound awkward as he said farewell to Halwen.

'Well, I shall see you at the festival then.'

She smiled her lovely smile at him.

'Of course. I hope your nose feels better by then; you'll not want to look grumpy in front of everyone.'

Gawain's brow furrowed.

'In front of everyone?'

Anna gave his arm a quick squeeze and there was a wicked glint in her eye.

'Oh, did Mother not tell you? She spoke to Elgan before he came around and put in a kind word for you.' She nudged his ribs, and Gawain didn't know if he wanted to kiss her or strangle her. 'You're to be the Summer King tomorrow.'

Chapter Four

Folk often said that women made poor archers. It took strength to draw a hunting bow, they said, therefore in hunting and in war alike, the bow was clearly a weapon better suited to a man than to a woman. They might have had a point. But those folk had clearly never met Darina. Mhari watched her string her great yew bow and wondered how many men in her warband could shoot it as far, or as accurately, as Darina could. Darina wasn't bulky or mannish, indeed, the fair-haired woman was a good stone lighter than Mhari herself, but there was a subtle strength in her lean frame that only a fool took for granted. None of the others' bows could match the power of Darina's weapon, and many looked as feeble as toys by comparison. It would surely be Darina's arrows that would make the most kills today, and Mhari tried not to envy her for it. *When it comes to spear and sword, then it will be my time.*

She touched Brathir's hilt for good fortune, then cast her eyes around to make sure all was in readiness. The Picts had come right to the edge of the trees and now lay or crouched in a long line, almost invisible in the half-light of the dawn. Morning mist was trailing along the open valley ahead and, less than one good bowshot away, their enemy was slowly waking up. The Lothians had stupidly set their camp directly in her warband's path, and while they might just have been able to sneak their way around, that would have been a coward's choice; the Thunderer would think twice about blessing them if his warriors shirked from battle. Besides, these Lothian bastards were on Pictish land and had to learn what fate awaited trespassers.

All along the line, waiting quietly in the shadow of the trees, her warriors watched the southerners like wolves watching a flock. Conn was nearest to her, his long limbs sprawled across the dewy ground, and though his hair hung down over most of his face, he was staring through the strands with a burning intensity. Mhari saw his fingers flexing on his spear, and when he saw that she was watching him he turned his head and grinned. Mhari smiled back, feeling her own heartbeat begin to quicken. Every one of them was eager for the off, eager for blood, though for all the noise they made, they might as well have been an army of ghosts; the little pinewood was as silent as a pyre-side.

Of course, once again, the Grey Woman was staying well clear of the action. She'd cast her bones to be sure the foe had no magicker with them, then declared the battle safe to enter and melted away into the trees. Temar was almost certainly hanging back as well, and Mhari didn't regret either of their absences. So long as the Grey Woman's predictions were correct and Temar's men were willing to fight, Mhari couldn't give a broken stick what they did while the warriors fought.

She kept eyeing the southerners as the early-risers began setting cook-fires for the morning porridge. Mhari wondered idly who had brought them here; Hardhand had not been heard of for months and more, and few of Lot's warlords scouted so far north. The shields lying beside the travelling packs all bore the Red Fox of Lothian, but there was no other sign of who these warriors might be. Then she saw him, a tall man with close-cropped hair, a shaven face, and a red tunic that looked bright even in the grey of the morning. *Peleus*. Mhari had only ever seen him once, and that from a distance, but she knew him by reputation. Some grandsire of his had been a man of the legions, and Peleus liked to emulate the Romans of old by scraping his face and bathing too often, and by chasing away Picts whenever he saw the opportunity. Unlike most of Lot's warlords, who were content to fight raiders and then raid back in turn, Peleus apparently held dreams of conquest, and wished for Lothian to rule all the way to the world's edge. *An arrogant fool. But a* skilled, *arrogant fool.*

Mhari decided quietly that she would kill him herself, and up close if she could do it. Peleus was a very well-thought-of man, and it never hurt to remind her warriors of just why she was in charge. Being canny was all very well but no-one led Picts without being good at killing, and slaying the well-reputed Peleus would do her own reputation a deal of good. She felt herself smiling at the notion, but then focused her mind on the task ahead of them.

They'd been fortunate enough to kill the Lothians' watcher before he could raise the alarm, but soon enough the others would wonder where he'd gone. Her warband had the numbers, but if the southerners became wise to them they would form a shieldwall, which was the bane of any Pictish force. Part of Mhari sometimes wished that she could train her own people to fight like that, but it was a fool's notion; the Picts were the bravest fighters on Danu's Earth but they had no love for discipline, and it was discipline that made a shieldwall. Besides, a Pict lived for the glory of combat, and what glory was there in standing behind a linden-wood board and jabbing at the enemy until he went away?

But craven or not the shieldwall was a dangerous enemy, and they had to attack now before the southerners had a chance to form one. In any case today was Beltane, a time for the Old Gods to show their might, and when a gentle wind rustled through the trees Mhari knew those gods were telling her it was time. The warband would all be in position by now, and to wait longer was to court disaster. *Time to make work for the ravens*. She turned her head and nodded to Darina, who smiled and nocked an arrow to her string. Mhari did the same, and along the line her archers shifted position or rose to one knee and readied themselves. There were only a handful of targets so far, a sentinel or two and some bleary-eyed men, but it was enough for them each to score a kill if Taranis was with them, and Mhari touched Brathir's pommel for his blessing.

Darnia might have been the best markswoman of them but Mhari was the chief, and she would loose the first arrow. She took a slow breath and sighted on a man who'd wandered to the little camp's edge, and was currently fishing his member out from his trews. Mhari kept her eye on him as he started to piss, raised the bow slowly and drew in the same smooth motion. She released with a tiny exhalation.

The weapon thrummed gently, and before the arrow struck its mark Mhari was on her feet, and within a heartbeat a dozen more shafts were whizzing towards the camp. She saw her arrow strike home in the pissing man's stomach, while other shafts thudded into various chests and legs. One, which must have been Darina's shot, went clean through a sentinel's eye.

Mhari began to sprint, her long legs covering the open ground in great loping strides. She nocked and loosed another arrow on the run, though it flew wide of its mark and whipped harmlessly past a southerner's head, but as her blood began to race and the Thunderer's strength coursed through her, Mhari decided she didn't care a damn for one arrow. She dropped the bow and drew out Brathir, and as the distance closed she screamed her people's war-cry.

'Garnaith!'

The name of their ancient king, so revered he was practically a god, echoed from all around her as the warband charged the unprepared camp. She could feel Conn's presence beside her and knew his blood would be pounding as hard as hers, desperate to get to grips with the enemy. Alarms were being called, men were scrabbling for their weapons, and Peleus had grabbed a shield and started bellowing for men to form on him; but it was too late. Within seconds the Picts had crashed into the Lothians like a wave on a wall of sand, and Mhari was the first of the northerners to draw blood.

The first man to face her was groggy and slow, and was still bending to pick up a spear when Brathir smashed into his mouth. Blood and teeth flew as the steel sliced halfway through his head, and the man's feet went out from under him as his scream became a gurgle. Mhari didn't break her stride and kept pelting on through the camp, with Conn and the others close behind. Her next four kills barely counted since the men were armed only with blankets, and though the easy butchery didn't last long, it lasted long enough. Peleus' numbers had perhaps been equal to Mhari's to begin with, but nearly half of them had been slain or disabled before they had a chance to fight back. Now Pictish warriors were cutting down the rest, and the result of the battle was already a foregone conclusion.

A lone spearman tried charging her but Mhari batted the weapon away, and before he could draw back for another lunge she grabbed the haft and hauled herself towards him with Brathir aimed for his midriff. None of the Lothians had been given time to don their mail, and the steel rammed through the soft flesh of the southerner's belly. He grunted as the blade went in, then shrieked as Mhari twisted it and yanked it free, opening the wound wide and sending blood gushing to the grass. He dropped to his knees and Mhari screamed out her war-cry again; revelling in savage joy as her second blow crushed his skull.

The next man to come at her came charging in from her left, but Conn's spear spitted him before he closed into her range. She smiled as her lover drew the weapon out and cracked the haft into the southerner's head, dropping him to the earth like a clubbed hog. Another spearman appeared and this one they took together, with Mhari darting one way and Conn the other, forcing him to choose which one to face. He decided to make a grab for Conn's spear, and when he reached for it Mhari sent Brathir through the back of his leg. His cry was cut short when Conn's spearpoint impaled his throat.

Mhari looked about eagerly for more foemen to kill, but all she saw nearby were her own panting warriors. There was sporadic fighting here and there around the camp, but the battle seemed all but over already. Peleus was still alive and calling men to him, and three or four of them were even trying to form a shieldwall, but it was far too little and far too late. She watched as the warlord cut down one of her raiders, she couldn't tell who, then started battering at Darr with his Lothian shield. Mhari fixed her gaze on Peleus and bared her teeth in a grin. Her heart was still pounding with battle-lust, and she wasn't finished yet. She saw Conn looking at her and winked at him before dodging around a cook-fire and sprinting towards the would-be-Roman.

Taranis must have been watching her because though the men around him died like flies, Peleus himself was still standing when she reached him. His shield had managed to hold off Darr and the others, and Mhari shouted at Temar's man as she sped towards the group.

'Mine!'

Peleus turned at the sound, and Mhari took Brathir in both hands and swung it at his neck with all the power and weight of her charge. His shield came up at the last possible second but he'd had no time to put his shoulder behind it, and strong though he was, Mhari's momentum was stronger. Brathir slammed hard into the painted wood and the warlord stumbled off balance. Mhari stayed on him and hacked down at his shoulder, and was rewarded with a splash of red and a cry of pain, followed by the dull thud of the shield slipping from his wounded arm. She tried to press on and cut for his head, but despite his bleeding arm Peleus' instincts stayed sharp, and he brought his sword up to parry and then counter-cut with blistering speed. Mhari backed off a pace.

Though she kept her eyes on Peleus she knew the whole warband would be forming a circle to watch this fight. The battle was as good as over, and this was a final bout of entertainment for them before the corpse-looting started. They could easily have just rushed him of course, and had she not called out her challenge, Peleus would already be feathered with Darina's grey-fletched arrows. But she *had* called out a challenge, and now it was down to her to prove, once again, that she was still the chief. *Let the Grey Woman's spells try to match* this*!*

Mhari bellowed at the warlord and feigned a lunge at his head. His dodge was predictable, but when she brought Brathir around for the real attack Peleus moved like a wary cat, blocking the cut and swiping at her stomach in a single fluid movement. A lesser swordfighter would have been disembowelled, but Mhari was quick too and side-stepped at the last instant. The sword still clipped her ribs, but her furs were thick and the strength of the cut was spent, and the worst the blow could cause her was a bruise.

Her warriors were cheering now, calling out her name, or to Garnaith or the Thunderer. She was sure Conn's voice would be shouting louder than any of them but she didn't dare let her mind turn to him; there was killing to be done. Peleus came at her again, this time with a war-cry on his lips as he tried to rush her. He was a strong man, and if he closed the gap and made this a grapple then he would dominate Mhari with his strength. So she didn't let him. As he came on she crouched low and swiped at his legs, and before Peleus could slow or swerve, Brathir bit deep into one knee. His war-cry became a shout of pain as the leg buckled under him, and Mhari wasted no time in gloating. Even lamed this could be a dangerous man, and she hadn't become a chief by taking chances.

As he toppled she brought the sword up again, and without a second's hesitation she rammed it hard into his throat, bellowing Garnaith's name as the steel ripped through Peleus' windpipe. The warlord's eyes went wide and blood streamed down his neck, and Mhari almost felt the sword dragged from her grip as the dying man crumpled to the dewy ground. The cheering swelled but Mhari wasn't finished yet; her blood was up and she had a point to prove. Peleus was still gurgling his life away when Brathir hacked into his neck again, and then *again*, until on the third swing his head finally came free, and Mhari took it by the hair and held it up for all to see.

'For Taranis!'

The cheers grew deafening, and though the grisly offering felt slack in her hands, and gore dripped stickily from the man's ragged neck, Mhari didn't care a damn. She had killed a warlord of Lothian, and she knew the Thunderer would honour her for it. She threw her head back and screamed to the clouds, and her warriors all joined her in a chorus of savage delight. Even when blood dripped on her face Mhari couldn't help but grin at the sky. The sun had barely risen, and already it seemed that this would be a fine Beltane.

Killing the Lothian wounded hadn't taken long. As she'd expected, Temar had skulked back to the men guarding the slaves and livestock before the fighting started, and only now had he been brave enough to come into the camp. *Useless bastard.* The flat-faced fool had amused himself by spearing a few dying men, and had tried to torment one of them by blinding him with a knife, but the Huntsman was showing pity to his own and the southerner died as the first eye was taken. Mhari wondered quietly how low her opinion of Temar would sink before she wound up killing him in frustration, and the answer was worryingly inconvenient. *You need the warriors, just remember that.* When they got back north and the tale of this fight was told, Temar's mother would encourage more warriors to join Mhari's band, and if enough of them joined then Mhari could justifiably be called a warlord; it was worth putting up with the lumbering toad until then.

She wandered over to where Conn was trying on a taken mailshirt, and her lover smiled as she approached him and pointed to a bundle on the ground.

'That one might fit you; looks like it was made for a youngster.'

From someone else those words might have implied some disrespect, but from Conn it was simply the truth. The Lothians didn't approve of women fighting in their wars and tall though Mhari was, finding a mailshirt to fit her had been a challenge. *Damned fools, why do they waste half their people for no good reason?* Apparently the Romans had been the first to say that womenfolk should not be fighters, and the southerners had abandoned their old ways like dogs submitting to a trainer. Even with the Romans gone they still sent only men to war, while the Picts had retained the good sense to muster all the warriors they could field when they were needed. *Since when has a pair of teats meant that you can't fight?* She sighed to herself; it was just one more reason why Lothian would fall one day, it was only a question of when.

Mhari nodded to her lover and thrust Brathir into the ground before leaning down to pick up the metal shirt. It was heavy, but when worn she knew the weight would be spread out across her shoulders, and she heaved it over her head with a grunt of effort. Conn, in his typically subtle way of showing affection, slipped behind her while her arms were up and slid his hands around her body. He reached for her breasts but only had time for a quick squeeze before she released the weight of the shirt and let the metal rings drop with a jingle. The steel came crashing down on Conn's hands and he swore as he drew his arms back. Mhari smirked as the mailshirt settled comfortably on her shoulders, then turned to face her lover with one red eyebrow raised.

'Was that perhaps not the wisest idea you've had?'

He tried to give her a smile but it was spoiled a little by the way he massaged his thumb.

'I couldn't resist.'

Mhari held back a grin. She too was feeling the lust that was so common after a battle, but she couldn't help taunting Conn a little. She stepped in close to him and ran a hand down his chest, then enjoyed the look of shock when she grabbed hold of his manhood.

'Try, my love.'

She wasn't squeezing as tightly as she could, but it was enough to make him grimace as he nodded. She smiled as she released him, then grabbed the back of his neck and drew him down into a hard kiss. He returned it with a will, wrapping his arms around her and crushing her body to his, and Mhari wondered if anyone would notice if they disappeared into the trees for a while. Of course, it was at that moment that the Grey Woman made her presence felt.

'Did I not say that all would be well?'

Mhari resisted telling her exactly what she could go and do; frustrated or not, it was madness to openly disrespect a druid. *Even one as strange as her*. Mhari broke off the embrace, though Conn cheekily grabbed her rump before she stepped away. She slapped his backside in return and then turned her attention to the Grey Woman.

'I see that seven of ours are dead, as you foretold.'

The acknowledgement was grudging, but genuine. Difficult though she could be, the druid knew her work. The Grey Woman bowed her hooded head.

'My thanks, but mayhap this was not the battle which first I saw. We must be wary of any assumptions.'

It was an irritating answer, but Mhari was becoming accustomed to those. She nodded respectfully, then shrugged as if unconcerned.

'I am always wary.'

As ever, the Grey Woman acted as though she'd known what Mhari would say, and she bowed again, gesturing at the bloody plain.

'This was a fine beginning, Mhari mer Raghnal, you have been a credit to your folk. But we must not linger here.' She gave Mhari a long look and despite herself, the chief was drawn into her too-wide eyes. 'You must gather your strength quickly for the raiding to the south. Great events are already in motion.'

Chapter Five

By dawn the pipes and drums had already been playing all night, and the beat would not stop until Bel's chariot had crossed the sky and the great festival was done. A score of bards and younger druids would take their turns to play over the many hours until the sunset, and even then the music wouldn't end. The evening celebrations would continue well into the night, and eventually holy music would give way to bawdy songs, as ritual duty blended seamlessly into drunken revelry. But that time was still a long way off, and Gawain intended to enjoy every moment between now and then. All the same he was feeling nervous. If he was ever going to impress Halwen it would be today, and combined with the pressure of the whole of Dun Edin watching him, and all the gods as well, he couldn't help but feel a fluttering in his stomach.

He was waiting in the shade of the fortress' north gates, where the long procession down the hill would begin. From the Dun itself all the way to the open field past the town, the path had been decorated with ribbon-draped poles and flaming torches set into the earth, and soon he would walk that path in his role as the Summer King. Burian, who'd been chosen as Winter King, was already making his way down that path, followed by his drummers and the dozen Winter Dancers. Gawain could hear the merry booing of the townsfolk outside, and he could imagine his friend shaking his blackthorn rod at the crowd and pulling faces at the children as they jeered his menacing progress. *Only a few moments more, and it will be my turn.*

One of the novice druids put the final touch onto Gawain's costume, standing on the very tips of her toes to place a crown of cherry branches on his head. It was already a good sign from Bel that the cherry trees had ripened early, and dark red berries winked out from the woven wreath. Gawain stooped down to help her put the crown on him. His braided hair, weighted down by green ribbons, swung awkwardly about his face, and he swiped some of them back as the druid settled his crown in place, whispering a quiet prayer. For all his love of Halwen Gawain couldn't help noticing how pleasant it was to have the young woman so close to him, and out of loyalty he did his best not to look too hard.

The novice stepped away and smiled. Like every other girl today she wore a crown of daisies in her hair, but she was otherwise dressed simply in a druid's robe.

'Are you ready?'

Gawain told himself he was and nodded once. He'd been washed with morning dew, draped in his green-and-gold cloak, and his hair and limbs festooned with a score of matching ribbons. One half of his face was painted bright green and he bore the sword-length hawthorn rod of the Summer King in his right hand; he was as ready as he was likely to get. He flexed his hands on the rod and nodded.

'Ready.'

She smiled again and beckoned to a trio of drummers who'd been waiting for him, all draped in the bright colours of the Summer King. They struck up a merry beat and cheers began sounding from the people outside. Behind the drummers a group of druid novices, six men and five women, cast off their pale robes and readied themselves for the procession. The girl who'd helped dress him hurried over to join them, and Gawain couldn't help looking as she too let her robe slip to the grass. Like the others she wore nothing beneath it but the painted green marks of summer, and Gawain completely failed not to stare.

He growled at himself for being so shallow. Today might be a day to celebrate fertility, but he knew full well he ought to be thinking more about the union of the God and Goddess, and less about the sway of this young woman's hips. All the same, he was a young man standing before a group of naked women; holy thoughts were not going to be paramount in his mind. He tried to look instead at the naked men who were with them, and it did something to quench his ardour when one of the more… gifted men started dancing, and his manhood began flopping about like a great fish on dry land. Gawain looked away and quietly thanked Bel that the dancing druids would be *behind* him in the procession.

The cheering outside grew louder, perhaps touched with a tinge of impatience, and Gawain squared his shoulders and said a final prayer to Bel and the Huntsman to be with him. He felt a little guilty for ignoring Christ today, but no Roman god could say that Beltane was about them, and he hoped that Christ would understand that. Even if Father Iain would be scowling at them all day.

With that final prayer Gawain stepped through the archway, and the nearest of the townsfolk roared with approval as the Summer King strode into the early morning sunlight. He waved his hawthorn rod above his head and grinned at the cheering crowd. Gawain had been watching Beltane marches his whole life and had seen Gaheris perform these rites a year ago, and so he knew he had a high standard to meet in this role. Halwen might not have been there to see it, the Spring Maiden would follow after him, but it was important to give the crowd and gods a good show on the march, and so he leaped and danced and laughed his way along the path, feeling all his wariness vanish as he embraced the attention, and the simple joy of the festival.

Following after him came the drummers and the Summer Dancers, then the sound of pipes met his ears and he knew that more players would be emerging from the Dun. He grinned, feeling happy and free as he capered down the pathway with his braided hair flying wild about his face. A little way ahead of him he saw the winter procession dancing their way down, and when the hill steepened he even spied Burian at their head, leaping around like a giant frog and growling at the onlookers. Not to be outdone, Gawain started making great jumps into the air, roaring merrily every time he landed, to the cheers of the laughing crowd.

In his head Gawain knew that the way from the Dun to the town was no short walk, and even had he not made the trek a thousand times, the sheer number of poles and ribbons that had been prepared was proof enough of the distance. Yet it seemed to take no time at all. The progress of the Summer King felt like it was over in a matter of heartbeats, and before Gawain knew it they'd reached the open field at the far end of town, where long trenches had been dug and filled with brush for the Beltane fires. The crowd had broken up a little on the walk as some followed the Winter King, some the Summer King, and some the Spring Maiden who came after, but now they gathered in one great circle marked by yet more coloured poles, and waited for the next event. Gawain was sorely tempted to turn and look behind him to catch a glimpse of Halwen, but such behaviour was inappropriate, and he had a role to play.

Across the ring from him, at the north side, Burian and his white-painted dancers were leaping and twirling to the beat of their drums, and the Winter King slowly edged around until he stood with his back to the west. Gawain did the same, leading his dancers and drummers until their backs were to the east, and the path down which they'd come lay halfway between them. Burian was clearly enjoying himself, grinning like a madman as he waved the blackthorn rod. The white paint covering half his face was stark against his swarthy skin, but the harsh contrast only served to make the Winter King look more menacing, and more than one child was hiding behind their mother's skirts. Gawain watched him dance and threw back his head in a dramatic laugh, and the folk nearest to him bellowed approval as he embraced his Beltane persona. All his nerves had melted away as he lost himself in the revelry, then he caught sight of Halwen, and his heart began to hammer.

The Spring Maiden had appeared at the foot of the path, followed by her own drummers and dancers. She wore crimson ribbons and a crown of primroses in her red-blonde hair, and the bronze rings in it sparkled in the morning sunlight. The paint on her face was just two red lines on either cheek, and they somehow made her more beautiful, not less; they made Gawain think of the warpaint her Pictish ancestors would have worn, and the fierce spirit that lurked behind those lovely eyes. As befit the Spring Maiden, her dress was a rich red hemmed with golden-yellow thread, held in at the waist with a woven belt. Gawain's confidence almost faltered at the sight of her, but when Burian started his capering again he joined in as smoothly as he could.

The Winter King danced before the Spring Maiden and beckoned her to come to him, to hide herself away in the depths of winter's cold. Gawain leaped forward and spread his arms wide, a gesture to tempt spring to be reborn in Bel's fire.

Naturally, both boys tried to outdo each other in the wildness of their dancing, and Gawain's carefree joy returned as he fell into the familiar routine of competing with his friend. The crowd cheered for summer and booed for winter until, as was her role, Halwen gestured to the circle so that the two kings could fight it out. Gawain and Burian both bowed and stepped away, and the crowd around them began to clap in time with the beat of the drums. The united noise would drive away any wicked spirits who would seek to interfere, as well as giving the dancers a single beat as they made circuits of the ring.

Gawain and Burian returned to the east and west sides and cast aside their coloured cloaks to face each other bare-chested. There was a moment or two of posturing, but at a signal from the drummers the two kings locked eyes and shouted out a challenge. They charged headlong towards each other, and the battle for the Spring Maiden began.

Gawain had sparred with Burian a hundred times and they knew one another's reach to within a hair's breadth, so while the rods they held were thick, there was no chance at all of either king being hurt; that wasn't the point. They swiped at each other and clacked the sticks together, all the while dancing and posturing as they sought to impress the crowd. The grinned at each other as they played at fighting, slapping one another's legs and backsides with the rods and howling comically at every stroke. More than once, to the onlookers' delight, Gawain lifted Burian fully off his feet, and he would kick his legs wildly as he pretended to attempt escape. It was difficult not to laugh, as most of the clapping crowd did, and Gawain tried to remember there was a seriousness to this as well; if the gods thought they were simply playing for its own sake, Bel or one of the others might grow angry, and deny them a good spring no matter who won the 'battle'.

Of course, the winner was a foregone conclusion. After an enjoyable few minutes of trading blows the drumming sped up and they both recognised the signal. Burian took a final few swings with his blackthorn rod, then opened his arms wide in an obviously foolish taunt. Gawain took the opening and leaped forward, slicing the hawthorn rod an inch in front of Burian's chest. The Winter King cried out and made an elaborate show of staggering around, clutching his heart. Gawain held his hands up in triumph as the crowd roared for summer, and after a suitably dramatic amount of 'dying', Burian dropped the rod and threw aside his mistletoe crown. The Winter King fell flat on his face and Gawain cheered with the others before striding over to where Halwen waited.

All through the fight he'd been lost in the joy of Beltane, but when he saw Halwen again his legs felt weak, and he fought to keep walking like a victorious king. When he reached her he dropped down to one knee and lowered his head; the Summer King begging the Spring Maiden's favour. For the first time since the procession began the crowds and pipes fell silent, though the drums continued their steady beat. This moment was always tense, since there was no guarantee that the Spring Maiden would accept the Summer King. It was expected of her of course, but in the past there'd been girls who, for whatever mad reason, had refused the Summer King's hand. The druids said that the gods sometimes spoke through the maiden to foretell a poor year to come, and the danger of a refusal was something that always brought terror to a community.

Halwen paused for what felt like a lifetime but eventually put a hand below Gawain's chin and lifted his face to look at her. She was smiling at him, which alone was enough to make his heart pound desperately hard, and when she reached out and took his hand he was sure it would burst from his chest. Her words were nearly drowned out by the roaring of the crowd, but Gawain just about heard what she said.

'Welcome, King of Summer.'

He bowed and gave the proper response.

'I am honoured, Maiden of Spring.'

Druids approached them bearing torches, one each from the Summer and Spring Dancers, and Gawain set aside his hawthorn rod to take one. Halwen took the other and, hands still clasped, they made their way to the fire-trenches. Her fingers felt small and cool inside his grip, and Gawain wanted to squeeze her hand but feared he might hurt her if he did. He thought he could feel her squeezing his but he couldn't be sure, and he didn't dare look at her to find out.

When they reached the trenches the crowd quietened once again. Druid Elgan, his grey hair crowned with oak leaves, stood patiently between the trenches, waiting for them. Wordlessly he raised his long staff in both hands and arched his back to look up at the sky, where Bel's chariot was rolling up from the east. For the first time that day Gawain began to feel the real presence of the Old Gods, and for a moment he even forgot about Halwen as he tossed his torch into the brush. Halwen lit the other trench with hers and then, as the Beltane fires began to flicker up at them, the novices who'd formed their dancing parties took torches from the crowd and skipped along the trenches, spreading the holy fire all along their length. Far more heat came up at them than any newly-lit fire should generate, and Gawain was sure that Bel or Gorfannon was stoking the flames with godly power.

The smell of the fires was strong and pure, and Gawain took a deep breath of the smoke. Beside him he heard Halwen do the same thing, and this time he was *sure* she was squeezing his hand, though whether it was with affection or out of fear of the nearby gods, he couldn't guess. He tightened his fingers just a little in response.

Elgan lowered his staff and crossed over to them, his face grave. He shifted his staff so that he held it one-handed, then raised both arms to the heavens again.

'Let the Sacred Marriage be made! Let the year be born again!'

With that, druids came to relieve them of their wreaths of cherry and primrose, to replace Gawain's with a set of antlers and Halwen's with a crown of willow branches. Once again, Gawain had to bow down to let the druid put on his headdress, and when it was in place his whole body tingled for a moment. *The Huntsman is with me.* The pipes remained silent and the drummers slowed their beat as Elgan made his final proclamation.

'The Spring Maiden is made the Goddess, and the Summer King the God! They are Danu and Cernunnos, they are Mother and Father!' He met first Halwen's eyes and then Gawain's. 'The Marriage is made, let Beltane begin!'

Gawain had thought the cheering was loud when they'd started all this, but that had been a whisper compared to the roar that greeted Elgan's words. All of Dun Edin called out to the gods, and Gawain swallowed his nerves and turned to face Halwen. The holy fire reflected gloriously in her eyes, and though he was sure she was as unnerved by Danu's presence as he was by Cernunnos', her smile was almost mischievous as she leaned forward. Gawain held his breath. This was a moment he'd dreamed of for longer than he cared to think, and finally it was here. He could *feel* that the gods were around him and that they wanted this as much as he did; for the God and the Goddess to be joined together as one.

The distance between them closed and he held her hand that much tighter, and before he even knew it her lips were touching his. They were soft and warm, and gods or no gods all he wanted to do was stay there and keep kissing her, and the rest of the festival could take care of itself. But he dutifully broke away after only a second or two, and then grinned like a fool when he saw Halwen was still smiling at him.

Elgan gestured for them to walk and so the God and Goddess began another procession, this time walking in-between the burning trenches. The dancers fell into step behind them, and soon enough all of Dun Edin would walk the fires too, along with all the sheep and cattle from every farm within sight of the hill. It would take all day, but all would be blessed as the year was reborn, and the Beltane fires would still be burning long into the night. Gawain would be among the first to be finished though, and from there it was on to dancing and feasting and who knew what else? His heart was racing as he walked on, his hand still clamped onto Halwen's. A few years ago Elgan had said that the Beltane fires smelled of hope and renewal, and that to breathe their air was to breathe in essence of the gods themselves. Gawain didn't know about that. What he did know was that he'd never smelled anything that made him as happy as the thick smoky scent of those burning trenches. To him, the Beltane fires smelled of pure joy.

The feast was held up at the fortress, where long tables had been set up around the great bonfire in Dun Edin's main yard. Each one was long enough to seat a hundred diners and more, but still plenty sat on boxes and barrels, and all the children ate on the grass. Nobody minded the overcrowding. It was only on the great festival days that the Dun was packed so solid, and tonight everyone was so filled with Beltane spirit, and Beltane mead, that the air of happiness wasn't stifled by the press of so many bodies. Gawain took another swig from his mug and smiled. The massive bonfire, which had been burning since before he'd left that morning, was still bright against the darkening sky, and men and women and children alike danced around it, singing to the gods of home and harvest.

Gawain and Halwen had been seated at the very centre of the highest table, with even the king and queen placed further along to make way for the God and Goddess. He looked and saw that Lot was laughing at some jest of his wife's, and the looks they kept exchanging gave him the uncomfortable feeling that there would be noise from his parents' chambers tonight. It was all well and proper he supposed, it being Beltane and all, but still he didn't relish having to hear what they got up to. *Maybe I can find some excuse to go back late?* With a little luck they might be finished by the time he got to his own room. He looked sideways at Halwen and wondered if there was any chance that *she* might be that excuse.

In the old days the God and Goddess had always coupled at Beltane, and plenty of other folk would be doing that tonight; was there some charming way he could ask Halwen if she wanted to too? A hopeful part of him remembered that the Picts still celebrated Beltane in the old way, and Halwen was of Pictish blood. *She did pass on that kiss, remember, and when we kissed at the fires it felt right.* Truth be told he'd have been happy enough if she just told him he could kiss her again, but the idea of doing *more* caused a stirring that made him grateful that the table was there. He took a breath and forced himself to calm down before he embarrassed himself.

After a few moments' careful study of a hunk of bread Gawain's ardour began to calm, and he felt it safe to turn and look at Halwen again. His queen for the night was currently waving down one of Lot's guardsmen, and Gawain felt an irrational pang of jealousy until he realised what Halwen was doing; after a few whispered words the guard removed his cloak, and between the two of them they wrapped it over young Gareth's shoulders. Gawain leaned forward to look down the table at his brother. Thanks to Gaheris, tonight he'd been permitted his first taste of Irish uisge, and it would seem he'd enjoyed it rather more than was healthy for a boy his age. The youngest of the king's sons lay slumped with his head perilously close to his stew-bowl, snoring contentedly with a trail of dribble down his chin. The heavy cloak Halwen draped on him made Gareth look even younger and smaller than he already was. *He's barely three years her junior and he might as well be her babe.* Halwen wiped the dribble away with a corner of the cloak, then sat back and saw Gawain looking at her. The smile she gave him was distinctly motherly, as if she'd just tucked in their child, and Gawain decided to interpret it as something good. He smiled back.

'He's had a drop more than is good for him, eh?'

Halwen sighed.

'At least he's not roaring nonsense or retching his guts up as some will tonight.'

Gawain wasn't sure if she was making some subtle hint to him, but he put down his mug nonetheless. He wasn't drunk yet, but he'd had a fair bit of both Gaheris' Irish uisge and Beltane mead, and it might be that his chances of impressing her would be much improved if he slowed down. Instead of drinking he picked up a bowl of strawberries and offered them to Halwen, who picked one out and happily popped it in her mouth. As a rule Gawain wasn't over-fond of fruits, especially when there was perfectly good pork right in front of him, but he took some as well to be companionable, and the pair chewed for a moment while he tried to think of what to say. Fortunately, Halwen spoke first.

'Where has your sister disappeared to?'

Gawain turned around and made a show of searching the table, though he had a fairly shrewd idea where she had gone.

'I'm not sure.'

And it was true, he wasn't *sure*, he just confidently suspected. Not long ago he'd seen her and Burian walking together by the fire, and they'd been gone from there for quite some time. Gawain hoped quietly that whatever they were up to they were being cautious, or at the very least being discreet. Beltane or not, if they were careless then Lot would be unamused, not least because there would be nothing he could do about it.

At Beltane the usual rules of conduct between the unwed didn't apply; it was a festival of birth and re-birth after all, and in times past, promiscuity had been actively encouraged during the rites. Any girl, wed or not, who fell pregnant by making love at Beltane could never be rebuked by a father, or even by a cuckolded husband, and the child would be considered a blessing, not a bastard. However, though the custom was still honoured, Gawain doubted if Lot would be pleased if Anna and Burian were careless tonight. A little quiet intimacy was one thing, but the king and queen had plans for Anna, and the Bernicians were far more strictly Christian than the Lothians; they would not react well to a bride-to-be who carried another man's child.

Gawain took another strawberry then deliberately dropped it, and when he bent beneath the table he touched a hand to the cool earth. He whispered a quiet prayer to Mother Danu that Anna would not be foolish, and after a moment's pause he mumbled the same prayer to Christ. The God of Rome might not have much power tonight but he was a god who valued chastity, and it couldn't hurt to ask for him to watch over her as well.

He came back up and held up the strawberry he'd retrieved, smiling a little awkwardly, but Halwen didn't seem to mind and simply helped herself to another. Gawain sighed under his breath, wishing he knew what he could say that would be suitably impressive. A glance down the table showed him Gaheris busily seducing some black-haired girl, though the noise of the feasting was too loud to hear what he was saying. *Pretty sod probably doesn't have to say* anything, *he just winks at them and their dresses melt away.* He turned his attention back to Halwen. The notion of anything happening between them both excited and, for some reason, terrified him, and he kept wracking his brains for something to say. Once again, Halwen spoke while he was still thinking.

'I was sure I saw her talking with Burian earlier?'

There was mischief in her voice, and Gawain knew she was thinking the same thing he'd been. He shrugged, affecting disinterest.

'Was she? I didn't notice.'

He was tempted to mutter another prayer to Danu but it would have been obvious. Halwen smiled, clearly not fooled.

'Anna is a sensible girl; I'm sure she will be cautious.'

She patted Gawain's hand and he tried not to look too pleased about the simple touch. He decided there was no point in trying to hide his thoughts about Anna though, and found himself frowning as he answered.

'Beltane or not, if Burian pushes his luck with her he will lose teeth for it.'

Halwen raised an eyebrow.

'Hardly the attitude you should be fostering in your position.' She gestured to his crown. 'If anything we should be encouraging them; if folk can't give in to their natural wants tonight, when else can they?'

Gawain's breath caught as his mind started racing with possibilities. Was Halwen suggesting what he thought she was? Her wonderful eyes were fixed onto his, but he couldn't read anything in them. In the firelight she looked lovelier than he'd ever seen her, and he found himself picturing what it would be like to take her hand and guide her somewhere quiet, to take off that crimson dress feel her soft skin beneath his hands. He wanted to curse men like Gaheris, who always seemed to know what to say to girls at times like this, and he cudgelled his brains for a response that might result in *them* giving into their natural wants. For good or ill, Halwen went on before he could answer, her voice becoming something comforting.

'Whatever they get up to, no real harm can come from it. If they are merely,' her eyes grew almost wicked, '*playful*, then no-one need know about it. And if they couple together there is no certainty that she will fall pregnant.'

Gawain was tempted to remind her that men and beasts alike were more fertile at Beltane, but she headed him off.

'And even if she does, your father can bluster all he wants but it will fade. You know him better than anyone; he'll not stay angry for long.'

Gawain wasn't as confident about that as Halwen was. It was true, his father's rages rarely lasted, and as far as the child itself was concerned he'd be willing enough to raise it. But he had alliances to make for the future of their house, and Anna's marriage was a part of his planning. Gawain decided not to mention his doubts to Halwen though; if the gods intended for something to happen then this was no night to be resisting their will. Instead he smiled and tried to sound casual.

'I suppose so. And you are right; tonight is the night for such things.'

He tried to read her look to see if she caught his meaning, or rather, to see if she *agreed* with it. She opened her mouth to answer and Gawain prayed that her northern blood was growing heated, but before she could say anything a serving man in front of them tripped and careened into the table, almost tipping his platter over them both. Gawain half-stood and caught the dish before it could skitter across the board, his hand driving straight through a chicken and leek pie. It was still piping hot and he bit back a curse as he whipped his hand out again, sending pieces of pie flying everywhere. He muttered oaths as he blew on his fingers.

The serving man, a blonde-haired Saxon, stammered an apology but Gawain waved him away, resisting the urge to shout at him. Mabb, who'd been snoozing beneath the table, perked up and started trying to lick Gawain's pie-covered hand, but he flung a piece of chicken at him and the hound seemed contented with that. Halwen chuckled into her sleeve, but when Gawain sat down she called for water to be brought and started wiping off and bathing the burned hand. Gawain was too angry and embarrassed to appreciate the feel of her hand on his, and a voice from down the table only added to his chagrin.

'Gawain my boy, once the chicken is in the pie there is no need to wring its neck.'

Gawain turned to see that Father Iain had joined them at the high table and was smiling over at him. He gave the priest a nod and his best attempt at a friendly smile. Despite the pain in his hand, and the accompanying embarrassment, it was good to see that Iain had reached the point in the day when he would relax and join in with the others.

As he did at all such festivals, Iain had spent the majority of the day looking vaguely uncomfortable and insisting to everyone that what they were really celebrating was *Christ's* re-birth, and that the older rites were just a different way to honour him. Iain was a well-liked man and so no-one had argued with him, but nobody had taken the idea seriously either; Christ had his place and it was not at Beltane. Eventually, as happened around this time at every festival, Iain had given up on correcting them and settled down to eat, contenting himself with handing out God's blessings whenever someone approached him.

He was sitting beside Druid Elgan and they each raised their wine-cups towards Gawain. Gawain picked up his mead with his good hand and returned the toast to the holy men, quietly pleased that he'd done well by both of them today; he'd apparently done a fine job as Summer King at the rituals, and before that he'd scrubbed the floor of Iain's church until the stones practically shone.

Iain was sitting close to the king and so Gawain assumed that Bishop Dyfan was either too disapproving or, more likely, too sotted to attend himself. Like Iain, old Dyfan officially disapproved of Beltane rituals, but the bishop enjoyed ogling the dancers and drinking the wine, and most years that would overcome his religious reservations. But apparently this year even that was beyond him, and Gawain doubted if anyone regretted the bishop's absence.

More food was brought around, this time a steaming platter of beef and onion pies covered over with thick strips of bacon. Gawain very deliberately sat back and sipped his drink, determined that if this server slipped he'd not be fool enough to burn himself again. But the man placed the dish down with care, and cut a thick slice each for the God and Goddess. He made as if to present Halwen's slice to her but Gawain forestalled him and passed it over himself. She smiled sweetly and once again Gawain cursed himself for not knowing what to say. Everything she'd said and done made him sure that she was fond of him, but he couldn't think of a way to share his own feelings without looking like a slack-jawed fool.

He was about to throw caution to the winds and try kissing her hand, it always worked wonders for Gaheris, when Ulfric came staggering up to them and gave an elaborate bow.

'My lord and lady, a merry Beltane to you! Eostre's blessings!'

His words were slurred but he wasn't *quite* drunk enough for Gawain to think he'd had too much. Ulfric ruffled the sleeping Gareth's hair affectionately, then grinned and fell to his knees in front of their table, his elbows on the wood and his cup tilting precariously. He leaned forward and, in the manner of drunks everywhere, convinced himself that he was whispering without actually lowering his voice.

'Did you see where Burian went off to, eh?' He gave Gawain a hugely over-done wink. 'I think your sister will be celebrating the old-fashioned way this year.'

Gawain, already annoyed at the interruption, glanced hurriedly along the table to where the king and queen sat. Gods be thanked they were still laughing together and didn't seem to have heard. He hissed at his friend.

'Keep your bloody voice down!'

The young Saxon shrugged and took a swig from his cup, then leaned forward again.

'As you say.'

He'd barely lowered his voice but a little was better than nothing, and Gawain was eternally grateful when Halwen changed the subject.

'What did you think of our dancers today, Ulfric? Did any of them tempt *you* to celebrate the old-fashioned way tonight?'

Ulfric guffawed.

'There were some lovely girls and no mistake.' He nodded to Gawain. 'But I couldn't concentrate on them, not with that dancer of yours leaping all about them.'

The drunken Saxon narrowly avoided smacking his head on the table as he spread his hands apart.

'His snake must have been that long!'

Gawain would have liked to draw the conversation away to something else, but then Halwen chuckled as well.

'I know the one you mean; when he jumped I thought he'd blacken his eye with it!'

Ulfric wheezed out a laugh and Gawain tried to join in, though it felt rather awkward with Halwen there. Among his friends he'd have happily traded jokes about the lucky young druid, but sitting beside Halwen it was a rather less amusing subject, especially since he was still hoping she might want to be intimate with him tonight. *If you can ever think of a way to ask her, that is*. Gawain was nervous enough about the prospect already, and talk like this made things a hundred times worse; he didn't consider himself badly endowed, but if he and Halwen went off together and she was still thinking about that dancer, then she'd be in for some disappointment when *his* clothes came off.

He growled to himself and tried to sound at ease.

'Swinging that low, I'm surprised the dogs haven't tried to take a bite of it.'

It wasn't particularly funny but Ulfric laughed anyway.

'My da must have them well-trained not to steal sausages.'

Gawain knew for a fact that this wasn't the case, but it was Halwen who answered.

'Maybe he just trained them not to bite snakes?'

Ulfric guffawed drunkenly and for all that Gawain loved his friend, he started wishing very hard that he would bugger off and let them be. Apparently the gods were listening, which shouldn't have surprised him tonight, and Ulfric started heaving himself to his feet. After an uncertain few seconds he steadied himself and drained his cup in one long draught. He struck his chest and belched.

'Well, I can't boast an adder, but there must be *some* girls tonight who'll be content to stroke a grass-snake.' He grinned stupidly. 'I think I'll go and find them.'

Gawain gave him what he hoped was an encouraging smile. 'Huntsman's luck!'

Ulfric bowed his head, almost overbalanced, and then straightened up again. He pointed to the antlers on Gawain's headdress.

'That's *your* luck for tonight, my friend. But I'll take what you can spare.'

He smiled at them both and staggered away, and Gawain tried not to let his relief show. Of course, he was now back to trying to think of what to say to Halwen, and he'd still yet to think of something that was both charming and sincere enough to get his message across to her. He wanted her to know how he cared for her, but he wanted to say it in the manner of a strong man, not some love-struck puppy. *Why is it so much easier to be assured when all you have to do is fight someone?* Gawain's nerve never failed him in the training yard, so why did his legs turn to water around Halwen? *Because the gods have a sense of humour.*

Gawain stared hard into the central fire. *But* you *are the God of Beltane tonight, and she is your Goddess.* He clenched his hand around his cup and steeled himself. *Just be bold. Be honest.* The prospect of her rejecting him was terrifying, but one lesson he'd learned from the yard was that indecision was death. *Time to put it into practice.* He took a deep breath to calm himself and turned to look at her, ready to tell her exactly how he felt. Mercifully, it looked like she was about to speak first anyway, but then her smile vanished and her lovely face froze in shock. A moment later Gawain realised the cause of it, and his heart seemed to skip in his chest; the drums had stopped.

The drums had been playing since long before dawn, and were supposed to continue uninterrupted until Bel's chariot rose tomorrow, but now neither drummers nor pipers made a sound. The overcrowded yard had fallen completely silent, and when Gawain turned to face forward again, he saw why. A massive horse had entered the yard, bigger even than Durro, and was trotting towards the central fire at a quite unnerving speed. Every soul at the tables stared open-mouthed as the beast made no move to circle the great blaze, and then the rider, who was hard to see in the evening light but looked easily as big as Gawain, suddenly put his heels to his mount's flanks and the trot became a gallop.

Panic spread through the watchers as he thundered towards the flames, but before anyone could move or even call out a warning, the great beast ducked its head, let out a defiant neigh, and threw itself over the mighty blaze. Screams burst from all around him but Gawain simply stared, unable to look away. It was as if the flames parted from their way as horse and man leaped through the Beltane fire to land with perfect control on the other side, neither one seeming the least bit unsettled. They came to a halt mere feet before the high table, and Gawain got his first proper look of this fearless man. He was tall and imposing, and dressed completely in green.

Chapter Six

With the fire behind him the stranger's face was hard to see, but the torches at the high table were enough for Gawain to make out his form. What he saw was extraordinary. The Green Man was both tall and broad, his large frame draped in a heavy cloak and mantle that seemed to be stitched out of leaves, with a lining of thick white fur. Beneath it Gawain saw the glint of what looked like a shirt of greenish bronze scales, long enough to cover his legs down to the knee. His fur-trimmed gloves were also green, as were his trews and even his boots. On his head he wore an open-faced helm with antlers affixed to the temples, and Gawain couldn't have been the only one to wonder whether this might be Cernunnos himself, come to Beltane at their summoning. He felt the weight of his own meagre crown on his head and wished that he could take it off, but doing that would only serve to make him look more foolish.

The face beneath the antlered helm was dominated by a green beard woven through with leaves, and at a closer look Gawain saw that even the mane of his massive horse looked green in the flickering light. In one hand the Green Man held a holly bough, a common gesture that a warrior came in peace, but the long-handled war-axe slung at his back was sending another message entirely. With his free hand he removed the helm and tucked it under one arm, letting a great tangle of green hair fall down about his shoulders. The tables all around him were as silent as a pyre-side, and when the Green Man spoke his voice seemed as loud as a thunderclap.

'Who is master of this hall?'

It was inconceivable that anyone in Britain didn't know whose hall this was, but still Lot, looking far more composed than any man there had a right to be, stood up. Gawain saw the fire-light glinting on his father's red hair and golden torque, and had never been more impressed by the man than at that moment; for all anyone there knew, the King of Lothian was talking to a god.

'I am Lot ab Efrawg, and I am king here.' His voice was remarkably steady, and he gestured to the high table. 'You join us at the feast of Beltane. Sit and be welcome, and we will talk of your business later.'

The king had spoken with perfect courtesy, and terrifying though he was, the Green Man bowed his head and returned it.

'My name is Verdis of Maes Gwyr, and I give you thanks for your welcome, King Lot.' He paused for half a heartbeat. 'But I did not come here to feast.'

Even with his helm removed the stranger's face was bathed in shadow, but Gawain was sure he saw his eye flick towards him, and once again he felt foolish for wearing his antler crown.

All around him he felt the people of Dun Edin growing more frightened by the Green Man's words, and he felt Halwen's hand close tighter around his. He squeezed back, and when he risked a sideways glance he saw that her face was deathly pale, though she was doing a fine job of not showing fear in her expression. Further along he saw that Gareth had woken up, and his brother was staring open-mouthed at the Green Man, the sight sobering him up better than any water-dunking could have done. Gawain's heart was hammering hard but he straightened his back and resolved to keep a brave face.

But Gawain's attempt at seeming brave was as nothing next to his father's. Everyone knew King Lot to be a man of courage, he'd proven it against Irish, Saxons and Picts time and again, but this sight must have been frightening even to him. Nonetheless, though he was unarmed and facing a man who was likely some spirit or sorcerer, the king's voice was steady to the point of threatening.

'This is the fortress of Lothian, friend. And if you have come here seeking battle, Verdis of Maes Gwyr, be warned that our warriors will be glad to oblige you.'

He had maintained a courteous tone, despite the defiance, and the Green Man continued to match it.

'I do not doubt it. I have heard many tales of the might and courage of the Men of Lothian.' He held up the holly bough. 'Though I have arms enough for battle, I tell you by this that I do not come here for war. I come here only for a simple test; a game, of sorts.'

It was not Lot but Queen Morgause who spoke next, and like Halwen she was pale but hiding her fear well.

'What manner of game would you play?'

The Green Man tipped her a short bow.

'A game for Beltane, lady.' He turned back to face the king. 'Today your people played at the battle of Summer and Winter, but I ask you this; how gravely did your folk see that battle, a battle fought with sticks wielded by a pair of beardless boys? With how much reverence for the Old Gods was this mighty conflict fought?'

Gawain resented the tone but he kept his face blank and his eyes fixed on the stranger. The truth was that part of him wanted to shrink away from his words; he and Burian had indeed thought little enough about gods when they'd fought each other. For his part, Gawain knew he'd felt the touch of the gods only once or twice over the whole long day, and that most of it had been spent celebrating, or trying to think of what to say to convince Halwen to kiss him again. Was this stranger some fae who'd been watching them, unseen, and noted their lack of respect for the Beltane rites?

Lot answered with the same voice as before, courteous but strong.

'And you are here to speak for the gods?'

The Green Man's answer was part-threat, part-warning.

'Better that I speak with words than the gods speak with actions.'

Before Lot could reply Father Iain stood up and, after crossing himself, addressed the stranger with anger in his voice.

'Do not think to utter threats here, Verdis of Maes Gwyr. Christ is with us, and if you mean harm to our folk then I swear on the Holy Cross you will be struck down as a servant of evil!'

Gawain was convinced that the Green Man would meet anger with anger, but instead he raised his empty hand, palm up.

'Peace, priest. I do not come to fight the God of Rome, and I harm no man who would not harm me in return.'

Before Iain could say any more to him the Green Man raised his voice and spoke to the whole assembly.

'My game is a simple challenge; a single fight with a single champion. It need not even be unto death, but only unto the first true blow. If my challenge is accepted then the gods will know your worth and that you would do them honour by fighting a true battle today. The year will be a blessed one for all your people, a year of peace and plenty.' He gave another of his tiny pauses. 'Should this challenge be refused, they shall know how little you regard them, and how hollow your reputation.

And your year will be a cursed one, fraught with famine, plague, and death. All this, I give as my oath. Will no brave man come forth to meet my challenge?'

It was concerning but it did indeed sound simple, though Gawain knew there must be more to it than that. With gods and fae, it was never simple. Lot spoke the thought aloud.

'Lothian is peopled only by the brave, but I suspect that there is more to this game of yours?'

The Green Man nodded his leafy head.

'Should I win this contest, then the man I beat shall be my slave until next Beltane, when again we shall play this game. Should your man win, then whatever blow is struck upon me today, at next year's fires I shall attempt to return that blow. On the champion if he is willing, on his kinfolk if he is not. And then the game will be played anew.'

The silence was total. Someone had to fight him, that was certain, but the prospect of becoming slave to what was either a sorcerer or some manner of fae was daunting to say the least. Gawain had heard tales of such beings all his life, and the frightening ones far outnumbered the happy ones. And even if the Lothian man won and the year was blessed rather than cursed, this game would have to be played again next year, and then presumably every year until the Green Man tired of it. *Unless of course, our champion strikes a killing blow?* But even discounting his otherworldly nature, a glance at the Green Man's size, and the war-axe slung behind him, *and* his evident courage for having jumped the fire, made Gawain doubt the chances of any mortal champion killing him.

He ground his teeth together. Why had he not taken his role as Summer King more seriously? He knew Father Iain didn't approve but Beltane was supposed to be an appeal to the gods, and Gawain's task today had been to honour and embody the Huntsman, not just play-fight with sticks with his friend. *And think of nothing but kissing the Spring Maiden.*

The Green Man's gaze went up and down the high table, eyeing the royal family and the various lords of Lothian. Gawain had the unnerving feeling that they settled on him for a moment, but worse still was when they lingered on Gareth. For a heartbeat or two the silence reigned on, until at the exact same instant both Drustan and Gaheris stood up from their seats, clearly ready to accept the stranger's challenge. Gawain didn't even realise it when his own voice called out first.

'I will do it!'

The shocked looks from around him were nothing compared to the surprise this was to Gawain. One moment he'd been sitting down clutching Halwen's hand, the next he was on his feet and his mouth was answering the challenge. *What in Bel's name are you doing?* Whatever instinct had made him stand was certainly not born of his wiser self, but the answer in his head made a twisted sort of sense. *You are the one in the crown. You are the one who should have taken your role seriously.* He frowned, not wanting to agree, then the voice spoke again, more angrily. *And you are the one who put Gareth in danger yesterday. Real warriors endanger only themselves, and only at time of need. If you think that's what you are, then prove it.* Well, it was a time of need alright, but a baser part of him was wishing very hard that there was some other way to prove his worth as a warrior, and that Drustan or Gaheris had been half a second faster. But they hadn't been, and there was no way to back down now without dishonouring his king.

Halwen's grip was almost crushing his fingers but he didn't dare turn to look at her. If he did then she would see that he was having second thoughts, and Gawain dreaded the thought of Halwen thinking him a coward. *No, just let her think you a fool instead!* Apparently what little sense he had was arguing back against the part of him that had made him stand up, but there was no time now for self-debate. *Indecision is death*. Despite the coldness on his neck and the hollow feeling in his legs, Gawain put all the menace he could muster into his voice.

'I am Gawain ab Lot, and I accept your challenge.' He was sure that sounded weak and so he added a taunt the way champions normally did. 'Take your guard if you dare.'

Halwen's grip tightened even further but Gawain kept his eyes on the Green Man, who nodded once and swung his leg around to dismount from the massive horse. When he took a pace forward Gawain could swear he grew in size, and the war-axe on his back glinted wickedly in the firelight. The mass of green hair fell forward as the huge man bowed, and when he straightened up there was a smile beneath his great bush of a beard.

'Well met, Gawain ab Lot.' The smile became a grin. 'I dare.'

Drustan, after a furious glare at Gawain, agreed to fetch a mailshirt and a war-axe, and the wait for him to return was mercifully brief. Gawain could tell that Halwen and his mother both wanted to tell him to back down and take the shame, and that his father and Gaheris were longing to berate him for his stupidity, but nobody spoke a word. It was far too late now, and they all knew it. As for himself, Gawain simply stood still and tried not to show fear as the Green Man's eyes bored into his.

He'd set aside his crown and stepped back from the table ready to arm himself, and was sorely missing the touch of Halwen's hand on his. In the absence of that he clenched his fists tight and did his best to muster up some confidence. Now that they were both standing he saw that though the Green

Man was indeed large, he was only a little larger than Gawain himself, and some of that bulk might be accounted for by the heavy cloak. Added to that, when he first laid down his challenge he would almost certainly have been expecting to fight a swordsman, rather than a fellow axeman, and that would mean a very different kind of fight to the one he'd been prepared for. Gawain was strong and skilled, and fae or not the Green Man was sure to underestimate him. *If I can just catch him quickly and land one solid blow, he's bound by oath to leave us be for a full year.* They were already promised a fertile year just for accepting the challenge in the first place; in all, there was every good reason to be confident. So why did his legs keep wanting to buckle?

Gawain heard the jingling of mail as Drustan hurried back to them, and he tried to slap his mind into focus. *You are strong, fast, and well-trained, and you only need to land one blow. You can do it.* The sight of the Green Man, tall and sinister in the flickering light, made him want to second-guess that conviction, but Gawain snarled at his doubts to shut their damned whining. He was committed now; there was no more point in worry. Drustan moved to stand in front of him, his dark face almost black in the dying light, and he grunted for Gawain to raise his arms. He did as he was bidden and the champion helped him into the mail. It rested comfortably on his shoulders and the weight was reassuring. A solid strike with the war-axe would still put him down, but even a glancing blow from such a weapon could gut an unarmoured man, and the iron rings could be enough to save his life.

The neck of the mailshirt was opened wide to make it easy to put on, but once it was in place Drustan stepped behind him and began closing the leather straps on his upper back. Gawain felt him lean in a little closer than he had to, and when the champion spoke his voice was the quietest whisper.

'His cloak is heavy about his shoulders. He'll not weary himself with overhead cuts; keep your guard for low sweeps.'

Gawain gave a tiny nod, hoping that this fae or sorcerer, or possibly just madman, had not heard the advice. Once the shirt was in place Drustan handed him his axe, and grumbled beneath his breath.

'Bloody axes.' He sighed and clapped Gawain's shoulder. 'You're a damned fool, boy. Huntsman's luck.'

Gawain nodded again, feeling a little emboldened by the feel of his axe in his hands. It was slightly heavier than those most men used, and the long haft was worn smooth by years of practice. He hefted it once and then rested it on his shoulder, then began the long walk around the table to where the Green Man stood before the fire. He measured his stride carefully, not so slow as to seem frightened, but not so fast as to seem like a servant rushing to his master. *I am Gawain ab Lot, the son of a king, answering a challenge in my father's fortress.* He rounded the table and stalwartly refused to look at anyone, especially Halwen. If he met her eyes he knew his mind would flood with visions of the Green Man killing him before he could kiss her again, and he couldn't afford to be afraid now. He took slow breaths as he walked, drawing on all the focus and courage he could summon, and when he came within ten paces of the fire he halted and found his voice was strong.

'Shall we begin?'

The Green Man had moved closer to the blaze and appeared as little more than a dark shadow against the flames, but Gawain saw his opponent nod and heard the rustling of the leaves in his hair.

'We shall.'

Gawain brought the axe into a two-handed grip and the Green Man did the same. He could feel his heart beating like a maniac's drum, but Gawain realised with a jolt that it was born more of excitement than fear; because the Green Man was doing exactly what Drustan had said. While Gawain's axe was held conventionally across his chest, with the head just above his right shoulder, the Green Man was holding his weapon lower, where it would be harder for him to strike down or clash hafts. *Drustan was right, the cloak restricts him!* Gawain grinned, confidence flooding through him as he knew just what he had to do. When the Green Man swung low he would dodge, then all he need do is step to his off-side and bring his own axe down upon the stranger's neck. *He'll be expecting you to charge in rashly or to hesitate after he comes for you. So don't do either! Focus on this one blow and you have him!*

He fixed his eyes on the Green Man's shadowy form and thought of nothing but his movements. The whole population of Dun Edin was watching them but so far as Gawain was concerned they might have been alone on a mountain-top. The only things to see were the man and the fire, the only sounds to hear were the rustling leaves and the crackling wood. The pair began to circle, the Green Man likely trying to get his back away from the fire, but Gawain headed him off, blocking his path. He was sure he saw a tiny smirk on the other man's face, but the light was so dim it was hard to tell. *I don't need to see his face. I'll see his head when it's rolling at my feet!*

He almost laughed in anticipation of what was soon to come, but when the moment came it was almost too fast for him to know it was happening. The Green Man did exactly what he'd hoped he would and swung low, in what looked like a lazy arc towards Gawain's midriff. Without even thinking Gawain threw himself clear and stepped around, bringing his axe up as he moved. He heard his own voice scream out, felt the axe swing downwards, felt it strike something hard, and then the steel blade was buried in the turf and the whole yard was erupting in a cheer. Gawain looked and saw the great fur-lined cloak now had no head atop it, and for a second he raised his voice to join the others. Then the cheer caught in his throat, and he was sure he was going to be sick. The Green Man was still standing. And he was holding his own head!

Even in the shadow of the great fire there was no mistaking it; the Green Man had dropped his axe and was holding his head in both hands, clutching it close to his body, just in front of his stomach. Gawain wanted to turn and run as his courage bled out of him, but for some reason his legs wouldn't move. All around him the merry cheers were turning to oaths and screams, and while some folk began to flee or hide, most were too stunned to do anything but stare. The Green Man smiled at him and, quite casually, pushed his head back up until it sat on his shoulders once again. Gawain felt his hands shaking on the haft of his axe, but somehow he managed to haul the blade from the ground and hold the weapon in front of him again. He had no idea what he was supposed to do now, but apparently the Green Man was not at all concerned. He raised his arms above his head and called out in a booming voice, so loud and commanding that even the terrified screaming ceased.

'Enough!'

He laughed; this man who'd just had his head hacked from his body actually *laughed*!

'Well struck, Gawain ab Lot, well struck indeed!'

Gawain knew he ought to say something to that, but his throat felt dry as a year-old bone and all he managed was a croaking sound that he was fairly sure no-one heard. The Green Man just kept smiling, but then Father Iain's voice sounded from the high table.

'Be gone from here, demon!' Gawain looked over and saw that the priest was unarmed but had one hand on the wooden cross about his neck. 'Your sorceries will not protect you from the wrath of God! Be gone, or be struck down by the power of Christ!'

Iain looked ready to vault the table, and Gawain felt a stab of fear for him. The Green Man was either a fae or a sorcerer, and this was the very worst night to rely on Christ's power for protection. And if the Green Man took offence at Iain's words, what might he do to the old priest? Gawain tried to tell his feet to move but they were rooted to the earth. Fortunately, as before, the stranger simply held up a hand.

'I am no demon, nor am I an enemy to you or your god. But I shall go.'

He faced the high table and fixed his eyes on Lot. The king, who was on his feet, continued to keep his fear hidden beneath anger and pride.

'And your game?'

The Green Man shrugged, and his massive cloak rustled oddly.

'The blow was fairly struck, and the game won. A blessed year and a merry Beltane to you all!'

No-one knew quite what to say to that. There was perhaps a tinge of relief in the air but the yard remained deathly silent, and clearly nobody felt like this was a merry Beltane any more. The Green Man seemed unperturbed and simply heaved himself back onto his horse. The great beast shook its head and the rider leaned down towards Gawain, who was still standing frozen to the spot.

'We shall face one another again next year, if you are willing?' He gave him a broad wink that was somehow both playful and menacing. 'Perhaps when next we meet, *I* shall strike the first blow?'

Gawain tried to answer him but only managed another dry croak. What had just happened? He still couldn't understand it, any of it, and even the confusion was drowned by an icy-cold fear. The Green Man didn't seem to mind however, and without another word or so much as a glance at anyone, he gently urged his mount around the fires and made for Dun Edin's gate. Within moments he had passed into the shadows beyond the flames, and moments later Gawain saw his silhouette disappear through the open gateway.

As soon as he was gone the muttering began, first in frightened whispers and then louder as men and women grew confident that the Green Man was truly gone. People rushed towards Gawain and he heard Gaheris and his parents begin asking him all sorts of things, but he didn't say anything. He couldn't. His mind seemed to have numbed and he just stood there dumbstruck, the axe-haft slipping from his nerveless fingers. He didn't even notice when Halwen's soft hand touched his.

Chapter Seven

King Lot remained outside to speak to his people, and attempt to smother the panic that threatened Dun Edin's yard. Gaheris stayed with him, as did Elgan, while Drustan did his best to escort Gawain inside without making him look too much of a milksop. For himself, it was all Gawain could do to walk in a straight line without his legs buckling, and he barely heard a word of his father's speech. He barely registered anything at all until they reached the royal chambers. Drustan sat him down on a bench near the fire, and only when Gawain looked up did he see that Iain, Halwen, and Morgause had all come with them. He didn't want them to see him so shaken, especially Halwen, but at the same time their presence was comforting; even sitting down he felt unsteady.

He watched in silence as, without being bidden, Halwen set about warming wine in a little brass cauldron. He heard the queen advising her on what herbs she should put in, though Morgause's eyes never left her son. Gawain could see fear in them but it was tightly controlled, and her face gave no sign of anything but a quiet, motherly concern. He felt a hand on his shoulder and saw that Iain was standing over him. His voice was low and soothing, though Gawain was sure that he too was afraid. *What fool wouldn't be?*

'Rest easy now, my boy. You have won through, thanks be to God.'

He smiled as he made a grateful sign of the cross, though Gawain was not much reassured. Christ might indeed have helped him win the sinister game, but rarely had Gawain felt less like a victor. *I took his head off and he smiled! He just put it back on his neck and* smiled*!*

Drustan was loitering nearby, looking unconvinced by the priest's words, and Gawain noted that the champion had picked up his little antlered crown. It looked a feeble thing compared with the great helm the Green Man had worn, but Drustan was holding it carefully, his thumb gently rubbing against it, presumably in the hopes of appeasing the Huntsman. He cleared his throat gruffly.

'You faced a champion of Cernunnos and beat him, lad. You should be proud.'

Though praise from Drustan was a rare thing, today it sounded hollow. No-one there looked particularly proud. Halwen came across to him with a mug of steaming wine, and when she pressed it into his hands she let her fingers linger on his.

'Drink, it will help.'

Ordinarily Gawain would have tried to bluster away the implication that he needed help, but it would fool nobody tonight, least of all Halwen. He nodded his thanks and took a short draught. The wine was almost hot enough to burn his mouth, but not quite, and the mingled flavours were pleasant on his tongue. He felt the warmth travel all the way down to his belly, and after a couple more sips some of the shock began to ease away. Halwen sat beside him and gave his hand a squeeze, and that more than the wine did much to calm his nerves. For once he didn't feel over-excited at her touch, he'd made enough of a mess thanks to those feelings already, but it was cool and comforting and his heartbeat finally began to slow. He looked to Iain again.

'What was that man, father?'

Iain looked a little uncomfortable at the question.

'If he was some forest spirit, then perhaps Druid Elgan would be better informed about his nature than I.'

Drustan nodded slowly.

'Some envoy of the Huntsman would be my guess.' He looked up and gave what looked like a forced smile. 'With his challenge met, we can look forward to a blessed year.'

Now that the danger of the fight was over Drustan seemed less concerned than the rest of them, though even he looked far from relaxed. Iain gave him a sidelong look.

'If I may say so, Lord Drustan, I believe you are being too dismissive about all this. For all that we know, young Gawain has just survived a battle with a demon.'

Once again the priest crossed himself, but Drustan answered unconcernedly.

'Demons are rare, father. And if he *was* a champion of the Huntsman then we can trust his word. Besides, if he is fae and we obeyed the rules of his game, he can hardly come back again tomorrow. If he is someone to fear we likely have at least until Samhain to prepare for him.'

Iain looked unimpressed but Drustan did have a point; Samhain, like Beltane, was a time when the boundary between the spirit world and the mortal world was thin, and thus the time when fae creatures were at their strongest. Gawain frowned and spoke up for the first time.

'The Green Man didn't say he was from the spirit world. He said he was of Maes Gwyr.'

Calling him simply '*The Green Man*' was odd, but Gawain didn't feel comfortable using the stranger's name. There was a chance that he was simply some mortal sorcerer, but if he was fae then speaking his name aloud could bring terrible bad luck. Iain shrugged his shoulders.

'I've not heard of such a place. It must be somewhere north of Anthony's Wall.'

Drustan threw in what he must have known would be an unwelcome comment.

'Unless Maes Gwyr is in some part of the Otherworld?'

Iain looked unimpressed, but Morgause stepped in before the two could go any further.

'What he was and where he came from can be discussed tomorrow. He is gone for now, let us be glad of it.'

The two men shared a quick glance then bowed almost simultaneously.

'As you say, my queen.'

'You are right, lady.'

Morgause nodded in acknowledgement. In all likelihood she would be on Drustan's side if it came to an argument, but she gave no indication of preference and simply turned back to her son.

'Are you…'

But before she could go on the door to the chambers opened and Lot, Gaheris, and Elgan walked in. Everyone bowed their heads respectfully, and Lot's first words were to his wife.

'Is he alright?'

Morgause nodded.

'He seems to be.'

Lot nodded back.

'Good.'

With that he rounded on Gawain.

'What were you thinking you damned fool? You might have been killed!'

He'd refrained from shouting, presumably because he'd just been working to calm everyone else down, but the anger in his words was palpable. Of all of them it was Halwen who responded first, looking up at the king with the defiant eyes of a Pict.

'Lord, Gawain was only…'

But Lot silenced her with a glare. Spirited though she was, Halwen was still a smith's daughter addressing a king, and she looked away as good sense outweighed her boldness. Lot turned back to face Gawain, the anger in voice tinged with weariness.

'Why did you do it, boy? Must I bore a hole in your head and *pour* some brains into you?'

In truth Gawain hadn't been thinking when he'd taken the challenge. He'd simply heard the Green Man issue it and then heard himself answer it. All the same it had been the right thing to do, and surely there'd been something admirable in doing it? He felt his cheeks grow warm, and his fear began to dissipate as defiance came to the fore.

'*Someone* had to take the Green Man's challenge.' He pointed at Gaheris and Drustan. 'You would not be berating them had they accepted it.'

Morgause answered in a measured voice.

'Drustan and Gaheris are both blooded men. You are not.'

Gawain wanted to argue but Father Iain spoke up in agreement.

'No-one doubts that what you did was brave, my boy. But you have not seen real combat before and this was a foolish risk of your life. It is only by God's grace that we are scolding you tonight instead of mourning you.'

Once again the priest crossed himself, and a moment later Lot and Gaheris dutifully did the same. Gawain copied them, as did Halwen, though unsurprisingly, Drustan, Morgause and Elgan did not. It was the druid who spoke next.

'The good father is right, Gawain. You risked life and soul tonight in a challenge that was not yours to take.'

Gawain tried to sound respectful as he argued back, and nodded towards the antler crown in Drustan's hand.

'I was wearing that; this challenge was *exactly* mine to take.'

Halwen spoke again from beside him, courteous but not quite meek.

'The Green Man said that his challenge was because of our battle between Summer and Winter. He might have picked out Gawain anyway?'

Lot gave her a sharp look, but Morgause spoke before he could rebuke her.

'I wish it was not so, husband, but young Halwen has a point.'

That seemed to give Lot pause but Gaheris leaped in instead, glaring angrily at his brother.

'He wouldn't have had the chance to pick you out if you'd just kept your bloody mouth shut!' He jerked his head towards Drustan. 'We were only an eye-blink slower to stand up, and once the challenge was accepted one of us would have taken him.'

Gawain felt his temper shorten at Gaheris' tone.

'Or you would have died in the attempt. I won this because…'

He was about to say that he'd won because the Green Man had been expecting to face a sword and not a skilled axeman, but Elgan cut him off.

'You *won* in only the very loosest sense, Gawain.'

The druid's tone wasn't harsh but he was right of course, and Gawain looked away, embarrassed. Both Gaheris and Lot looked like they wanted to voice their agreement, but once again it was Morgause who spoke first.

'All this can wait. My son has done a brave and foolish thing, as men of Lothian are wont to do.' She flicked a steady look at her husband and Gaheris. 'You can berate him for it in the morning. But keep in mind that he did nothing that you would not have done had you been a moment faster to volunteer.'

Neither man dared argue with that. Morgause turned her eyes back to Gawain.

'Whatever else, you have had quite a night. You need to sleep.'

His mind was still working hard through a mixture of fear, dread, and frustration, but for the most part Gawain agreed with her; he felt weary enough to sleep for a month, assuming he'd be able to. He nodded and began to stand, but then Halwen's voice came from beside him.

'May I sit with him, lady?'

For a moment his pulse quickened at the prospect of being alone with Halwen, then he remembered that he was in no state to try to seem charming. All the same, it would be pleasant to have her with him. Morgause thought for a heartbeat, then first raised his hopes and then crushed them again.

'You may, dear. But Elgan ought to go with you too, to make sure this Green Man has placed no hidden curse on my son.'

Gawain wasn't sure if Halwen looked genuinely disappointed, or whether that was just what he wanted to see. Elgan seemed unconcerned either way and simply bowed to the queen.

'Of course, lady.'

If Father Iain was put out by not being asked for his help too then he hid it well, and there was no trace of bitterness in his voice.

'I shall be sure to pray for you, my boy.'

Lot gave him a short nod of thanks, his anger apparently diminished for now, and Gawain made himself smile at the priest.

'Thank you, father.'

He took Halwen's hand again, hoping that his own palms hadn't grown sweaty in the warm room, and was about to stand up when a nagging thought needled him.

'Druid Elgan, do you know where Maes Gwyr is?'

Elgan's brow furrowed in thought.

'I have never been there but I was sure I recognised the name when he spoke it. I believe it is north of Anthony's Wall, somewhere near the eastern coast.'

Iain was polite enough not to crow over Drustan for his comment about Maes Gwyr being in the spirit world, but Gawain did note a little smile on the old priest's face. Lot cocked his head at his son, suspicion in his eyes.

'Why do you ask, boy?'

Gawain didn't really want to voice his next thought. He wanted to go to bed with Halwen holding his hand, and forget about the Green Man and his damned challenge. He wanted to doze off wondering how he'd prove his worth to Lot and Gaheris tomorrow, and either go and fight the Irish with his brother, or to go north to join Peleus. He wanted to drift into sleep imagining how he would go on to do valiant deeds, and come home in glory before the autumn leaves fell. And he'd imagine how happy Halwen would be to be the wife of a hero of Lothian. But he couldn't do those things. His mind had no space for pleasant fantasies of the future.

Iain had once told him a tale of a king who hung a sword over his throne with the point dangling over his head. That was how Gawain felt now, and he would feel that way until next Beltane unless he did something to change his fate. He stood up very slowly. His legs felt weak but he steadied himself and took a deep breath before speaking.

'Because I need to go there.' Everyone's eyes widened, either in shock or simple disbelief, but he forged on. 'The Green Man said he would return next Beltane to challenge me again, and if I refuse he will challenge one of my kin.'

He glanced towards Gaheris but he was really thinking of Gareth, and somehow he knew that Gaheris was thinking the same.

'I will not sit and wait for a year with the Green Man's axe hanging over my neck. I will go north to Maes Gwyr.'

The thought frightened him but he reminded himself firmly that he'd won the last challenge, and this time he'd be ready for him. *And I* will *win again*. He forced confidence into his voice.

'I will take the fight to him.'

Apparently, that was the wrong thing to say. Gawain saw the anger re-kindling in his father's eyes, and King Lot fixed him with a glare.

'Have you lost what few wits you ever had, boy?'

The king closed his eyes for a beat and took a slow breath to compose himself. When he spoke again the anger was still plain upon his face, but his voice had calmed. A little.

'Each time I think you cannot grow stupider, you somehow succeed in proving me wrong.'

Gawain felt himself redden again and snapped out an answer.

'Do you have some better plan? Beyond sitting here and waiting for the Green Man to return and play some other game with us?'

Lot glowered.

'*If* he returns. We cannot know that he will.'

Beside the king, Drustan spoke up respectfully.

'Lord, if he was a spirit of the Huntsman then he will keep his oath. Cernunnos does not lie.'

Lot didn't look at his champion and just waved a dismissive hand.

'If he returns then you and Gaheris can chop him apart and that will be an end to it.'

Gawain couldn't help feeling irritated that he, the man who'd actually struck a blow against the Green Man, had been left out of that statement.

'I am the one he faced today and he said himself that I am the one he will challenge next time. This is for me to deal with and I will do just that.'

He felt Halwen's hand squeeze his, and though her words were gentle there was firmness beneath them.

'You'll deal with it by travelling gods only know how far north, and searching dangerous lands for a dangerous man who has sworn to return here in any case?'

The king gave Halwen an approving look and Morgause stepped up beside him.

'If all you will do with your father is lock horns, will you listen to *her*, at least?'

Gawain looked down at Halwen and wanted to say something pleasant, but she was wrong in this; they all were. He didn't want to be running off and risking his neck either but it was the right thing to do, why couldn't they see that? Damn it all he was trying to be responsible, and all they could do was slap him down for it. Despite Halwen's warm voice and her beautiful gaze, he shook his head at her.

'I'll not wait here like a hog awaiting slaughter.'

Lot scoffed.

'At least a hog has the sense not to chase after the butcher.'

Gawain turned to him and felt stubbornness outwrestle his good sense.

'Well this hog has tusks! I have to do this, Father, and there is damn-all you can say to stop me!'

As soon as the words came out he knew he'd been a fool to say them. Lot drew himself up, Gawain sometimes forgot just how large a man he was, and took a menacing pace towards his son.

'Damn-all I can say?' His voice became almost a bellow. 'You *dare* speak so to your father and your king?'

He pointed a finger between Gawain's eyes, and his voice lowered into something dangerous.

'Take that tone with me again, boy, and I swear to Bel and Christ you'll feel this.' He clenched his fist and held it two feet from Gawain's face. 'We'll see how bloody bold you are when all you can eat is soup!'

Gawain was torn between the instinct to back down and the instinct to dare him to try it, but was spared from choosing which to follow by Morgause's intervention. She stepped smoothly between them, placed a palm on the king's chest, and spoke a single word in her low-pitched voice.

'Husband.'

Gawain knew that tone; it was the not-quite-scolding tone she used when she wanted to tell Lot he was in the wrong without undermining him in front of people. It was a subtle tone, halfway between appeal and disapproval, but in twenty years of marriage Morgause had perfected the art. Lot paused and took a slow breath, and Gawain tried to stay calm in his response.

'I'm going, Father. Will you tie me to a post to keep me here?'

Lot grumbled.

'Why waste good rope on fools?'

The queen's answer was somewhat kinder.

'Do you truly wish to ride off and try to get yourself killed?'

Gawain turned his eyes to her. It was a lot harder to speak angrily to his mother but he tried to keep up his resolve.

'I have to do this. If nothing else, if I don't face him then sooner or later he'll challenge another man, either here or in some other town. And the next man he challenges he may kill.'

He felt a flash of inspiration and turned to Iain. The argument would be flimsy to Morgause but Lot and Iain would have to listen.

'Father, doesn't Christ say that it's holy to risk your life for other people?'

Iain looked rather awkward as he spoke the verse.

'*Greater love hath no man than this; that he lay down his life for his friends.*' He continued very quickly. 'But that need not be the case here, and I sense the sin of pride...'

But Halwen interrupted him, pulling Gawain around to face her.

'Lay down your life?'

There was fire in her hazel eyes but a hint of appeal in them too. She was angry, but it was born of fear for him. Gawain had no time to enjoy that knowledge and spoke softly as he met her gaze.

'I don't mean that I *intend* to die, I meant only...'

But now it was Gawain's turn to be interrupted as the king's voice sounded again, loud and aggravated.

'Enough of this!' He scowled at Gawain. 'You are not Christ surrendering to the Cross; you're an idiot boy chattering about things he does not understand. And you can talk until your tongue drops off, you are not going anywhere.'

Gawain squared up to his father, stubbornness overriding his instinctive fear of him.

'I am going, and you will not stop me.'

Lot looked like he would strike his son but Drustan spoke quietly from beside him.

'Lord, is it for us to keep a warrior from seeking a just challenge?'

Lot half-snarled at the champion.

'He's no warrior yet.'

Drustan's voice remained calm.

'And he never will be if he is not tested. It's an unusual method to be sure, but what better test for a warrior than a challenge from an emissary of the Huntsman himself?'

Lot gave him an angry look but, to Gawain's astonishment, Father Iain took Drustan's side against the king. The old priest let out a resigned sigh.

'Lord, short of breaking his legs I cannot see a way of preventing your son from going. With that being so, the best we can do is ensure that he is sent into this madness well-prepared.' He fidgeted with the cross about his neck for a moment, then seemed to come to a decision. 'I shall go with him, by your leave, to provide guidance and God's protection against the demon.'

The look he gave Gawain said very clearly that he didn't want to be travelling to the wild north on a fool's errand, and that he disapproved of both the mission and his attitude. But the fact that he was willing to do it made Gawain feel a little flush of gratitude. Lot was growing red-faced and he rounded on the priest, but then Drustan spoke again from his other side.

'Iain can guard his soul if he wishes, but if Gawain is going close to Pictish land he'll need a man to guard his back.'

Gawain and Lot both looked at him wide-eyed, and for a moment it looked as if Gaheris would say something too, but Gawain never heard what it was. Lot growled like a cornered dog and barked before anyone could say more.

'Enough, I say!' He fixed Gawain with a stare and pointed to the door. 'Get yourself from my sight before I take up a cudgel and batter some sense into you!'

Gawain met his eyes and for a foolish moment he considered defying his word, but he thought better of it and turned away. He stormed from the room without a glance at anyone, and didn't look up until he'd left the hall and felt cold air on his face. He hadn't realised how hot it had been in the little chamber, and he closed his eyes for a moment and let the cool breeze calm his temper. He took a slow breath through his nose, taking in the faint smell of the distant fires, and let it out again through his mouth. Without asking them to, his feet began wandering around the hall towards the training yard, and his mind raced while his body strolled.

Why couldn't they understand? The Green Man had made it clear that this was at least partly Gawain's fault for not taking his role seriously as the Summer King. He'd done the right thing in taking the challenge, then done the right thing in out-manoeuvring the Green Man, then tried to do the right thing again by volunteering to go and face him. Why then, after all that, were they all treating him like a fool? *Maybe because you're rushing off to fight a man who will almost certainly kill you?* Gawain suspected that the voice in his head was making a valid point, but he shoved it away. This was what warriors were supposed to do, and Drustan agreed with him; they took up challenges to keep others from harm. The Green Man had looked at Gareth tonight, he knew he had, and if Gawain didn't face him then who knew what might happen to his brother? What if the Green Man chose to challenge someone else next Beltane instead of facing Gawain again, or what if he fought Gawain and won and then decided to fight Gareth the next year?

He kicked angrily at a stone and watched it thump against the well-worn ground before clattering from an archer's barrel. It was so quiet, and on a night when the noise of drums and revelry ought to be echoing from the fortress walls. He guessed that most of the townsfolk had gone home, and those living at the Dun were either clearing up the tables in silence or had retired to their beds to dwell on the evening's events. Gawain clenched his fists at the thought of them, partly in anger and partly in shame. If he'd just paid the gods their due respect this mess might not have occurred. Instead he'd worn the raiment of the Summer King but treated the whole thing as little more than a chance to kiss a pretty girl, and he'd been shown his fault in no uncertain terms. *So, what now?*

Gawain frowned as he walked. He had at least shown willingness to accept his fault, and it seemed to him that the Green Man insisting on fighting him again was pressing the point too hard; he'd been in the right to challenge them for not honouring the gods, but once that challenge had been accepted he ought to have let things lie. Instead he was threatening to return and fight again, and when that happened he might decide to change the rules of his damned '*game*'. So it made good sense to track him down and fight him first. The notion was a frightening one, but it was the best plan he could think of in the mess that had become his life. Why couldn't his father just understand that?

His anger was fading into sadness, and he might have started feeling sorry for himself if Halwen hadn't come running up behind him. She wasted no time in sharing her thoughts.

'What were you thinking?'

Halwen was gentle by nature but there was Pictish fire in her eyes. Gawain tried not to let his frustrations sharpen his voice.

'I was thinking that I was doing the right thing, which I am. This is for me to take care of and that is what I'll do.'

Halwen pointed back towards the hall.

'You know your father is in there cursing the day you learned to speak?'

Gawain pretended not to be bothered by it.

'He'll shout himself hoarse and then Mother will calm him down. He will see things my way by tomorrow.'

Halwen folded her arms.

'And are we all supposed to lose our sense overnight, or is it just him?'

Gawain took a slow breath. He didn't want to be arguing with her.

'There is no real choice, I...'

But she cut across him, and Gawain thought he saw the glint of a tear in her eye.

'No choice but to run off into the north and get yourself killed by a fae?'

She looked like she wanted to say more, but she broke off and turned her head at the sound of shuffling footsteps. A moment later two figures came walking around the hall's northeast corner. It was hard to make them out at first, but the watch-fires on the wall were still burning dutifully, and soon enough Gawain recognised Burian and Ulfric. Halwen quickly turned away again and rubbed her eyes with the sleeve of her dress. By the time the other boys reached them she had composed herself, though her attempt at light-heartedness felt rather hollow.

'Burian; has Anna worn you out already?'

Gawain was too preoccupied to take offence and he couldn't tell if his friend blushed at the question. He merely gave them an awkward half-smile and Halwen looked away, embarrassed for having asked. Both Burian and Ulfric were looking stricken, and it was the Saxon who asked the obvious question.

'What happened?'

Gawain really didn't want to go over it all again but he gave them a brief explanation, from when he'd taken the Green Man's head to when his father had banished him from sight. His friends watched him silently for a moment, and Gawain felt the need to defend his decision.

'If the Green Man *is* some kind of fae then he'll be at his strongest at Beltane and Samhain. If I can find him and challenge him at some other time his powers will be weakened.' They still said nothing and Gawain went on, half to convince them and half to convince himself. 'Next time I take his head the damned thing will stay off, and we'll never need to fret about him again.'

The silence that greeted him was acutely uncomfortable, and when Ulfric broke it, it was with the last words Gawain had expected.

'When do we leave?'

Gawain stared at him, but before he could comment he heard Halwen swear from beside him. By the time he turned to face her she was already walking away, and even as he took a step to follow her, her voice snapped over her shoulder.

'Don't!'

He almost went after her anyway but he realised it would only make things worse. Instead he looked back to his friends, and Burian repeated the Saxon's question.

'Well, when do we leave?' Gawain opened his mouth but Burian went on before he could speak. 'You say he came because we did not honour the gods? Well, I was Winter King today and did not take the duty as gravely as I should have.'

He tactfully didn't mention that he too had doubtless been thinking only of his own lusts, and Gawain was grateful for the omission. With all his other worries tonight, he didn't want to be thinking about what follies Burian and Anna had been getting up to. He turned his eyes to Ulfric, who shrugged his shoulders and tried for a carefree smile. It was forced, but well-meant.

'I may be holier than you two, but if you're going north of Anthony's Wall you'll need all the help you can get.' He raised a brow at Gawain. 'Isn't that why you brought us Saxons up here in the first place?'

Gawain did his best to smile back. Ulfric's father had been among the Saxon mercenaries King Lot had hired to help fight the Picts, and even Drustan, who spoke of them with such distain, would grudgingly admit that Saxons could be useful in a fight. *And a fight is what we'll have*. Challenging the Green Man might be for Gawain alone, but reaching Maes Gwyr could be an adventure in itself. He'd only the vaguest idea of where to go, and if it was beyond even the Venicones lands then he'd be risking the wrath of the Picts when he travelled. Peleus did a fine job of keeping those lands as safe as could be, but raids were still common and the further north he went, the more dangerous it would become.

He looked at his friends. The nobler part of him wanted to tell them not to risk themselves and that this task was his alone. But now that the arguing was over the hot-headedness he'd felt in the hall was giving way to anxiety, and the prospect of having his friends with him was so welcome he didn't dare tell them to stay. *Not that they would. They're as stubborn as you*. He felt warm in his heart as he looked at their faces; both set and determined, and both hiding their fear so well that a man who didn't know them might think them genuinely unafraid. But Gawain did know them, and the fact that they were afraid and still resolved to come made him want to grab them both in an embrace. Instead he simply smiled at his comrades.

'We leave tomorrow.'

Chapter Eight

Both Iain and Drustan kept true to their offers, and it was a company of five that made ready to leave the next morning. It was warm and sunny, a bright day full of birdsong and the fresh scent of grass, and Gawain felt a pang of guilt at how ungrateful he was for the gods' blessings. But whether the fine weather was the work of Bel or Christ or Danu, he couldn't feel gratitude to any of them today. He tightened the straps that held his bedroll to the horse's flank, and tried not to let his anger bubble to the surface. Gossip about his mission had spread like fire in a haystack, and half the Dun had turned out to see them off. But not the king. Lot had not deigned to leave his hall to watch his son depart, and had even refused to grant the company mounts for their journey; Morgause had eventually persuaded him to allow them three pack horses for their gear, but the five would be walking the many miles to Anthony's Wall, and however much further it was to Maes Gwyr.

He growled to himself as he fixed the belt. It was rare for the old man to hold a grudge but Gawain strongly suspected he would be holding onto this one, and the perverse part was that this time Lot was angry not at something he'd done wrong, but because of something he was trying to do *right*. He looked over towards the hall, half-hoping to see his father in the doorway, but there was no sign of him. Gaheris had not come out to bid him farewell either, though Gawain hoped that was more out of loyalty to their father than because he genuinely didn't care.

Anna and their mother had come and he was grateful enough for that, even if Anna's farewells weren't only for him. His sister had her arms wrapped around Burian's neck, and the swarthy youth was holding her just as tight. When they broke off and she kissed his cheek Gawain saw his sister's eyes were bright, and he felt his heart ache like a day-old bruise; in part for her, and in part because Halwen too had refused to bid him farewell. He walked up to them and didn't have to ask before Anna answered him.

'I'm sorry, Gawain. I tried, but...'

He nodded, understanding. Anna had gone to Halwen early to try to talk her around, and Gareth was likely still with her even now, pleading Gawain's cause. But he hadn't expected her to come; Halwen was proud. There was some cold comfort in knowing that she cared enough to be angry at him for risking his life, but that did little to outweigh the sadness of not seeing her.

Anna put her arms around her brother and squeezed.

'You two can make amends when you get back.'

Even at so young an age, Anna was learning their mother's craft of keeping emotion from her voice. All the same, Gawain knew she would be saying it only partly to encourage *him*, and mainly to comfort herself with the assurance that he would be coming home. He returned the embrace and tried to remain confident; he'd beaten the Green Man before, he could do it again.

'Just be sure to keep other men away from her while I'm gone.'

Anna leaned back and smiled up at him.

'I will try.'

Before Gawain could break off the embrace she moved in close again, and her whisper betrayed a flicker of fear.

'I know you'll be safe. But watch over Burian for me.'

Gawain was sure that she knew as well as he did how little future there was in their relationship, but it was no more doomed than his would be with Halwen. He whispered back.

'I will.'

He felt the tension leave her shoulders and she stepped back.

'Huntsman's luck to you.'

Given who the Green Man's patron god was, *'Huntsman's luck'* was perhaps not the best of sayings to use, but Gawain reasoned that if Cernunnos really wished him harm, he'd have made the Green Man faster with his axe last night. He smiled and nodded thanks to Anna, then stepped over to where his mother awaited him. Like Anna, the queen was wearing a deep blue dress, and the long lines of the skirt served to emphasise her impressive height. Her black hair seemed to draw the sunlight somehow, and shone as brightly as the gold torque about her neck. She gave him a small smile before embracing him.

'All good fortune go with you, my son.'

Gawain hugged back.

'Thank you, Mother.'

They parted and, though the queen was far too dignified to whisper, her voice lowered a little.

'Are you sure you must do this? It is not too late.'

Gawain held back the urge to frown; it *was* too late, and they both knew it. Or rather, it was too late to back down without doing irreparable damage both to his own fledgling reputation and to the honour of the House of Lothian. Morgause might forgive him, even speak up for his decision, but in a twisted way Gawain knew that the one way to make his father respect him even less would be to back out of all this now. He smiled at his mother's kindness.

'I am sure. And when I come back, you and father can enjoy scolding me about it some more.'

She hugged him again, saying nothing. Gawain didn't like to think about how hard he was making things for her. He'd heard from Drustan that Gaheris had picked out a dozen raw spearmen and would soon be taking them west to fight the Irish. With him leaving in a matter of days, and Agravain still down at King Uther's court, Morgause would have only Gareth and Anna left to her when Gawain left. It was every mother's fate to see her children drift away, but it was not a fate that many mothers welcomed. Gawain squeezed her tightly, trying to convey love, apology, and gratitude all at once, and he waited for her to break off the embrace first. When she did she was dry-eyed and composed, as ever, but there was warmth in her smile.

'Make us proud, my boy.'

Gawain returned the smile, trying not to let thoughts of his father spoil their moment together. Morgause might be made proud if he came home having bested the Green Man, but it would take more than surviving a fight to make King Lot proud of him now.

'I will try.'

She touched his cheek gently.

'That is all any man can do.'

Gawain knew that if he kept lingering here he would say or do something to make a fool of himself in front of all Dun Edin, and so he bowed and took his leave, determinedly not looking back as he made his way to the horses. Burian met him on the way there and nodded his head towards the crowd.

'It's not right that a Saxon should get that kind of embrace; not when he can't appreciate it properly.'

Gawain followed his gaze and saw that Ulfric was saying his farewells to his family. Ekbert the kennel master was looking on proudly, as was young Harald, Ulfric's brother, but it was his mother that drew the eye, as she always did. Elswid was well past forty but she was fair of face and had a figure that every boy in Dun Edin would stare at when she passed. Like her husband she was a Saxon, and had the same straw-coloured hair as Ulfric, but on her it was something delicate, and it fell in long curls onto a chest that her green dress was struggling to contain. She was currently smothering Ulfric in an embrace, and for all his loyalty to Halwen Gawain couldn't help agreeing with Burian; it was an enviable position to be in.

'It does seem to be wasted on him.'

Burian smiled.

'Do you think if we asked her nicely, Elswid might wish us a farewell too?'

Gawain slapped a hand on his friend's chest, only half jesting.

'Well *you* can bloody well stick to watching.' He jerked his head back towards the hall. 'For some strange reason my sister seems to have grown fond of you, so you behave yourself.'

Burian gave him a sceptical look.

'Would you rather I went back and paid Anna some more attention?'

Gawain scowled, but mainly at himself. Burian and Anna had seemed genuinely caring towards each other, but he still didn't like to think about what sort of attention Burian might already have given her. He grabbed the front of his friend's tunic and pulled him a step closer.

'Just keep your hands to yourself.'

He didn't glare at him all that hard and in truth it was a pretty feeble threat, but he couldn't think of much else to say. Fortunately Ulfric soon came jogging up to them, and the pair were able to turn their mockery on him; familiar banter was infinitely preferable to having to talk about what was actually happening. Burian grinned.

'Did your ma pass on any message for me?'

Ulfric smirked.

'She did,' he feigned a confused look, 'something about how you shouldn't feel embarrassed; a knife is as good as a sword in the right hands?'

Burian answered without a pause.

'In Elswid's hands any sword becomes a spear.'

Despite his nerves Gawain snorted.

'Well, hopefully not yours, Ulfric; I don't think Father Iain would approve.'

They reached the pack horses and a deep voice sounded from the other side of the nearest beast.

'From what I've seen a Saxon will stick his wick in anything warm, why let a little thing like blood get in the way?'

Gawain saw Drustan straighten up from where he'd been securing his pack, and Ulfric answered without thinking.

'Why plough *our* mothers when…'

He stopped himself short. Had he been speaking to Burian or Gawain he would have said something obscene, but Drustan was not a man one spoke to in such a way. The champion's face was blank as slate and Ulfric began to stammer an apology, but Burian spoke up first.

'I'm sure he…'

Drustan waved him to silence.

'Never mind that.' He looked to Ulfric. 'You get some leeway because your da is that rarest of things; a decent Saxon. He's lending us this fellow.'

He let out a quiet whistle and Gawain grinned as Mabb trotted happily around the horse. The huge wolfhound seemed far cheerier about this mission than any of them were, even cheerier than they were all pretending to be, and Gawain ruffled his ears affectionately. Like the chatter with his friends, the gesture was comfortingly familiar. Drustan looked on blank-faced, and Gawain wondered what must have been going on in his mind. He had volunteered to come along because he'd thought the challenge was a just cause, but it must have been gnawing at him that he was defying the will of his king. He said nothing and went back to preparing the horses, and Gawain felt some of his forced good humour bleed away. He hadn't wanted his decision to affect anyone else.

The three friends lent their assistance to Drustan, packing up blankets and cooking pots, waterskins and hard cheese, dried meat, salted fish, and a long string of Una's sausages which they carefully packed out of Mabb's reach. Morgause had given Gawain a purse of silver in case they had to purchase food on the trip, but the further north a man went the fewer and further apart the towns became, and they'd be relying heavily on packed supplies and whatever game they could bring down.

Gawain secured his hunting bow and checked that the leather bag which held the strings was closed tight, then looked about to see whether Father Iain was anywhere near. He knew the priest would be joining them but Gawain hadn't seen him all morning and they would soon be ready to leave. He walked over to Drustan to ask if he knew anything, but at that moment Druid Elgan came up to give Drustan a blessing, and Gawain decided not to interrupt. Instead, with the champion distracted, he quickly checked the cloth-wrapped war-axe he'd strapped to the pack horse. Drustan would see it eventually but the longer Gawain could stave off his disapproval, the better; he might have used it to great effect last night, but nothing would ever persuade the champion of the virtue of an axe over sword or spear.

They would all be bringing ash spears with them too of course, Drustan would have it no other way, and Gawain also wore the sword his father had given him to mark his fifteenth year. It wasn't a decorated blade, he'd not earned such a thing yet, but it was well-made and had bronze in the pommel, and Gawain had been madly proud the day the king had presented him with it. *And now you're taking it on a mission in defiance of his will.* Gawain shook the thought away; he was in the right, and Lot would understand that one day. Maybe.

Drustan bowed his head to the druid then scooped up a bundle and threw it underhanded at Gawain. He caught it and felt the cool rings of a mailshirt shifting in his grip. It almost slithered free of his hands but Gawain got control of it just as similar bundles were thrown at Ulfric and Burian. Drustan did not waste words.

'I'll not have the horses burdened with them; you can wear these on the march, it will make you stronger.'

The boys nodded and looked at each other, but before they could organise who would don his shirt first Drustan spoke again, an edge of impatience in his tone.

'And you can get used to putting them on and taking them off yourselves. The neck-straps are a bugger to fasten the first few times so you'll need the practice.'

Drustan was already wearing his mail, along with the long scale coat that marked him as one of the king's elite, so there was no way for him to demonstrate. Gawain suspected that was deliberate. The three boys struggled their way into the shirts, acutely aware of how many people were watching them, and Gawain decided to leave the neck-straps open until they were out of sight of the crowd. He sighed as the mail fell into place. All that was left now were the shields.

He looked at the rather sorry-looking wooden boards and felt another little flash of anger. They would not be carrying shields that bore Lothian's Red Fox, either by Lot's command or because Drustan felt uncomfortable carrying the king's emblem on a mission he had condemned. Instead they would be taking plain shields of unpainted linden-wood, and without the bright colours to adorn them they looked sad and lowly things. Gawain tried not to see it as an ill-omen that he'd be making his first foray north without bearing the emblem of his house. *As if this wasn't going to be hard enough, we have to leave a measure of our pride behind as well.*

He was just reaching down to pick one up when a familiar voice came from across the yard.

'Not that one.'

He looked up to see Father Iain walking briskly towards them, his long robes flapping around his calves. The priest had a staff in his right hand and a pack over that shoulder, presumably holding his bedding and cloak, but Gawain's eye was drawn to what he held in his left hand. It was a large shield, painted white with a red device; a five-pointed star, cleverly drawn in a continuous line that linked the points across the shield's centre. Gawain had the vague impression that he'd seen such a star before, though he couldn't remember where. The priest laid the shield's rim on the grass but stopped Gawain before he came close.

'Take care, the red is still wet.' He pointed at the symbol with the hand which held his staff, and Gawain noticed that his fingers were also stained red. 'This star was chosen by King Solomon as a mark of faith and fidelity, and has become a holy symbol of Christ's protection. The points are the Five Wounds, the Five Joys, and the Five Virtues of a holy warrior.'

Grateful though he was, Gawain felt a little embarrassed. He'd *heard* of the Five Joys, and was fairly sure he knew what Christ's Five Wounds were, but the only thing he'd truly understood was the Five Virtues of the warrior; honesty, courtesy, valour, devotion and benevolence. He'd learned those virtues as a boy, both from Drustan and his father, and had been made to remember them. They seemed simple enough in theory, but now that he was heading out on a warrior's mission, Gawain suspected they might be difficult things to live up to in practice. *A good thing to have a reminder of them on the shield, I suppose.* He'd have preferred to carry the Red Fox of course, but Iain's gesture had been immensely kind and he bowed his head to him.

'Thank you, father.'

Gawain noted that Drustan was looking on with mild disapproval but he said nothing, and Iain smiled warmly.

'You are welcome, my son.'

He must have seen something in Gawain's face because he nodded towards the green-and-red banner flapping above the watchtower.

'I know that you would sooner carry your father's emblem. And I know that you are as angry with him as he is with you.' He put a hand on Gawain's arm. 'But you must each of you try to forgive the other.'

Gawain scowled, and Ulfric and Burian both busied themselves in picking up the other shields; if their king was about to be disrespected, better that they were out of earshot. Gawain kept his voice low anyway.

'He is in the wrong, why can't he...'

But Iain held up a hand and Gawain stopped.

'To my mind you are both in the right and both in the wrong. Who is *proven* right will be for God to decide.' He softened his tone a little. 'But your father is angry with you because he fears for your safety, and brave men hate being made to feel fear.'

Gawain suspected that Lot was principally angry for having been defied in his own hall, but Iain continued before he could voice his thoughts.

'Why do you think he is allowing us all to travel with you, if not because his anger is born of fear?' He nodded towards Drustan. 'If he commanded his champion to remain at Dun Edin then Drustan would be oath-bound to obey. And he could easily have the rest of us detained under guard until you had gone. Well,' he smirked, 'perhaps not *me* but certainly your friends there. He has not done so, and has allowed himself to be defied by all of them, because his first concern is that you survive this ordeal.'

Gawain didn't know what to say to that, and even glanced over at the hall, half-expecting to glimpse Lot standing in the doorway to see him off. But only Anna and the queen could be seen at the hall, and he shoved away the foolish thoughts about his father. The king might indeed be concerned for his son's life, but he'd be far too proud to come out and watch Gawain and the others defy his word. Gawain hefted the shield and noted that on the inside, in between the grips, was painted a simple figure of a woman in blue, presumably the Virgin Mary. It seemed that as well as reminding him of his virtues, the shield would keep the blessing of Christ's mother close by him. Drustan wouldn't think much of that, war was a place for war gods after all, but Gawain was grateful; on this journey he'd need all the blessings he could get. He pushed the doubts to the back of his mind and tried to embrace the fact that he was travelling north on a noble quest, and frightening though it was, he couldn't deny it was also exciting. If he could hang on to that feeling instead of his sadness, this whole affair would be a damned sight easier to bear.

Drustan let out a short whistle and when Gawain turned the champion gave him a curt nod. It was time. Gawain returned the nod and slung the shield across his back as he paced over to Burian, who handed ash spears to him and to Ulfric. Burian took up his own spear and, with a final wave towards Anna, slung his unpainted shield before taking the reins of the nearest horse. Drustan was already leading the first of their beasts towards the gates and Burian fell into step behind his uncle, followed shortly after by Ulfric and the next horse. Iain spread his arms and spoke a few quiet words of prayer before walking over to join them, and Gawain took a final look behind him.

Gareth had joined his mother and sister and looked like he wanted to run up to Gawain to say his farewells, but he checked himself awkwardly and simply waved with the others. Gawain did his best to smile as he waved back, trying not to think about Halwen, who Gareth had clearly not persuaded to come and say farewell. He was about to turn back to the gates when he saw a shape in the hall doorway and, at a second glance, saw sunlight glinting from a golden torque. For a mad moment he thought it might be Lot after all but then, squinting, he made out long hair and a beardless face, and recognised Gaheris. His elder brother did not wave, and Gawain turned away without acknowledging him. Whatever his reasons for coming to watch him go, Gaheris hadn't even bothered to step out of the hall and nod, and Gawain wasn't going to pander to him by turning back. Instead he strode towards the gates with the others, giving half-smiles and nods to the townsfolk who'd gathered to see him off.

When they reached the gates he was sorely tempted to turn around one last time. Maybe Gaheris or Gareth wanted to say something to him after all, or maybe Lot or even Halwen had changed their minds and were just waiting for him to turn? Gawain grunted at himself and shucked the strap of his shield. If they wanted to talk they could have done by now, and looking back would just make him seem like a hesitant boy. And he wasn't a boy today. Today he was a man, heading out from Dun Edin with spear and shield the way Gaheris and Agravain had, and that was something to welcome, not something to grieve over. Gawain forced his fears and sorrows aside and embraced his sense of adventure as the little company marched through the fortress' north gates. Halwen, his father, and all the rest of it he could deal with on his return. For now he was Gawain ab Lot of Lothian, heading out on a mission to vanquish a dangerous foe. *And a foe you've beaten once before, remember. You can do it again.* For all his many cares and worries Gawain actually felt a grin spread across his face. *Yes, and next time I'll be sure his bloody head stays off!*

Chapter Nine

With only a vague idea of where they were going, it was agreed that the sensible route was simply to make for the coast of the Short Sea and follow it northwest. Once the sea narrowed they would have the choice of selling the horses and taking a boat to the northern shore, or keeping the beasts and trekking around the coastline past Anthony's Wall. Elgan had said that Maes Gwyr was somewhere in eastern Venicon territory, and once they were out of Lothian lands they could search the settlements for a guide to the Green Man's home; a simple enough plan when spoken, but Gawain doubted if finding their destination would be quite so easy.

All the same the journey had at least been pleasant so far, and they'd made good time in reaching the coast. The weather had been clear, and though clouds were now massing in the northern sky, Gawain had to admit it was an agreeable walk. All around them the fields were green with the health of spring, and the air blowing from the Short Sea was fresh and bracing. Looking hard, he was sure he could almost see the opposite coast by now, and it surely wouldn't be long before they found a boatman willing to ferry them. He shrugged his shoulders as he walked, making his mail jingle and shifting the weight of his shield. Carrying all his war-gear was taking some getting used to, but Gawain was strong and hadn't complained about the burden. Unlike Ulfric.

His Saxon friend was no weakling, but he was the slightest of the three youths and grumbled at the weight of his mailshirt and shield, particularly after midday when the sun grew hot. Bel's chariot was long past his zenith by now and the air was thick and humid, and Gawain could hear Ulfric muttering to himself every time he shucked his shield. Neither Gawain nor Burian had offered to help him, that would be a far worse insult than any comment about his mother, but all the same Gawain felt a little guilty that he was able to enjoy his walk while his friend suffered in the heat.

Beside the Saxon, leaning heavily on his staff, Father Iain looked as tired as if he too carried pack and shield, and periodically exchanged a sympathetic gripe with Ulfric. Drustan, naturally, did not tire, and Gawain knew that the champion would happily have picked up their pace, but he plodded along at the speed of their slowest members, occasionally berating Ulfric for his weakness but never going so far as to make them speed up. *He knows we lads would run if he made us, but Iain is long past running age.* The two men had their differences, but there was still such a thing as respect.

A few hours before dusk he called for a halt at a pine grove, and Gawain lashed the pack-beasts to a bough before joining the others on the grass. Drustan and Burian both looked fresh as stream-water, but Ulfric looked grateful to be able to sit for a while, and Iain looked quite ready to lie down and sleep. The old priest groaned aloud as he bent his knees to sit, and he leaned back against a pine-trunk with a satisfied sigh. Mabb trotted up to him and began nuzzling Iain's hand, and the priest smiled as Gawain came to sit with them.

'You wait until you reach my age, my boy. You'll learn to appreciate the simple joy of sitting down after a walk.'

Gawain smiled back.

'By the time I'm your age, father, I'll be a warlord with a hall full of warriors to do my walking for me.'

Drustan gave him a sceptical look and threw a waterskin at him.

'Warlords who let their men do all the work do not stay warlords for long.'

Gawain caught the skin before it could smack him in the face, and Drustan continued with a snort.

'Be grateful you're not a Pict; if one of their chiefs gets lazy, his first warning is a knife in the back.'

Gawain's eyebrows went up as he brought the skin to his lips. 'Are they truly that savage?'

Drustan nodded.

'If one of King Lot's warlords is no bloody good then either his men desert him or Lot strips him of power. If a *Pict* warlord is no bloody good then his second man just kills him and takes his place.'

Gawain took a swig and heard Iain tut beside him.

'I've heard tales where they give their former chief's head to their pagan gods afterwards.' He raised a hand towards Drustan and his voice was casual but sincere. 'Meaning no offence to you, lord, but pagan rituals can be brutal.'

If Drustan was offended he gave no sign of it. If anything, Gawain suspected that he himself was the one most embarrassed by the priest's remark. Iain had baptised Gawain after all, which meant he'd surely want him to agree with him about such things, but Gawain didn't wish to offend Drustan or the Old Gods any more than he wished to offend Iain or Christ. He was sure that both men understood the dilemma and wouldn't judge him for keeping silent, but all the same it was a relief when Drustan spoke first.

'Some can be, I'll grant. The Picts love the Thunderer more than the Huntsman, and Taranis has a great love of blood.'

He tapped his sword-hilt for Cernunnos' favour, and Gawain tried to do the same without Iain noticing. He probably did, but he didn't say anything. Gawain covered the movement with a question.

'Did you ever see heads offered up for sacrifice when you fought the Picts?'

Drustan's face was expressionless as he answered.

'I saw heads thrown at our shieldwall, though whether that was ritual or just the Picts being vicious bastards, I couldn't say.'

Gawain saw both Burian and Ulfric lean forward a little, though they tried not to make it obvious. Most warriors loved to tell tales of their exploits but Drustan, despite appearing in many other men's tales, rarely spoke of his own experiences unless it was to teach them something. If he was about to be coerced into telling a tale of the war, then this was a moment to savour. The champion's eyes flicked to them and he must have seen their eagerness, but he sighed rather than scolded.

'Fancy a bloody tale, do you?'

Every boy liked to hear stories of battle, but Gawain and Ulfric both nodded anyway. It was Burian who spoke though, his voice so low and grave that for a moment he sounded very like his uncle.

'Tell us about the battle where my father died.'

An uneasy silence fell over the company. Drustan watched his nephew for a moment, and Gawain wondered if Burian had asked too much of him. Then the champion nodded.

'Very well. But I'll sing no legends. We've walking to do and I am no bard.'

The boys nodded again, Burian still looking very serious. Drustan shifted where he sat and let out a long sigh before he began.

'It was after the fight at Gwaedlyd Hill. The king was heading north…'

But before he could get further Mabb stood and began sniffing at the air. A moment later Ulfric had risen to one knee and was holding a hand to his lips. The Saxon's eyes and ears were keen and a second later he cocked his head, listening hard. Gawain felt himself tensing ready to fight but he worked hard to sit still. He scanned the trees slowly, barely moving his head as he sought any sign of movement in the ferns. His spear was leaning against a tree and his axe was still stowed on the pack-horse, but his sword was at his side and would be more use in close quarters anyway. He wondered who their enemy would be; there would surely be no Picts this far south, but while the king's harsh laws meant banditry was rare, that didn't mean the roads could not be dangerous.

Father Iain cast his eyes about nervously as Ulfric strained his ears. Mabb still seemed more curious than concerned and Drustan had not moved from where he sat. To an outside observer the champion seemed completely relaxed, but Gawain knew that he would move quicker than a cat if threatened. Burian rose very slowly and began walking casually towards the horses, though whether he was going to find his bow or his spear, Gawain never found out. At that moment he heard a rustling from his left and Gawain acted without thinking; without waiting for any signal from Drustan he turned and sprang for the ferns, and his sword was half-drawn and his face set in a snarl before he realised what the noise had actually been.

Halwen's eyes went wide as he came at her, and her hand flew to what looked like a long-handled knife at her belt. Gawain checked his movement before he could draw the weapon, and a moment later Halwen relaxed her hands, though her face remained deathly pale. A surge of guilt went through Gawain for having frightened her so, and he forced his expression into something less feral as he looked down at her. She was wearing a wide-hooded cloak and what looked like a boy's tunic and breeches, neither of which fitted her particularly well. For all the shock of seeing her, Gawain couldn't help but notice how strong Halwen's legs looked in the trousers, which seemed to be strained to breaking point over her thighs.

It seemed his heart was slow to realise that there wouldn't be a fight, and it continued to hammer hard and send hot blood tingling through his limbs. Gawain's words came out in an awkward huff.

'What are you doing here?'

Halwen gave him a slightly forced half-smile, which became more genuine when Mabb sauntered up and started licking her fingers.

'It is good to see you too, Gawain.'

Gawain faltered for a moment and was trying to think of what to say when he spotted the red-haired youngster trailing behind her. He blinked in surprise.

'Gareth?'

His brother nodded nervously, and Gawain was grateful that Drustan rose to his feet and took over the questioning.

'What are you doing here?'

The words sounded a lot calmer coming from him, though there was an edge of impatience behind them. Both newcomers looked at him sheepishly and it was Halwen who stepped forward to answer.

'We neither of us said our farewells to Gawain, and with this task being a dangerous one, we wished to farewell properly, on good terms.'

Gareth nodded along beside her.

'So we thought we would catch you up, and maybe walk with you as far as Anthony's Wall?'

Drustan eyed them disapprovingly. Gawain, now that the surprise was fading, felt himself torn between gratitude and frustration. It felt wonderful that Halwen was no longer angry with him and just the sight of her was a delight, but the whole thing was so awkward and uncertain as well, to say nothing of the problem of Gareth. Halwen was, generally, a sensible girl who would say her farewells, maybe grant him another kiss if he was lucky, and then go. Gareth on the other hand might convince himself that he ought to be coming with Gawain the whole way, and getting him to go back home would be an unpleasant conversation. Gawain wondered whose idea it had been to come after them, and surmised that Gareth and Halwen had probably persuaded each other into it. *A foolish thing to do. But then who are you to judge?*

Iain appeared beside Gawain, leaning on his staff, and fixed his grey gaze on Halwen.

'Does Sibeal know where you are?' He looked to Gareth. 'Or the queen?'

Gareth didn't look at Iain as he shook his head. Halwen was marginally bolder, but still didn't quite meet the old priest's eyes.

'We left a message with Anna so they would know not to fret.'

Gawain could tell that Burian wanted to say something but his uncle cut across him. The edge in Drustan's voice had grown keener.

'We have no need for bystanders where we're going. Say your farewells now and get yourselves home.'

Halwen opened her mouth to speak but then, as if it had been waiting to interrupt her, there was a distant rumbling of thunder, and a moment later the first lazy drops of rain began to fall. Within seconds they multiplied, and it was clear to everyone that this would soon become a downpour. Iain looked over at the champion.

'They were fools to come after us, Drustan, but we should not turn them back in this weather.' He gestured north, where shepherd's huts dotted the grassy land down to the coast. 'The afternoon is all but gone anyway, we can shelter in one of these dwellings overnight and send them back home in the morning.'

The words were kind but like Drustan's there was sternness beneath them, and the priest gave no illusions about their new companions being welcome. Drustan looked for a moment like he might object and send them off regardless, but Halwen was a woman and Gareth a king's son; he could hardly turn them away into a storm. The champion gave the priest a curt nod and, ignoring Halwen and Gareth completely, stamped back to where he'd left his shield and spear.

'Get your things and move.'

Ulfric and Burian did as they were told, and Iain turned and walked towards the horses. Gareth looked up at Gawain and smiled a little, and despite all the awkwardness Gawain smiled back.

'Well, come on then, if you're coming.'

Gareth beamed and hurried over to help Iain with the pack-horse. Gawain flicked his brother's hood off and ruffled his hair as he passed, earning him an indignant grunt from Gareth and a warm look from Halwen. When he turned to look at her he was lost for words but Halwen, sensibly, spoke for him.

'We'd best get moving.'

Gawain nodded.

'We had indeed.' He jerked his chin towards the grey-looking huts. 'I only hope we find an empty one.'

While sleeping in a cramped space with Halwen might be intriguing, Gawain drew the limit at sharing it with the whole company *and* a shepherd to boot. Something told him they might spoil the experience for him.

As it happened, the very first hut they found turned out to be abandoned. It was small by the standards of a house but large compared to most shepherd's huts, and the travellers piled into it gratefully. To Gawain it felt as if the rain had grown heavier with every step, and all of them were soaked through by the time they got under cover. Drustan brusquely ordered Gareth and Burian to tend to the horses, and they wisely refrained from grumbling as they went out to do his bidding; the champion had barely spoken a word since the newcomers' arrival, and though he'd not bawled any of them out yet, Gawain knew it was just a matter of time.

The hut was a low-ceilinged structure of wattle and thatch, barely large enough for them all to crowd into it and sit, and certainly too small to be able to change clothes comfortably. Gawain would have been hesitant to remove much more than his mailshirt in front of Halwen, but even the simple act of untying its straps was near impossible in the cramped space. They all struggled out of their wet cloaks and boots and made the best they could of it, edging their way around until everyone had a section of wall to their backs and could put their legs out in front of them. Drustan even began making a tiny fire in the centre, though his efforts were frustrated when Gareth and Burian came back and everyone had to shift to make space for them and their gear. He grunted at his nephew.

'You tied them up safe?'

From the look on Burian's face it was clear he was holding back a sharp response, but Drustan was too busy with the fire to see it.

'We did. They even have some shelter under the tree.'

Drustan snorted.

'I'm sure when they learn to talk they'll thank you for it.'

Once again Burian bit his tongue. Drustan's annoyance was not for him, and he knew it. Gawain liked to think it wasn't for him either, but that was wishful thinking. Even had this whole affair not been his fault to begin with, their unwelcome guests had come because they'd wanted to say farewell to *him*. He would not be blameless in Drustan's eyes. *Given the choice, he'd probably have* us *tied beneath the tree and keep the horses in here.*

There was no real door to the hut but the shepherd kept a wicker screen beside the entrance, and with a great deal of shuffling and muttering they managed to get everyone into the dry and push the screen across the opening. They left a narrow sliver to allow potential smoke to escape, though Drustan was still cursing quietly as he worked to start a fire with damp wood and no space. Nobody dared to offer help or advice. Iain busied himself fetching out food from their packs, and Halwen got something dangerously close to a look of approval from Drustan when she produced a loaf of bread and a hunk of cheese for herself and Gareth. Unwelcome though she might be, at least she'd come prepared.

Eventually Drustan got a smoky little fire going. It was far too small for cooking but it gave them light while they ate and took the chill from their bare toes, and soon enough the combination of the fire and the press of bodies meant the whole hut grew pleasantly warm. Gawain shifted himself about and tried to get comfortable, or as close to comfortable as any of them were likely to get tonight. He was quietly pleased that he'd wound up sitting beside Halwen, and he enjoyed the feel of her body so close to his, but it was hard to appreciate any sense of intimacy when his brother, his two friends, a giant wolfhound, a frowning priest and an irate warrior all sat within ten feet of them. Nonetheless Gawain embraced the moment as best he could, and when they finished their meal and Halwen leaned into his shoulder, it was a miracle that he didn't grin like a fool.

Though for all the contentment he felt being close to Halwen, the silence was undeniably uncomfortable. Despite the hut being packed full of people who'd known each other for years, the only sounds were the gulps and chews as they ate their meal, the crackling of Drustan's little fire, and the constant pattering rain from the storm outside. No-one seemed to want to be the first to start a conversation, and so risk Drustan losing his temper. Gawain frowned to himself. If someone didn't do something soon, they were all in for a very long night.

He fished about in his pack for the little lump of ash he'd brought from Dun Edin and, as casually as he could, he began whittling at it with his knife. Gawain was no great craftsman but that wasn't the point in this, and he hoped that Drustan would catch the meaning of what he did. The champion's eyes went from the wood up to Gawain, then flicked quickly to Iain and back again. It was true, Iain wouldn't approve, but Christ was a god who loved peace and Gawain was on his way to battle; it made sense to appease the right god for the right things.

Drustan made no comment on Gawain's whittling but he took a slow breath and broke the silence in a voice which, if not exactly cheerful, sounded relaxed and at ease.

'So, I was speaking of the fight after Gwaedlyd Hill?'

Gareth and Halwen were merely surprised by the sound, but Ulfric's and Burian's eyes grew as large as hens' eggs. Drustan was reluctant to tell tales in the best of moods, and he was far from being in the best of moods. They said nothing though, and it was Iain who commented first.

'Would such a tale be appropriate here?'

He tried to be subtle in the way he glanced at Halwen, but in such cramped quarters it was hard to do anything unnoticed. She looked over at the priest and spoke with no trace of malice.

'Is it inappropriate because I'm a woman, father? Or because of my grandmother?'

Iain looked taken aback by her directness and while Drustan didn't smile, Gawain could tell he was amused. The priest hesitated for only a moment and then answered calmly.

'Either, or both, I suppose. Hearing a bard sing of bygone battles is one thing, but this…'

Drustan interrupted, his voice completely impassive.

'I've had women swing blades at me while baying for my soul, and I've cut those women down as eagerly as I've cut down any man. It makes no difference to me. As for the girl being part Pict?' He shrugged. 'If we refused to talk of it before anyone of Pictish blood, then only pigs and goats would hear stories of the war.'

He prodded the little fire with a stick, then pointed it first at Burian and then back at himself.

'We two look about as different from a Pict as any man could.'

Gawain wasn't sure what point he was trying to make, but the statement was certainly true. Burian's skin was darker than the swarthiest Pict, and Drustan's was even darker than his nephew's. Descendants from Roman auxiliaries were a common enough sight in Dun Edin, but even among the scions of Syrians and Sarmatians, Drustan and Burian stood out in the crowd. The champion went on.

'But even we have the blood of the far north in our veins. Look back through my grandmother's line and I'll bet a gold ring to a tin pot that you'll find Pictish blood there somewhere. Aye, and likely some Brigante and Venicon too. And if it's true for us, then it's true of all Lothian.'

He was right, of course, though Gawain wasn't sure he liked the idea of having Pictish blood in him. But then, if it ran in Halwen's veins too then he supposed it couldn't be all that bad. He suspected that Gareth had never thought of things this way, and he gave the champion an appealing look.

'Even in us?'

He gestured towards Gawain. Drustan nodded.

'King Lot has blood in him from every part of the Hen Ogledd, and he'd be the first man to admit that to you.'

Gareth looked rather crestfallen.

'But we're the Royal House of Lothian. Shouldn't that mean...'

Iain gently interrupted him.

'No man is of only one people. Queen Morgause is of Kernow remember, and she has Roman and Silurian blood in her as well, which means you do too. We all of us have the blood of many tribes in our ancestry. Unless a clan marries brother to sister it must always include outsiders, and that is no bad thing.'

Gareth didn't look much comforted and Iain did his best to cheer him.

'Having savage blood does not make you a savage.'

Halwen, who was sitting near to him, smiled and gave Gareth a friendly shove.

'I should hope not.'

Gareth returned the smile, and Iain leaned back a little.

'Indeed. Remember, Gareth, it is a man's soul that defines who he is, not his blood.'

Drustan's mouth twitched a tiny fraction, and Gawain was sure that if he'd blinked he would have missed it. But he didn't miss the fact that Drustan's next words, though they sounded like support for Iain, did not quite agree with him either.

'True enough, father. Only a fool can judge by blood alone; it's what a man does that shows if he's worth a damn.'

Iain must have noticed the subtle disagreement, but Drustan jerked his chin at Ulfric before the priest could say anything.

'Unless he's a Saxon, of course; they're *all* worth as much as a eunuch on a wedding night.'

Ulfric shook his head but he was well-used to Drustan's empty jibes and contented himself with scratching Mabb's floppy ears. Iain looked rather more disapproving, partly at the crudeness in front of Halwen, but Gawain suspected it was mostly because he'd hoped to elaborate to Gareth about how his soul defined him. Gawain liked Iain a great deal, but the man rarely missed a chance to lecture the youngsters about their souls. He made no effort to interrupt however, and Drustan turned his attention to Halwen.

'Now then, since your Pictish blood is recent I shall ask you plain; will you take it ill if I tell a tale of when Lothians killed Picts and Picts killed Lothians?'

Halwen had of course heard such stories all her life, though admittedly she would have heard them in a bard's song rather than from a veteran across a campfire. She answered very courteously.

'I will not take it ill, and I am as curious as the others.'

Drustan nodded, and Burian, Ulfric and Gareth all shifted forward expectantly. Gawain probably would have done the same, but that would move him away from where Halwen leaned on him. He still watched the champion eagerly though, his knife and block of ash completely forgotten. Drustan didn't start immediately, and for a few moments the only noise was the crackling fire and the rain outside, then he let out a breath and began his tale.

'Well, we had beaten back Drest ab Drest at Gwaedlyd Hill, and Lot was taking the main army and half our Saxons in pursuit. The rest of the mercenaries and about fourscore Lothian men were sent east to secure the river, myself and your fathers among them.'

He nodded briefly to Burian and Ulfric. Gawain didn't feel left out for Lot not being a part of this story, and he doubted if Gareth did either. They'd both heard every tale of their father's exploits a hundred times over, either from the man himself or from some bard or former warrior who wanted to flatter the king. This story was something new, and there was certainly no flattery in it. Gawain settled in to listen, and enjoyed the simple way that Drustan told his tale. He spoke of how Alva mer Colm had ambushed them, and how twenty men had died before a shieldwall could be formed. He spoke of how Ekbert had fought on his right side in that wall, and how the Saxon had saved his neck a dozen times when the Picts tried to break their line. There was no exaggeration in the story, no effort to make it seem heroic or glorious, it was simply a man who had been there recalling what had happened. Yet somehow, and he had no idea why, Gawain found he was still enthralled.

Drustan went on to tell how Burian's father, Beinon, had been struck down by a Pictish axe, and though Burian had listened dry-eyed, the champion put a hand on his nephew's arm as he told that part. Like the rest of his tale there was no glorification; Beinon had fought hard, he had protected his shield-brothers, and when he fell Drustan and Ekbert had slain the man who killed him. A simple story, but one that Gawain knew he wouldn't forget, and from the proud looks on Burian and Ulfric's faces, he knew that they wouldn't either. *Why do bards play with words so much when this is all they need to do?* Most of the bards who made the songs hadn't seen the battles themselves; perhaps they didn't know the simple truths, or perhaps they just didn't care? Gawain decided that when his story was told, he would want it told simply, the way Drustan did. If a tale was worth telling, he decided, then it didn't need embellishment.

As gripping as the story was, by the time Drustan was finished they were all of them feeling drowsy, and Gawain saw that Gareth had already fallen asleep. Halwen too was beginning to nod, and he took care not to move her too much as he reached for his lump of ash. He'd given up on the whittling almost as soon as Drustan began to speak, and it would be several evenings more before it resembled anything other than a hunk of hacked wood. A furtive glance at Iain told him the priest's eyes were closed, so Gawain quickly put the ash to his lips before tucking it away in his pack. Across the fire, Drustan nodded approvingly. Gawain nodded back, trying not to feel guilty for deceiving Iain.

He pushed away the thought, he was doing no harm to the old man after all, and soon enough he might have good cause to be glad he'd made the gesture. He leaned back against the wall of the hut and let out a quiet sigh. The noise of the storm was restful in his ears, and he surprised himself by not thinking more about how his own tale would be told one day. After Drustan's recounting he was convinced his mind would be full of nothing but the battles to come and the great deeds that he would do, and how he'd need no flattering bard to make him sound impressive later on. But he didn't think about that. He didn't think about the Green Man either, and the very real chance that the next time they met, one of them would die. He didn't even think, as he often did at night, about Halwen, and the softness of her lips or how her skin would feel beneath his hands. Instead he thought only of how pleasant it was to feel her head resting on his shoulder as she drifted off to sleep, and how warm his feet were before their little crackling fire. It was strange indeed but he didn't object to it at all, and Gawain closed his eyes and marvelled at how contented he felt tonight. It wasn't even spoiled when he learned how loudly Halwen snored.

Chapter Ten

'So, how did my son acquit himself?'

Mhari hated herself for what she had to say, but she had little enough choice in the matter.

'He killed his share, lord.'

It was the closest thing to an honest answer that she could give. Temar *had* stabbed a few Lothians after all, even if the flat-faced cur hadn't been bold enough to join in the charge. Calling it his share was a fair stretch of the truth, but given who she was speaking to, Mhari forgave herself the lie. *I could have said far worse.* Alva smiled down from her high seat, and beside Mhari, Temar grunted an insincere thanks to his chief.

Alva mer Colm had the same large build as her son, though the old warlord had run to fat in her later years, and great folds of it hung down from flabby arms and a bulging paunch. Her hair, which had once been as black as the jewels around her pudgy throat, was now liberally streaked with grey and had even receded from her brow in some places. Like Mhari she wore the swirling tattoos of a warrior on her cheeks but her many wrinkles now spoiled the pattern, and the bright blue had faded with time. *Like the rest of her.* Her rheumy eyes had to squint to see anything more than a few feet away, and Mhari knew the old woman found it hard to walk without her stick. It was enough to make Mhari want to weep for her.

For as long as she could remember, Mhari had gorged herself on tales of Alva's countless exploits, and now the mighty warlord was a sagging shadow of what she'd once been, and Mhari's admiration was slowly fading into pity. Alva didn't even have the comfort of strong children to succeed her, since both her daughters had died young and Temar, no matter what half-truths Mhari told, was a gutless, useless waste of good mountain air. It was hard to believe, but it seemed that dragons could sometimes birth worms.

Alva nodded appreciatively.

'I am proud to hear you speak well of him.' She transferred her squinting gaze to Temar. 'Keep learning from this one,' she gestured towards Mhari, 'and you will be a credit to us all in good time.'

Temar didn't seem impressed but there was a murmur of approval from the warriors around them. Alva's longhall housed some twoscore of her finest fighters, all of whom knew Mhari's reputation, and most of whom would be keen for their future lord to learn the art of war from her. Temar bowed and gave a hollow little smile.

'My thanks, Mother. I shall learn.'

Alva smiled back at him. Mhari could never work out whether Alva was deliberately blind to Temar's many faults, or whether her mind was slowly growing simple in old age. It took no great thinker to work out Temar's worth, yet the old warlord seemed oblivious to his failings. Mhari would have given much to tell Alva exactly what she thought of her boy, but however much Alva might be fond of Mhari, Temar was her blood and she wouldn't forget that. Instead Mhari had to make up half-truths about the useless bastard, and keep him with her on the raids for the sake of his mother's warriors. *Like a lump of gold hung around a swimmer's neck.*

The old warlord went on.

'You say you intend to make larger raids now? I suppose you would have me send more warriors to take with you?'

It was a question to which Alva already knew the answer; Mhari could have sold her slaves off anywhere, but Hengraig was where Alva was and so they had come here. Their profits from the raids might tempt a few roaming warriors to Mhari's warband, but oath-men from Alva would be far more reliable. Even if some of them wound up under Temar's command.

Mhari made sure to project her voice so none of the warriors in the hall could miss her words.

'We mean to tug at Lot's beard, lord, and raid further south again. Any warriors keen for reputation would be welcome to join us.'

Given that every warrior worth the name was keen on reputation, Mhari knew she had the attention of her audience. Alva knew what she was doing of course, and her voice took on a slightly teasing tone.

'I hear you killed Lord Peleus all by yourself?' She waved a hand at her people and grinned at them. 'Are you sure you wish to share glory with this rabble?'

Her warriors called back a series of objections, heavily seasoned with boasts about their prowess in battle. They all knew how well Alva truly valued them of course, but few warriors missed a chance to brag about their deeds, and if there was loot and glory to be gained by going with Mhari, they would want her to know their worth. Mhari bared her teeth at Alva.

'Your rabble may not have my skill, lord, but I'm sure I can find a use for them.'

There were more calls from the warriors around them but they were silenced by Alva's bark of laughter.

'I don't doubt you find a use for that one.' She pointed a finger towards Conn, who was looking particularly handsome in the red cloak he'd bought with his share of silver. 'Or if you can't, send him to me and I will.'

Conn gave the warlord a roguish wink and answered for himself.

'Alas, lord, Mhari values my spear too highly to leave it behind while she does battle.'

Alva sighed.

'At her age I'd have had you battling with it all day and all night.'

Mhari grinned, at least in part because Temar was so obviously discomforted by his mother's flirting.

'I will be sure to bring him back in once piece for you to admire, lord. But if I'm to keep him in fine cloaks then I will need to keep up my raiding?'

Alva gave her an approving smile and Mhari knew she had won her point, and Alva would be granting her more warriors. And then the bloody Grey Woman appeared out of nowhere and yet again stole the credit from under her.

'It would be wise to send your warriors, Alva mer Colm. All the signs say that the riches gained will be vast, and there will be glory enough to share amongst all who come with Mhari mer Raghnal.'

Smug bitch! Her words were pointless, the bargain was all but struck, but now men would say that the Grey Woman's voice had been the one to persuade the warlord. The druid still wore her mist-coloured cloak but had lowered the hood inside the hall, and her hair shone red in the light of the longhall's fire. Her strange eyes looked up at the high table, and Alva looked back at her, intrigued.

'You have read signs of this?'

The Grey Woman nodded.

'I have, lord, in ash and in bone, and each sign I have read spoke of glory to the south.'

Alva turned and looked to the gnarled druid who sat to her left. He looked old enough to have shared drinks with Caesar, and when he spoke his voice was thin and croaking.

'What ash and bone suggest, the wind and sky confirm.' He waved a frail-looking hand towards the rafters, above which the storm could still be heard. 'For three days and three nights Taranis has raged above us, lusting for blood and for battle. Mhari mer Raghnal made him proud at Beltane, and he will follow her south.'

Despite herself Mhari felt grudgingly glad that the Grey Woman had spoken after all; the words of the old druid would give even more heart to Alva and her people, and had the Grey Woman not spoken of signs then the old man might have stayed silent. Alva's face became serious as she looked down at Mhari.

'You have some fifty warriors with you now, do you not?'

Mhari nodded, though only thirty or so were oath-bound to her. The rest were Temar's men. Alva looked about the hall and then back to Mhari.

'I think I can find a score of men who'd be willing to go with you.' There was a rumble of approval from the benches. 'And a score to fight under Temar as well.'

That was met with rather less enthusiasm, and Mhari guessed smugly that the keenest warriors would be flocking to *her* once the talking was done. Alva either hadn't noticed or chose not to react to the half-hearted response her son received, and instead spoke directly to Mhari.

'I am sure my boy will be a fine chief under your tutelage.'

Mhari doubted that, but her doubts took second place to the sudden tingling in her belly. If Temar was being recognised as a chief, and Mhari was still considered to be his superior, then that meant…

Alva spoke before she could finish the thought.

'Where exactly will you be raiding, Lord Mhari?'

For a moment Mhari was too busy enjoying her new title to respond, and by the time she took a breath the Grey Woman had spoken for her.

'We make for Tahrnax.'

The silence that followed her answer was, Mhari hoped, because the hall was impressed at their daring. In truth it had taken some persuading from the Grey Woman to convince Mhari to risk it, but frustrating though the druid was she had led them to good targets thus far. Even so, the more cautious of Alva's warriors would find their enthusiasm waning thanks to this news; Tahrnax was unnervingly close both to Anthony's Wall and to Maes Gwyr, a place said to be haunted by dangerous spirits. Tahrnax itself was allegedly protected by ghosts, though it was also rumoured that the lord's hall was filled to bursting with gold and silver. *What will win out, caution or greed?* Plenty of Alva's people still seemed keen to join her, and after a quick look around Mhari was confident that she'd have more than enough volunteers. *Greed then.*

Alva nodded, impressed.

'I should have expected nothing less of you, Mhari.'

Mhari got the very real feeling that Alva was growing fonder of her than she was of her son, which showed that dotage hadn't quite caught hold of the old warlord yet. She winked down at Conn again but kept speaking to Mhari.

'Just be sure to bring this one back with you. Too many of my men have the faces of pigs and I need something pretty to look at.'

Once again Temar looked uncomfortable and Conn just gave her a charming smile. Mhari jerked her head towards her lover.

'If the warriors you send with me fight well enough, I'll have Conn show you his scars when we get back.'

Alva's smile grew wide.

'I shall hold you to that, Mhari.'

Before Mhari or Conn could answer the old warlord gestured to a grizzled warrior at the end of the high table.

'Gomer.'

The man slowly stood and turned to a serving table behind him. Alva went on.

'I had every faith in the both of you,' she glanced first at Mhari and then at Temar, 'and had these ready for when you came back in glory.'

Gomer strode around the table and approached Temar. He handed him a scabbarded sword that looked, if not the equal of Brathir, then at least a good quality blade. The bastard didn't deserve any such gift of course, but he bowed his head in thanks and busied himself in buckling it on. Mhari thoroughly approved of the distain on Gomer's face as Temar fumbled with the buckle, and when the old warrior approached Mhari he seemed a good deal more comfortable. He passed the new lord her gift with a nod.

It was a shining steel helm, its cheek-pieces edged with polished bronze, and the inside lined with red leather. Dominating the cap was a ram's skull, fitted so that the eye sockets, which had been carefully widened, would rest before the eyes of the wearer. The bone had been so cunningly worked that Mhari was sure her vision would be no more impaired than when she wore an unadorned helm, and she held it by the curling horns and bowed deeply to Alva.

'A fine gift, lord. I thank you for it.'

Alva bowed back, affecting to ignore the fact that all her son had done was nod.

'You have earned it, Lord Mhari. I shall speak to my warriors and find those most fit to join your raid.' She put a hand to her belt, and Mhari guessed that she was touching the steel of a sword or dagger. 'Taranis go with you.'

Mhari put a hand gently on Brathir's hilt and, at that very instant, the Thunderer rumbled his blessings from above them, loud and fierce and long. A cheer went up from all around her, and Mhari grinned to herself. She decided she could put up with Temar and the Grey Woman, at least for a while longer. Mhari mer Raghnal was a warlord now, and the gods themselves were throwing their power behind her. All the ghosts of Tahrnax and Maes Gwyr would be no match for Mhari with Taranis guiding her sword. *And soon enough, King Lot himself will learn to fear me.*

Chapter Eleven

Gawain supposed that, depending on how you looked at it, things had either gone extremely well, or extremely badly. The weather had only grown worse, and though Drustan had appealed to Danu and Iain had prayed to Christ, it seemed that for now Taranis remained the master of the skies. The Thunderer had thrown so much rain at them that the road had become one long mire, and a trek that ought to have taken only one more day had taken them the best part of three. Men and horses alike would slip and grow stuck in the sucking mud, and the sheer misery of the pounding rain made the walk a hard slog instead of a pleasant stroll. All hopes of taking a boat across the Short Sea had been dashed, and the plan now was to make for Anthony's Wall and cross the Avon Du further west. And of course, it would have been impractical to send Gareth and Halwen back on their own in such conditions.

Much to Drustan's irritation it had been agreed that the pair would stay with them as far as Pencardden, where horses could be bought and a friend of Drustan's sent back with them. Gareth had, in a wonderful display of contradicting himself, both insisted that he was old enough to escort Halwen home on his own, which he wasn't, while also insisting that there was no harm in his going with them further north. Understandably this had only shortened Drustan's patience, and the champion was back to barely speaking when they ate, and on the walk itself he was silent as a pyre-side.

He strode ahead of the little company, using his spear as a walking staff, and all Gawain had seen of him since breakfast was the back of his hood and the plain wood of his slung shield. It was strange, and sad, not to see the Red Fox adorning it, but he told himself the proud creature would look forlorn in the driving rain anyway. Everything else certainly did. The wide green country had turned to dull grey, and the beautiful sea to a churning mass of black water. Mabb's fur and the horses' manes were both a grey bedraggled mess, and they walked with their heads bowed low against the wind. Ulfric was staggering and muttering curses every few steps, and Gareth and Halwen were struggling to maintain even an easy pace. The pair leaned against one another for support, and Gawain would have helped, but his hands were full helping Father Iain.

The old priest was in by far the worst condition of any of them, and was the principle reason why they'd covered so little ground. As willing as his spirit was there was no denying the age of his limbs, and unlike Drustan he had never been accustomed to long marches even in his youth. He leaned half his weight on his ash staff and the other half on Gawain, and though he did his best not to complain aloud, his laboured breathing made his struggle painfully clear. Gawain tried to remind himself that coming along had been Iain's own idea, not his, but nonetheless he couldn't help feeling a stab of guilt each time he winced; no matter whose decision it had been, Iain wouldn't be here if not for him.

He looked ahead of them to where Halwen trudged through the mud, and told himself he shouldn't feel guilty for her either. True, she too was out here because of him, but it hadn't been Gawain's doing to bring her here, nor was it his fault that the weather meant she couldn't return yet. Besides, it meant having her leaning on his shoulder at night, and if anything could make their dreary camps into something cosy, it was that.

Iain coughed from beside him.

'I suspect I will not like the answer, but is there any sign of it yet?'

Gawain shook his head. Drustan had said they would make their next halt when they reached Anthony's Wall, and Gawain knew he hadn't been the only one straining his eyes for a sight of it. The rain made it hard to see very far, and he kept hoping that the wall might be just out of sight through the haze, but so far all he'd seen was yet more mud.

'Nothing yet, father. But it can't be far now.'

They were empty words, and they both knew it, but he hoped Iain appreciated the gesture. The priest nodded, sending drops of rain pouring from his hood.

'You know, my boy, a wiser man would have stayed in his nice warm church and let you youngsters go adventuring on your own. Sometimes I forget how very ancient I am growing.'

Gawain smiled at him.

'Bishop Dyfan is ancient, father. Druid Elgan is ancient. You are just a normal man who likes to bellyache.'

Iain made a half-hearted effort to shake his fist and almost overbalanced.

'Were we on dry land, that sort of cheek would earn you a caning.'

Gawain heaved some more of the priest's weight onto his shoulder.

'When next we stop, I'll be sure to thrash myself thoroughly for you.'

Iain nodded.

'You do that, my boy. You do that.'

The effort of talking was tiring the old priest even more, and he soon fell silent again. Gawain plodded on, his eyes scanning the horizon for any sign of the wall, or of Burian returning with some game. Drustan had told his nephew that in this rain all he'd do was ruin a good bowstring, but some fresh meat would do wonders to raise their spirits, and so Burian had disappeared into the mist anyway. For a moment Gawain envied him the freedom of roaming off to hunt, then remembered that he had a more important role here. He shifted his arm more comfortably under Iain's and kept on walking.

It seemed to take days but it must only have been a few hours before Anthony's Wall came into sight. Gawain grinned and Iain crossed himself, thanking God for the respite, but Ulfric sounded unimpressed.

'Is that it?'

Gawain supposed he had a point; the word *wall* was perhaps a bold term for it. The northernmost frontier of the old Roman Empire, and the border of Lot's kingdom, was just an earthen bank stretching from east to west. There had once been a timber palisade above it but most of that had either collapsed or been scavenged for building material, and now all that remained was a long grassy mound. Gawain had never seen the Great Wall to the south but Gaheris had said that, crumbling though it was, it was still a wonder to behold. Clearly the Romans who'd come this far north had been a less ambitious breed. Drustan growled over his shoulder.

'Expected a palace, did you?'

Ulfric shrugged his rain-soaked shoulders.

'I expected a stone wall at least. That's just a pile of mud and turf.'

Drustan's growl became a bark.

'That pile of mud and turf is a damned sight better than anything a Saxon ever made, now shut your noise.'

Ulfric didn't dare press him any further and held his tongue. Gawain sensibly did the same, and the company trudged on in silence until they reached the bank. A young oak was growing on the Lothian side, and Gawain and Ulfric set about stretching spare cloaks between the branches to form a shelter. It wasn't much, but it was enough for Iain to sit down out of the rain, and Halwen and Gareth were shoved under it with him. Drustan leaned against the trunk, half-covered, while Gawain and Ulfric squatted down nearby, sheltered only by hoods and tree-branches. They did little good, and Mabb shaking his fur only spattered them further, but neither one said anything to complain. The champion's voice was curt.

'We won't stop long. Once Burian gets back we'll cross over and make for Pencardden.' He looked down at Gareth and Halwen. 'You two will wait out the storm there.'

Gareth nodded obediently, and Halwen bobbed her head.

'Of course.' She paused for a moment before reaching out a hand. 'May I?'

Drustan grunted and fished in a pouch at his belt. A moment later he tossed her a whetstone, and Halwen caught it with a nod of thanks. They would be crossing into the safest part of Venicon territory, but still Drustan had insisted that they all keep their weapons keen. Halwen drew out her dagger and started sharpening it, using long even strokes the way the champion had shown her. The weapon had apparently once belonged to her Pictish grandmother, and it was a thing of beauty; the hilt was polished rowan inlaid with silver, and the elegant blade tapered to a needle-sharp point.

Halwen leaned half against the tree and half against Gawain's leg as she worked, and damp though she was Gawain enjoyed the contact. He did his best to ignore the rain and thought about the road ahead. They ought to reach Pencardden before nightfall and from there they could cross the Avon Du. He didn't look forward to Halwen leaving them but it would be for the best, and with a little luck she might kiss him goodbye. After that they would have to double back east again but with good fortune and a break in this weather, they might make good time on their way to the Short Sea. *And then what?*

Gawain had been avoiding thinking too hard about that, and he brought up his shoulders and folded his arms. *Whatever happens once you find the Green Man, you will deal with it.* He'd been quick enough to beat him before, and this time he'd teach the bastard the error of playing games with sons of Lothian. He embraced that pride and the sense of confidence it gave him, and started leaning a little more casually against the oak's trunk. All would be well, and within a moon's turn he would be back at Dun Edin. And Halwen would be there waiting for him.

The light was fading by the time they finally reached Pencardden, and combined with the constant downpour it was hard to see much of the Venicones village. From what Gawain could make out there were a few houses on their side of the Avon Du, but the majority of the people seemed to live on the north bank. The vague shapes of many homesteads could be seen across the swollen river, while on this side there were perhaps a dozen wattle houses and a single long barn. Short wooden jetties stuck out into the water, and beside them a fleet of fishing boats bobbed and rocked in the storm. Looking first at them and then at the rushing river, Gawain suspected he would not enjoy the crossing that was to come.

As they drew near to the settlement a lone figure came hurrying towards them. When he got to within a few paces Gawain saw he was a man around Gaheris' age, tall and thin as a spear, with a black shadow of a beard across his cheek. He recognised Drustan, and the company paused as the pair clapped each other's shoulders, sending drops of rain flying from their cloaks.

'Good to see you, Oran.'

The man, presumably Oran, smiled.

'Drustan, what brings your old bones north?'

The warrior jerked his head behind him at the miserable party.

'A fool's errand.'

Gawain resisted the urge to say something to that, even when Oran leaned around Drustan to look at them.

'A fool's errand that needs three spearmen and Lot's champion?'

Drustan shrugged.

'If a man wants a thing done right he must do it himself.'

Oran smiled again.

'Very true.' He beckoned to Gawain and the others. 'Well, whatever it is you'd best press on.'

They did as they were bid and Gawain, still half-supporting Iain, muttered to the priest.

'We'll soon be inside now, father.'

Iain nodded, breathless.

'A good thing too, my boy. I'm sure I've forgotten what dryness feels like.'

Halwen, who'd been looking at the priest rather anxiously, forced a smile and nudged his other shoulder.

'I can't remember how to walk without my feet squelching!'

The priest gave a half-hearted smile back, and Gawain somehow became even more besotted with Halwen than he already was. Even in all this miserable rain, she still had time for a kind word to an old man.

Drustan walked ahead of them beside Oran.

'So, how's your da these days?'

Oran sounded amused.

'Fat and lazy, and wise enough to be out of the rain. He'll want you to be staying with him tonight.'

Gawain could only see the backs of their hoods but he knew that Drustan would be scowling.

'We're better off staying this side of the river tonight. Five of us are heading north but, with your leave, we'll be leaving the boy and the lass with you until the storm passes. I'll pay for their keep while they wait, and if you send a man to escort them to Dun Edin the king will pay him good silver for it.'

Halwen looked mildly irritated, but stayed silent as Oran shrugged.

'Any friend of yours is welcome here, of course. You needn't think about paying to feed them.'

Drustan nodded, then called behind him.

'Burian!'

Burian handed the reins of his pack horse to Ulfric then jogged up to join his uncle. Drustan pointed to Oran.

'Give the man your hares. The least we can do is give Eirys something for her stew.'

Burian had spent all day trying to keep Mabb from filching the two brace of hares he'd shot, and failed to hide his resentment as he handed them over to Oran. The Venicon half-turned to him and Gawain saw him smile companionably.

'Very decent of you.' Burian nodded once and Oran ignored the mild discourtesy. 'But it's only right that you come and share them with us. We can send your youngsters back across in the morning.'

Gawain knew Drustan wouldn't approve of that, but neither did he want to insult his host.

'As you say.' He gestured towards the boats. 'Are you still as poor a steersman as you used to be?'

Oran's smile became a grin.

'Worse. I un-learned what little I knew in case I had to ferry your ungrateful hide again. But since you brought some inoffensive folk along with you, I may let older hands do the work this time.'

Gawain looked over at the boats and he was sure they'd grown more rickety-looking in the last few moments. A distinct unease came over him at the thought of clambering into one in this weather, but Halwen was still nearby and so he kept the worry from his face. Drustan called out to them again.

'Alright, get yourselves down to the bank and start unloading the beasts.'

Father Iain, who'd clearly been hoping that the day's trials were over, didn't quite manage to bite back a groan. Gawain beckoned Gareth over to him.

'You and Halwen stay with the father while we sort the baggage.'

Gareth was half Gawain's size but he did his best to get under Iain and support his weight. Halwen lent her help and Iain, looking both grateful and a little embarrassed, sneezed and muttered a blessing to them both. Gawain joined Ulfric and Burian as they took bags and blankets from the horses and laid them in the boat, along with their shields and spears. Given how swift the river was running they would all gladly have removed their mailshirts, but a single glare from Drustan was enough to dissuade them. *We'll just have to make sure we don't fall out.*

The boat was one of the largest tied up at the jetty, and was crewed by two youths and a toothless man whose years might have numbered anything from forty to sixty. Oran introduced him as Talorg, and when Gawain and Ulfric offered to lend their hands to the oars, Talorg spat into the river and growled incoherently. Oran translated his grumbling.

'He has little trust for strangers helping on his boat, and he is not fond of Lothians.'

Gawain kept any comment to himself and clambered aboard with the others. Ulfric led a rather reluctant-looking Mabb, who, like Gawain, had apparently noticed how much their ferry rocked every time a new body stepped onto it. A few moments later Talorg had untied their moorings and shoved them off, and Gawain resolved not to hold onto the rail. The current was strong but they struck out at an angle upriver and the young oarsmen managed to keep them from being washed off-course. Gawain sat near the stern, flanking Iain on one side while Gareth sat on the other in case the priest should feel unstable on the water, though if anyone seemed truly ill-at-ease, it was Burian.

Almost as soon as they entered the current he seemed ready to hurl his guts up, and he held the rail with a grip of steel. By then Mabb had forgotten his uncertainty and was sitting calmly at Ulfric's feet, and the Saxon grinned at Burian and made a show of standing up on the shaking deck.

'Eostre's arse, man, it's only a river!'

Burian grunted at him to go and do something that he wouldn't normally have said in front of Iain or Halwen. Gawain wondered if he ought to apologise on his friend's behalf, but Drustan's voice sounded before he could.

'If you like boats so much you can find your own and bugger off back to Saxon lands.'

Ulfric grumbled and sat, while Oran chuckled from the boat's prow.

'From a man of your complexion, Drustan, telling other folk to go home is a wee bit bold!'

Gawain knew he wasn't the only one taken aback by the Venicon's words, but the champion simply smiled at him.

'We can't all be cousin-humpers like you, Oran; some families like variety in their blood. Anyhow,' he jerked his chin at Ulfric, 'much as I'd love to ship this little sod off to the arse-end of nowhere, his da would never forgive me for it. He's grown fond of him for some reason.'

Ulfric grinned and then Drustan, his mood improving by the chatter with his friend, reached over to the young Saxon.

'Of course, I could hardly be blamed if he decided to swim there?'

He gave Ulfric a short shove, but caught hold of his tunic in the same movement and yanked him back before he could topple. The jest led Ulfric and Gareth to bark with laughter, but the movement shook the already rocky boat, and Burian groaned and doubled over in his seat. Gawain tried to take his mind from things.

'Just think of something else until we're landed.'

Burian looked up at him and tried to smile.

'I could try thinking about your sister, but then I might unbalance the boat.'

Halwen put a hand on his arm before Gawain could answer that. She looked as soaked and uncomfortable as Burian was, but still she stood up and moved over to sit with him.

'Maybe try thinking of Anna with her clothes *on* for a change?'

Burian smirked.

'It won't annoy Gawain as much, but I can try.'

He cast his eyes down and stared hard at the planks in front of him, and Halwen put a comforting hand on his shoulder.

Oran stood and came striding up to them, as steady on the swaying deck as he had been on solid ground.

'Try to look up instead of down, you'll feel better for it.'

Burian bobbed his head and tried to follow the advice, transferring his gaze to the hazy far shore. Oran nodded then turned to Gawain.

'He will be alright soon enough.'

Gawain suspected Oran was about to ask about why they were heading north, and decided to distract him with a question; Drustan might want to explain their endeavour himself.

'So, do you have many Picts raiding up here?'

Gareth and Ulfric leaned forward, eager for a tale of battle, but the Venicon chuckled at the question.

'Picts? My friend, we are not at the world's end just yet! The only Picts we see are those coming south to trade.' He waved his arm vaguely towards the distant bank. 'Our kin further north are the ones who face the raiders. Lucky for us, your king's patrols head out often enough that the Picts don't dare to raid this far south.'

Iain, who despite the storm seemed far more relaxed now that he was sitting, looked at the Venicon curiously.

'I have heard that your people have a great lord at Ystre Lyn. Does he not send his own warriors out to patrol the borders?'

Oran's brow furrowed.

'He'd sooner have his warriors tucked in safe at his hall. The chiefs down south don't give a damn for the chiefs up north. They would sooner pay off the Picts than go and fight them.'

Gawain raised an eyebrow.

'Does that work?'

Oran shrugged.

'Sometimes it does, sometimes it doesn't.' He sighed. 'It pains me to say it, but our kin up north need your boys more than any of us care to admit. Just don't say that aloud when you meet my da.'

Gawain nodded. A part of him felt proud that Lothian men were helping these folk, but he suspected he wasn't all that justified in his pride; his father sent men to fight the Picts to keep them far from Lothian lands, not for the benefit of the Venicones. Father Iain often said that it was the duty of the strong to protect the weak, but also that a man's motives mattered more than his deeds alone. King Lot only helped weak folk for his own purposes.

He looked out at the swollen river as it buffeted their hull, and was glad that Drustan spoke before he had to think of a response to Oran.

'Corra mac Cathair is raiding again so we sent most of our spearmen west with Lord Gaheris. But Lord Peleus will be getting more men soon.'

Oran snorted at him, but did it with good humour.

'Old Peleus is only a mouse-hair better than the Picts. He would sooner turn all our land into Lothian, and have us all bowing to your king.'

Gawain had heard similar stories about Peleus' ambitions, and Drustan made no effort to deny them.

'Any news of him?'

Oran nodded.

'Half his men are still at Ystre, he took the other half on some jaunt up north. Right now he's likely planting a standard or pissing on a tree, or whatever else you boys do to mark your territory.'

Despite himself Gawain felt an urge to defend his fellow Lothian, and was about to make some proud remark when Drustan gave a tiny shake of his head. Instead of leaping to Peleus' defence the champion smiled at their host and raised his head up to the storm, closing his eyes as rain soaked his face.

'Well, at least it will be well-diluted piss.'

For all its rockiness the crossing was over before anyone vomited, and the company all thanked Talorg for his service. The toothless Venicon nodded but said nothing, and Oran led them into the town. Pencardden was said to be a fairly large settlement, but Gawain saw little of it through the driving rain. He saw the badger skull mounted near the outskirts to ward off ghosts, he saw a handful of wattle homes and some pens full of soaking goats, but that was more or less his whole impression of the place until they reached the hall.

Oran's father was the chief of Pencardden and his longhall was at the centre of the settlement, a simple enough place but one filled with good cheer and warm welcomes; and more importantly, a roaring fire-pit. Aeddan himself was a tall man and Gawain suspected he'd once been as slim as his son, but time and easy living had given him a considerable paunch, and his great jowls would shake whenever he laughed. Which was often. He had greeted Drustan like a long-lost brother and, once their sopping cloaks had been taken by his servants, he embraced each of the others in turn. The cheery man held onto Halwen for perhaps a heartbeat longer than he did the men, but then ignored her completely when Mabb came bounding up. He fussed about the hound with a wide grin on his face, and the moment they sat down he began feeding him table-scraps.

Gawain and the others were invited to sit with him, and each was given a platter of bread and pork and a mug of sweet mead. Iain looked rather disapproving when Aeddan asked them to pour out a measure for the local sprites, but he complied politely with his host's wishes and then crossed himself fervently afterwards. Once the formalities were done, Aeddan promptly began a long conversation with Drustan which seemed to consist mainly of reminiscences and friendly mockery. The rest of the company were largely left to their own entertainment, and given how very weary they all were, there was little by way of conversation. Burian was still feeling queasy from the crossing and had no appetite for the pork, though when Odran's wife came around with her stew he dutifully managed a bowlful.

Halwen was, inexplicably, looking as beautiful as ever and had none of the bedraggled look that the rest of their party had. They had none of them removed their cloaks since the foul weather had begun, yet while everyone else looked like half-drowned rats, Halwen's hair somehow still shone, and the bronze rings in it still winked in the firelight. She sat between Gawain and Odran and spoke politely to their host's son.

'Do you know much of the lands further north?'

The slender man shrugged.

'For the most part I am a river-man and the river runs east, but I have travelled north a little way. After two days' walk it becomes wild country and few would go that way alone.'

Halwen nodded, and spoke without a trace of self-consioustness.

'My grandmother was a Pict. I have always wondered what her land was like.'

For a suspicious moment Gawain wondered whether she had followed them less for the sake of saying her farewells, and more because it was an excuse to see the lands that lay north of Lothian. He told himself not to be so damned selfish, she could have two reasons if she wanted after all. Odran seemed to care as little as Drustan did for Halwen's Pictish blood.

'What I've seen of it is beautiful, but a dangerous place for outsiders.' He smiled. 'Perhaps you should take your grandmother with you for protection.'

Halwen was courteous enough not to make him feel awkward by mentioning that her grandmother was dead. Instead she smiled and steered the topic away, and soon enough Odran was talking of river-trade and boatmanship.

Gawain was too tired to think of much to say at all and so, mainly to avoid staring jealously at Halwen, spent a little time whittling his lump of ash. It could now just about be recognised as something akin to a head and body, and thankfully Father Iain had either not noticed what it was or had realised and simply not commented.

The evening went by swiftly enough and as the fire died down they were assigned places where they might spend the night. Iain and Drustan were of course given pride of place and would share a straw bed in the chief's rooms behind the hall. There were no spare mattresses for the others to sleep on, but furs and blankets were brought out to pad the hall floor, with more still to cover their guests as they slept. Gawain took his bundle to one corner of the hall and felt a little surge of hope when he saw Halwen following him. The room was spacious enough that there was no need for them all to crowd together as they had done, yet still she was choosing to sleep close to him, and he could feel his heart begin to race.

Burian, having seen the pair walking, took Gareth by the shoulder and led him to the corner furthest away from them, and when Ulfric caught the hint he led Mabb over there as well. Gawain tried to be subtle in his nod of thanks, and though the low light made it hard to see across the hall, he was sure that Burian answered with a grin. Gawain's heart fluttered as he started struggling with his mailshirt's neck-straps, and he almost shuddered at the touch when Halwen reached up to help him with them. He tried not to let his thoughts run away with him. True, Halwen had shown quite clearly that she was fond of him, but neither one of them had actually spoken about how they felt. A false step here could ruin everything.

When the mailshirt was finally off, and he'd removed his boots and done his best to dry his feet, Gawain lay on the blankets and pulled the furs up over him, and waited with his heart in his throat. Halwen said nothing as she too took off her boots and lay down. Then she shuffled up beside him. The feel of her body next to his had Gawain stirring within seconds, and he felt himself flush and turned his hips a little, half-hoping that Halwen hadn't noticed. The other half of him was hoping very much that she *had*.

Slowly he felt her draw closer still, and her arm reached across his chest and touched the side of his face. He knew his cheek was rough with stubble but Halwen didn't seem to mind, and she gently turned his head until he was facing her. Even in the dim light her eyes seemed to shine, and they stared into his as she moved in closer. They closed half a second before her lips met his, and the moment the kiss began, Gawain returned it with a passion. His one arm wrapped around her waist while the other reached up to her hair, and when he ran his fingers through it the red-gold strands were sleek and soft. He pulled her close to him, and though he tried to limit his strength he still felt her gasp at the force of it. But she didn't stop. Her mouth stayed on his and she pressed close to his chest, and Gawain moved a hand down to her leg and squeezed the tight muscles beneath the trews. He felt Halwen hesitate for a moment but then she kissed him again, albeit with less passion this time, and he took that as a signal to carry on, his hardness almost painful as he imagined what must come next. He moved his lips to start kissing her slender neck and let his hand reach slowly beneath her tunic. Her skin was warm to the touch, and his heart hammered fit to burst as he cupped the soft flesh of her breast. That was when Halwen froze.

She leaned away from him and Gawain quickly drew his hand back, and he felt a sickish feeling as her eyes met his. He didn't know what he was seeing there but it was something uncertain, and dangerously close to dislike or even anger, and he began stammering some clumsy words of apology. Halwen raised a hand to silence him and spoke in a rasping whisper.

'Gawain, I…' But she seemed to struggle for words. 'We…'

She tailed off awkwardly and moved further away, and Gawain all but growled at himself as she turned her back and brought the furs up to her neck. The foolish optimist in him took heart that she hadn't slapped him or stormed off, but if anything her staying so close made him feel even worse. He rolled to his back and cursed himself. It had been going so well, so perfectly, and then he'd rushed at her like a half-mad bullock and offended her in the worst way. Now even though Halwen was lying there next to him, for all the closeness he felt she might as well have been back at Dun Edin. *You've made her hate you.*

He was tempted to get up and go and sleep with the other boys. They would mock him for his clumsiness but at least Halwen might feel more comfortable. But then, would she take that as further offence, as if he now hated her too? He decided it was best just to stay where he was, and pray that Halwen would forgive his foolishness. After a moment's consideration he determined that Christ was the best god for this; he was a god who valued purity, and his priests preached forgiveness for sins.

Gawain didn't have a cross to hold and so he turned his head and squinted for where his shield lay propped against the wall. It was facing out and so the Virgin Mary couldn't be seen, but he focused on the star and prayed silently to Solomon's god. The star looked back at him with stark red lines, and Gawain found himself counting off the Warrior Virtues in his head;

valour, honesty, courtesy, devotion, and benevolence. Well, he'd thought himself devoted to Halwen but he'd failed her in that, and he'd hardly been a paragon of honesty or courtesy either. He'd yet to have the chance to be valorous or benevolent, but even if he was as brave as Gaheris and as kind as Father Iain, he doubted it would make up for his failings in the other three.

He stared up at the shadowed roof-beams and listened to the storm, wishing that he could speak to the woman lying so close to him he could hear her breathing. But he had lost the right to. All his life Gawain had wanted to live up to the virtues of a warrior, and he'd failed in more than half of them without even seeing a battle. He had let himself down in the shallowest way he could think of. And he'd lost Halwen's regard, perhaps forever.

Chapter Twelve

He awoke with a start and for a moment Gawain just lay there, not knowing what had shaken him from sleep. Then Mabb barked again, and a moment later he heard a distant but unmistakable scream. Gawain's eyes widened and blood pounded through his limbs as he threw off the furs and leaped to his feet. Across the hall Burian and Ulfric were stirring too, and Mabb's barking soon woke up the others. More shouts and screams sounded from outside the hall, and Gawain didn't even look at Halwen as he threw his mailshirt over his head; his guilt would have to wait. He buckled on his sword, grabbed his spear and shield, and was halfway to the door before he realised he'd left his boots behind. But it was too late to turn back now.

He called to a terrified-looking Gareth.

'Stay here! Keep Mabb with you!'

He didn't linger to see if his brother had heard, and rushed outside with his friends close on his heels. The night sky was clouded but he could just about see around him, thanks to the fires that raged on half a dozen roofs. The rain had softened to a mere drizzle, and though in most places the soaked thatch would refuse to catch light, where the fire *had* caught it was now blazing fiercely, casting a horrid red light over the panicked settlement. Some detached part of Gawain's brain thought that the fires must have been started with oil or fat of some kind, but he banished the thought as a useless detail; the fires had been started, and that was all that mattered.

The others were clearly unsure what they should do now, and Gawain realised they were both looking at him. He blinked once or twice and then nodded.

'Follow me!'

He set off through the mud at a loping run, heading away from the river. Despite Oran's casual assurance Gawain was certain this was the work of raiding Picts, and if they were Picts then it made sense that they were coming from the north. Even as he ran, his bare feet sliding in the mud, he chided himself for the simplicity of that idea; they might have come from the north initially but they could easily have spread out to surround the houses, and there was no way of knowing where they might be now. But then he saw the first of the armed men.

The Pict, assuming that was what he was, carried only a one-handed axe, but the weapon was already bloody, and Gawain wondered for a heartbeat if whatever Venicon he'd just killed had been someone who could fight back. Then a burning heat filled his chest, and before he even knew it Gawain was charging the Pict with a wordless bellow. He had no thought of looking around to see if the man was alone, nor did he call out to the others or think of forming some sensible defence. All he saw was an enemy in front of him, and when the Pict's eyes met Gawain's he felt like he was looking right into the raider's soul, and he knew he was about to send that soul screaming to the next world.

Gawain led with his shield and when he reached the Pict his bloody axe thudded dully into linden-wood. He thrust the spear out beneath the shield-rim, aiming his stab low. The spear's tip was a leaf-shaped blade a foot long, and the steel plunged easily through the soft flesh of the raider's belly, followed by more than two feet of the ash spear-haft. The Pict screamed and tried to clutch at the weapon, but Gawain slammed his shield into his face, and when he stumbled back Gawain dragged the spear free, ripping it from the wound in a welter of gore. The Pict collapsed and in the back of his mind Gawain knew he was already dead, but his mind was no longer in control, and he thrust the spear down at the fallen man. After six or seven pointless stabs into the corpse Gawain finally took a clumsy step back. He was breathing hard but his blood was on fire, and he raised his spear and shield and screamed to the clouds in a voice he barely recognised.

'Lothian!'

He didn't know if they were drawn by his shout or if they were nearby anyway, but when he looked around he saw three more Picts hurrying towards him, two carrying short axes, the other brandishing a battered-looking sword. All three were draped in heavy furs but none wore mail, and Gawain noticed that the swordsman had swirling tattoos over both his cheeks. He bared his teeth at the raiders and set his shield ready, the spearpoint resting on the rim.

'Come on, you bastards!'

They did not disappoint him. The three men bellowed some strange war-cry as they charged, and the first to reach him was one of the axe-men. Gawain dispatched him the same way he had his first kill, only this time he wrenched the spear back quickly, and was readying himself for the next man when Ulfric appeared on his right. The Saxon lunged at the charging Pict, and when the raider dodged aside Gawain thrust his spear at his face. He jerked his head back and bumped awkwardly into his comrade, and by then Burian had appeared on Gawain's left. Between them they made a tiny shieldwall and charged the unbalanced raiders. Gawain and Ulfric brought the other axe-man down between them, and Burian's spear gutted the tattooed swordsman.

The corpses splashed in the mud, and the stench of their bowels opening made Gawain want to gag. He stepped back a pace but kept his shield up as he'd been taught, scanning around for any sign of danger. Fires still blazed but he saw no Picts nearby, and in that moment of pause Gawain felt icy fear clutch his heart. For the first time since waking up his mind had time to think about what was happening, and he realised that what was happening was terrifying. This was supposed to be a safe little town, Oran had said so, and now God only knew how many Picts were running loose here, burning and killing as they went. *And now you too have killed.* Gawain looked down at the corpses he'd helped to make and for a moment he was sure he would vomit. He even felt the bile rise up in his throat but he forced himself to take a breath and swallow the foul-tasting fluid.

Drustan's voice called him to his senses.

'Lothian to me!'

The call was loud but perfectly calm, and Gawain and the others flocked to the sound without thinking. The champion was standing outside the longhall, and just the sight of him was enough to cow Gawain's fear. Drustan had cast aside his cloak and the firelight shone from the polished scales of his armoured coat. The cheek-pieces of his helm were closed, and he carried spear and shield so naturally that he might have been born holding them. His dark-skinned face was almost invisible, with only the gleam of his eyes and the flash of his teeth to show that this wasn't some ghost in human garb. Gawain wondered how any Pict could look on him and dare to fight.

Standing with him was Aeddan, dressed only in his shirt and trews, along with Oran and a rather lost-looking Father

Iain. The noise of panicked shouts and women's screams still echoed from the darkness, but Drustan spoke as calmly as if they were seated at a hearth-side.

'Gather your warriors together, and quickly.'

Oran was staring open-mouthed into the night.

'How is this…?'

But Drustan cut across him.

'Never mind the how, we have work to do. We cannot know their numbers and we must gather our strength.'

Aeddan's jowly face was a mask of horror but he nodded and shoved his son's shoulder.

'He is right. Find Einon and the other warriors, tell them to come to the hall at once and we'll see off these whoresons.'

Oran dashed off into the dark without a word, though Gawain worried quietly how much use those warriors would be. Oran had said himself that Pencardden did not suffer raids, so what experience would the warriors have? Some might have travelled north to fight before now, and some might be veterans of old wars with the Picts or the Irish, but most would surely be old men or green boys. *Like us.*

Drustan must have had the same doubts, but he stopped shy of stating them outright.

'We've no knowledge of their strength, lord; for all we know they are enough to overwhelm your warriors.' He gave Aeddan a look which, while it did not lack respect, told him very clearly who was in charge. 'We must get the women and children to the waterfront. They can take boats to the south bank and wait there until this is done. The warriors will guard their retreat and then join them.'

Aeddan clearly didn't like the thought of abandoning his hall but he nodded and started calling out commands to anyone who could hear him. Drustan turned to Iain and spoke quickly.

'Father, gather those who cannot fight and get them to the boats.'

Iain didn't question him, and just as Gawain opened his mouth to speak of Halwen, both she and Gareth appeared from the longhall. Gareth was holding Mabb by the collar, and though Ekbert had trained him well enough that he didn't try to charge off, the great hound was clearly keen to get into the fight. *All the better that he stays with Gareth, then.* Gawain almost pitied the Pict who tried to fight his way past those fangs. The pair had their packs on their shoulders and Gawain guessed that one of them, he assumed it was Halwen, had realised that running was their only choice. Both were wide-eyed but they were keeping composed, and Gareth even tried to sound defiant.

'Where are they?'

The slight boy was holding Gawain's war-axe over his shoulder, despite it being far too heavy for him to use, and he set his jaw and did his best to glare. It would have been comical on some other day, now it just made Gawain afraid that his brother would get himself killed. He leaned his spear into the crook of his shield arm and took Gareth by the shoulder.

'Never mind them. You get Halwen down to the river, and any other women or children you find along the way. You can do that?'

Gareth hesitated.

'I want to…'

But Gawain cut him off.

'If you say the word *fight* I will knock your teeth in right now!' He took a breath and forced himself to speak calmly. 'You'll be more use protecting the womenfolk, now go!'

Gareth blinked but nodded, and Gawain forced a smile as he ruffled his brother's hair.

'Get going. We'll be with you soon.'

The youngest Lothian nodded again and began to usher Halwen away. For a moment Gawain thought she was going to stop and say something, but then she turned away without looking at him and went with Gareth and Mabb. Iain set off as well, heading into the town and calling out for the Venicones to flee to the river. Gawain watched Halwen disappear into the night, then Drustan's voice snapped his mind into focus.

'You three, follow me.'

The champion moved off at a jog, heading roughly northward away from the longhall. Gawain, Burian and Ulfric kept pace with him while Aeddan stayed where he was, bellowing for his warriors. Gawain's heart was pounding hard but surprisingly almost none of it was fear now, and as he ran he felt his hands start to tingle as keenness for battle flowed back into him. He had his wish granted soon enough. They'd barely gone twenty paces when a pair of brand-wielding Picts came loping around a corner, laughing as they set more homes alight.

The raiders skidded to a halt at the sight of spearmen, but to their small credit they did not run away. One man was bolder than the other, and he yelled his war-cry and charged while his fellow hesitated. Gawain grinned and locked shields with Burian, and as the first man came at them Burian's spear lashed out at his belly. He dodged to the side and tried to fling his brand at their faces, but it bounced from Gawain's shield in a shower of sparks, and Burian's second thrust drove home into Pictish guts.

Gawain had no time to see the man drop because his comrade was coming hot on his heels, and this one grabbed for Gawain's spear-haft as he attacked. His instincts were quick, and the Pict caught hold of the ash, but Gawain barged forward and the star-painted shield slammed into the raider's chest. The shove sent the Pict sprawling, and when he tried to rise, Gawain and Burian lunged in together, impaling him through the neck and torso. He fell to the mud with a choking rasp.

When Gawain looked up he saw that Drustan or Ulfric had killed another of the raiders, and that Venicon warriors were rushing between the houses, heading towards the longhall. Oran was among them, and while only a few of the men carried shields, Gawain saw more than one who looked formidable enough to put up a fight. *We may not need to flee this place after all.* Drustan nodded to them as they passed, then waved with his spear for his tiny warband to move. The fight had been brief but still Gawain was breathing hard, and he took in a gulp of air before following him. The champion called over his shoulder.

'Let Aeddan's boys form a strong force at the hall. We move forward and…'

But the words died in his throat as they rounded a corner. In between what looked like a group of tradesmen's houses there was an open space of flat grass, presumably used for festivals. Gawain would have laid good odds that the Venicones had celebrated Beltane here, and he thought he saw the outline of fire-trenches in the gloom. Only days ago their Summer King would have walked their Spring Maiden through this space. Tonight, that space was filled with their tribe's worst enemies.

Better than a score of raiders were milling about its edges, either looting the tradehouses or trying to set more fires, and Gawain realised that the men they'd seen so far were just stragglers from the main group. A glance at the enemy's real strength told him they had no chance at all of holding them. Drustan signalled silently for them to fall back, but then a Pict spotted their movement and called out to his fellows. A second later an arrow flew towards the little group, but Ulfric raised his shield and it thudded into unpainted wood. Drustan turned and shoved the Saxon back.

'Run!'

They turned and fled, and a heartbeat later Gawain heard a roar as the Picts gave chase. Drustan stayed behind them and bellowed to Ulfric, who ran half-blindly in the front.

'Get to the hall!'

Gawain glanced back and almost slowed when he saw a Pict closing in on them, but Drustan slew the man without so much as glancing at him, and they kept on running for the hall. Mercifully it was a not a long or complex way back, though when the longhall came in sight Gawain felt his heart sink to his feet. There was no safety here. Aeddan had gathered only nine men, almost none of them with shields and only one with a war-spear. The Venicon chief looked furious.

'The others all fled with their families. Either that or they're dead already.'

Drustan didn't slow down as he answered.

'Too many to fight here. Fall back!'

Aeddan nodded and pointed southwards with a broad-bladed sword.

'Back men, back!'

Gawain looked to where he'd indicated and saw that south of the longhall several storehouses stood close together, with blessedly narrow gaps between the buildings. A shieldwall there would be flanked within minutes of course, but it was marginally preferable to standing in the open where they would be overwhelmed in seconds. He followed the Venicones as they fled, and Aeddan called out as he passed the hall.

'Make for the…'

But his words became a gurgle, and when Gawain snapped his head around he saw a grey-fletched arrow transfixing Aeddan's neck. The chief fell to his knees but before he even hit the ground Drustan was shoving Gawain in the back.

'Move!'

He sprinted, expecting every second to feel an arrow punch through his spine, but somehow he made it to the alley, and Drustan bellowed to the warriors.

'Shieldwall!'

Those men with shields locked them together, and Gawain shoved himself between Ulfric and Burian and did the same, his spear resting ready on the rim. He was still gasping for breath, and trying hard not to think that he'd just watched a man die who was laughing and joking only hours ago. He could feel Ulfric shaking beside him, and he nudged the Saxon's shoulder with his own. Ulfric looked up at him and Gawain gave him what he hoped was an encouraging nod. There was no time to see if Ulfric nodded back.

The Picts charged them, howling their strange battle-cries and brandishing swords and axes that glinted in the light of the fires. The alley was only wide enough for four men to stand abreast, and half a dozen raiders tried to rush them all at once. One died on Burian's spear, but the one who faced Gawain was canny, and parried the spearpoint down before dashing inside its range. The Pict slammed his weight into the shield, and Gawain felt his bare feet slip in the mud as he tried to hold him. A sword-blade clanged twice on the shield's iron rim, but then Gawain regained his footing and shoved back hard. Young though he was, few men could match Gawain's strength and this time it was the Pict who was unbalanced, but before Gawain could spear him one of his comrades came charging forward.

He was stunned to see that this one was a woman. She had pale blonde hair and must not have been much older than he was, and any hint of femininity in her face was masked by a feral snarl. In the second it took for Gawain to regain his wits, the Pict hacked her sword at him, aiming to split open his skull. The shield came up but it was poorly timed, and Gawain felt the sword glance from the wood and slam down on his shoulder. The mailshirt held true but the weight of the blow was enough to numb the arm, and Gawain felt his spear slip from his fingers. The Pict screeched in triumph and kept on cutting, and Gawain ducked low behind the shield, struggling to free the sword from his belt as her blade hammered down on linden-wood. After a futile heartbeat he pushed upward with the shield, brought his knee up high and stamped down through the woman's front knee. She cried out as the leg buckled, and Gawain put both hands on the shield and bellowed as he thrust it at her face.

'Lothian!'

The Pict flew backwards, and Gawain darted back into line with an awkward skip, hauling his sword free as he went. His arm ached but he fought to ignore the pain as Drustan's voice sounded from nearby.

'Give ground, stay in line!'

Gawain had heard those commands a thousand times in the training yard, and he locked his shield with Burian's and started shuffling back. They couldn't stay where they were, the Picts would surround them and trap them in short order, but they'd checked their enemies' initial charge and so long as they stayed together, the little formation might just make it to the waterfront alive. A glance at the muddy ground showed him that three Picts had fallen in the assault, and the rest were hovering outside of spear-range, their eyes burning with hate. Gawain glared at them, and found himself wishing that they'd attack again. He brandished his sword even as he fell back, and flashed his teeth at a flat-faced Pict that dared to look his way.

'Lost your nerve, have you?'

Drustan growled from along the line.

'Shut your noise!'

But Gawain's blood was up, and he taunted the raider again.

'What's wrong you gutless bastard? Scared of a bootless boy?' He waved a foot at the enemy, then bared his teeth and spread his arms. 'I am Gawain ab Lot! Come try your hand, you dog-humping milksop!'

Drustan shoved him in the back.

'I said shut your noise you damned fool! Close up.'

Gawain did as he was told and settled for glaring at the flat-faced man, praying quietly that these bastards would tempt their fates and charge. He told himself it was because he wanted to keep the Picts occupied while Halwen escaped, but that noble reason was a half-truth at best. The fact was that he'd finally learned what men meant when they spoke of battle-lust, and the blood was racing through his limbs, driving away the fear and the pain. All he wanted to do was kill these whoresons one by one.

But Drustan's command came again, and Gawain forced himself to obey.

'Give ground! Stay tight back to the water!'

The line kept creeping back, and some of the Picts began to edge forward after them, but it wasn't until they were clear of the alley that the raiders struck again. The moment the little shieldwall was no longer anchored by buildings Picts began to rush them, some from along the alley they'd retreated down, and some having circled around charge the Venicones in the flanks. The wings of the wall curved backwards but still when the Picts struck, the line barely held.

Warriors with ragged furs and tattooed faces flung themselves at Gawain, and he blocked and shoved and stabbed around his shield, snarling curses at the enemy that even he couldn't understand. He kept as tight as he could to Burian and Ulfric, but it was hard to fight and retreat and keep a formation all at once, and Gawain wasn't the only one who struggled to maintain the wall. Twice he saw Venicon warriors correct themselves just an eye-blink too slowly, and get hacked down by angry Picts as a result. One of them, a man who'd seen sixty years if he'd seen a day, was disembowelled by a raider and left to bleed, and his pitiful screams followed them as the line shuffled back towards the river.

Gawain's ears were full of a roaring that drowned out the terrible noise, and even his own war-cries echoed oddly in his head. He bellowed another one as he struck at a man trying to pull down Ulfric's shield, half-severing the Pict's hand before the Saxon barged him over. He fell to the mud and writhed there, clutching at his arm, but the line was still moving backwards and Gawain had no time to finish him. He spat at him instead, calling his mother a whore and his father a bastard, though he doubted if the wounded Pict heard him. The rest of the raiders had become cautious again now, and were loitering out of easy range and spreading themselves out. Gawain took a quick glance around. Only three or four of the Venicon warriors were still living, though Drustan, Ulfric and Burian all looked to be unharmed. The champion was looking grim, his eyes darting from side to side, and a second later Gawain realised what he was thinking.

They were still a good fifty paces from the water, and from the sounds of it the women and children were still loading themselves onto the boats. With eight men facing twenty there was a chance, albeit a small one, that they could form a tight circle and survive another attack. But the Picts knew that too, and why assault a shieldwall when there was easier prey to be found? Already Gawain could see raiders slipping past them to make for the river, and just as he was about to shout to the others, Drustan bellowed the exact same thought.

'Break ranks! Get to the river!'

His father had once told him that nothing was more terrifying than to feel your shieldwall break, and the hollow jolt in Gawain's stomach testified to the truth of it. The savage joy of the battle-lust started bleeding out of him, and he turned from the milling enemy and bolted for the water. He could feel the others running beside him, and he could see the black water and the bobbing boats ahead, but all his thoughts were for the shouts and jeers coming from behind him. He didn't dare to turn, not even when an arrow whipped past his shoulder, but kept on running on the muddy ground, praying desperately that he wouldn't slip.

There was almost no light at the riverbank save for a few torches carried by fleeing townsfolk, but Gawain followed the sound of Mabb's barking until he spotted a familiar face. Iain was standing in what looked like Talorg's boat, a flickering brand in one hand and Mabb's leather collar in the other. A second glance showed Gareth and Halwen standing behind him. From what Gawain could see, it looked like most of the boats were already mid-river with their cargo of Venicones, though Talorg's had yet to leave the jetty. Gawain waved his aching arm.

'Go!'

Iain looked back at him but he didn't obey. The old priest simply beckoned with the torch. Gawain growled as he ran.

'Damn it, cast off!'

There were other boats still untaken, at least one of which was large enough to hold four men, but still Gawain's words were ignored and all he could do was keep sprinting for the water.

He had almost reached it when he saw Oran take an arrow in the ribs, and the chief's son toppled into an empty boat, his body thudding hard on the deck. A woman's scream came from somewhere on the river, but there was little light over the water and Gawain couldn't see where she was.

By the time they reached the jetty only one Venicon warrior remained with them, and the wall they made across the planks looked pitiful. They locked their shields together and began to edge back towards Talorg's boat. The Picts took their time in following. Only a dozen or so bothered to stay to face off with the warriors, while the rest dispersed along the riverbank and started slaughtering anyone who'd been too slow to escape. Gawain watched, helpless, as the flat-faced man he'd tried to goad grinned like a child and slammed his sword through an old woman's skull. Bile rose up in his throat again, and Gawain grimaced as he swallowed it back. If they broke from the wall they would all be killed, he knew that, but that fact did nothing to ease the shame of watching unarmed Venicones being butchered. The strong were supposed to protect the weak. But they didn't. Here the strong stayed in their shieldwall and inched back towards the boat, while the Picts facing them laughed and jeered, and helpless villagers were put to the sword.

They were only paces from the boat when Gareth leaped out of it and came hurrying towards them, and Mabb strained against Iain's grip as he tried to follow. Gareth had at least put down the war-axe, but he now held a strung bow and was fumbling to notch an arrow to the string. Gawain glanced back at him and growled.

'Get back in the damned boat!'

The sudden noise made Gareth drop the arrow.

'I can help!'

Drustan stole the words from Gawain's mouth.

'Then help from the bloody boat!'

Some of the defiance left Gareth's face, and a moment later it was replaced by terror. A great roar had gone up from the

Picts on the bank, and a pack of them had begun to charge up the jetty. Gawain did his best to sound offhand.

'Get back in the boat, you're too pretty to be killed by an ugly mob like this!'

Gareth's voice shook as he answered.

'I'll go and find myself a handsome killer, then.'

He backed off towards the boat, and Gawain felt quietly proud of his brother's attempt to seem unafraid. But this was no time for pleasant thoughts. He turned to face the charging Picts and, on a sudden impulse, kissed his shield. The Huntsman was normally the best god for a man facing battle, but Christ's symbols had protected Gawain so far tonight; it seemed right to ask the God of Rome to stay with him. *Assuming Christ can stand against Taranis.*

The Thunderer's rain had hardened enough to blur his vision, but Gawain saw that the first man coming at him was brandishing an axe above his head. He barged forward just as the raider drew his weapon back, and when the shield crashed into the charging Pict's face, Gawain swung his sword low. The steel hammered into the Pict's leg, and he cried out and fell as the blow crushed his knee. Battle-lust began to burn in him again, and Gawain took another stride forward to finish the crippled man off. He heard Drustan shout something as he brought down the killing stroke, but the words were lost in the chaos of the fight.

He was out of the wall and with Picts on either side of him, but Burian and Ulfric were keeping them occupied, and the one in front of him was fool enough to hurl his axe instead of using it to hack. Gawain swayed aside and dodged it with ease, then thrust forward with the sword, aiming for the foolish Pict's eyes. The raider was quick and pulled back from the blade, and Gawain took another pace forward and punched his shield-rim into his chest. The Pict coughed and fell, but before Gawain could press on he felt a hand on his shoulder and a weight hauling him back. Burian let out a grunt of effort, and Gawain shot him an angry look as he reluctantly reformed their tiny wall. But then Burian pushed him back even further, and he and Ulfric closed up before Gawain could re-join the line. He was about to ask what in hell they were doing when a cry from behind him made him turn.

Gareth was lying on the jetty with blood drenching one side of his face. Even as the rain washed it off more seeped out from his temple, and Gawain saw with a jolt that the axe he'd dodged was lying at his brother's side. Halwen had taken up his bow, Mabb was barking wildly, and Iain was straining as he tried to drag the boy into the boat. Gawain rushed over with tears in his eyes. *Please, Bel and Christ and Danu, don't let him be dead!* When he reached Gareth he threw his sword into the boat and lifted his brother one-handed onto his shoulder. He turned back to where the warriors still fought and heard his voice crack as he shouted.

'We have to go!'

With Iain's help he stepped carefully into the boat, wary of his balance as the little vessel rocked. On the jetty, he heard Drustan shout for the others to retreat, and a moment later Ulfric was tossing his spear into the boat. Burian was a pace behind him but a Pict was hard on his heels, and he had to duck behind his shield as an axe hacked down at him. Gawain was too encumbered to help but Drustan was at his side in a heart-beat, and his sword slashed down in a smooth arc that took the Pict's head from his shoulders. The champion bared his teeth as his nephew stood up again. Then an arrow appeared through Drustan's neck and the warrior's eyes went wide. He dropped to his knees with a bloody cough.

Burian and Gawain both shouted at once, and Ulfric tried to make a grab for him as Drustan began to fall, but Talorg had finally cut the mooring lines and was pushing the little boat from the bank. Mabb howled and struggled desperately to leap from the boat and attack, but Iain and Talorg between them just managed to hold him back. Gawain set Gareth down and reached a hand out to Burian.

'Come on!'

But Burian was reluctant to abandon his uncle, and didn't even notice that more Picts were bearing down on him. He was still staring down at the body when one raider got within two strides of him, but an arrow, presumably shot by Halwen, struck the Pict low in his side and he cried out and fell to the boards. The gap between the boat and the jetty kept widening and Gawain shouted again.

'Burian come on!'

His friend blinked a few times and seemed to come to his senses. He took half a pace back, eyed the distance, and sprang from the jetty in a massive leap. The Pictish archer took him while he was still in mid-air. Gawain saw the grey-fletched arrow thud dully into Burian's ribs, and the impact jarred his momentum and sent him flailing into the water. Ulfric scrambled to the rail and held out his spear, but Burian made no effort to reach for it and the current had already caught hold of him. The Saxon bellowed to Talorg to turn the boat but the Venicon simply mumbled as Ulfric yelled and swore. Gawain shouted at the unmoving Burian to hold on, but the darkness on the river was near-total, and within moments he was invisible.

Gawain wanted to scream in frustration, but then another Pictish arrow buried itself in the boat's planks, and he knew that they were still far from safe. The gap between the boat and the jetty had become too far for a man to leap, but the Picts standing on it could still be seen, and at least one of them held a bow. Beside him Gawain saw Halwen send another shaft at them, but either her first shot had been lucky or she had lost her aim with this one, because the arrow sailed harmlessly over the raiders' heads, and one of them even laughed at her effort. Gawain squinted and saw it was the flat-faced man, and a moment later he had cause to hate that man more than he'd ever hated anyone.

Two of the Picts were already stripping Drustan of his armour, but the flat-faced man waved them away. With his eyes still on Gawain the man undid his trews, paused for a moment, and then smiled at the fleeing Lothians as he pissed on the corpse of King Lot's champion. Gawain screamed at him, wordless, meaningless screams of rage and hatred. This weasel, this bastard, this coward of a Pict was shaming the greatest warrior in all of Britain! Tears burned his eyes and beside him he could hear Ulfric hurling curses in the British and Saxon tongues alike. Even Iain was shouting that the Pict's soul would burn in hellfire for his crimes, and Gawain was on the verge of vaulting over the rail and swimming back there, just to gut that one miserable swine. Then something hard punched him in the right thigh, and when he looked down he saw a grey-fletched arrow stuck clean through his leg.

Rage was still burning in him, and without thinking Gawain dragged the arrow clear and flung it at the jetty, spitting and cursing at the vanishing Picts. He didn't know how long he kept shouting at them, but they were well out into the darkness of the river by the time he stopped. Gawain stood there and panted for a moment, then he remembered that Gareth had been hurt in the fight and spun around to check on him. The movement hurt horribly, and he lurched awkwardly before looking down at the source of the pain. Even in the darkness he could see that one leg of his trews was soaked through, and by the time he realised that the fluid must be blood, Gawain was already falling.

Chapter Thirteen

It was cold when Gawain awoke. He felt as if an icy breeze was slicing through his mail, but when he shivered it sent waves of pain crashing through his leg and back. He was half-sitting, half-lying on the deck of Talorg's boat, and something on the rail was digging painfully into his spine. He tried to shift his weight away but that just sent a jolt through his leg, and so he stayed put and just grimaced at the discomfort. The sky was slowly brightening to a pale grey, and he guessed blearily that he must have been asleep for some time. There was almost no noise to be heard, just the lap of water against the planks and the occasional blackbird's caw. For a little while Gawain just sat there, and the gentle rock of the river almost lulled him to sleep again. Then he remembered what had happened and his eyes snapped open. *Gareth!*

He put his hands on the deck and tried to push himself up, then the lesson he'd failed to learn about moving reasserted itself, and pain shot through his leg like a red-hot knife. He grunted and fell back again, though the fall was slowed by someone catching him and easing him down to sit. The hands on his shoulders were so small they could only be Halwen's, and when he turned his head he saw her face was lined with concern.

'You mustn't move.'

Looking down, Gawain saw that his aching leg was bound up in blood-soaked cloths, and he decided she was probably right. His voice rasped as he sat back down.

'Gareth?'

Halwen's voice was flat.

'Still asleep, the axe only clipped his head and the bleeding has stopped. Father Iain says he will live.'

Gawain let out a breath.

'Thank God.' He tried to smile. 'The axe didn't spoil his looks, I hope?'

Halwen didn't quite smile back, but her features softened.

'The scar will just make him more dashing.'

Gawain nodded awkwardly, and a silence stretched between them. Thoughts of Burian and Drustan came into his head in that silence, though he was too exhausted to embrace any anger at the Picts for killing them. All he managed to feel was a bleak sort of emptiness in knowing they were gone. He wondered how he would tell Anna that Burian was dead. Would she hate him for it? Gawain could hardly judge her if she did; who else was there to blame? On top of that his guts were twisted with guilt for what had happened to Gareth, and as if all *that* was not enough, it seemed that Halwen could barely stand to look at him. *Well, for that at least I can apologise.*

He shuffled a little, ignoring his throbbing leg as he tried to meet her eyes.

'Halwen, I...'

Before he could go on she took his hand and met his gaze, her brow furrowed. Her fingers were cool, and when she spoke her words were neither soft nor sharp.

'You are sorry. I know.'

Part of Gawain wanted to stop talking and leave things there, but it would be cowardly to let her do his apologising for him. Besides, Halwen's tone had been very detached, as if she only half-believed what she was saying. He leaned towards her and tried again.

'I truly am, for everything. Will you...'

He'd been about to ask if she would forgive him, but then the grey sky tilted sideways and Gawain felt himself swaying, his head suddenly very heavy. Halwen's hand tightened on his.

'Careful now.'

She helped to ease him back down but his vision still swam, and it took a few slow breaths before he could see clearly again. He wished Halwen wasn't seeing him like this; he felt horribly weak, his hands were cold and clammy, and he was making a terrible mess of trying to make amends.

Before he could speak again he felt a waterskin being pressed to his lips, and without thinking he began to drink greedily. Halwen stopped him from gulping down too much at once and forced him to take only a few short sips. It was a frustrating way to drink, Gawain hadn't realised how thirsty he was, but at the back of his mind he knew this was the sensible way to do it. She had let go of his hand, and Gawain was missing it, but she stayed close to him and that was something. Once again, he tried to ask forgiveness.

'Halwen, will...'

But again she cut him off, holding the skin to his lips.

'Drink.'

As before she did not sound angry, but there was no hint of a smile on her face either. Gawain wondered if her dejection was born more because of the way he'd betrayed her trust last night, or because of the battle they had just barely survived. She'd not been close to either Drustan or Burian, but he knew she would be feeling their loss, and only a madman would not feel melancholy after witnessing the slaughter at Pencardden. *But that doesn't mean she isn't angry with you too, and with good cause.* Gawain sipped the water and readied himself to speak again, but before he could begin the sound of creaking planks made him look up.

Father Iain was walking towards them from the bow, and Gawain knew that forgiveness would have to wait. The old priest picked his way around ropes and oars and made a valiant attempt to wipe the grimness from his face.

'Gawain my boy, you are as stubborn as ever. I'd feared we might have seen the last of you.' He leaned down and closed his eyes as he put his palm on Gawain's brow. 'God be praised.'

Gawain nodded to him when Iain opened his eyes again.

'Thank you, father.'

Iain managed a tiny smile but it soon faded away. Gawain saw that the old man's eyes were dark-rimmed and red, and he wished he could say something more to him. He felt Halwen shift away to make space and Iain thanked her with a nod before easing himself down to sit. His joints clicked, and Iain grunted but didn't complain.

'Your brother will live, God-willing, though both you and he have lost much blood. We must find a place to land and see you properly cared-for.'

It took some effort, but Gawain straightened up where he sat and looked down the length of Talorg's boat. Ulfric was standing at the prow, peering out over the mist-covered river, while old Talorg himself lay slumped and snoring beside the Saxon. In the middle of the boat lay Gareth, his head wrapped in a dark cloth that was even more stained than Gawain's bandage. The boy's eyes were closed but his chest rose and fell evenly, with Mabb's head resting over his heart. Even curled up and sleeping the great wolfhound looked enormous, and Gawain was reminded yet again of how very small Gareth was. *And he came running into this madness because of me.*

Neither of Talorg's rowing lads were anywhere to be seen, which presumably meant they'd either abandoned their master to die or been butchered by the Picts. Gawain didn't want to know which one it was. Around them the river was still swollen by the storm, but the rain had stopped and it was almost eerily quiet. Gawain's eyes still felt weak but he strained to look about them. There was no movement on either shore, and Iain answered his thoughts before he could voice them.

'Aeddan told me yesterday that there are fishing settlements on the north bank.'

Gawain nodded.

'Did he say how far off they were?'

The priest let out a sigh.

'It would make little difference if he had. I'm afraid I have no notion of how far we've come overnight.' He gestured to the water. 'The current was swift but I am no waterman to judge our speed or calculate what distance we have covered.'

Once again the priest managed a momentary smile and he nodded his head towards Talorg.

'I tried asking our Venicon friend but he was not helpful in his answers.'

Gawain frowned but it was Halwen who spoke the question.

'Then how do we know if we have passed these settlements already, father?'

She looked only at Iain, and Gawain bit back the urge to just blurt out his apology now. It wouldn't be right to make her feel awkward in front of Iain, and he was in no hurry to confess what he'd done before the priest. Iain shrugged.

'We do not know. But I do not doubt we will find some fisher-folk who will give us aid and shelter. We must simply have faith.'

Halwen gave him an uncertain look and Gawain couldn't hold back his doubts.

'Faith, father?'

Iain's face broke into a small but genuine smile.

'Gawain my boy, all is as God wills it. What happened last night was a tragedy but it has not shifted you from your course.' He waved an arm at the river around them. 'We had intended to cross the Avon Du and head east; thanks to these currents, we are doing just that. In spite of the trials that the Devil sent our way, still we are on the path to strike down this Green Man.'

The priest looked at Halwen and Gawain in turn, meeting their eyes with the sincerity he always exuded when he spoke about God.

'The Lord works his miracles in mysterious ways. You,' he pointed at Gawain, 'you have survived this terrible trial because you are on a mission to vanquish a great evil. Christ will find a way for you to fulfil that mission, and that means he will send someone to give us aid.'

He spoke with such certainty that Gawain found himself thinking of the shield that had kept him safe last night, and wondered if Christ might indeed be the right god to help him fight the Green Man. But then, Drustan had thought the Green Man was an emissary of the Huntsman, and while that certainly didn't make him benign, if he served Cernunnos then he couldn't be purely *evil* either, and so would it be right to ask for Christ's help to defeat him? Iain surely thought so, but wouldn't it be better to best the Green Man with courage alone? That would have been Drustan's advice. Gawain frowned to himself. Thinking about this was confusing, and remembering Drustan was painful, and so Gawain simply nodded his thanks to Iain and cast a quick sideways glance towards Halwen. Her face was still blank, and while he saw no anger in her, she had still yet to look him in the eye. He sighed and Iain, mistaking his meaning, gave his hand a friendly pat.

'Have faith, my boy. You will see.'

The priest sat back and watched the river go by, and despite his drained appearance Gawain saw confidence in his eyes; God would come to their aid, and that was all that mattered. He envied him that faith, but he couldn't feel it himself. Ever since last night everything had gone so horribly wrong, and if God was watching him at all then his attention felt more like punishment than guidance. But, given that they were floating down a river with no idea of where they were, and hoping to find an enemy who might very well be the death of them, Gawain couldn't think of much else to do than follow Iain's stoic example. He ground his teeth against the pain in his leg, leaned back against the little boat's rail, and waited patiently for God to send some fishermen to their rescue.

Iain was admirably humble about it when his prediction came true. When Ulfric had spotted the fisher-folk and the Venicones welcomed them over, the old priest had given all credit to God, and had accepted their help with modesty and courtesy. Despite none of them being Christian, and despite Iain's efforts to talk them into becoming so, the Venicones had taken a liking to the priest; in exchange for a silver piece they'd been more than happy to take Gawain and Gareth to their settlement to be cared for. Ulfric and a fisherman named Yorath had grounded their boat, still containing a half-asleep Talorg, and headed east and north towards the Venicones' home. It had taken no small amount of struggling in Gawain's case, but both the Lothian brothers had eventually been loaded onto Yorath's cart, and Gawain had promptly fallen asleep with his head on a rolled-up cloak and his nostrils full of the smell of trout.

He drifted in and out of wakefulness, and every time he fully woke he brooded on all that had happened. If he'd only restrained himself when kissing with Halwen, she might still look at him as she once had. If he'd only stayed in the shieldwall on the jetty, that axe would never have flown at Gareth. If he'd only done his duty properly as Summer King, he wouldn't have one of Cernunnos' spirits to face in the first place. But it seemed Gawain's mind thought only of girls and glory, and here was where they had landed him. *Maybe some god is trying to tell you to stop courting trouble and show some damned restraint?* If he was, Gawain thought the message might finally be getting through his skull. He just wished he hadn't had to learn the lesson in such a way. His leg throbbed painfully but he chided himself each time he winced. Drustan and Burian were dead, he had no right to whine about an arrow-wound.

He couldn't guess for how long he dozed, but Bel's chariot was past its height when they arrived at their destination. Unlike Pencardden, this settlement looked as though it had been built with defence in mind, though the state of it told Gawain there'd been no danger here for some time. The whole village was surrounded by a tall grassy bank, with a muddy ditch before it that was still half-full of rainwater. There was no palisade, and woodland had grown far too close to the perimeter for a serious fortification, though as they crossed the earth causeway and through the bank, Gawain saw that the place was not entirely without defence.

An oaken post had been set on either of the entrance, and mounted on each one was a fleshless human skull. The sightless eyes watched them as the party entered the village, and though Gawain couldn't see him from where he lay, he knew that Father Iain would be crossing himself. Many old fortresses had a ghost-ward of some kind, even Dun Edin had fox and wolf skulls on the gate-towers, but Gawain had never heard of a place that used human souls as their guardians. He hoped that Gareth or Halwen had taken his little carving from Aeddan's hall, and when they passed the leering skulls he crossed himself just to be safe.

Inside the village looked much like any other, though the houses all looked well-built and maintained, and there was ample space between each one. He guessed that most of the menfolk must still be out hunting or fishing, but there were women wandering here and there, and dozens of children scampering about in the mud. Gawain saw a pair of older girls, perhaps a year or so younger than Gareth, looking strained as they tried to steer a herd of goats into a pen while simultaneously trying to control a gaggle of younger siblings. He found himself smiling as the little ones exasperated their elders' efforts, remembering the trouble he'd enjoyed causing for Gaheris when he was a boy.

Some of the villagers exchanged greetings with Iain and the fishermen, but nobody hindered them as they trekked towards the longhall. It was a small thing compared to Aeddan's hall at Pencardden, but like the rest of the settlement it looked solid and well cared-for, sitting squat and strong on what could just barely be called a hill. As they approached it a youngish man appeared at the doors and came hurrying down the slope towards them. He was dark-haired and long-faced, and dressed in a red wool tunic and breeches. He nodded towards Yorath.

'Who are these folk?'

He sounded curious more than challenging, and their fisherman friend explained where they'd been found and the sorry condition of the Lothian brothers. He declined to mention the silver that Iain had given him, but then, the man in red hadn't asked him about it. After a quick glance at the cart he turned to Iain and gave him a polite bow.

'I am Cethin, the steward of this hall.'

Iain returned the bow and proceeded to introduce them all. Ulfric and Halwen bowed respectfully, though Gawain managed only a nod. Gareth had still not woken fully, and mumbled something that might have been a greeting or might just have been meaningless sound. Gawain hoped the steward would not take offence. Cethin didn't seem to, and smiled at them pleasantly.

'I'm sure my lord will be happy to let you stay here, and we have wise folk who can tend to your hurts.' He turned back to Yorath. 'Will you send for Old Brisen to come to the hall?'

The fisherman nodded and gestured to one of his boys, who hurried off into the village. Cethin looked ready to say something else to them, but at that point Yorath nodded his head towards the longhall, and Gawain saw a pair of figures walking towards them. It was still a struggle to see very far but they soon came within easy sight, and Gawain saw it was a man and a woman. The man was tall and seemed to be in his late prime, with silver in his brown hair and a very long, prominent nose. He wore a green tunic edged with swirling black patterns, and a heavy red cloak trimmed with what looked like bear fur. His fingers glinted with rings, and the torque about his neck was of heavy gold. He was a striking-looking man, straight-backed and smiling, but Gawain's gaze didn't linger on the lord.

The lady walking beside him looked to be somewhere between thirty and forty, and had a dignified beauty that took his breath away. She had thick black hair that fell to her waist, set off perfectly by a slender silver circlet about her brow. Her figure seemed only modestly curved, but her deep red dress was so tightly-bound that it was difficult not to stare at her. Her narrow girdle was a twisted braid of green and gold, and her long sleeves were embroidered with black patterns that matched those on her lord's tunic. Her face was fair, and though Gawain was sure she wasn't really any more beautiful than Halwen, there was a something in how she held herself which made her almost enchanting.

It was the man who spoke first, and his voice was deep and strong.

'Greetings. It is rare indeed that we have guests in this place.'

Iain bowed to the man, who was clearly the lord here.

'My name is Iain, lord. May I first assure you that we come here as friends.'

The lord let out a friendly laugh.

'Were you anything but friends you would never have crossed the ghost-ward.'

He stepped forward and clapped Iain on the shoulder before putting a hand out to Mabb. The wolfhound's collar was still held by Halwen but she let him lead her forward a pace as he investigated the stranger. For a moment or two the hound seemed unsure, then he sniffed the lord's hand and shoved his head under it to be patted. The smiling man ruffled Mabb's ears and looked back up at Iain.

'As friends, you are of course welcome in my hall. My name is Berlak ab Myrd ab Gilleasbuig ab Donnchadh ab Tahrnax.'

Iain wasn't the only one of them to blink at that, and the lord smiled again.

'You may call me Berlak, my friends. And this,' he placed his other hand gently on the woman's arm, 'is my dear wife. May I present the Lady Luned mer Creuddlad?'

There was another round of bows and introductions, and Gawain worked hard not to stare too hard at Luned. When she'd bowed her dark eyes had been on him, and he'd been sure he would fall into them and drown if he wasn't careful. *Damn it man, behave yourself!* Bad enough he'd insulted Halwen by pawing at her like a lustful dog, now here he was gawping at another man's wife.

Their actual dog seemed rather less enchanted than Gawain, and Mabb neither asked for nor was offered any attention from the lady. Gawain strongly suspected that Mabb was a more sensible soul than he was. Berlak and Luned approached the cart and the lady cast an eye over the brothers. When she spoke, her voice was almost as deep as a man's.

'The young one will need Brisen's care before he grows feverish.'

Cethin bowed to her.

'She has already been sent for, lady.'

Luned gave a short nod of approval.

'Thank you, Cethin.' Her dark eyes went back to Gawain again, and he resolved not to let himself be lost in them. 'This young man I shall tend to myself. Danu-willing his wound will not fester and my skills alone will return to him his strength.'

Gawain couldn't help but wonder how it would feel to have this woman touch him, and he cursed himself a second later and flicked a guilty glance towards Halwen. But she was busy helping Yorath to unload their packs and if she noticed or felt anything about the interaction, she gave no sign of it. Gawain looked back towards Lady Luned and tried his best to keep his mind on God or Halwen or anything else but those deep dark eyes. She smiled at him and leaned forward across the cart, and when she spoke again her voice was rich, and smoother than honey.

'Welcome to Tahrnax, Gawain ab Lot.'

Chapter Fourteen

Gawain had wanted to stay with Gareth but the old woman Yorath's boy brought limping up to them, presumably Brisen, would have none of it. She commanded Yorath and Ulfric to carry Gareth to her hut and made it abundantly clear that she was to be left in peace to tend to him. Iain had tried to compromise with her and, after some fairly brusque words, she eventually conceded that Halwen could accompany Gareth on the promise that she would not get in the way. Judging by the look she gave to Iain, Gawain guessed that Brisen was not over-fond of priests. Yorath and Ulfric did as they were bid, and Gawain watched as his brother was carried off around the slope, with Halwen and Mabb trailing a pace or two behind. Part of him wished he could have spoken with her before she went, but then again, what would he have said?

Once Brisen was gone Berlak, ever smiling, made polite apologies for the healer's rudeness.

'Her words are short but she is the finest healer we have. She will tend to him well.'

Luned's mouth turned up at one corner.

'Well, your second-finest healer had best get to work as well.' She turned to the steward. 'Lord Gawain is a rather large young man, Cethin; we will need some strong backs to carry him.'

Gawain tried not to smile at being referred to as *lord*, and held up an open hand.

'I needn't be carried. I just need a good man to lean on.'

Iain took a step forward but Luned waved to Cethin before the priest could speak.

'Very well. Cethin, lend him your shoulder.'

The steward bowed and offered Gawain a hand out of the cart. It was awkward but eventually he found himself standing on his good leg, leaning his other arm heavily on Cethin's. Within ten paces of their journey he was regretting his brash assurance; hot pain shot through his wounded leg with every hopping step, but he clenched his teeth and told himself it was too late to change his mind. Iain appeared at his side and, tired though he was, lent what support he could. Gawain wished he could check over his shoulder and be sure that Halwen wasn't witnessing this indignity, but then he remembered that she likely wouldn't have cared.

He was frustrated and miserable by the time they reached the hall. His leg was on fire, and his jaw ached from biting back obscenities. Despite himself he'd still muttered a few vile words about Picts, archers, and his own stubborn stupidity, but neither Iain nor his hosts had seen fit to rebuke him for it.

Luned led them inside and through the main hall to the rooms beyond. Gawain caught glimpses of tables and tapestries, and a large fire-pit with a blackened spit running across it, but the only thing he really noticed about the place was how damned *long* it was. He was sure that from the outside this building had seemed barely half the size of Lot's hall, yet somehow the walk from the door to the rear chambers took them a full year to complete. They passed into a short corridor that divided up the rooms, and, typically of Gawain's luck, the one they were bound for was the one furthest from the hall.

Iain and Cethin got him there with much grunting and sweating, and by the time Gawain was finally laid down onto a bed, all three of them were breathing hard. It was Cethin who recovered first; standing up straight and doing his best to look composed in front of his mistress. Luned smiled at him.

'Thank you, Cethin. I think the good father here might appreciate a place to rest, and a perhaps cup of warm wine?'

The steward bowed and offered a hand to Iain, who was leaning against the timber wall and panting. Iain waved it away and straightened up under his own power, bowing his head politely to them both.

'My thanks. A brief rest would be welcome, though I would lend what help I can with Gawain.'

Luned smiled at him.

'Of course, and I shall be grateful for your help. Cethin, take the father to the hall and give him a seat by the fire until the wine has boiled.'

Cethin bowed again and made towards the door. Iain gave Gawain a brief pat on the arm and then nodded to Luned before following Cethin out. Luned closed the door behind him and turned to face Gawain. The light from the little fire seemed to dance in her dark eyes, and for all his weariness he felt himself stirring as she approached him. She sat down on a stool beside the bed, and when her hand reached towards his leg he almost shuddered. His hostess smiled.

'Try not to move, lord.'

He did as he was told, and when she started unrolling the blood-soaked cloth he was almost glad of the pain; it gave his mind something to focus on besides Luned's touch. When she saw the wound she tutted and glanced up at him with a frown.

'I assume whoever bound this did not clean it first?'

Gawain shook his head.

'I don't know, lady. I awoke with the wound bound up.'

She nodded, her eyes already back on his leg.

'It does not seem so. We must ensure it does not fester. Clench your jaw.'

Gawain was glad that he obeyed straight away, because without preamble the lady took hold of his trews and drew them down his legs. He told himself to welcome the pain again but it was hard to do as fire shot up his thigh. Luned tossed the bloody garment aside and reached behind her for a bowl and cloth. After a few moments the pain dulled to a steady throb, though that meant there was less to focus on when Luned began washing his leg. Gawain tried to think of the pain, or about shieldwall drills or scrubbing floors, but despite all his efforts he felt himself hardening at her touch, and though his tunic mostly covered it there was no chance that Luned didn't notice. Her dark eyes flicked up to him and her lips twitched into a smirk.

'Now may not be the *best* time for such things, lord.'

Gawain was glad the light was dim enough to hide his blush.

'Forgive me, lady.'

Luned shrugged and went back to her work.

'I shall consider it a forgivable flattery.'

Gawain nodded, somehow both grateful and ashamed at the same time. Half of him, the better half, was glad that she'd taken no offence and was now trying hard to calm his ardour. The other half was wishing madly that Luned's hand would stray further up. He clenched his fists and shut his eyes, hoping that if he didn't look at her it might help. She kept speaking as she worked, and he felt the odd flash of pain as she prodded around the wound.

'The arrow missed the bone at least, and went in and out neatly enough. Whatever fool took it out made a real mess of it.' Another stab of pain shot through him at a touch. 'Both wounds were torn. Thank Danu the head wasn't barbed.'

Gawain deliberately said nothing; he didn't feel like admitting he'd been the one to draw out the arrow. Luned went on, speaking half to herself.

'Washing this out will not be pleasant.'

She had set aside her cloth and her hand now simply rested on his thigh, and for all his raging guilt Gawain felt his hardness returning. He tried desperately to think of Halwen and the loyalty he owed her, but the baser part of him was screaming that she didn't want him anyway, and this beautiful woman's hand was just inches from his manhood. He didn't know if he imagined it, but he was sure for a moment that he could feel her hand sliding up his thigh, and all the pain and guilt in the world couldn't block out his eagerness for her to reach just a little bit further.

A shuffling step sounded from outside half a second before the door opened, and Gawain's eyes snapped open, his heart in his throat. Mercifully Iain's eyes were focused on the overfull bowl in his hands, and Gawain had a moment to prepare himself. He cast his mind back to Beltane and pictured the young druid with his great swinging member. Even that image wasn't enough to destroy his arousal completely, Luned's hand was still so *close*, but it calmed him enough to make his enthusiasm less obvious in the flickering light, and when the old priest came closer Gawain was fairly sure he didn't notice. Shame was washing over him like cold water, which helped to douse his ardour a little more, and he remembered Iain's lessons that no matter where a man went, God could see all. He only hoped that God hadn't been watching too closely for the past few minutes.

Luned nodded a greeting to the priest and finally let go of Gawain's thigh. She took the steaming bowl from Iain, and the last of Gawain's arousal vanished as the smell of it struck his nostrils; it was as if someone had boiled a man's foot in his own sweat. He wrinkled his nose and Luned gave him a chiding look.

'What does us good is rarely pleasing.' She pushed the bowl under his chin and the pungent smell was overwhelming. 'Drink.'

He looked at her and there was amusement in her eyes.

'Dian-gift tastes worse than it smells.'

Gawain wondered how that might be possible, but then she placed the bowl's rim on his lips and tipped it, and he discovered it was *entirely* possible. The steaming drink made him want to gag but Luned was relentless, slowly easing sip after sip into his mouth until the bowl had been drained and Gawain felt ready to vomit. Iain's voice spoke comfortingly from behind her.

'You'll be glad of it in a little while, my boy.'

Gawain grunted.

'I'm glad enough that drinking it is over.' He grimaced. 'I think I'd sooner be shot again.'

Iain lifted an eyebrow.

'If you were shot again, you would have to be healed again. And then you'd have to drink this again.'

Gawain scowled at the priest's logic but had no answer for it. Despite the lingering taste in his mouth he was becoming pleasantly light-headed, though the drink hadn't tasted like wine or ale. He leaned his head back on the straw-stuffed mattress and let out a long sigh. Luned stood up from her stool.

'We will leave you a few moments to let the Dian-gift do its work; then I shall clean the wound.'

Gawain murmured in thanks, and let his eyes slowly droop closed.

He'd no idea whether it was minutes or hours later that he opened them again, but when he did Luned was sitting down beside him with another steaming bowl. Despite his drowsiness he dreaded the thought of another draught of her medicine, but then he realised there was no foul smell this time. Iain appeared at his side with a silver cup and the priest put it to his lips.

'It is wine this time.'

Gawain smiled a little stupidly, thoroughly approving of this new treatment. Iain's face was grave but the wine was fine and strong, and when Gawain drained the cup Iain immediately refilled it. By the fourth cup Gawain had decided that being wounded really wasn't that bad after all, and he was just beginning to enjoy himself when the priest pushed a folded belt into his mouth and told him to bite down. Gawain wasn't sure why he should but he did as he was told, and for some reason Iain held his right hand very tight. Luned was doing something with the steaming bowl but before he could look at her Iain was leaning his free hand on his brow, forcing Gawain to look straight up. The priest spoke in a very low whisper.

'It will be over soon.'

Gawain wanted to tell him that he was perfectly fine, and was on the verge of taking the belt from his mouth to reassure the old man. Then white fire raged through his wounded leg and he gripped Iain's hand so tight he was sure he'd crushed the bones. The priest said nothing, but right then he wouldn't have noticed if Iain had been bellowing out a sermon. Agony like nothing he'd ever felt was burning through his leg, and the belt stuffed between his teeth was all that stopped Gawain from screaming.

At some point he must have fainted, but when he awoke there was a pleasant smell of stew in the air. He was fairly sure his dreams had been unpleasant but whatever they'd been they were fading fast, and Gawain's thoughts were now occupied by his aching leg and rumbling belly. Looking up he saw that Luned was standing with her back to him beside the table. For a moment his eyes lingered on the long lines of her legs, but she turned before he could shame himself by staring.

'At last. You have slept the whole night and half the morning.'

She brought over a bowl of stew and a silver spoon, and Gawain shuffled painfully until he was half-sitting. He took the food gratefully and, after waiting for a nod from his hostess, began to eat. Gawain neither knew nor cared what the soft-boiled vegetables in the stew were, but he wolfed them down as eagerly as he did the chunks of chicken and bacon. He felt as if he hadn't eaten in days, and when he thought about it, he realised he didn't really know how long it had been since the supper at Aeddan's hall. For all Gawain knew, he *hadn't* eaten in days.

Between mouthfuls he did his best to remember his courtesies.

'Thank you, lady. How fares my brother?'

Luned poured out two cups of water and placed one within his easy reach.

'He is awake, though still weak. Brisen is taking good care of him.'

Gawain let out a sigh. He'd been afraid that Gareth's wound might be more serious than all had thought, and he whispered prayers of thanks to Danu and Christ. Luned went on as if reading his thoughts.

'The Goddess was kind to him, though your priest insists on giving credit to the God of Rome.'

Gawain smiled up at her.

'He'd be a pretty poor priest if he didn't.'

Luned shrugged.

'I suppose so. Your Saxon friend is thanking some goddess of his own for your recoveries, but then I suppose he'd be a poor *Saxon* if he did not.' She sniffed. 'As if there was such a thing as a good one.'

Gawain felt a little awkward at that but kept his tone polite.

'Is Ulfric making himself useful?'

Luned nodded, albeit with a slightly reluctant look.

'As useful as a Saxon can be, I suppose. When he came to ask after you Berlak invited him to go hunting with him. I've no doubt the man himself will be little use, but that hound of his had a cunning look about it.'

Gawain kept eating for a moment, almost afraid to ask the question, then he swallowed and tried not to sound too hopeful.

'Did Halwen come asking as well?'

Luned blinked and then seemed to understand.

'The girl who came with you? Not that I know of. At least, I have not seen her at the hall.'

Gawain did his best to hide how dejected that made him feel. He knew he'd offended her terribly but still he'd half-hoped that she'd be concerned for him. Luned was watching him expectantly and Gawain hurried out an answer.

'She dotes on my brother, no doubt she wanted to stay with him.'

He didn't meet her eyes as he told the half-truth, and Luned made no comment. He finished his meal in silence, though when he set the bowl aside he realised his chin was damp with stew. His stubble there was slowly becoming a real beard, and he quickly looked around for a cloth; he'd met many men who let food get caught in their beards and was in no hurry to follow their example. Before he could find anything to clean himself with, Luned leaned close to him and began dabbing at his chin with a square of linen. Her thick hair smelled of lavender, and

Gawain was uncomfortably reminded of the fact that all he wore below his waist was a bandage. He adjusted his tunic and spoke quickly.

'So, does your husband have any warriors here?'

It was a question he really ought to have asked earlier, given that there were marauding Picts nearby, but the thought had completely slipped his mind. Luned had finished cleaning off the stew but made no attempt to move away from him. Instead she sat down on the bed with a hand resting casually on his shoulder.

'There are one or two old spearmen, I think. But we need no warriors at Tahrnax.'

Gawain focused on the silver band around her brows, trying hard not to look at the firelight in her eyes.

'The Picts who attacked Pencardden were many and savage, your people should be ready in case they come here.'

Luned's honey-smooth voice showed no trace of concern.

'We are safe here.'

Gawain frowned, remembering what her husband had said about the ghost-ward keeping enemies at bay. It was true that such things were potent, and one made with human souls would be powerful indeed, but what if it wasn't enough? Luned smiled, seeing his thoughts once again.

'Do you truly think we could live a stone's throw from Maes Gwyr if our ghost-ward was not unbreakable?'

The stew in his stomach suddenly turned to icy water, and Gawain struggled to keep his question conversational.

'Maes Gwyr is near here?'

If Luned heard the fear in his voice then she made no comment on it.

'Why yes, it's just over the hill.'

She pointed as if to indicate the direction but Gawain couldn't be sure where she meant; he wasn't certain which way the room faced. But whichever direction Maes Gwyr was in, it was somewhere nearby and that was enough to make his heart flutter. Perhaps Iain had been right about God putting them on the right path, though if he was, Gawain couldn't help wondering how Cernunnos felt about the God of Rome interfering in the business of his emissary. *You're in enough trouble as it is without getting caught in the midst of a god-feud!*

Luned was looking at him curiously and Gawain considered spinning some lie to cover his discomfort, but something told him it would be wasted effort; Luned struck him as a woman who would be difficult to deceive. He told her, in brief, about Beltane and the challenge of the Green Man. He swept over the more embarrassing details but even so, Gawain suspected he did not come across as particularly clever. Luned listened patiently, and when he finished her dark eyes were concerned.

'And so you seek to fight an emissary of the Huntsman?'

Her tone was gentle, but it did imply that only a fool would do such a thing. Gawain nodded, making the same argument he'd made to his father.

'If I don't fight him now, I'll only have to do it when he returns next Beltane, and if I fight him at Beltane I'll have to face him at the height of his power.'

Gawain might have beaten him once, but who knew what the Green Man might do now that he knew not to underestimate him? *And if he kills me, who will he challenge next?* He shook his head.

'No. Best to fight him now and finish him before Samhain.'

Luned was so close to him that they'd been speaking in little more than whispers, but now her deep voice grew quieter still, and her eyes looked away from his for a moment.

'He may yet kill you.'

Gawain had grown accustomed to not thinking about that, and tried to look casual as he shrugged.

'Should the worst happen, Gaheris or one of the others will try their fate with him next year.'

It was hard to sound confident about that, and Luned saw through his attempted indifference. She placed a hand over his.

'You are brave, lord.'

Her eyes met his again as she spoke, and some of Gawain's fear seemed to melt away, replaced almost instantly by a mixture of lust and guilt. Luned shifted a little where she sat, and the feel of her body next to his made him want to put his arms around her and draw her close. She kept her gaze fixed on him and leaned down to stroke his hair, her voice the barest whisper.

'Don't think about death, Gawain.' She ran her fingers through his hair and let the other hand drift across his chest. 'Though I'm sure fear is a stranger to a man like you.'

Gawain swallowed, scrabbling through his mind for something to say. Nothing came to him, and Luned leaned so close to him that her lips were bare inches from his.

'You are bold man, a strong man.'

The hand that stroked his chest moved gently down his torso, and Gawain was hard as oak within a heartbeat. Luned's eyes closed as her lips began to brush his, and he longed to draw her into a kiss. Then a voice roared in his head. *Stop this, damn you!* This was another man's wife, and he was a guest in their home! What of the virtues of a warrior, what of devotion and courtesy? What of the honour of the House of Lothian? What would his father think, or his mother or Anna or Iain? *And what of Halwen?* She may have turned her back on him but he couldn't turn his back on her.

With what felt like gargantuan effort he put a hand on Luned's shoulder and held her at bay. Her dark eyes opened and he saw a line appear between her brows.

'Is something wrong?'

Given where her hands and lips were, most of Gawain thought that something incredibly *right* was about to happen, but his bloody better self was in control. He didn't feel at all grateful for that, but he supposed he ought to.

'I mean no offence, lady, but you have a husband.'

He felt her shrug more than he saw it; his eyes were lost in hers.

'What Berlak does not know will not vex him.'

Her hand began inching down his body again and Gawain was sure his heart would burst it was hammering so hard. He wanted so very badly for her to reach lower, and it took all his effort to put his hand on hers and stop it.

'Lady, you are truly lovely, but we must not do this.'

For the briefest moment he saw something flash in those dark eyes, but then she sat up a little, her face unflustered.

'As you say.'

Gawain let out a sigh that was part relief and part frustration, and was completely unprepared when she swiftly leaned in again and kissed him. It was brief, all *too* brief, but there was heat and passion in it beyond anything he could describe. When Luned sat back up there was a mischievous smile on her face.

'But do not think we are done here.'

She glanced down at the bulge beneath his tunic and gave the cloth a stroke so gentle she might almost not have touched it at all. But she *had*, and the feeling was enough to make Gawain let out a gasp. She chuckled and stood, leaving him aching for her touch despite all his good intentions, and her hips swayed intoxicatingly as she walked towards the door. Just as she opened it she turned back to him, with a smile full of wicked promises.

'I shall see you later, my lord.'

Chapter Fifteen

It wasn't a pleasant experience, but with Cethin to lean on Gawain just about managed to hobble to the longhall's main doors. His leg ached horribly but he knew he had to get himself outside, and to his credit the steward did not complain as they shambled through the hall. All the same both men were panting by the time they breathed fresh air, but for Gawain at least, the effort had been worth it; the sun was just dipping towards the green hills in the west, and the afternoon breeze on his face was wonderfully refreshing. The storm seemed to have finally abated, and Gawain instinctively murmured his thanks to Danu for calming Taranis. Of course, considering who he was coming to fight, it was the Huntsman's temper that he really ought to be worrying about, but that concern was less immediate than the storm.

Gawain sighed and leaned against one of the oak pillars flanking the door. Perhaps his performance in battle would do something to endear him to Cernunnos? No god was obliged to favour anyone of course, but for the most part the Picts liked to revere the Thunderer, while most Lothian warriors were loyal to the Huntsman instead. Well, for all that the Picts had won the fight at Pencardden, Gawain liked to think he'd given a good account of himself in combat, and when Lothian warriors won glory Cernunnos tended to smile on them. Would he smile on Gawain for fighting well, or would he be better served in keeping Christ as his patron? It had worked well enough so far, after all. Gawain shook his head. What use was there in trying to guess the motives of gods?

A serving-man appeared with a three-legged stool, and Cethin helped Gawain to sit down beside the doorway. The movement was awkward, but it felt good to take the weight off his leg. Cethin remained standing, his hands clasped behind his back.

'How is the ache, lord?'

Gawain tapped his hand gently on the injured limb, well away from the wound itself.

'A great improvement on how it was, thanks to your mistress.'

Cethin gave a small smile.

'Lady Luned saved my boy's life when he was a newborn. She is skilled, is she not?'

Gawain nodded, not quite trusting himself to comment. The fact was that, weak though he felt, Lady Luned was fast becoming far more of a worry than two little holes in his leg. He'd barely managed to resist her advances the first time, and she had left him in no doubt that there would be a second. What if he gave in to her the next time she tempted him? Or even if he didn't, what if next time she took offence at the rejection and decided to spin some tale to Berlak that would see them all cast out or worse? He'd been a fine host so far but Gawain had no real idea who he was or what he was capable of. *And you were a guest in his home for less than a day before you kissed his wife.*

Iain had been right, as he so often was; Gawain needed discipline. His lack of that simple virtue had led to too much grief already without making things worse now. Thinking on his impulsiveness made him cast his eyes about the village, hoping to catch a glimpse of Halwen among the bustling locals, but her red-gold hair was nowhere to be seen. He turned back to Cethin instead.

'Your lady tells me you have no fear of raiders here?'

The steward looked as unconcerned by the idea as Luned had.

'We live far from where the Picts usually roam, and Tahrnax is well-warded.'

Gawain pressed him a little.

'Picts were roaming just up the river only yesterday.'

It took Cethin a moment to respond to that.

'An oddity, I'll grant. But Tahrnax is no easy place to roam to.' He gestured to the tree-covered slope beyond the outskirts. 'We are hidden from the world, neither on the way *to* nor on the way *from* anywhere else. Even were we not protected by the wards, an enemy would struggle to find us, let alone threaten us.'

Gawain frowned. He could remember only a little of the journey here from the river, but it was true enough that Tahrnax was not a settlement a traveller might stumble across by accident. All the same, Gawain hated to think of this peaceful place meeting the same fate as Pencardden. *They had thought themselves safe as well.* He shivered a little, and lied to himself that it was the breeze. He'd spent most of that fight too caught up in battle-lust to be afraid, but he knew that he'd only pushed down the fear, not conquered it; it was hard to remember that night without feeling cold in his gut.

It was a gloomy path to tread, but Gawain couldn't help but wonder how many of Aeddan's people had survived. Though he'd seen boats shoving off and heard voices on the water, he couldn't guess how many of the Venicones had escaped to the southern shore, or how many might have hidden themselves until the Picts had slaughtered their fill. But he'd seen what happened to those too slow to flee, and the memory filled him with shame. The strong were supposed to protect the weak, yet he'd stood and watched as unarmed women were cut down by blood-maddened savages. *And while that flat-faced coward pissed on a hero's corpse!* He felt a pressure behind his eyes but refused to let tears fall. Instead he ground his teeth and clenched his fists, and swore to himself that, should he survive this and make it home, he would talk to Lot and make him send more help to the people here. *And I will come with them.*

Cethin had seen him shiver and must have thought it was from cold, because he put a gentle hand on his shoulder.

'Do you wish to go back inside, lord?'

Gawain smiled at him.

'Not just yet. A little more air would be good, I think.'

The steward nodded and the pair lapsed into a comfortable silence. Gawain stared absently at the villagers going about their business, and tried planning what he'd say to his father when he returned. Lot didn't have the men to garrison all of Venicon territory, but he could easily send out seasoned warriors to arm and train the locals. At Pencardden there'd been barely a handful of fighting men, and the shieldwall they'd made had only held thanks to Drustan's leadership. The Venicones living this far south were woefully unprepared for the emboldened Picts, and Lothian could do much to ready them. *And I could make a start right here.*

Gawain flexed his knee and though the pain was bearable, it was still highly unpleasant. There was no way he could face the Green Man until his condition improved, and while he waited for it to heal, he and Ulfric could train the men of Tahrnax in the way of war. Neither of them was an expert but they were both well-taught and had at least a little real experience; their training would be a great deal better than nothing should the Picts come raiding downriver. He would have to ask Berlak's leave of course, but his host had seemed a genial sort, and it would be in his people's best interests. *And his too, if it keeps you out of the hall and away from his wife.*

He was wondering how he could best bring up the subject when Cethin's voice dragged his mind to the present.

'Look there; the lord is back.'

Gawain looked up and sure enough, Berlak was striding through the grassy bank, with Ulfric just behind him and Mabb trotting along in the rear. On their shoulders the men held a long pole, from which a red deer swung back and forth as they walked. It was an impressive-looking beast, and both Berlak and Ulfric were smiling smugly at their kill. Gawain, with a helping hand from Cethin, stood up as they approached the hall and saw that as well as the swinging deer, both men had a brace of hares tied to their belts.

Mabb came loping up to nuzzle Gawain's hand, his tail wagging so hard it slapped at Cethin's leg. The steward made no comment. Berlak kept one hand on the pole to steady it but reached out with the other to clap Gawain's shoulder.

'Good day, young lord. I trust your leg is healing?'

Gawain nodded politely as he ruffled Mabb's ears.

'It is, lord, thanks to your lady wife's good care.'

Berlak smiled, though the expression was somewhat spoiled by traces of dried blood on his face and grey-flecked beard.

'She is a rare wonder, my Luned. Even now she will be working her magic in the kitchens; we have fine cooks here but Luned has so many talents and she is ever-generous with them.'

Despite his best efforts Gawain wondered briefly what talents Luned might have shared with *him* earlier, but he shoved the fantasy away and hoped the guilt didn't show on his face. He couldn't let Berlak suspect that anything had happened between them; should the fight with the Green Man end badly, the others would need Berlak's help to get safely home again. *And so you will lie to him? What of your own sin in all this?* Gawain didn't much like the voice of his conscience, but it was right. For all the practical reasons for keeping this a secret from Berlak, there was no keeping secrets from God. Amends had to be made. But how?

A sudden flash of inspiration struck him and Gawain shuffled a pace closer to his host.

'The lady is indeed most busy.' He leaned forward and planted a quick kiss on Berlak's cheek. 'From her, lord. Welcome home.'

He saw Ulfric give him a confused look but Berlak simply smiled at the gesture.

'Most courteous of you, my friend, and I am glad to be back.' He jerked his head behind him. 'Now then, I've made your Saxon comrade haul our prize for quite long enough. I'm sure her sister will be halfway prepared for tonight by now, and we need to get this beauty hung up in her place.'

Ulfric was indeed looking tired of holding the weight up, and he nodded gratefully at their host's back. Gawain bowed his head.

'I shall see you inside, lord.'

Berlak smiled and started walking again, though he nodded down at Gawain's bare feet as he passed.

'Cethin, find the young lord some boots, would you?'

The steward bowed.

'Yes, lord.'

Berlak and Ulfric disappeared into the hall, though Mabb stayed behind, still nuzzling at Gawain's hand. Cethin turned to his guest.

'Shall we go inside?'

Gawain was tempted to stay where he was and wait for Halwen to come up to the hall, but there was still no sign of her anywhere and besides, he didn't want her to feel ambushed. He nodded once, then gave Mabb a quick scratch behind his ears before ushering him towards the door. The hound gave his fingers a final sniff and then obeyed. Cethin offered Gawain an arm and he took it gratefully, feeling a little better than he had done when they'd come out; passing on the kiss might not be much of a gesture but it was something. Hopefully God would appreciate the effort, and Gawain now had a plan for something useful to do while his leg healed up. He tried to maintain that positive mood as he hobbled into the hall. *All you have to worry about now is how to make amends with Halwen, how to keep yourself from being seduced by Luned, and how to defeat the un-killable emissary of the Huntsman.* Things were certainly looking up.

The smell of roasting venison would have made his mouth water if he hadn't already been eating. For such a small community it seemed the people of Tahrnax didn't lack for food, and even as the prize course cooked over the fire-pit, plump loaves of bread and great bowls of hare stew were already being passed around the tables. Serving women walked back and forth with pitchers of spring mead that that never seemed to need refilling, and at the high table they even had Roman amphorae of rich red wine. To Gawain's eyes it seemed that half the village had been invited to eat in Berlak's longhall, and not one of them seemed unused to the idea. Apparently their host's generous spirit was not limited to his guests.

Gawain curled his toes inside his new boots. According to Cethin they were an old pair of Berlak's, but the soft leather felt barely worn and they fitted Gawain as if made for him. So far he'd taken great care not to spill anything on them, but he took comfort in the knowledge that if he did, Mabb would clean the boots long before Berlak noticed. The grey hound was sitting patiently at Gawain's feet and so far had eaten easily as well as those sat at the table. Both Gawain and Berlak had been slipping him morsels since they sat down, and Ulfric had already commented that Mabb would soon grow too fat to hunt.

The Saxon was sitting on Gawain's right while Luned sat to his left, her leg brushing dangerously close to his. Beyond Luned sat her husband, and after him sat Iain, Halwen and Gareth. Gawain had seen his brother briefly before they sat down and, despite his pallor, he seemed hearty enough. He'd had no chance yet to speak with Halwen. They'd exchanged nods and a polite enquiry about his wound but that was all, and Gawain had hoped that they could sit together so that he could finally apologise and start making amends. But Berlak himself had shown them to their places on the bench and his guests could hardly complain about it. He frowned into his mead as Ulfric finished his story.

It seemed that Berlak was both a fine tracker and an expert marksman, and had brought down the deer with a near-perfect shot. *Just what I need in a man I've almost cuckolded; a gift for marksmanship.* The lord himself smiled pleasantly through the tale, then sent crumbs flying as he waved his bread at Ulfric.

'Now then my friend, you are too modest. Your own arrows caught three of these beauties for us.' He lifted a silver spoon with his free hand, picking up a chunk of hare-meat from the stew. 'And rarely have I seen finer shooting. It is well that you are so young; I don't doubt that Vortigern would have made terrible use of you back in my time.'

Ulfric bowed his head, flattered by the compliment, but Gareth gave their host a curious look.

'Vortigern, lord?'

Berlak smiled at the youngest Lothian, and began recounting the history of their once-great enemy. Vortigern had been a half-Saxon, half-Briton who had declared himself Wide-Ruler of all Britain, in the days when King Lot was a young man. He had united a great host of eastern men, most of them Saxons, and made war against the other kingdoms of Britain in an effort to conquer it. Lot, along with the kings of Bernicia, Elmet, and half a dozen other kingdoms, had united against him under Uther Pendragon, and after much bloodshed Vortigern had been defeated. It had all ended when the Pendragon had faced Vortigern in single combat; Uther had taken the Wide-Ruler's head, and been acknowledged as the High King of Britain by his peers.

Gawain had heard this tale before and only half-listened to it, though Berlak was a fine story-teller; he never bragged of his own deeds, or even mentioned them at all, but he spoke of those battles and marches in the voice of a man who had clearly been there. The story took some time to tell, and Gawain soon finished his bread and stew and started working on a duck-and-chestnut pie. Gareth was so engrossed in the tale that he lost half his pie to Mabb, who plucked it from the table like a thief swiping a purse. The hound nudged it back to where he'd been sitting and devoured it noisily beneath the table.

When the story finally ended Gareth's eyes were wide.

'I only wish I was old enough to have been there, lord.'

For the first time since their arrival Gawain saw Berlak's smile falter, but he composed himself quickly enough.

'Wars have a habit of repeating themselves, young Gareth. I don't doubt you will see such a thing in your time; it is the fate of most young men.'

For all his smiling there was still a line between his brows, and he seemed grateful when his wife moved to a new subject.

'It is not the fate of most young women though, Danu be thanked.' She turned to Halwen. 'What brought you into this tangle, my dear? You were not seeking battle at Pencardden, I trust?'

Gawain could see little of Luned's face but her tone was pleasant enough, if not quite as friendly as her husband's. Halwen answered in the same voice.

'Gareth and I had only meant to travel part of the way. We would have turned south again at Anthony's Wall, but the storm and the Picts had other plans.'

Luned nodded and then tilted her head.

'Are you kin to the young lords?'

The pause before Halwen's answer was brief but undeniably awkward. Gawain saw Iain lean forward to intervene but Halwen answered first.

'Gawain and I are good friends, we were Summer King and Spring Maiden this Beltane.'

Gawain felt a tiny touch of relief; at least she'd said *are* and not *were*. Halwen went on with her answer, relaxed and confident.

'I'd never travelled north of Dun Edin and decided to accompany him for part of the journey.' She smiled and ruffled Gareth's hair. 'And Gareth here would be at a loss without me.'

Gareth seemed torn between indignation at being treated as a child and the instinctive joy every man had for Halwen's smile. Berlak chuckled and gestured towards the youngest Lothian.

'A strong lad like this one? I'm sure he could wander the wilderness with nothing but a pointed stick; Brisen tells me he was stamping about like a fenced bull the moment she'd bandaged his head.'

Gareth looked away, clearly pleased and a little embarrassed by the compliment, and Berlak turned his attention back to Halwen.

'Not that we are not delighted to have you here with him, my dear. Tahrnax has been brightened by your presence.'

Halwen bowed her head, and the rings in her hair glinted in the firelight.

'You are too kind, lord. And your home is a beautiful place.'

For a moment Gawain felt a stab of irrational jealousy, but then his inner self slapped him down. *You're jealous of a smile and a compliment when you've already kissed this man's wife?* He felt he ought to be saying something to continue the conversation, but fortunately Iain spoke first.

'Lord, I'm told that Maes Gwyr is not far from here. Would you be able to direct us?'

Berlak nodded.

'It is just northeast of us, father, over the hill.' He turned to look at Gawain. 'Luned tells me you intend to challenge Lord Verdis?'

Gawain blinked.

'You know him, lord?'

Berlak moved his shoulders a little.

'I've not seen him myself but folk know to avoid his home; he is a servant of the Huntsman.'

Gawain saw Iain cross himself and though Berlak did not react, he didn't miss Luned's silent disapproval.

'I have little choice but to go there, lord. He challenged me at Beltane and I must meet him in combat soon.'

Berlak frowned at him.

'It strikes me as a dangerous mission. I don't suppose I could dissuade you from it?'

A part of Gawain wanted to be talked out of it, but he banished the doubts from his mind. This had to be done, and he'd beaten the Green Man before; he could do it again. Luned answered the question before Gawain could.

'It strikes *me* that Lord Gawain is not a man easily discouraged.'

It was said innocently enough but all the same Gawain almost blushed. Berlak still hadn't quite managed to regain his smile but he gave Gawain a kindly look.

'But you must stay here and until your leg is healed, in that I will brook no refusal.'

Iain spoke up from beside him.

'We would not want to over-stretch our welcome, lord.' He gestured at the feast around them. 'You have been kind enough to us already.'

Berlak, predictably, waved a dismissive hand.

'You are welcome here for as long as you have need, father.'

Iain nodded.

'You are kind, lord. We are more than willing to pay for our keep.'

He patted the purse at his belt, but once again Berlak waved the idea away.

'I do not lack for wealth, and no host worth the name would take silver from wounded men.'

Iain looked both suitably grateful and a little discomfited, and Gawain took the opportunity to speak.

'Then let us be of use, at least?' Berlak turned to face him and Gawain rushed into his offer. 'Your wards here may indeed be strong, lord, but with Picts raiding so far south it would be wise to prepare for the worst. Ulfric and I would be happy to train some of your menfolk in the way of war?'

He had mentioned the idea to Ulfric before they sat down, and the Saxon nodded his head.

'They might be glad of the chance to learn, lord? May Wodan forbid it, but the Picts may have magic of their own that might counter your wards?'

Gareth piped up from along the table.

'I can help too, lord.'

Truthfully Gareth had only received the most basic of training, but Gawain supposed it would be good to make him feel useful. Not that most grown men would listen to the advice of so young a boy; it would be a challenge to make them listen to himself and Ulfric. *But it will do them good, and it will get you out of this hall and away from temptation.*

Berlak looked indifferent but his tone was courteous.

'Our wards have kept us safe so far, but I see no harm in men learning to fight should they wish.' He called over to Cethin, who was taking his meal on a table just below theirs. 'Cethin, how would you feel about our friends here instructing the villagers in warfare?'

The steward looked up and shrugged.

'It might be worth learning, lord, by your leave.'

Berlak returned the shrug and faced Gawain again.

'Very well, young lord. Any of the menfolk who wish to be trained shall be welcome to, and you will have my thanks for it.'

He was clearly just being polite and didn't care one way or the other, but Gawain thanked him for his permission all the same. The conversation turned to other things and soon became what Gawain was sure was a very clever discussion between Iain and Berlak, though he struggled to understand most of what was said. They spoke of gods and histories and rituals, and for all his efforts to follow their talk he soon lost interest in it.

After two more courses of meat, including a delicious haunch of venison, the serving women began bringing out a sweet dish. It was apparently Luned's creation; a hard biscuit flavoured with nuts of some kind, topped with soft cheese and covered in early blackberries drizzled with honey. Gawain, who was rarely fond of sweet foods, consumed three of them in quick succession, covering his hands with honey in the process. Mabb helpfully licked them clean, and Gawain hoped quietly that the honey wouldn't make him ill; a pile of dog vomit on his rushes would be a poor way to repay their host.

Berlak broke off his conversation with Iain to turn and smile at his wife.

'My dear Luned, these are by far the best you have made.'

Luned returned the smile and touched her husband's arm, though her leg rubbed against Gawain's.

'I have to occupy myself somehow when you are off at your hunting. I only wish I'd been finished in time to greet you home.'

A flutter of panic went through Gawain and he spoke quickly before Berlak could say anything.

'I did pass on your kiss, lady.'

Both lord and lady turned to him, and with her face away from her husband Luned's lips twitched in a tiny smile. Gawain didn't dare react to it and a moment later she gave a deep-throated laugh.

'You are a courteous young man, Gawain.'

She beckoned to her husband and tapped a finger to her cheek, and Berlak smiled and dutifully kissed her. Luned turned from him and fixed Gawain with her dark eyes before leaning in to pass the kiss on. It was brief, though not so brief that he didn't smell the lavender in her hair, and was no more than a chaste peck on his cheek, but all the same Gawain was sure his face reddened. Luned smirked as she backed away again.

'My husband's thanks for your courtesy, young lord.'

She was entirely at her ease, and Gawain couldn't help but wonder if he was not the first man to take her husband's place while he was away. He flicked a quick glance at Halwen but she seemed uninterested by the exchange, and if anything that made him feel even worse. A little hint of jealousy might have been awkward but at least he would have known that she cared; a kiss from a host was meaningless in itself, but Gawain would still have felt a twinge of resentment had Berlak been kissing Halwen.

But no-one made any comment, no-one even changed their expression, and Gawain forced himself to stay blank-faced as the talk continued. Luned's leg continued rubbing gently against his, and he told himself firmly that he wasn't enjoying it. The thought of her coming to his chamber again did *not* make him excited, and he would *not* entertain the fantasy of her dress falling to the floor, and Luned telling him to run his hands over the soft skin of her body. His better side growled at him and forced the image away. He was Gawain ab Lot, and damn it all he would discipline his mind and comport himself as befit the son of a king! But Luned's thigh continued to rub against his, and he wondered just how much say his better side would have in this matter.

Chapter Sixteen

Mhari almost pitied the young Venicon, but she reminded herself that he was a lickspittle to the Lothians; he'd earned no kinder fate. The bound man was tall and thin as a spear, and was beginning to stagger as exhaustion took its toll. It wouldn't be long now. *If he's lucky someone will cave his head in before Temar gets any ideas.* The Venicon swung his sword, but yet again it struck nothing but air. His left wrist and ankle had been lashed to the table, and any attempt to cut his leashes was met by a spear jab to his face. He'd already lost an eye to one such a lesson and had long given up trying to escape, though it seemed some tiny spark of spirit still lived in him; enough to keep him swinging the sword at his tormenters at any rate. Darr, the latest of the Picts to take their turn with him, dodged the captured man's blade with ease and laughed as he ducked in and rammed a punch into the Venicon's injured side. The prisoner cried out as the warriors laughed, and Darr's knuckles came away bloody.

Mhari took another drink and looked away from the display. She wasn't averse to harsh lessons for those who grovelled to the southerners, but Temar and his cronies revelled in such torment far more than they revelled in battle, and that made them less than warriors. Temar was laughing the loudest and hurled his empty beaker at the prisoner's head. It broke on impact and the Venicon fell to his knees, blood trickling from his ear.

Mhari leaned back in the chief's chair and sighed, raising one boot onto the table. Beside her, Conn half-watched them as he cleaned his nails with a dagger-point.

'Imagine if Temar was that fierce in an actual fight? We'd all be dining in Dun Edin by now.'

Mhari snorted but said nothing; she was still fuming at the antics of the gutless imbecile. Temar's warriors had been told to scout south of the main warband as they made their way towards Tahrnax, and even that simple task had been beyond him. Rather than watch for trouble and report back, Temar had led his men into Pencardden and got a dozen of them killed for no reason but his own vanity. Most of the locals had fled across the river so there were no decent slaves to take, and there was barely a sniff of silver to be found. The raid had been a pointless waste of Pictish lives, yet here Temar was, behaving as if he'd won some great victory. *At least the warriors he lost were* his, *not mine*. When the time came for Mhari to deal with him, the fewer men Temar had behind him, the better.

She took another sip of spring mead. It was pleasant-tasting but she couldn't enjoy it, any more than she'd enjoy sleeping indoors tonight instead of out on the hills; the simple fact that Temar had been the cause of it was enough to ruin the luxury. A part of her wished the Grey Woman was here. Her prediction about only seven deaths had been proved wrong, which meant she would either have to lose face by admitting to the mistake, or condemn Temar's actions for going against their prophesied path; the path which led to riches and glory. However she chose to play it, it would be good from Mhari's point of view, but their prophetess had vanished to the woods to commune with her spirits. Mhari, as ever, found this suspiciously convenient.

She didn't doubt the Grey Woman had knowledge of the spirit world, but her disappearances always seemed to coincide with when there was hard work to be done.

Mhari drummed her fingers on her leg and stared blankly at the ram's-skull helm on the table. She'd come down to Pencardden purely to keep watch on Temar, and by the time Mhari and her people had arrived all the fighting had been long over. She had yet to wear her lordly gift in combat, and until she did Mhari couldn't truly call it her own. Conn saw her staring and nudged her chair with a foot.

'If you're thinking of wearing that in bed tonight, I'll need some stronger drink before we start.'

Mhari snorted again.

'I'll give you a choice.' She took the helm in one hand and turned it to face him. 'Would you rather have this looking *down* at you, or *up* at you?'

Conn considered the horned skull for a moment, then winked at her.

'*Back* at me.'

Mhari held her cup out, her mood lifting a little despite herself.

'Refill this and we shall see.'

Conn made a pretence of hurrying with the jug and Mhari actually smiled for a moment. The expression vanished when she heard the jingling steps of Temar's approach, and by the time she'd turned to look at him her face had become sour. Even the man's appearance was a disgrace; Temar, despite the fact that it was both undeserved and obviously too small for him, was strutting towards her in a shirt of polished scales that had once belonged to King Lot's champion. The flat-nosed bastard was telling anyone who'd listen that he'd killed him in single combat, and even now men were boiling the flesh from his skull so that Temar could have it as a cup.

Mhari struggled to keep the disgust from her face. She was certain he was lying about the fight, Drustan ab Hywel had been a legend of a man, but the only ones present had been Temar's henchmen, and they were backing his story to the hilt. Mhari could feel her hands wanting to clench and she fought to keep her fingers relaxed. The lie was pathetic, but Alva would believe it because she wanted to believe it, and when they travelled back north she would heap gifts and glory on her worthless son and call his killing of Drustan the equal of Mhari's killing of Peleus. She felt her nostrils flare. *If she calls him lord for this then Alva or no Alva, I'll cut his balls off right there in front of her!*

The big man swaggered up, plonked himself on the table, and swivelled on his rump to dangle his legs over Mhari's side. He wasn't quite drunk but he was well on the way to it, and what was probably supposed to be a dynamic manoeuvre looked clumsy and childish.

'So, have you decided yet?'

Mhari gave him a level look. He wasn't interested in what she thought, and had only asked so that he could make his own argument again.

'I am still thinking, I'm sure you have heard of the concept?'

Temar scowled.

'You should be grateful that I told you at all.'

Mhari met his eyes with a raised brow. Temar looked like he wanted to spit, but he acquiesced all the same.

'Lord.'

She nodded, satisfied for the time being.

'You told me exactly *because* I am the lord here, and because I am the one best suited to deal with this.'

The scowl didn't leave Temar's face. The one good result of his foolishness here, apart from Mhari having a bed to sleep in tonight, had been Temar's report of a red-haired youth who'd claimed to be a son of King Lot. According to Temar he had escaped downriver with a few companions, and though he didn't know how far he might have gone, or even what side of the water he might have landed, it was still something worth knowing. When the Grey Woman returned Mhari would have to press her into finding out where he'd gone. The Avon Du had been running swift that night, and if his boat had remained on the north side then this boy could prove a valuable prize; whether Mhari ransomed him or killed him, it could only serve to swell her reputation.

Temar, predictably, launched into the argument he'd already made.

'We should track him down, lord, and send his head north for my mother to mount in her hall. Men would come from miles about to see it.'

Mhari sighed. It was a stupid and ingratiating idea, and one that could easily prove more trouble than it was worth. The Picts were not ready for a full-scale war with Lothian, and it was one thing to kill Lot's son in combat, but quite another to put his head on a spike for the whole world to see. Lot would send Hardhand north along with every warlord and spearman he had, and even Alva would have no choice but to flee for the mountains.

Temar pressed on.

'If we send Mother the head of King Lot's son, she will fill our helms with silver.'

And name you a lord, or so you hope. That alone was enough for Mhari to dismiss the idea, but there was another very simple argument which Conn obligingly made for her.

'Or we could take the head to his father still attached to his body, and Lot will fill our helms *and* our boots with gold.'

He was still fastidiously cleaning his fingernails, holding his dagger just shy of the point, and barely glanced towards

Temar as he spoke. The big man scoffed and spoke in the tone of someone who knew everything.

'Ransoms are messy. Lot could play us false and have us killed once we handed him over.' He tapped a meaty paw on his chest, leaving grease-stains on the scale coat. 'My way is better.'

Conn shrugged, still barely deigning to look at him.

'Your way is *easier*, Temar, that is not the same thing.'

Temar straightened his back and tried to look intimidating, but Conn met his glare with indifference.

'Have you something else to say, or did you just need to stretch?'

Mhari smirked as Temar reddened. He pointed a thick finger behind him, where Darr was still tormenting the bound Venicon.

'Maybe me and my man there will stretch your neck between us until your pretty head breaks off?'

Everything about Conn spoke of relaxed disinterest, but Mhari saw him subtly shift his grip on the knife. He couldn't miss at that range if he tried, and if Temar made a false move he'd be dead in a flick of Conn's wrist.

'You boys can try, but best of luck catching me.' He winked. 'I'm a quick bastard when I want to be.'

Temar was, of course, too stupid to see the danger he was in, and Mhari was tempted just to let things unfold. But that would be foolish; Alva might like Conn's face, but that wouldn't stop her peeling the skin off it if she found out he'd knifed her son. Temar growled and shifted his weight.

'You won't be quick with my boot on your throat you little…'

But Mhari smoothly drew her own knife and held it to Temar's thigh, and the touch of the steel gave him pause. Her voice was calm and quiet.

'Finish that threat, Temar, and on tomorrow's march I'll be wearing your bollocks for earrings.'

Now it was Conn's turn to smirk as Temar's face contorted. If he'd had any brains he would have realised Mhari was bluffing, but he was a fool and a coward and after a moment's glaring he held up his hands. Mhari moved the knife away and carried on as if nothing had happened. *I may have a quiet word with Darina tomorrow; a stray arrow in the next raid could solve a good many problems.*

A cry from the hall gave them all an excuse to break the tension, and Temar pretended to be unworried as he twisted to look behind him. It seemed the fight was finally gone from the Venicon, and Darr had pinned him down and started cutting at his remaining eye. Temar pushed himself from the table, clearly eager to join him, but the damned fool turned to speak again before leaving.

'I'll send some of my men across the river in the morning, lord. We'll be ready to head east before midday.'

Mhari held back another sigh. Why could he do *nothing* right?

'No need. We'll head east first thing.'

There was no point in crossing the river to chase a few scattered Venicones and besides, word of this would spread and there were Lothian warriors at Ystre Lyn. The longer they tarried here, the better the chances of those men coming downriver to punish them for Temar's stupidity, and Mhari's warband would need perfect conditions and the luck of the gods to survive a clash with them. *No, we make for Tahrnax with all speed.* It galled her to be running, but she told herself it was temporary. Tahrnax was said to be as wealthy as it was haunted, and once she'd raided it she'd have silver and reputation enough to gather more warriors to her; enough to take those whoresons on and win. *And think what a name you'll make when you come back and take Ystre Lyn itself?*

It was almost enough to make her grin, but a warrior must be patient and she smothered her ambitions for now. Temar gave her a scornful look.

'Scared the southerners will come chasing us?'

Mhari tried and failed to keep the distain from her voice.

'If they do, I don't doubt you will be the first to step up and fight them?'

Temar sneered.

'Just because you lack the nerve, don't think…'

But Conn snorted and interrupted him.

'You wouldn't know nerve if it smacked you in the face and then stabbed you in the arse.'

Temar made to step forward, and though Mhari wasn't looking she was certain Conn was ready to throw his knife at an eye-blink's notice. *Not here, not now.* She put up a hand and met Temar's eyes.

'Enough. Get back to your men.'

For half a heartbeat she thought he might stand up to her, but then the gutless cur backed down and stormed away. She turned in her seat to scold Conn for provoking him, but her lover was in no mood to be told.

'You can argue patience all you like but it won't change the fact; he needs dealing with.'

Mhari let out the sigh she'd been holding in. Conn was right of course, but his timing was poor.

'He does. But we can't do it here.'

Conn shrugged.

'I know you're fond of Alva but if we don't do it soon he will drag us all into ruin.' His eyes became deathly serious. 'I'll wait a while. But if you do not deal with him, then I will.'

Mhari ought to have been annoyed by the ultimatum, but if anything his intensity made her that much keener to get him to bed. She leaned closer to him.

'Damned right you'll wait.'

She reached out and grabbed the front of his tunic, and Conn didn't resist when she pulled him close.

'But I'll deal with *you* first.'

Conn gave her one of his roguish smiles.

'Finally, my plan comes to fruition.'

Mhari drew him into a kiss but broke it off when a scream came from the blinded Venicon. Looking into the hall she saw that Temar and Darr were giggling like children as they held the poor bastard's feet in the fire-pit. Mhari bit back a curse. Conn was right; they'd have to deal with Temar soon.

Without a word she stood, walked to the pit, drew Brathir from its sheath and hacked it down through the screaming man's skull. His noise stopped at once and Mhari spoke to the hall before Temar could say anything, keeping her voice light.

'Bel's teeth, can you not find something *quiet* to do?'

For a moment she glared at Temar, daring him to object, but the coward said nothing and she leaned down to wipe Brathir clean on the Venicon's tunic.

'We have a long walk in the morning and I plan to do some humping before I sleep.'

At least half the warriors in the hall laughed or whistled, and Mhari grinned at her oath-men as she sheathed the sword and began walking towards the chief's rooms. Conn had risen from his seat and was now leaning against the doorframe that led to them. He smiled at her and Mhari winked back. When she reached the door she turned to face the hall again, and put a hand over her heart in mock courtesy.

'Apologies, my friends; we will *not* be quiet!'

She smiled as the hall rang with the friendly laughter of her warriors, though she couldn't ignore the fact that not everyone joined in. Around the fire-pit was a gaggle of distinctly sour-faced men, and sourest of all of them was Temar. *Conn is right; we must deal with him soon.*

Chapter Seventeen

Gawain supposed it was a mercy that Luned hadn't come to him in the night. He'd sat on the bed and worked on his carving as he prayed to Danu and the Huntsman, then he'd stared at the red star on his shield and prayed to Christ, saying the same words to each god; *keep this temptation from me*. It seemed that one or all of them had answered because Luned had not made an appearance, and Gawain told himself he was grateful to them; even if he *had* barely slept and had woken up hard as a spear.

He shook the thought away. It was a blessing that she'd not come to him, whether he appreciated it or not, and today he had work to do. The men of Tahrnax were training in an open space between the houses, and Gawain dreaded to think what Drustan would be saying were he here; they did not lack for enthusiasm but the concept of fighting as a unit was completely beyond them, and once again Gawain shouted the same two words that he'd been shouting all morning.

'Stay close!'

Some of those who heard him tried to obey, but it was like wrangling a pack of untrained dogs. There were about thirty men there in all, each one happy enough to practice fighting even if he had no idea how badly he was doing it. More had wanted to come, but several of the volunteers had been far too young or far too old to fight. Gawain had allowed only one greybeard to stay, purely because he'd been a warrior in his youth and was still capable with a spear, even if he'd never stood in a shieldwall before. *And he looks old enough to have waved the Romans off.* Gawain had turned away nearly all of the youngsters, including Cethin's son, partly because they were not yet strong enough for this, but mainly because of Tahrnax's dismal lack of weaponry. There were barely enough makeshift shields and training staves to go around as it was without trying to arm children as well.

Happily, Berlak had given Cethin leave to join them for the morning, and the steward was proving to be an invaluable assistant. He had as little actual ability as any of them, but all of Tahrnax looked up to Cethin as if he was the lord himself, and his approval of Gawain meant the locals didn't question the orders of a half-bearded youth. He was standing in the midst of the fray even now, trying to encourage his fellow Venicones to remember Gawain's instructions and keep together, though only those nearest to him seemed to hear over the racket.

The two groups of men had begun as opposing lines, one bearing shields and long staffs to train as a shieldwall, while the other held light staves and were instructed to charge wildly the way the Picts did. In theory the shieldwall group, despite being smaller, ought to be holding them off with ease. In practice the men of Tahrnax seemed far keener on the *idea* of this training than in actually doing what they were told. The moment the two groups clashed all of their careful drills disappeared like smoke in a breeze, and yet again the scene had devolved into chaos. Gawain shouted at them again.

'Shieldwall, stay close!'

Cethin did his best to comply, as did Yoreth the fisherman, but even with Ulfric standing with them their group still dissolved into a formless mass of fighting men, and Gawain soon gave up trying to salvage this exercise. He waved his arms and bellowed.

'Enough! Give ground!'

Mabb, who'd been trailing behind him as he watched the madness, gave a couple of supporting barks. It was probably that as much as Gawain's shout that told the men to stop fighting. The two groups backed away from each other and Cethin's group even tried to form something like a line as they withdrew. It would have looked better if half of them hadn't abandoned their make-shift shields in the melee. Gawain saw them lying about all over the churned-up ground, and let out a frustrated sigh. The crude boards were no match for good linden-wood shields, but they were still a damned sight better than blocking an axe with bare flesh, and the men had simply dropped them without a thought.

He waved to the two groups and tried to keep the irritation from his voice.

'Pile your weapons and rest for a moment.'

The men smiled or nodded at him and set about doing as they were told, heading over to the water-butt Cethin had ordered brought out. They clapped one another's backs and traded jokes, and it was difficult to stay angry at them when they were so clearly enjoying themselves, but Gawain reminded himself that a Pictish warband might be only days away, and ward or no ward he had a duty to prepare them for the worst. His leg was aching, and he limped over to the stool Cethin had set out for him and sank onto it with a grunt. Mabb followed after him, and the moment Gawain sat down the great hound shoved his head under his hand. Gawain absently scratched the wolfhound's ears, trying to think on the positives of all this.

The steady clang of the hammers from the village smithy told him that at least his spearheads were coming along. Given how close the Picts were there was no time to make long, leaf-shaped blades like the one that graced Ulfric's spear, but simple iron points were easy enough to make, and both the smith and his lad had been willing enough to help after Cethin put in a good word. Away to his right he heard the rhythmic thumping of arrows striking marks, and when he looked that way he saw that the archers were honing their skills well. *And putting my would-be spearmen to shame.* There were several decent hunters in Tahrnax and they'd been happy to teach what they knew to Gareth and some of the youngsters, and even a few of the womenfolk. Gawain sighed wistfully as he watched them practicing; Halwen was standing with them.

He'd still not had the chance to be alone with her, and seeing her without being able to talk to her was a torment. They'd shared a brief greeting when he'd first arrived this morning and he'd felt no hostility from her, but there was no real warmth between them either. She was shooting well, as was Gareth, though neither was the equal of the local hunters. From what Ulrfric had said they might well have benefitted from Berlak's instruction, but the lord had shown no interest in their training and had gone out hunting again at first light. Cethin doubted if he'd be seen again before dusk. Gawain watched as Halwen put three arrows into a barrel within a finger's length of each other, and hoped quietly that she'd never have to send those arrows into men. For all his arguments that this training was necessary, and that the danger to Tahrnax was both real and close, still Gawain would be happiest if fate proved him wrong. This place was so peaceful and the people here so contented; he dreaded the idea of them sharing the fate of Pencardden. *But that is why you must prepare them.*

Gawain supposed he ought to get back to that preparation and heaved himself to his feet. He wobbled a little but corrected himself without jarring the leg, and he made his way slowly to the water-butt with Mabb trotting at his heels. As he hobbled his way across the muddy grass, Gawain wondered how long it would be before he walked comfortably again. *And how long before you're fit to stand against the Green Man?*

On that front he was torn. Suppose he became fit enough to face him before the men of Tahrnax were fit to fight the Picts? It felt that the right thing to do would be to make for Maes Gwyr as soon as he was able and not trespass on their hospitality for longer than he had to. On the other hand, didn't he have a duty to see these men properly trained before he left them, rather than risk them fighting the Picts half-prepared and getting themselves slaughtered for their trouble? It wasn't a pleasant thought but there was always the chance that the Green Man would kill him when they fought, and then what would happen here? Would Ulfric stay and continue the training, or would he feel duty-bound to get Halwen and the others home as soon as possible, and take the news to King Lot of his son's death? Gawain frowned. It was a depressing dilemma and no mistake. He looked over at the milling men, all blissfully unaware of how terribly they were doing, and decided that, for now at least, they needed him more than he needed the Green Man.

At midday they took a long respite, and Cethin ordered food to be brought out from the longhall. It was impressive how much had been prepared for them, not just bread and cheese but several chickens too and mounds of fat little sausages. Naturally, Mabb had gone around most of the men looking suitably starved and had won himself so many sausages that he now lay with his head resting on Gawain's feet, looking smugly stuffed and sleepy. More than one of the locals was looking similarly full, and Gawain hoped they wouldn't all be hurling it up again when he started to push them later, because push them he must. The men sprawled about happily, most of them still under the impression that everything was going well, and Gawain hadn't the heart to tell them just how wrong they were in that. Their spirit still far outweighed their ability to listen, and he almost dreaded what trials the afternoon would bring.

The sun was pleasantly warm without being too hot, and Gawain tried to relax in it before having to get back to work. A little group had gathered around him, and Cethin looked up from his food to speak.

'I know we have a long way to go, but I think the men are progressing well.'

Ulfric looked cynical but Gawain decided not to stamp on Cethin's optimism.

'They will get there in time. How often can they be spared from their usual work?'

Cethin gestured towards the eating crowd.

'We still need our farmers and fishermen of course, but some can spare more time than others. I have cut down their tithes for this month to compensate any shortfall in production.'

Gawain's eyebrows went up and he wasn't alone. Ulfric and Halwen both looked shocked as well, and even Gareth looked a little confused. Gawain asked the question.

'Did Berlak order that?'

Cethin had taken another bite of cheese and so simply shook his head. After a moment he swallowed the morsel and explained.

'The lord pays little mind to such things, he leaves them to me.' The steward shrugged. 'He is barely here anyway.'

If anything that only made things more confusing and Cethin answered his guests' looks.

'Lord Berlak has kin all over the north and is forever visiting here and there on some errand or another. Before now we've gone half a year and more without seeing him.'

It made sense then that the people here treated Cethin with such respect; for much of the time he must have been their lord in all but name. Gawain wanted to ask what Luned thought of this but was too ashamed to speak her name aloud. Fortunately, Ulfric spoke the question first.

'Does his lady not rule whilst he is gone?'

Once again Cethin answered with a shrug.

'Sometimes, though she is often away with him, or on her own visits.' He looked around at the peaceful village and sighed. 'But it is always better here when they are home. It feels right.'

There was a brief pause where no-one really knew what to say, then Halwen cocked her head at Cethin.

'Does your lord have kin among the Picts?'

Cethin's brow furrowed.

'Not that I am aware, but he has so many people to visit I suppose it is possible.'

As he looked at her his eyes fell to the dagger at her hip, and he looked back up at Halwen's face.

'Do *you* have kin among the Picts, lady?'

Halwen's smile was polite rather than warm, but all the same it was a beautiful thing to see.

'My grandmother was of the far north, though I do not know of any Pictish kin still living.'

Cethin looked thoughtful for a moment, and Gareth spoke up defensively.

'But Halwen is of Lothian, born and raised with us.'

The scar on his temple did lend a certain roguishness to Gareth's face, but he was still a slender boy and Cethin was clearly not intimidated. He answered politely.

'It makes no difference to me, young lord. No-one can bear blame for their ancestry, and even among the Picts there are decent folk.' He smiled at Halwen. 'I do not doubt that your grandmother was one of them.'

Halwen smiled back, a little more warmly this time.

'She was. And the north is as beautiful a land as she always said.'

Cethin bowed his head to her.

'You are too gracious, lady.'

Gawain tried to ignore his habitual stab of foolish jealousy. Cethin hadn't been staring at Halwen or making any effort to pursue her, and so far as Gawain knew the steward was merely being courteous to a guest, but still it was hard to watch her being charmed by another man. *As if* your *charms are so much more preferable!* He decided to drag the conversation back to the training; Halwen wasn't his sweetheart anyway and he had no right to feel jealous.

'If some of your lads can be spared for it, their time might be well spent in making more shields? This practice is all very well but will be little use if only half of your men are properly armed.'

Cethin nodded his agreement.

'I have two of our lumber-men splitting planks even now. I have lent them what spare hands I can and, with a little good fortune, we should have enough shields to arm the remainder of the men in a few days' time.'

Gawain had to admit, Berlak had been a wise man to make Cethin his steward. He took a sip of his ale and nodded.

'Good. No doubt a few more will break during training, and the more we have available, the better.'

Ulfric let out a snorting chuckle.

'What your boys lack in skill they make up for in fervour; they've been battering those things to bits all morning.'

Cethin smiled at the half-compliment and repeated Gawain's words.

'We shall get there. And we appreciate the both of you lending us the benefit of your knowledge.'

Gawain felt his pride swell a little. True enough he was still young, but he had fought in a shieldwall and come out of it alive, and now older men were looking to him for advice on war. It was a pleasant feeling. He glanced towards Halwen, hoping she'd be looking impressed, but she was nibbling at a hunk of bread and seemed indifferent to Cethin's words. The little surge of happiness was doused and Gawain struggled to keep up a smile.

'You are more than welcome.'

Cethin smiled back but Gawain suspected he had noticed the way he'd looked at Halwen. Though he still had half a leg of chicken left to eat, the steward rose smoothly and drained the last of his ale.

'I think I will finish this in the shade.'

He gave Ulfric a quick look as he left and the Saxon picked up the hint. He too rose to his feet and gave Gareth's arm a tap on the way up.

'Come along,' he beckoned Mabb to him, 'let's give this lazy beast some exercise before he turns from hound to pig.'

Mabb didn't look keen on the idea but he dutifully stood and plodded over to Ulfric. Gareth got up as well and gave Mabb's ears a quick rub.

'You're not going to make him run are you?'

Ulfric snorted.

'And get my boots ruined with dog-vomit? A gentle walk about the houses is what he needs.' The Saxon tapped first his own midriff and then Mabb's. 'I suspect it's what we all need.'

Gareth nodded and turned to Gawain.

'Coming?'

Gawain shook his head.

'I may walk a little later.' He put a hand to his leg. 'But I'd slow down a snail at my pace.'

Gareth nodded and looked to Halwen before Ulfric could pull him away.

'How about you, Halwen?'

Gawain held his breath. This would be the deciding moment; Gareth might be oblivious but everyone else there, probably Mabb included, knew that this was a chance for Gawain and Halwen to be alone. Would she want that? The tiny pause seemed to last for days but eventually she spoke.

'I'll finish this first.' She held up her half-full cup. 'Go on and I will catch you up.'

Relief tinged with fear rushed through Gawain as the others left them. Halwen wanted to talk; now he just had to work out what to say to her. She looked up at him from where she sat and Gawain came out with it before she could say anything.

'I'm sorry for what happened.'

The words came out in a clumsy blurt and Gawain almost looked away, but he forced himself to keep his eyes on hers. Halwen didn't look angered but she didn't answer either, and so Gawain went on, slowing down a little.

'I meant no disrespect. I was overcome for a moment but I know that is no excuse.' He swallowed anxiously. 'Will you forgive me?'

Halwen paused only for a moment before she answered.

'You are right, that is no excuse.' Gawain felt his heart sink but then she gave him a small smile. 'But yes, I will forgive you.'

Gawain's heart went from sinking to flying in the space of an eye-blink and he felt himself struggling not to grin like a fool. He bowed his head.

'Thank you, Halwen.'

She shuffled across the grass until she sat close to him, then put her hand over his.

'Just don't press your luck in future.' She gave his hand a squeeze. 'Nothing good ever comes of rushing.'

Feeling her hand touching his again was wonderful, and Gawain wondered what he ought to say in response. Gaheris would have come up with something witty, and he tried to think what his brother might say in his place.

'I will try to restrain myself in future.' He gave what he hoped was a charming smile. 'If you'd like to join me in the longhall tonight, I swear to resist you as much as any man could.'

Halwen gave him a slightly odd look, and a moment later took her hand away from his.

'As much as any man could?' She sighed, clearly exasperated. 'Gawain, I…'

She didn't seem to know what to say next and rose from where she'd been sitting. Gawain felt a flutter of panic in his chest and rose too, albeit more awkwardly.

'I only meant…'

But she held up a hand and there was a glint of Pictish fire in her eyes, and Gawain wisely stopped talking.

'I know what you *meant*, but…'

Once again she seemed lost for words and Gawain was about to try to defend what he'd said, but the sound of soft footsteps came from behind them, and he turned to see sunlight shining from Iain's bald head. He was walking down from the hall with a confused look on his face, and Gawain only hoped he hadn't heard their conversation. His expression became concerned when he drew close.

'Is something wrong?'

Halwen was flushed but she waved a hand at the priest.

'Nothing a walk won't cure. Excuse me, father.'

With that she turned and walked briskly across the grass. Gawain cursed himself but put on a blank expression for Iain's sake.

'Just a disagreement, father. I spoke more harshly than I should have done.'

He was about to suggest going after her to apologise but Iain forestalled him, clearly not fooled.

'I think young Halwen would appreciate a little time alone before you speak again.' He gave Gawain a level look. 'And you might benefit from taking time to consider your words and actions.'

He didn't know how much the priest had deduced but he and Halwen had hardly been discreet in how close they'd been, and Iain had surely noticed the recent tension between them. Gawain nodded.

'You are right, father.'

Iain looked like he was about to launch into a lecture about lust and pride, and while it might have been deserved Gawain was in no mood to hear it. He was angry, half at himself for having said something to offend Halwen, and half at Halwen for having taken it the wrong way. Damn it all, she *knew* he'd just wanted to apologise, she'd even forgiven him for what happened at Pencardden, why did she have to take offence at an ill-judged jest? Why couldn't they just go back to how they were? He spoke before the priest could start his lecture.

'I had best get back to the men, father. They learn slower than bludgeoned sheep.'

Iain frowned and instead of disapproving of what was happening with Halwen, he disapproved of Gawain's attitude to the locals instead.

'We are still their guests, Gawain, and they have not been trained for battle the way you have.' He glanced over at the crowd of men eating their midday meal. 'And not all men are born to be warriors. That does not mean they should be looked down upon.'

Gawain was feeling low enough already without having to listen to Iain being right about something, and it was hard work not to snap at the old man.

'Yes, I know.'

Iain spoke evenly, making no comment on Gawain's tone.

'Then be sure that you keep that knowledge in mind.'

Gawain almost said something back but Iain went on before he could.

'I shall leave you to your work then. There are a few men here who will listen to the Word of God and I mean to encourage them.' He began walking away but then paused and turned his head. 'You would be wise to practice thinking before you speak and act, my boy. It will spare yourself and others a good deal of harm.'

Gawain wasn't sure if Iain was referring to his short words just now or to the problems between him and Halwen. *Probably both*. He sighed as the priest turned away again, regretting having shown him such insolence. As before he almost chased after him to apologise, but that would probably fly in the face of the advice he'd just given and so Gawain decided to stay put. Or rather, he decided to get back to work.

He let out a breath and started plodding down the slope to where the would-be-spearmen were eating. It would strain his nerves to watch their antics again, but he resolved to be as patient as he could with them. Besides, if he was lucky, getting frustrated at them would take his mind off the bloody mess he'd made of everything else.

Chapter Eighteen

Halwen had barely spoken a word to him at supper, and Gawain had fumed quietly through the meal; they'd been so close to making amends and now they were back to awkward silences again. He sat up in his bed and hacked at the little carving, spoiling a good deal of his earlier work as the knife bit into the ash. At least some of his anger was justified; the townsfolk had remained blithely complacent through the long day's training, seeing it more as a pleasant diversion than anything to be taken seriously. Their confidence in the wards around their home was unshakable, and the notion that any Pictish druid could undo them was simply inconceivable to them. Gawain knew little enough of the druid's art, but all the same it seemed a hugely naïve attitude.

His leg throbbed and, he set the mangled ash aside and flexed his knee a few times. He didn't know why that helped to ease the ache but it did, and he supposed that was all that really mattered. Without the carving to focus on he started thinking about the real source of his foul mood, and he genuinely couldn't decide if he was angrier at Halwen or at himself. The original fault had been his, and he'd handled the apology poorly but at least he *had* apologised. He'd done his best to make amends, so that surely ought to count for something? But apparently not.

Apparently Halwen could forgive him his actions but his clumsy jest afterwards was enough to make her angry again.

For a while he pondered how best to broach the subject with her tomorrow, then he snorted at his own ridiculousness; he was sitting here worrying about naïve villagers and a harmless quarrel when, just over the hill, the Green Man was waiting to fight him. Gawain was still undecided whether he ought to face him as soon as his leg was healed, or whether he should prioritise the training of the local men instead, and wait until they were competent before he left. He had until Samhain before the veil grew thin, which meant there was no great hurry to get the fight done. He had time enough to train them to a decent standard before the Green Man's power would swell again. But the men of Tahrnax didn't seem over-concerned about their danger, and his first priority ought to be to face the challenge he came here for, shouldn't it? Was it fear or duty persuading him to delay? No matter how much he thought on it Gawain couldn't decide what he should do, and Halwen's angry face kept interrupting his thoughts.

He was tempted to go back to his whittling, but a glance at the ash lump told him that was a bad idea. The deer was finally beginning to take shape, and his frustration from tonight had mutilated it enough already. *You have to calm down.* Iain was, as always, right; his mind needed discipline. Gawain closed his eyes and took a deep breath, trying to focus his thoughts. He hadn't got far in that attempt when he heard the door open, and the worst distraction imaginable came strolling into the room.

Luned looked as beautiful as ever in a long red dress, the silver band at her brow glittering gently in the firelight. She smiled at Gawain and without a word his hostess untied the green-and-gold girdle about her waist. Gawain took in a breath but she forestalled him.

'This was given to me by my grandmother many years ago.' She approached the bed and handed the belt out to him. 'She told me it carries a protective enchantment. I would have you wear it when you go to face your challenge.'

Gawain was a little lost for words and knew that his reply came off as oafish.

'You needn't… already you are too kind, I could not…'

But Luned waved him to silence and placed the girdle on the table.

'It would surely be the height of discourtesy to refuse so great a gift?'

She was right of course, and Gawain bowed his head.

'My thanks then, lady.'

In all truth, he'd been so busy half-hoping and half-dreading that Luned would kiss him again that the sudden gift had left him puzzled, especially since for a moment he'd thought she was about to undress right there in front of him. He told himself that it was a good thing that she hadn't. Luned lowered herself to perch on the bed but made no move to get close to him, and Gawain tried to stay relaxed as she spoke on.

'You and your Pictish girl seemed unhappy this evening?'

Gawain wasn't sure how much he ought to say of that and kept his answer vague.

'I gave her some offence a few days' past, and made a poor job of apologising for it.'

Luned's brows drew together.

'I cannot picture you wishing to cause offence to anyone.' She gave a smile that was part-teasing, part-contrite. 'Even when they make you feel awkward, still you behave with courtesy.'

A little touch of relief went through him at that; it seemed Luned was at least aware of how inappropriate she'd been.

'I try to be courteous, lady. But I did show her great disrespect.'

He looked away from her dark eyes for a moment, but he could tell that Luned was still frowning.

'Hard though that is to believe, did you not say you had apologised for whatever slight you did her?' When Gawain looked up he saw that she was smiling again. 'That is more than many a young man would do, and especially a young lord.'

It felt good to hear her say that. He *had* tried to make amends with Halwen after all. True, he'd botched it, but surely the intent had been the important thing? He met Luned's eyes and there was understanding there, and sympathy. She gave his good leg a pat and slowly stood up again.

'That girl should appreciate what she has in you, young Gawain. Few lords would countenance a smith's daughter treating him with such disregard, let alone the son of a king.'

For all his care for Halwen, Gawain couldn't help agreeing. He had admitted his mistake and asked her forgiveness, and that was indeed a great deal more than most lords would have done. It felt good to have someone tell him he wasn't in the wrong and he looked up at Luned to thank her for her understanding. But just as his eyes met hers, Luned's hand went to a tie at her shoulder, and a moment later the red dress was sliding down her body. The cloth barely rustled when it hit the floor, but Gawain wouldn't have noticed if it had clanged like a dropped cauldron; beneath the dress Luned was naked, and Gawain stared at her perfect body open-mouthed, all power of speech abandoning him as he took in the image. He hardened instantly.

Without a word Luned stalked towards him, her movements so graceful they were almost cat-like. Gawain could almost hear her purring as she reached the bed. There was no preamble; her lips met his the moment she came close enough, and one hand began deftly untying his trews. Luned's free hand found one of his and placed it gently over her breast, and

Gawain squeezed without even thinking. The flesh was soft but firm, and before he knew it, he was returning her kiss with vigour. Luned let out a satisfied moan, and when she took hold of his hardness Gawain gasped in reply. He kept kissing and caressing as Luned slowly began to stroke, and the feeling was something incredible and wonderful. A voice in his head was telling him to stop all this, but Gawain told it firmly to shut its damned noise.

How long that went on he couldn't say, but after a time Luned broke off the kiss and shuffled a little, moving her kisses down to his neck, and then his chest. For a moment Gawain felt disappointed that the movement took her perfect breasts out of his reach. Then her mouth moved lower, and his heart began hammering fit to burst. But the wild joy didn't last.

Now that she was no longer atop of him Gawain could see across the room again, and he almost cursed aloud as his eyes fell on his shield; the red star felt like it was glaring right into his soul. The holy symbol of the God of Rome and the warrior's virtues burned itself into his mind. Iain had painted that symbol himself to keep Gawain on a noble path, and now it stared at him in silent judgement. He was being dishonest and discourteous to a host who'd been kind to him, and behaving like a coward for stealing his wife's favours behind his back. He was betraying his devotion to Halwen who, quarrel or not, deserved his loyalty, and it was hardly an act of benevolence to treat one he cared about so poorly. *You are spitting on everything that Iain and Drustan would have you stand for.*

It took more effort than he would have thought possible, but seeing the shield had lent strength to the voice of his conscience, and Gawain put a hand under Luned's chin and raised her up to face him.

'Lady, we cannot. Forgive me, I…'

The flash of emotion in her dark eyes made him falter, but his hostess calmed within a heartbeat and whispered in her usual low voice.

'*Cannot*?' Her hand went on stroking him. 'It would seem to me that you very much *can*.'

Gawain put a hand on hers and, with some reluctance, drew it away.

'Say rather, *should* not, lady. You know the wrongness of this as much as I do.'

From the look on her face, that might not necessarily have been true. Or if it was, the voice of Luned's conscience was as quiet as a mouse.

'My husband will not be concerned by what we do, and your smith's daughter has been fool enough to reject you. Where is the wrong?' She smirked and placed a teasing kiss on his chest. 'Or has that priest of yours convinced you that all flesh is sin?'

She made as if to reach for him again but Gawain stopped her before she could.

'All *disloyalty* is sin; that is what matters.'

Once again he saw the briefest flash in Luned's eyes, but as before it was there and gone within a moment.

'Have it as you wish.'

She slid from the bed, still moving smooth as a cat, and Gawain forced himself not to stare when she stood and re-dressed herself. The green-and-gold girdle was still on the table but when he reached for it Luned saw the movement and raised a hand.

'Your gift still stands, young lord. If you are to face Lord Verdis you may be grateful for its enchantment.'

Gawain wasn't sure whether that was something he should do but he nodded nonetheless. His mouth was suddenly dry and when he spoke it came out as an awkward croak.

'My thanks, lady. Please do not think I mean you any offence, I…'

He'd been groping for words and was almost grateful when Luned interrupted him.

'Oh, I take no offence.' She smirked. 'Though I do wonder exactly what you will pass on to my husband this time.'

Gawain felt his stomach lurch. Passing on a kiss was one thing, but this had been a damned sight more than a kiss and there were limits to what his guilt could make him do! Luned laughed at his discomfort and took a step towards the bed.

'Amusing though it would be to watch you wrestle with that, I think I shall be merciful.'

She leaned forwards and planted a gentle kiss on his cheek. He hated himself for it but a hefty part of Gawain wished that she would stay there and do more, but he shoved the urge away with an effort. When Luned straightened again she was smiling.

'You may pass *that* on to Berlak.'

Relief managed to drown his lust, and without another word Luned turned and flowed gracefully to the door. The smile she gave as she left said more than any words could have done, and for all his frustrations, Gawain took comfort from one thing; if nothing else, tonight had made his decision for him. He'd resisted her twice already but he had no idea if he'd be strong enough to do so again. The longer he stayed here the more persuasive she would become, and the greater the chances of his falling to temptation and betraying God and Halwen both. He sighed and laid his head back, knowing full well that he would not sleep but glad at least that his doubts had been erased. There was nothing else for it; whether his leg was healed or not, tomorrow he would leave this place, and go to face the Green Man.

There was something comforting in the smell of woodsmoke. Gawain had no idea what made the smell so pleasant but whatever it was, he was glad of it this morning. He needed all the comfort he could get. The grass beneath his knees was damp with dew and his leg was starting to ache, but he kept as still as possible and tried to focus his mind. He kept his eyes on the carved deer at the centre of his little fire and whispered quiet prayers over the crackling blaze.

'Cernunnos, Lord of Trees and Beasts, Huntsman, Horned One, and God of War, hear me. I am Gawain ab Lot of Lothian, and this work of my hands is my gift to you. Whatever wrongs I have done to you and to others, I ask your pardon. I ask that you lend me strength and courage for the fight to come, that I may prove my worth against your champion, Verdis of Maes Gwyr.'

Gawain kissed his fingers and placed them on the grass, as close to the flickering fire as he dared. He didn't know how much heed the Huntsman would pay to his prayers but he'd be a fool not to appeal to him before a fight like this. Of course, by that same token, he'd be a fool to ignore the god whose marks were painted on his shield.

He had set the little offering-fire in the shadow of Tahrnax's north rampart, and had left the shield leaning against the bank. The picture of the Virgin was out of sight of course, but he fixed his eyes on the five-pointed star and whispered a second prayer.

'Father God, forgive me my many sins against you and against my fellows. I go to fight a man who would threaten harm to my people. Lend strength to my arm, Lord Christ, and courage to my heart in the trial to come. In the name of the Father, Son, and Holy Ghost, amen.'

He bowed his head and crossed himself. No doubt Iain or Elgan could have spoken more eloquent prayers, but Gawain hoped the two gods took his meaning. He took a long, slow breath, inhaling resolve and exhaling fear. The problem with following Iain's advice meant that, unlike when he rushed in hot-blooded, there was plenty of time for fear and doubts to cloud his mind as he considered his actions. Gawain had taken all night to think over his decision, and while he was sure it was right, overcoming his fear of facing the Green Man was no easy task. But this must be done, no matter what. He kept breathing slowly, drawing strength from the prayers he'd made and steadily banishing his fears. *The gods protect the right, and I fight with right on my side.*

Gawain stayed kneeling there for a moment longer, enjoying the smell of the woodsmoke, then he ground his teeth against the pain in his leg and slowly rose to his feet. His mailshirt jingled a little as it settled, though not enough to cover up his grunt. He felt Cethin take a pace towards him. The steward had been there when Gawain had snuck to the kitchen for a quick breakfast away from the others, and when he'd asked him where a good place for the offering-fire would be, Cethin had insisted on taking him there in person. Gawain held up a hand before Cethin could offer his help.

'I am well.'

The truth of that was negligible, but he refused to begin the last step of his task by leaning on another man's shoulder. *I should have begun this whole business alone; then Drustan and Burian would still be alive, and Halwen would be waiting in Dun Edin and thinking well of me.* He cursed his weakness for letting the others come with him, and anger dulled the pain as he stalked towards his weapons. Once again Cethin approached ready to help, but again Gawain waved him away.

He buckled on his swordbelt and slung his shield across his back, then took up his war-axe in his right hand. The green-and-gold girdle was tied to his belt, and enchanted or not, Gawain felt it was right that he wear it today. Whatever sins she might arouse in him, Luned had done him great kindness in healing his leg, and if she wished Gawain to wear her favour then he would do so. Before coming out he'd considered trying to hide it by wearing it beneath the mailshirt, but he'd quickly decided against that; better that Berlak take offence and Gawain face his displeasure than to add to his shame with one more deception. Cethin saw the coloured belt but made no comment on it.

The steward stayed with him until the fire consumed the little deer, then he doused the flames with a pitcher of stream-water. The pair began walking back towards the hall, and it was Cethin who broke the silence.

'You are sure you must leave today?'

Gawain nodded.

'I've little choice.'

Cethin didn't press him for details but still he looked concerned.

'Is your leg strong enough?'

Gawain grunted.

'I will manage.'

The limb hurt when he put weight on it, but he was able to walk and that was all that mattered.

A few paces further on Cethin spoke up again.

'I will not go into Maes Gwyr, but I will take you far enough to show you where it lies.' He gave an apologetic half-smile. 'You will have to forgive my lack of courage; we are raised to avoid that place.'

Gawain was grateful to have a guide even part of the way, and he nodded his thanks.

'You are kind, Cethin. And I do not think you lack for courage.' He tried to smile but didn't quite manage it. 'You are simply a sensible man.'

Cethin bowed his head and they continued to the hall in silence. Part of Gawain had wanted to just disappear without a word, but it would be cowardice to avoid saying his farewells, and it seemed that Cethin had seen to it that he had no choice in the matter anyhow.

Waiting for them outside the hall were Berlak, Iain, Ulfric, Gareth and Halwen, all clearly expecting him and unsurprised that he was armed and armoured. Gawain huffed out a breath, thanked his good fortune that Luned had not come out with them, and strode up to the group. Iain was first to approach him, worry written across every line of his face.

'Gawain, my boy, you are in no fit state to…'

But the priest suddenly stopped, as if he'd remembered some vital fact, and a very small smile twitched the corner of his mouth. He sighed before he spoke.

'I am not going to be able to dissuade you, am I?'

Gawain put a hand on the old man's shoulder. It felt thin beneath his black robe.

'No, father. It must be done and I will do it now.'

Rather than try to make an argument or lecture him, Iain simply reached up and gently drew Gawain's head down to his level. The priest kissed his brow and gave his arm a gentle tap.

'God go with you, my son.'

Gawain bowed his thanks before moving towards Berlak. Before he could reach his host, Gareth came scurrying up with Mabb close on his heels. Gawain scratched Mabb's ears and held up his palm before his brother could speak.

'You are not coming with me.'

Gareth paid no attention to the command.

'We're blood, Gawain. Don't think I'll let you go to this without me.'

Gawain shook his head.

'This is my task, and mine alone. You stay here and help Ulfric train the locals. It is important.'

Gareth was ready to argue but Ulfric spoke softly from beside him.

'Do you want this place to share Pencardden's fate?'

Gareth looked at his toes for a moment before answering.

'No.'

Ulfric nodded.

'Then best you stay with me and help prepare these folk.'

Gawain didn't know if Gareth knew it was all just a gesture to make him feel better, but he was a bright enough lad that he could probably guess. Once again Gawain tried and failed to summon a smile. He settled for ruffling the boy's hair.

'I will be back before you notice I'm gone.'

Even now Gareth looked like he might try to argue, but Halwen put a hand on his arm and, though she didn't speak, it seemed enough to persuade him.

'Alright.'

He threw his arms around Gawain but only stayed there for a heartbeat before backing off and turning his face away. Gawain hardened his heart and shared a quick embrace with Ulfric.

'Keep them working hard.'

The Saxon nodded.

'I will. You are sure…?'

Gawain clapped his shoulder.

'Yes. Stay here.'

Ulfric gave another nod.

'Very well. Wodan go with you.'

Gawain wasn't sure how many gods going with him would be too many, but then remembered that he was fighting a man who could lose his head and laugh about it, and rationalised that the more help he had, the better.

The last of his friends was Halwen, and Gawain hesitated for less than a second before stepping forward and embracing her; too much talk would only ruin things even more. He whispered in her ear before she could speak.

'I am sorry for everything, forgive me if you can.'

It was a struggle to let her go, he'd missed holding her so much, but he forced himself to release her after a final squeeze. It warmed his heart that she squeezed him back. Halwen said nothing as they broke off the embrace but there was softness in her eyes, and Gawain let himself feel a flutter of hope before moving on to his host.

While he wasn't exactly grim Lord Berlak was a long way from his usual cheery self, and the smile he gave Gawain looked strained.

'You have a heart of oak, young lord.'

Gawain touched his host's arm and kissed his cheek.

'You have been a more than generous host, lord.' He indicated the green-and-gold belt. 'Your lady wife offered me this token of hers for the challenge, I hope you do not object?'

Berlak's smile became a touch warmer.

'Of course not.' He clapped Gawain's shoulder with a sigh. 'It may seem an odd saying since you go to face Lord Verdis; but Huntsman's luck to you, my friend.'

Gawain nodded his thanks, then raised his voice and put all the hope he could into the words.

'I shall see you all before sundown.'

They responded with smiles and nods, hiding their fears as much as he was, and Gawain turned away before he could betray himself. Cethin was waiting patiently, a waterskin slung from his belt, and when Gawain began to walk the steward fell into step beside him. He knew the others would still be watching and stalwartly refused to limp. From what Cethin said Maes Gwyr was a short walk north over the hill, and Gawain suspected his leg would be burning long before they got there, but for now at least he would not show his weakness. He imagined Halwen's eyes on him as they reached the causeway over the ditch, and hoped quietly that she had indeed forgiven him. *You can come back and ask her when this is done.* The voice in his mind was positive, if not exactly convincing, but Gawain tried to heed it nonetheless. *You bested him once, you can do it again.*

A tingle shot through him as they passed the ghost-ward but Gawain did not shudder. He wasn't a frightened child on his first trip into the woods; he was the son of a king on his way to battle a champion. He had killed men in combat, he had held a shieldwall, and he had faced this Green Man before and taken the bastard's head. Gawain focused his gaze on the hills ahead, and stoked what courage he could find into a steady blaze. *This time he'll see what the sons of Lothian are made of. This time, his damned head will* stay *off!*

Chapter Nineteen

Tahrnax was no easy place to find, but thanks to the Grey Woman it was finally within their grasp. The druid had only returned to them at nightfall the day before, after Mhari's warband had spent most of that day blindly following the river east in the hopes she would re-appear. She had, and after consulting the bones she had insisted they travel through the night to reach their target. There'd been no small amount of grumbling but none had dared oppose her openly, and once Mhari made it clear that this was her plan too, the warband had trudged through the darkness in sullen silence. Now Tahrnax was finally in her sight, and Mhari had to admit, she was feeling nervous for the attack.

She crouched at the tree-line and watched as the ramparts grew clearer in the morning light. Stories of this place always spoke of dark powers defending it, and Darina's scouting had convinced her that they'd not been exaggerated; Tahrnax's ghost-ward had been made with human souls. When the archer had returned her face had been pale as milk, and Mhari had made sure she gave her news out of earshot of the others. Plenty of villages placed wards about their perimeter, but so long as a warband made a sacrifice to Taranis, or better yet had a druid with them, they could generally be passed in safety. But those wards were made from the skulls of stoats, badgers and the occasional bull, and the power they held was rarely enough to kill. Mhari had never even heard of a ward made with human souls, and a chill had gone through her at the prospect of facing them. *And what kind of savage bastard is their druid, to trap human souls into a ghost-ward?*

Naturally, Mhari had kept up an indifferent face in front of her warriors; the Grey Woman had been confident that she could break the wards and Mhari had encouraged her people to believe her. Their druid was not without power after all, there was every chance she could indeed bring down Tahrnax's defences and let the warband through unharmed. Nevertheless, Mhari was tempted to let Temar cross the boundary first.

She glanced down the line to where the cur loitered in a little gaggle of his cronies. He was still wearing the scale armour of Lothian's champion, and no doubt he'd be using Drustan's skull to drink Tahrnax's mead tonight. Mhari often wondered why men like Darr, who for all his faults was at least a bold fighter, followed this lying dog so loyally, then she answered her own question as she always did; greed. Temar was a shallow bastard but he had wealth to expect when Alva died, and men would always flock to the smell of silver. Coward though he was Temar at least *looked* big and strong, and once or twice Mhari had even witnessed him fighting capably. In the minds of Darr and the others that was clearly enough to justify hanging about him and pretending he was a war-leader.

Mhari felt the familiar surge of disgust and turned away from the sight of Temar and his men. Conn was right; she would have to deal with him, and soon, but it was a difficult proposition. If she waited until after his mother was dead Mhari risked facing a warband of men seduced by Alva's wealth, which was of course undesirable. On the other hand, if she challenged him or killed him out of hand *before* that happened then Mhari would lose Alva's favour, and that she was loathe to risk. She touched Brathir's pommel and whispered a prayer for the Thunderer's blessing. Hopefully Taranis would sympathise with her plight and guide some lucky Venicon's pitchfork into Temar's ugly face.

Tahrnax's wealth should at least mean Temar was near the front today. In theory all loot was divided up after a raid, but in reality most warriors pocketed the first silver they found. If his greed outweighed his natural cowardice, Temar might find himself far enough forward to be in real peril, and if the Thunderer listened to Mhari's prayers, some fatal accident might befall him. *And if not, there's always Darina.*

The lean-bodied archer was crouching nearby, and Mhari resisted looking in her direction. She'd been told to keep an arrow ready for Temar and was simply waiting for her lord's nod as consent to do the deed, but Mhari was keeping that plan as her final resort; if Darr or any of the others suspected Mhari's hand in Temar's death, she would either have to kill them all or risk Alva hearing that she'd had her son murdered. Mhari tapped her fingers on her sword's leather grip. It would have to be done one way or the other, though, and it would have to be done soon.

She frowned and tried to focus on the task ahead of her. *The way* she *does*. Mhari glanced over at their strange druid. Troublesome though she was, Mhari couldn't deny that the Grey Woman's concentration was enviable, and her powers in general were becoming ever more apparent. When she had returned to the warband she had dodged the question of her incorrect prophesy by saying the attack at Pencardden had not been part of their path, and nimbly avoided making Temar look a fool by making some comment on their sacrifice being worthwhile for what was gained. If that had been all then Mhari wouldn't have been impressed, but what she'd said afterwards had made the warriors' hair stand on end. Long before she'd had the chance to hear the news from them, the Grey Woman had told them all about Drustan's death at Pencardden, and had even known about Lot's son being among those who'd escaped. *Once Temar is gone and there is no dissent among my folk, I may actually be grateful to have this prophetess around.*

The woman herself was still sitting where she had planted herself at sunrise, a cluster of tiny bones in her lap and a wide circle of empty space around her. Apparently disabling the ghost-ward was no easy task even for her, and her brow was creased as she mumbled her incantations. Her eyes were on the earth bridge but they seemed oddly unfocused, and her lips had been moving silently since the moment she sat down. Mhari wondered for a moment what spells or curses she was casting, then decided that she didn't want to know; arcane knowledge often came at the cost of one's sanity, and Mhari was happy to live in rational ignorance of magic.

The bridge was too far off to make out the skulls but the whole warband knew that a ghost-ward would be there, and Mhari felt Conn shift in place beside her. His voice was a reverent whisper.

'Did she say how long it would take?'

Mhari shook her head and answered just as quietly.

'No. Only that we had to be here early.'

She wasn't looking his way but she could guess that Conn was frowning.

'She didn't…'

But he stopped suddenly and put a hand on her arm. Mhari kept silent instinctively and turned to look at him. Conn nodded towards the distant settlement. Two figures had emerged through the bank and were crossing the earthen causeway. They were far too distant to see clearly, and there was no real point in staying silent, but nonetheless she said nothing as she watched the pair walk. Mhari wished they'd been able to wait somewhere closer, the woods grew almost up to the ramparts further north, but the Grey Woman had needed a clear straight line towards the ghost-ward, and there'd been little point in arguing with her.

Mhari squinted as best she could at the two men. One seemed to be much larger than the other and was carrying an axe in one hand, but beyond that she could make out no details. Beside her, Mhari heard the gentle stretch of a bow under tension, and saw that Darina was testing her string. She'd yet to notch an arrow to it, over that distance even she would struggle to land two killing shots, but she made ready in case the men approached the woods. There was no need. The two men turned north and began trudging that way at no great speed, and the warband let out a collective breath. They were no real threat on their own, but if an alarm was raised before the Grey Woman was done, who knew what horrors Tahrnax's ghost-ward might unleash upon them?

As the men disappeared Mhari found her patience fraying, and she knew she wouldn't be the only one. She looked over to where the Grey Woman sat and wondered if she dared interrupt her spell-craft to question her. The druid must have sensed her look because she spoke before Mhari made up her mind.

'Soon.'

The effort of that one word seemed to strain her, and Mhari wisely neither answered nor questioned her, and instead turned her attention back to the distant bank. Beside her, Conn nudged her arm and held out a handful of vervain, and Mhari took it with a nod and tucked it into her tunic. Even warriors who didn't usually bother were wearing the purple flowers today, and Mhari wasn't too proud to join them; no matter how strong the Grey Woman's powers might be, anything that warded off ill-luck was welcome here.

She looked at the haunted settlement with a little thrill of anticipation. Mhari wasn't fool enough to feel no fear at all, but it was being drowned out by excitement as she imagined what was to come. If they did this, if she took her warband into Tahrnax and came out with its wealth, her name would be a legend in every corner of the north, and Mhari mer Raghnal would become Mhari the Bold, Mhari the Fearless, or Mhari the Ghost-Killer. She liked the sound of that. That was a title to make even Alva mer Colm green with envy, and every warlord of Lothian would soon learn to fear that name. Mhari smiled to herself as she drummed her fingers on Brathir's grip, imagining how it would sound to have that name cheered by her warriors. *Soon.* Soon they would be done here. Soon, Mhari's name would be roared to the morning sky.

Chapter Twenty

The sky had been overcast when they'd crossed the ditch, and by the time Gawain and Cethin made it halfway around the hill Bel's chariot was hidden by looming clouds. There was no scent of rain in the air, at least not yet, but all the same Gawain doubted that a darkening sky could be called a good omen. He forced his doubts away and trudged on, trying not to wince when he put weight on the injured leg. Cethin had led them in a long loop around the hill rather than trekking straight over it, and while Gawain was grateful for the gesture, even a gradual uphill climb was murder on the aching limb. A voice sneered in his head. *A bloody hill is beating you, and you think you're in good enough shape to face the Green Man?* He grimaced as pain shot through the leg and told the voice in his head to shut its damned noise; this had to be done, and whining about it would change nothing.

Cethin dutifully ignored his intermittent grunts and maintained a slow pace beside him. At a guess Gawain suspected they'd been going less than an hour, though already it felt like he'd spent half a day on his feet. The land around them was at least beautiful to look at, despite the dimness of the sky. The grassy hillside glowed with health, with great swathes of bluebells dotting it like patches on a blanket. The tranquillity of the place seemed almost mocking; Gawain couldn't help thinking how pleasant it would be to spend a spring morning up here with Halwen by his side, and instead he was trudging through it with his leg on fire, on his way to fight a man who would probably kill him.

It took an effort but Gawain managed to shove away his doubt; the man who expected failure would only ever prove himself right. *I will not fail. I mustn't.* He strode on across the slope and thought about Gareth. The Green Man had made it clear that he intended to return to Dun Edin, and that if Gawain didn't fight him he would fight one of his kinsmen instead. *And next time his game might not have such a harmless ending.* A vision came to him of the Green Man holding up Gareth's severed head, and he heard his mother screaming as clearly as if she'd been standing beside him. *No.* No matter what else occurred, he would not let that happen.

It did not take them long to circle the hill, and when Cethin's footsteps faltered, Gawain knew they were almost there. He looked over at the steward.

'If you wish to leave me here, I am contented.'

The normally-composed man was looking pale and nervous, but he shook his head.

'I will go a little further. Soon enough we will be able to see his hall.'

Gawain raised an eyebrow.

'His hall?'

Cethin nodded.

'I know of nobody else who lives there but yes, Lord Verdis has a longhall in the valley.'

Gawain thought he must be an odd sort of spirit to require a hall to live in, but then there was a chance that he was no Huntsman's emissary at all but a sorcerer of some kind. He might be a druid gone mad from too long in the woods, or a warrior possessed by some magic of dark trees. Gawain told himself it didn't matter.

'Very well.'

They walked on in silence and, true enough, only a short way further on Gawain caught sight of the Green Man's hall. It stood on the edge of a great dark forest that stretched across the valley floor and then up the northern slope. In shape it looked much like any other longhall, though the roof was low and seemed to be of turf rather than thatch. In front of the hall was an open space of grass with a wooden pen at one end, though Gawain saw no livestock in it, and his imagination painted an unnerving picture of what sort of beasts this lord might keep. A glance at Cethin made it plain he was uncomfortable being this close to the Green Man's domain, and the steward gave him an embarrassed half-smile.

'We used to dare one another to come this far when I was a boy.' He nodded downhill to what looked like a false crest. 'Not one of us ever went further than that.'

Gawain could tell that part of him wished he had the will to go further, but he had asked enough of Cethin already, and pushing him into something he so clearly dreaded would be unfair.

'I'm sure you will be needed back at the village.' He tried to keep his tone light but couldn't bring himself to smile. 'Your fellows need to get back to their training, and Ulfric cannot handle them all by himself.'

Cethin looked awkward. The excuse was flimsy and they both knew it, and Gawain did his best to sound both firm and friendly.

'This is my task, not yours. I must go down there alone, you understand?'

The older man nodded and cleared his throat.

'As you say.' He put a hand on Gawain's shoulder and met his eyes for a moment. 'May all your gods be with you, lord.'

Gawain clapped Cethin's arm and set off before things could become uncomfortable. Cethin wasn't a coward, but he didn't want to stay here and there was no reason to make him feel he had to. Gawain trudged down to the false crest, fighting back a grimace as the slope grew steeper. It was tempting to look back and see if his guide had stayed to watch his descent, but he decided he didn't want to; if he was still there it would only make Cethin feel guiltier to see him look. Gawain kept his eyes forward and walked on, whispering prayers to Christ and Cernunnos alike as the green-roofed hall drew nearer.

The valley was not deep, but the further down the slope he went, the closer the air seemed to feel. The sun was still obscured by clouds and Gawain could have sworn the morning had been brisk a few moments ago, yet the closer he got to the valley floor, the warmer he became. By the time the ground flattened out he was sweating beneath his mailshirt, and any trace of a breeze had long since vanished. He could almost feel the magic radiating from the longhall, and for a moment his gut felt cold despite the heat. Gawain thrust out his chin and made a point of increasing his pace, firmly ignoring his throbbing leg. He was *not* afraid. He could beat this man and he *would* beat this man. He would take his head, set it alight, then limp back to Tahrnax and collapse into Halwen's arms. The cold in his gut refused to vanish but he growled under his breath and kept going towards the hall. Just one fight and this would be over. One swing of his axe, and he could go home.

He was maybe ten paces from the longhall's doors when they creaked open of their own accord. The sight was unnerving but Gawain did not break his stride; he had Luned's green-and-gold girdle at his belt, he had the shield with its red-painted star at his back, and he had the blood of King Lot of Lothian in his veins. He called out to the blackness of the hall.

'You'll need more than some conjurer's trick to scare me off.' He spread his arms, holding the heavy axe high for his enemy to see. 'I am Gawain ab Lot! I am the man who took your head when last we met!'

There was silence from the hall and Gawain called again.

'Verdis of Maes Gwyr, you said that you would face me again. Here I am!'

For a moment there was no answer, and a mad part of Gawain dared to think that the Green Man was hesitating. But then a shadow appeared in the darkness of the doorway, and a moment later he saw the outline of a big man in a heavy cloak, with shaggy hair and a thick beard, and a long-handled weapon in one hand. It took every ounce of his courage for Gawain to keep moving forward, as the Green Man stepped into the light and bared his teeth in a wolfish smile.

'Greetings, Gawain ab Lot.' He too spread his arms. 'Here *I* am.'

The coldness in his gut threatened to spread to his legs, but Gawain battered the feeling down. The Green Man looked just as impressive as he had when last they met; still tall and wild with green hair and beard, and a cloak of evergreen leaves over his shoulders. He wasn't wearing his antlered helm but Gawain had clearly not caught him unawares. He wore his shirt of bronze scales beneath the heavy cloak, and everything in his bearing spoke of a man who'd been expecting trouble, and was unworried about it. Gawain stopped just out of striking range and planted his feet.

'You said you wished to face me again.' He tapped his axe on the ground. 'I thought I might visit *your* home for our second fight.'

It was hard to see behind the beard but Gawain thought the Green Man was smirking.

'So keen? I also said that I would return at Beltane. You would have been better served embracing your year rather than rushing to meet me again.'

He stepped from the shadows just as the sun broke through the clouds, and his many hues of green seemed to shine in the morning light. The attempt to intimidate him only angered Gawain, and he put scorn into his voice.

'A year of waiting with a sword above my head? A year to sap my courage as I wait for you to return and threaten me and mine once again?' He let the shield slip from his back and moved his axe into a two-handed grip. 'Better to strike you down now and have done with it.'

The Green Man looked completely unworried by the threat and took his time in hefting his own weapon. Even his leather gauntlets had a green tinge to them, and he ran his hand smoothly along the axe-haft as he answered.

'It is no easy task, and I will not stop you if you choose to leave now and postpone your fate. A wise man would turn and head back to Tahrnax whilst yet he could.'

Gawain bared his teeth.

'You are not the first man to call me unwise, and you won't be the last.' He gripped the axe tighter and bellowed out the last words. 'Take your guard!'

Gawain waited less than a heartbeat before striding forward. The Green Man made no move, and Gawain brought his axe up for a blow that would split his skull. Just as he moved into range and the axe began to fall, the Green Man released his grip and held a hand up in front of him. Gawain didn't see what he did, but at that instant there was a noise like a whip-crack and a sharp, choking smell, and a tiny burst of fire appeared from nowhere. Flames leaped from the Green Man's fingers, and Gawain jerked his head back in shock. A moment later the flames had vanished, but before he could attack again the Green Man's axe was moving, and it seemed his cloak was not restricting him today. Gawain was forced to back off; even if his mailshirt managed to stop the cutting edge, the blows being swung at him would be hard enough to break bones.

He retreated a couple of paces and brought his own weapon back to guard, and the Green Man did the same thing. Gawain's heart was hammering at the sorcery he'd seen, but he forced himself to stay calm and breathe slowly, his eyes on his opponent. What little face could be seen beneath the hair and beard seemed to be amused, and Gawain fought to control his anger at the sight. Slowly, the Green Man began circling to his left, and Gawain guessed that he was trying to angle him so that the sun was in his eyes. He kept his knees bent, ignored the pain in his wounded leg, and took care to mirror the movement slowly. *You can't afford to let him turn you around. You must attack first.*

The prospect of another flash of fire was daunting, but so was the prospect of Bel's chariot dazzling him, and Gawain lunged forward while the Green Man was still trying to circle. The axe-swing missed when his enemy ducked, but Gawain had expected that and smoothly switched the attack to a strike with the butt-end. Somehow the Green Man anticipated him and stepped in at an angle, his own axe-haft blocking Gawain's. For a dreadful moment their faces were only a hand's breadth apart, then the Green Man sprang back, surprisingly agile in his heavy cloak, and landed outside of Gawain's cutting range. He held up a hand and sunlight shone from the green-and-gold of Luned's girdle. Gawain felt coldness in his gut again.

'A fine trinket you had here, young Gawain. Though not yours, I think?' The Green Man smiled at him. 'Mortal strength is of no use here, my friend. It is not too late; lay down your axe and ask my pardon, and you may return to Berlak's lady unharmed.'

Gawain didn't answer. He didn't know exactly what enchantment the belt held, but whatever it was it was lost to him now, and in the hands of his enemy; he couldn't give him time to use it. With a roar he charged forward, hoping to catch the Green Man while he was gloating, but it seemed he had been ready for just such an attempt. Before Gawain could raise his axe to strike, his opponent was moving in and bringing his own weapon to bear. There was no way to pull back and so Gawain shoved forward and met the swing haft to haft, using the momentum of his charge to drive forwards. Magical though he was, the Green Man must have weighed less than Gawain did, and the force of the clash drove him back a stumbling pace.

His weapon was up again in an eye-blink, and he even smiled as Gawain pressed after him. But now Gawain was smiling too, remembering. *I beat you before, I will do it again*. Magic or not, if the Green Man could be unbalanced then he could be defeated. Fear of his sorcery vanished and Gawain felt the war-axe move smoothly in his hands, his muscles obeying the countless hours of training he had inflicted on them. He obeyed Drustan's lessons without any conscious thought, swinging with grace and power tempered with precision and control. The Green Man was forced to back away again, and then again, ducking and dodging desperately as Lothian steel glittered in the morning sunlight. Gawain dared to let hope flare through him as he closed in on his enemy, and when the

Green Man's cloak caught beneath his boot, Gawain bellowed in triumph and brought the axe down for a killing stroke.

Then the same whip-crack of sound, the same choking smell, and fire flashed a hand's breadth from Gawain's face. He cried out and rocked back on his heels, suddenly seeing nothing but white. Pain flared in his hand as something struck the fingers, and an eye-blink later the Green Man's axe slammed into Gawain's weapon, catching it mid-haft and sending it flying from his grip. Though he could barely see Gawain brought his fists up instinctively, and when he felt his enemy approach he swung a punch at what felt like head height. The blind strike was pitifully easy to dodge, and Gawain's hand met nothing but air. Before he could try again something solid cracked into his sternum, and as the wind rushed out of him he felt a boot sweep through his calf.

Gawain crashed to the ground and couldn't hold back a cry as his wounded leg screamed with pain. He tried to scramble up but the touch of metal on his throat made him freeze in place, his heart hammering. His sight was still marred with dark spots but he made out the shadow of the Green Man standing over him, a huge black shape against the sunny sky.

'A fine attempt, young Gawain. When you see your forefathers, you may greet them with pride.'

The cool metal vanished from his neck and Gawain heard the jangling of scales as his enemy raised the weapon to strike. There was nowhere he could move to, his leg was on fire, and he could barely even see his enemy. It was over. This was death. He tried to shout for Lothian with his final breath, or call Halwen's name or some prayer or curse, but all that came out as the war-axe fell was a wordless scream of defiance.

When the metal struck his neck it was surprisingly painless, and for a foolish moment Gawain thought he had died without realising it. Then he blinked again and realised he was still lying where he was, still battered and half-blinded, with an axe-blade on his neck that had just given him the lightest scratch. He squinted and tried to look up at the Green Man, but he was still a vague shape against the brightness of the sky. His voice, however, was unmistakably merry.

'I have landed my blow, Gawain ab Lot. And first blood is drawn.'

He felt the axe leave his neck, and Gawain put a hand to the tiny cut. Barely a speck of red touched his fingers, and when he looked up again, a leather-clad hand was reaching down to him. He took it without thinking, and with the Green Man's help he struggled to his feet.

Gawain stood there, his breath coming out in gasps, and stared at the man he had just been fighting. His sight was growing clearer with every blink but even so he was sure his eyes were lying to him. The leafy cloak was lying abandoned a few feet away, and his enemy's great mass of green hair had vanished. Gawain knew his jaw was hanging open but he didn't know what he could say; what had once been a spirit of the Huntsman had become merely a tall man with a brown-and-grey beard, and a familiar, jovial face. Berlak smiled, and Gawain kept staring, dumbstruck, as he clapped him companionably on one shoulder.

'Well done, my lad. Well done.'

Chapter Twenty-One

Mhari had been right about her helm's design; the skull's eye-sockets had been widened so well that her vision was barely limited at all, and even the weight of the horns made almost no difference to how the helm sat. Alva's gift truly was a fine piece of work, and today it would inspire terror in the people of Tahrnax. Mhari closed the cheek-pieces and tied the straps beneath her chin. The time had come. The Grey Woman had finally finished working her magics, and at Mhari's signal the attack would begin. Despite their druid's evident powers Mhari's heart still fluttered at the prospect of crossing a human ghost-ward, but to show hesitancy now was to court disaster, and she focused instead on the riches and reputation that lay beyond those posts.

She flicked a final glance at Conn and Darina, then rose from where she crouched and started running for the causeway. The rest of the warband broke from cover to follow her, and within a few seconds the first war-cries began to sound. Mhari supposed she ought to disapprove, she'd told them to keep silent until the ward was crossed, but the rest of the warriors were no doubt as wary of the spirits as she was, and if it gave them courage then she wouldn't reprimand them for it. The warlord upped her pace and screamed out with the others.

'Garnaith!'

The Picts reached the causeway without any sign of life from the village, and Mhari assumed they were either too slow to see their danger or too afraid to do anything but hide. She paused at the ditch, but only long enough to point the skulls out to those men she'd tasked with dealing with them; the Grey Woman had said that all the power of the ghost-ward was now locked in the skulls themselves. She had given the men herbs to sprinkle around the grisly totems, and once a fire was set upon them the magic in the bones would be rendered harmless. It would have been better if the Grey Woman had come with them to deal with this herself but, as usual, she was hanging back from the fighting and letting the warriors do the dirty work.

Mhari set her men to their tasks, and the moment the fires were lit she strode across the causeway with Brathir in hand. She felt a shiver as she passed the posts, their empty eyes seemed to follow her, but she stamped the fear down and put faith in Taranis, the vervain, and the magics of the Grey Woman. In that order. She crossed the boundary completely unharmed, closely followed by Conn and Darina, and the rest of the warband surged forward when they saw their leaders breach Tahrnax's defences. Darina had an arrow already nocked to her bow, and once they passed through the bank she looked to her lord for instruction. Mhari jerked her head southwards and the archer loped off in that direction; if Temar had to suffer an accident today, best that the instrument of that accident was a long way from Mhari when it happened.

The rest of the warband rushed into the settlement, which was filled with well-made homes in good repair. In themselves they hardly spoke of a life of opulence, but Mhari had yet to see a Venicon town where everything was in such good order; the roofs weren't thatched with gold, but the very fact that everything looked to be of such quality told her that this was a place where wealth would be found. Mhari ran past the houses with Conn at her side, and had just begun to wonder where all the people were when they rounded a corner and came to an open space at the settlement's heart.

It seemed that Tahrnax had been built around a low hill with a longhall sat atop of it. Like the other buildings it did not look grand but was clearly well-maintained, and Mhari didn't doubt that there would be silver aplenty hidden in its chambers. Her first instinct was to rush up the slope and kick the doors in, but it seemed the locals would take some dealing with first. Dotted about the hill were women and old men, all rushing towards the longhall at the top, while at the foot of the little hill were perhaps two score men, nearly all of fighting age and all of them armed. Only half of them carried shields, and those were unpainted and crude, but every man was armed with axe or spear, and behind those men stood a pack of archers with bows strung and arrows nocked. Mhari could tell that the sight of her was frightening them, but it was clear that at least some of these fools were ready to put up a fight. It seemed they'd heard the Pictish warcries and had gathered together and armed themselves rather than trying to hide or flee. *They did it damned quickly too.*

Within a heartbeat their arrows were flying towards her, and even as Mhari crouched she felt one glance from the skull on her helm. She shouted to the warriors behind her.

'Shelter!'

They obeyed at once and scattered towards the buildings as shafts began falling among them. Mhari guessed that the local hunters were either poor marksmen or were hesitant to kill men rather than beasts because most of their shots flew wide, though two of the slower-moving Picts were struck before they could find safety. Mhari saw Nerys stumble with an arrow through her calf, and Indulf went down screaming when a shaft pierced his cheek. Mhari and Conn both bounded for shelter and a second later were crouching behind a chest-high wattle fence. Her lover half-smiled.

'Well, why make things too easy, eh?'

Mhari growled.

'A *little* ease would have been nice.' She called out to the warband. 'A bare dozen have bows. Get behind them!'

A handful of warriors disappeared around the nearest house and began picking their way across the settlement. Hopefully Darina would already be flanking the Venicones as well, and there was no way the archers here could defend themselves from all sides. *No*, Mhari thought, *but then they don't intend to. They will fight from the hall.* She glanced around the fence and, sure enough, the archers and spearmen had joined the mass of bodies rushing up towards the longhall. Despite the setback of this resistance, Mhari felt herself grinning; the Venicones were too close together, too undisciplined, too panicked, and the archers would be hard-pressed to aim from the middle of a frightened crowd. She raised Brathir over her head.

'They're making for the hall!'

If her people couldn't understand that for the order it was, then they had no business calling themselves warriors. Letting armed quarry reach the hall would mean a hard fight in cramped doorways, while catching a fleeing mob in the open would mean easy slaughter with minimal losses. Mhari swung around the fence and charged, and every warrior worth the name was at her back within an eye-blink. Two arrows came sailing towards her but they struck nothing but dirt, and Mhari sprinted past them, heedless. She almost laughed at the panic in the Venicones' eyes as some tried to push forwards while others fled for the transient safety of the hall. *They are fools to try to fight us. But then, if they didn't, this would be a duller day.* Two men, far bolder than the others, outpaced their comrades and charged the Picts with shoddy-looking spears. It might have been admirable if it wasn't so stupid.

Conn was right beside her, and when the Venicones reached them he rammed his spear through the first man's neck. The fool dropped to the grass with a rasping gurgle. Mhari took the other with contemptuous ease, dodging his clumsy spear-thrust and hacking low across his belly. Brathir bit through flesh and scraped on bone, and the Venicon dropped his weapon to clutch hopelessly at his stomach. Blood and offal gushed onto his hands, but Mhari back-swung her blade and crushed his head before the dying man could scream. She and Conn exchanged grins and carried on up the hill, and scores of howling Picts came rushing up after them. Mhari could feel the battle-lust roaring in her veins, and once again screamed out the war-cry of her people.

'Garnaith!'

Chapter Twenty-Two

Gawain was still struggling to find words; the dreaded Green Man, the spirit or sorcerer who'd terrorised Dun Edin at Beltane and haunted his thoughts ever since, was the cheery old Lord of Tahrnax? His mind raced with a hundred questions but none of them seemed able to reach his mouth, and Gawain simply gawped at him in silence. Berlak, assuming that was this man's name at all, was still wearing his smile and carried on as if their conversation was the most natural thing in the world.

'I never lost faith in you, you know. Luned was convinced that you would fall to temptation but I knew better.'

Gawain blinked. He'd been beginning to worry whether Berlak would be quite so jovial if he knew what he and Luned had been up to, but apparently that was something else Gawain hadn't understood. He finally managed to give voice to some of his confusion.

'You sent your own wife to seduce me?'

Berlak waved a hand.

'That would be absurd. I sent her to *attempt* to seduce you.'

Gawain wondered if he dared tell Berlak just how close that attempt had come to succeeding, and decided it was best to remain discreet. His host gestured towards the green-roofed longhall and continued speaking as he made towards it. Without thinking, Gawain fell into step beside him.

'Verdis' challenge was all artifice, my friend, a trial of your resolve and courage, one that you passed not once but twice over. As for Luned's part, in all honesty that was her idea; a trial to test your sense of honour. In that too you have distinguished yourself.' He smirked. 'I suspect she is a little disappointed that you resisted her charms so easily.'

Gawain's first thought was that there'd been nothing easy about it, but again he kept the details to himself. Berlak seemed to be waiting for him to speak, and Gawain blurted out a clumsy question.

'How did you do it, lord? At Beltane I took your head from your shoulders, and just now you…'

But Berlak brushed the questions aside.

'I have learned many things in my time, though I'd be a fool to reveal my methods, would I not?'

Gawain felt he had to nod, though the memories of Berlak's magic were still unnerving to recall. The man himself was completely unconcerned and put a hand on Gawain's shoulder as they walked.

'You and I must talk, Gawain. There is much afoot that is of great import, and you have shown yourself worthy to be a part of my plans.'

For all his confusion Gawain felt a little flattered, and was about to speak his thanks when something caught his eye and he turned to look south. Above the grassy hill was a plume of dark smoke which could only be coming from Tahrnax. There was far more of it than would be produced by the cook-fires in the village and besides, the fires lit indoors had much of their smoke absorbed by thatch. He glanced at Berlak, who was still heading towards the hall, and pointed over the hill.

'Lord, the smoke?'

His strange host glanced up at the sky and barely shrugged his shoulders.

'Likely it is nothing. Cethin has been meaning to burn off the bracken at the south-east corner.'

Gawain frowned. The smoke looked awfully thick for a bracken-burning.

'Cethin made no mention of that.'

Berlak remained unworried.

'He is a capable man and runs things his own way.' He began steering the conversation back again. 'As I was saying, there is much to discuss and more to do. The day is coming when all Britain will need warriors of virtue, and I have spent much time and effort in seeking the best and boldest to become warlords when the time comes.'

Gawain knew he was probably supposed to thank him for the compliment, but he couldn't take his eyes from the smoke. He stood and stared at it with a cold feeling in his stomach; what if it *wasn't* just Cethin burning bracken? Berlak went on, though he stopped walking when Gawain did.

'I would have you become a man of substance in the Britain that is to come, Gawain. You would be the great pride of your house.'

Again, Gawain was sure he ought to be saying something polite but he simply nodded towards the smoke again.

'There are Picts raiding nearby, lord. It might be that they have found Tahrnax.'

A hint of impatience entered Berlak's tone.

'Your concern is appreciated but that is inconceivable. Tahrnax is far too well-protected to be attacked by a mere raiding party.'

His voice, indeed his whole being, radiated confidence, yet Gawain was still unsure.

'The folk of Pencardden thought themselves safe, lord. Ought we not go back and see for ourselves that all is well?'

Berlak answered dismissively.

'Tahrnax is not Pencardden. Now you must understand, King Uther will not live forever and when he dies every kingdom of Britain risks falling into chaos.'

But Gawain was only half-listening. He was thinking of the chaos he'd seen at Pencardden, and the flat-faced man who'd murdered unarmed women and desecrated Drustan's corpse. The people of Tahrnax were in no condition to fight them off, and Ulfric could hardly defend the whole settlement on his own. *And what of Halwen and Gareth, and old Father Iain?* He turned to face Berlak again.

'With respect, lord, I am going back to make sure. May we speak of this later?'

The impatience in the older man's voice became a fraction more pronounced.

'I would sooner not be ignored while discussing the fate of nations, Gawain. And I would hardly call it courteous to leave on some fool's errand when a man is trying to make you a great figure in this island's future.'

Gawain was all for becoming a great man in the future, but surely that could wait?

'Your pardon, lord, but I must be sure my friends are safe.'

Berlak looked irate and in truth, Gawain was growing frustrated himself. Whatever this grand plan was, why could it not wait until he'd checked that the village was not in danger? It was hardly a journey of days or some complex task, and if all was as safe as Berlak seemed to think then he could be there and back within the hour if he hurried. Yet it seemed his host was obstinate.

'They *are* safe, Gawain. Now I would speak to you of great things, or would you sooner not be a part of the future of your people?'

He didn't quite seem angry, but there was something about him that told Gawain he wasn't far from it. He was tempted to stay and listen, Berlak might dismiss him from whatever grand plans he had if he left, but if there was any chance at all that the Picts had followed them here, he had to make sure Halwen and the others were alright. He spoke as politely as he could.

'You must forgive me, my host, but I am going and I am going now.'

He paced back to where his axe had fallen and stooped down to pick it up. His hand still hurt, and leaning down brought a stab of pain to his leg, but he determined not to show it on his face. He bowed to Berlak, who met his bow with a glare.

'The men I seek must know obedience as much as courage. Do not presume anything of me if you leave here, Gawain.'

For a moment Gawain told himself that he was worrying for no reason, that Tahrnax was safe behind its ghost-ward and he was throwing a handsome gift in the face of a powerful man. But he dreaded to think what would happen if it turned out Berlak was wrong. He bowed again.

'Thank you for your hospitality, lord. It was appreciated.'

It seemed Berlak had nothing more to say to him, and Gawain turned around before he could make things any worse between them. He made towards the hill, noting with a jolt that the smoke had grown thicker, and quietly hoped his host was right and he was about to make a fool of himself over nothing. But something in his gut was telling him that this was no harmless bracken-burning; something was wrong, and he had to find out what.

His leg was burning when he crested the hill, but Gawain told himself he'd done the right thing in going over it rather than looping around. Cethin's way might have been easier on his injured limb but the direct route must have cut the time in half, and Gawain was in a hurry. His mind was a whirling mess as he trekked through the evergreens that crowned the hill, trying to make some kind of sense of the madness he'd landed in. Berlak had ridden to Dun Edin purely to test Gawain's nerve, or so it seemed, and hadn't seemed at all surprised that he'd come after him for a second fight. Had he known this would happen through his magics? Had Berlak been gambling on Gawain's impulsiveness to get the challenge done? He doubted if Berlak would have settled for waiting until next year, not if his grand plans were as urgent as he made out.

That was another thing that made Gawain think; what had he meant about King Uther? As far as Gawain knew the High King was no older than Lot and had always been called a strong and vigorous man. Surely it would be years before the Pendragon left this world and even then, didn't he have a son to succeed him? Gawain couldn't remember the boy's name but he was sure his father had mentioned that Uther's heir was either a man or very nearly one. Even if Uther died unexpectedly there was no reason for the southern kingdoms to suffer for it, let alone for his death to affect Lothian. So why had Berlak been so anxious that they speak of such things now, unless his sorceries had told him of some tragedy? *And even so, why did he come to me?*

He might have kept pondering on that but as he peered through the trees his mind was pulled back to the here and now. He couldn't see much through the canopy but he was sure that the smoke was growing blacker in the sky, and when he upped his pace and started hurrying downhill, he caught his first glimpse of red flame between the boughs. Gawain broke into a run and when the trees finally thinned he saw that at least four houses had been set ablaze, and there was some kind of commotion up near the longhall. It was too far away for him to make out details but it was more than enough to tell him that trouble had indeed come to Tahrnax.

Gawain's heart pounded hard as he thought of Gareth and Halwen, and he went from a steady lope to a dead sprint. He reached the north side of the bank with his leg screaming in protest but he ignored the throbbing pain and kept on running. Now that he was closer he could hear distant shouts and war-cries, but the thick bank and roaring fires muffled most of the sound. He considered clambering down the steep ditch and up over the rampart, but even the thought of it sent daggers through his wounded leg and so he kept on running, heading for the causeway at the best pace he could.

When the ramparts curved southwards and the causeway came into sight, Gawain was convinced that for all the evils befalling them, either Christ or the Huntsman was still with him; there were four men standing on the earth bridge, and despite the fact that a hulking youth in mail had just come running around the bend, not one of them seemed to notice his arrival. They were loitering at one end of the causeway, where fires had been set around the skulls that formed the ghost-ward, and a glance at their furs and weapons made it clear that these were Picts. He supposed that a more cunning warrior might have rolled into the ditch or dived for the trees, then crept closer to take the raiders unawares. But Gawain was making peace with the fact that he was, perhaps, not the most cunning of men.

He poured on as much speed as he could, and when one of the Picts finally noticed he was there, Gawain raised the war-axe and screamed at the pitch of his lungs.

'Lothian!'

The closest man was dead before he could raise his spear, his skull smashed to splinters by a two-handed swing. The force of the blow almost unbalanced Gawain but he twisted with the momentum, and when the next Pict lunged in his sword glanced harmlessly from the mailshirt. He was too close to kill with the axe-head but Gawain was still moving with the force of his first cut, and the Pict was caught up in the whirlwind. Gawain gripped him by the chest and spun him from his feet, then dug in his heels to steady himself for the next two. It seemed one of them was wounded already, his right arm bloody to the shoulder, and only the uninjured one dared to approach.

The Pict tried to menace Gawain with a long spear but he ignored the jabs and charged forward with his axe held high. It was possible for a spear to pierce mail but it was never guaranteed, and the Pict predictably angled his weapon up to impale Gawain through the throat. He saw it coming and struck the haft with his axe-handle, knocking it aside and gaining himself a crucial half-second. It was all he needed. Even without the momentum of a swing, the war-axe's head was deadly sharp, and Gawain had honed the edge only that morning; he punched the weapon forward and sliced the Pict's face in half, and when he cried out and reeled Gawain slammed the butt-end under his chin. He didn't know if the blow broke his neck, but when the Pict hit the ground he made no move to get back up.

The wounded man looked frightened and was still trying to draw his sword when Gawain took his head from his shoulders. A distant part of Gawain told him that was not an honourable thing to do, but it was quickly shouted down by the rest of him. Halwen and Gareth were still inside, and he had to get to them. The man he'd sent sprawling was still scrabbling to his feet, and Gawain took two short steps and brought the axe up in a swing that split the Pict's jaw. Gawain didn't bother to make sure the man was dead; he was out of the fight for now and there was no time to waste.

His leg was still throbbing but not nearly as badly as he'd feared, and Gawain ran across the causeway with all the speed he could muster. He didn't pause when he passed the skulls in their little rings of fire, and didn't even slow down when he saw Cethin's blood-drenched body in the ditch. There would be time for mourning later, but right now he had to keep moving. The Picts had fired the first few houses beyond the rampart, but he only spotted one or two dashing in and out looking for loot. One man saw him as he ran past but Gawain killed him without breaking his stride, hacking through his neck before he could cry out.

Gawain only slowed down when the village opened up and the hall came into sight. The scene was chaotic but it looked like the Picts were trying to rush a group of locals making a stand before the hall doors. At second glance Gawain saw that the men of Tahrnax had formed a crude shieldwall and were jabbing out with spears as Picts tried to hammer through them. He almost felt a swell of pride at their efforts, but it was quickly doused by fear for what would happen when that wall broke, as it surely would. Brave or not, the locals had no experience of this kind of fighting, and weight of numbers and Pictish savagery would wear them down sooner or later.

The attackers had surrounded the hall but Gawain remembered he'd only seen two rear doors to the place, both of which would be locked and barricaded by now. He could make out a handful of bolder Picts crawling on the roof, though even as he watched he saw one of them arch his back and tumble to the ground, and Gawain breathed a short sigh of relief. It seemed Ulfric had been wise enough to have archers ready inside the building, and the hall would at least be safe from men trying to squeeze their way through the thatch. All the same it was only a matter of time before the Picts broke in some other way, and then Ulfric and all the others would be butchered or worse.

The hall's doors weren't quite facing him, which meant the Picts weren't quite facing away, and Gawain fought the urge to charge straight up at them. *With that many foes, you should at least* try *to be cunning!* If he could attack from a better angle he could maybe blindside the Picts and cause confusion enough for Ulfric and the others to counter-charge. It was a slim hope, but when the alternative was seeing Gareth slain and Halwen ravaged, Gawain was ready to latch on to whatever hope he could. It galled him to move away from the fighting but he told himself it would only be a few moments' delay, and he hurried around the wattle wall of a house that was still intact.

He had just rounded it and reached a point where he could run up the hill unseen when a sound from within made him pause. It couldn't quite be called a scream, nor was it merely a whimper, but rather it was something in-between and truly horrible to hear. Gawain edged closer to the door and saw a man with a tattooed face standing in the opening, grinning at whatever was happening inside. Even had he not been a Pict and an enemy, Gawain could take a shrewd guess as to what was going on in there, and he felt rage burn in his chest as he threw himself at the raider.

The Pict saw him just in time to lift his sword, and Gawain's first swing was parried down. The tattooed man stabbed for his face but Gawain jerked back and sent a clumsy kick at his groin. The blow barely made contact but the Pict doubled forward instinctively, and as his head came down the axe came up and thudded wetly into bone and brains. Gawain tried to pull it out but the blade had bitten deep, and when the Pict fell the weapon was almost dragged from his grasp. He kept on trying to free it as he looked into the house, and though it was dark inside Gawain could see well enough to be disgusted.

A young girl, one of those he'd seen herding goats on his first day in Tahrnax, was being pinned on the floor, her woollen dress torn almost to shreds. She was too young to have a woman's figure, and seeing her nakedness would have made Gawain feel awkward had he not been so blind with anger. There was blood around her nose and mouth and she was weeping as she struggled hopelessly against the heavy-set Pict straddling her. He was older than Gawain by a few years, with a scarred left cheek and a solid build beneath his tunic. His fist had been poised to strike the girl again but he had frozen in place when he saw Gawain in the doorway.

The rage burned so hot that Gawain forgot about his axe and simply charged the would-be-ravisher with a wordless bellow. The scarred man was on his feet in the blink of an eye but Gawain grabbed him by the waist and powered through him like a bull, and the wattle wall cracked and buckled as the pair slammed into it. The scarred man was as strong as he looked, and he started thumping huge fists down on Gawain's back and neck. He was forced to let go to protect his head but he kept close to his enemy, barging forward with his forearms and elbows. The wall creaked again as the Pict was shoved into it, but then he shuffled sideways and swung a pair of heavy hooks before Gawain could close in again. The first punch thudded harmlessly into his armoured shoulder, but the second whipped around his guard and crashed into Gawain's cheek. The blow spun him, and by the time he'd righted himself the Pict had drawn a broad-bladed sword.

There was no time to be afraid. Gawain grabbed the nearest thing to hand, a heavy jug, and flung it at the big man's head. He swatted it from the air but the half-second's distraction was enough for Gawain to charge in again and grab him by the wrists. He forced the Pict's hands out and trapped them against the wall, then rammed his head forward and flattened the bastard's face. The Pict grunted in pain but couldn't bring his arms up to defend himself, and Gawain butted forward again, and then again, smashing the dense bone of his brow into the raider's nose and mouth. A bolder man might have tried to butt back, but Gawain wasn't surprised that this dog made no attempt to; the kind of cur who ravaged children was not the kind who relished fighting men.

Gawain screamed at him as he kept up the attack, and soon enough the Pict's face was little more than bloody pulp. The scarred man grew limp, his sword long lost, and before he could fall Gawain grabbed him by his belt and collar. He was a big man, but so was Gawain, and rage and battle-lust lent him a wild strength; he lifted the heavy Pict as though he weighed no more than a sack of oats. Gawain hefted him fully above his head for a heartbeat, then screamed out wordlessly as he slammed him head-first into the ground. There was a horrible crunching noise and the weeping girl cried out and bolted, but Gawain felt only savage joy at having dealt justice to this monster.

He was breathing hard, but he knew that if he stopped to rest he wouldn't stand up again. *And Halwen and the others still need you.* Gawain bounded for the doorway and, after a few moments' struggling, wrenched his axe free from the tattooed man's head. He looked up towards the hill. It looked like the shieldwall was holding for now, but it would crumble before long under the onslaught of the Picts. His whole head hurt from the scarred man's punch and his leg was throbbing painfully with every step, but Gawain forced himself to move. It hurt to run, but even if the effort killed him, these Picts would feel the wrath of a son of Lothian before he dropped.

Chapter Twenty-Three

They were half-trained and frightened but Mhari had to admit, these Venicones were putting up quite a fight. Time after time she had been forced to back off from the wall of shields, and though they were killing the defenders one or two at a time, her warband had already lost far more than the seven men the Grey Woman had promised. *I shall have words with her when this is done.* At least a dozen of her warriors lay dead from the spears and arrows of clumsy locals, and two more had died when a wolfhound tore out their throats. If many more went down then all the reputation Mhari would gain from this raid would be undermined by the losses she took in the process. *And most of them will be my own people.* Though Temar had given in to greed and joined the main attack, half of his oath-men had dispersed to loot the village and spared themselves this carnage. If this fight wasn't won quickly, there was a real danger of Temar's warriors equalling hers in number, and that Mhari could not allow.

She shoved forward and used Brathir to knock a spear aside before cutting down at the man before her. The steel bit into the crudely-made shield and even struck off a chunk of wood, but it failed to touch the Venicon standing behind it. These shields had no iron rims and Pictish swords and axes would hack them apart eventually, but that was hard work for her warriors and all the while spears were jabbing out at the milling Picts, with the bolder of the archers taking quick shots at them from the doorway. Mhari grimaced as she struck down again and took solace that at least the fools hadn't barricaded the door. Braver warriors would have formed their shieldwall and then barred the longhall's doors behind them, but these Venicones clearly thought that they would have to retreat before the Picts were driven off, and had left the doors open to let them fall back. *At least we won't have to batter our way through a barricade once these whoresons are dead.*

The spearman in front of her began backing off, cowering from her sword-strokes, but the man beside him came to his aid and lunged at Mhari's ribs, forcing her to dodge. If these spearmen had been experienced then the first man would have tried spitting her while she was on her heels, but they were farmers and fisher-folk and could barely hold their wall together, much less take advantage of openings. All the same, though her warband were taking fewer losses than they would against real warriors, the wall was enough to stave them off, and now and then a spearman would get lucky and a good northerner would end up gutted.

Mhari yelled out a war-cry and started forward again, and this time she felt Conn's presence beside her. She batted spears aside and stabbed Brathir around the nearest shield, earning her a cry of pain from the man behind it. His fellow came to his aid again and Mhari had to parry his weapon away, but Conn took advantage of the first man's wound and lunged forward before the Venicon could recover himself. His spear took the injured man in his side, piercing just below his ribs and driving deep into his belly. The Venicon grunted at the impact, screamed as Conn ripped the weapon free, and a moment later he was on the ground, his own spear and shield forgotten as he clutched desperately at his wound.

The wall tried to close up but Mhari barged into the opening with Brathir alive in her hands, and Conn followed a moment later, jabbing left and right with his spear. The Venicones around them panicked and Mhari could feel their spirit begin to break. This was it! The nearest man to her found himself trapped between Mhari and Eithni, and as he tried to defend against Brathir's swing he caught Eithni's long knife in the gut. Mhari pulled down his shield, butted her ram's-skull helm at his face, and then punched her sword-hilt into his eye. The Venicon cried out and dropped to his knees, and Eithni's blade opened his throat a heartbeat later. Bright blood sprayed over the two Picts, and as one they yelled out Garnaith's name. *They are breaking! We have won!*

But even as Mhari felt the victory in her hands, a sound from behind them made her snap her head around.

'Lothian!'

Chapter Twenty-Four

Gawain had held in the war-cry until he was only feet from the nearest Pict, and the raider had barely half-turned when the war-axe smashed through his skull. He dropped like a clubbed hog but Gawain didn't pause to see it, already bringing the axe back around for his next swing. The Picts ahead, even those who'd almost breached the shieldwall, were looking back in confusion and fear. He saw more than a few back away in panic or else flee from the fight altogether. *They must think that a whole band of men have arrived. After all, what kind of fool would charge into this chaos alone?*

Gawain took full advantage of their mistake. He kept shouting his war-cry as he charged up the hill, and within seconds another Pict lay dying on the grass. The press of men up ahead was thick but Gawain's only chance was to batter through them and get to the defenders, hopefully killing or scattering his share of enemies in the process. He swung the axe left and right and kept screaming like a man possessed, driving hard towards the longhall. For the first few moments the Picts were hesitant to come within range of the weapon, then they finally realised that Gawain was alone.

Though many had backed off, fearing that a real counter-attack was underway, most had stayed to fight and now realised that they faced not a warband of Lothian spearmen but a single youth with more brash than brains. Picts began to close in on him and though Gawain struck down as many as he could, he knew he'd soon be mobbed by simple weight of numbers. But then battle-cries came from the hall and he heard Ulfric's voice shouting for the line to move forwards. Gawain could just make them out over the heads of the Picts and he saw Ulfric, along with Yorath and a dozen of Tahrnax's would-be-spearmen, surging forward behind their shields to start driving into the Picts. They could never hope to overcome them, but the moment's confusion might be all Gawain needed.

More than half of the Picts facing him turned back to face the shieldwall, and Gawain roared and began shoving his way through the rest. There was little space to swing the war-axe but Gawain was trying to drive through them, not kill them, and he battered this way and that with the weapon's haft, occasionally drawing blood when he punched forward with the head. More than one Pictish sword cut around his defence, but he kept his guard high enough that they could only strike low, and the mailshirt turned the blades in a combination of luck and good steel.

He was closing in on the line now, and could even see Gareth and Halwen standing in the hall doorway beyond it. Both held bows though neither had a shaft nocked, and Gawain guessed that they had both run out of arrows. He wanted to wave at them to get inside but he couldn't afford to take a hand from the axe and so kept on driving forward. Gawain was almost there when he saw a broad-shouldered Pict hanging back from the fighting, and good sense abandoned him as he stared at the flat-faced man.

The thieving whoreson was wearing Drustan's coat of polished scales, though it was ill-fitting on his heavy frame. In one hand he held what looked like a well-made sword, but even in the chaos of battle Gawain noted how clean it was. He supposed that was a good thing, at least no-one had fallen to this cur yet, but nonetheless he viewed the bloodless weapon with contempt. *Craven bastard's probably waiting until only those who can't fight back are left!*

Gawain stalked towards the man and for some reason the nearby Picts made no effort to stop him. Indeed, the fighting immediately around them seemed to halt entirely, and he wondered if this dog might be some chief among them, and that the northerners wished to respect his being challenged so directly. If that was the case then the flat-faced man didn't seem keen on the idea, and looked as if he would sooner back off and disappear into his warriors. Gawain didn't give him the chance. He bellowed as he approached, raising his axe above his head.

'Lothian!'

Coward though he was, his opponent was fast for his size and he dodged aside quick as a hare. Gawain's heavy blow missed him but he brought the weapon back around before the flat-faced man could counter, and the sweeping cut narrowly missed taking his head. The swine tried to dart in for a lunge but Gawain jerked away and attacked again, this time aiming low. Once again the Pict dodged but he wasn't quite fast enough this time, and the axe thudded into Drustan's armoured coat. The blow caught the Pict at the end of its swing and had lost much of its power, and the well-made scales protected his flesh. Nevertheless, Gawain grinned as he saw the panic in his enemy's eyes.

In what was clearly a desperate move, the Pict came charging forward with his sword swinging wildly. The cuts were fast, and had Gawain backed off he might have lost the initiative, but instead he held the axe like a spear and jabbed forward as the Pict came at him. His face was flattened even further when heavy steel rammed into his nose, and his head snapped back with bright blood drenching his beard. Gawain doubted if he was bold enough to try another attack but he pressed on before the whoreson got the chance; this craven dog had dishonoured Drustan and he would die for it right now!

When the Pictish chief reeled back Gawain hefted the axe, and he swung it with all his weight in a massive upward arc. The steel head slammed between the raider's legs and Gawain felt the blade part flesh, crack bone, and then drive further up into the bastard's guts and belly. The Pict's eyes flew wide and he screamed in a voice so shrill it was almost painful to hear. Gawain tried to rip the axe free as he fell but the weapon was lodged tight, and the flat-faced man screamed all the louder as Gawain tugged on the haft. He might have kept trying despite the man's cries, but then Gawain looked about him. The Picts, who'd been content to let their chief fight and had probably assumed he'd win, were now looking at Gawain the way hungry cats looked at mice. They didn't seem enraged by their chief's death, but Gawain guessed they were all eager to be seen as the one who brought down his killer.

Gawain focused on the man directly between himself and the hall, a lean warrior with tattoos on his forehead. There was no time to draw his sword but if he could just barge past that man before he was swamped, there was a chance he might survive this and make it to the shieldwall. It was a small chance but it was all he had, and Gawain braced himself ready to charge. Then a voice screamed out from behind the man, high-pitched and furious.

'Lothian!'

The warrior half-turned and was almost knocked over as Halwen leaped on his back, one arm wrapping around his neck while the other stabbed down with her Pictish dagger. Her blows were frantic but they plunged into the man's neck and shoulder all the same, and Gawain charged forward before the other Picts could close in. A sword swiped at his back but the mailshirt protected him, and Gawain sprinted for the pair. Rather than waste time trying to pull Halwen from her enemy, Gawain simply grabbed the lean man by the waist and lifted, hauling both of them towards the shieldwall. It was no light weight but his pounding blood gave him strength, and Gawain carried the struggling pair a dozen paces before he had to let go. By then he was almost at the shieldwall, and when the lean man rolled away Gawain snatched Halwen's hand and dragged her towards the line.

By some miracle of Christ or Cernunnos they reached it without being cut down, and Ulfric opened a gap in the shields for them to come through. It was a close run thing, and a pair of Picts almost managed to follow them before the wall closed up again, but Ulfric was quick with spear and shield, and gutted one man even as he defended from the other. Gawain wanted to collapse on the spot and he dropped to one knee, breathing hard. Looking up he saw Gareth still standing by the hall doors, his bow abandoned and a spear held in both hands. The boy looked determined, and though Gawain's instinct was to shout at him to get inside, he knew it would do no good. *And at least he's not alone.*

Mabb was standing next to him, his weight slightly off one fore-leg but his face looking bloody and fierce, and behind them stood Father Iain with his heavy staff in hand. If the Picts breached the shieldwall they would all be doomed of course, but something about seeing Gareth with friends about him made Gawain feel better. Halwen had almost fallen when they came through the wall, and Gawain found himself smiling when their eyes met. All the tension of the last few days seemed to melt away and for a mad moment he thought of kissing her. But he shook the thought away; the fight was far from over, and he still had a duty to do.

Gawain stood up with a grunt and looked out over the ragged shieldwall. More Venicones had died but they were holding on, and he spotted Ulfric's straw-coloured hair at the centre of the line. He headed over to him, snatching up a dropped shield and drawing his sword as he walked. The Saxon was too busy fighting for any talk, but Gawain elbowed in next to him and started hacking at the charging Picts. All their hesitancy from earlier had vanished and if anything they were attacking with renewed vigour, hurling themselves at the wall and cutting wildly at anything they could. He managed to down one of them but the Venicon to his left was killed a moment later, and it was a desperate few seconds before the wall closed up again. Gawain growled as he ducked and stabbed and ducked again. *We cannot hold them. If every man here kills three of theirs, they will still outnumber us.*

Amidst his battle-cries Gawain found himself shouting curses, not aimed at the Picts so much as they were aimed at Berlak. This was *his* home damn it all, and for the sake of pride and his damned grand plans he had stayed sulking at Maes Gwyr instead of ensuring his people's safety. A few handfuls of flame or the sight of a living headless man would see these bastards off in moments, but instead he'd left his people help-less, and presumably his wife too. Gawain hacked down at a charging Pict and almost wished that it was Berlak's skull he was crushing. His damnable pride was going to get them all killed.

Another Venicon fell, and the Pict who'd killed him quickly turned his spear upon Gawain. He was a rangy warrior, hand-some and confident, and he used his spear with almost blinding speed. Gawain tried to shuffle into the breach and keep his shield up at the same time, but a thrust came up under his guard and slammed hard into his sternum. The mail rings held, but the force of the blow knocked the breath out of him and before he knew it he had half-dropped the shield. He saw the handsome man grin as he sent the spear-blade speeding at his head, but at the very last instant the deadly strike veered away. Gawain glanced right and saw that Ulfric had stepped forward and sent his own spear under the Pict's left arm, ruining the strike and drawing a sharp cry of pain. The Saxon drove forward, piercing the man's heart and dropping him to the grass, but before he could nod his thanks Gawain heard an ear-splitting scream.

Further along the line he saw a slender Pict in a crimson cloak and a helm topped with a ram's skull. The warrior bounded forward with incredible speed, and before Ulfric could so much as turn his head, a sword had swept up in a lightning-fast cut and opened the Saxon's throat in a spray of gore. Ulfric's eyes went wide and he fell to his knees, his hands flying to his neck. Blood poured between his fingers and the skull-helmed Pict hacked down before Gawain could move to stop him. The blow almost split Ulfric's head in two, and the straw-coloured hair turned red.

Gawain bellowed and, forgetting the shieldwall, hurled himself blindly at his friend's killer. The Pict was fast, maddeningly fast, and dodged his attack and countered with a swift cut at his head. Pure instinct brought the shield up and stopped it, but the Pict screamed again and brought the blade smoothly around, slamming the heavy steel into Gawain's side. This time the mailshirt parted, and though the cut was robbed of power Gawain felt the weapon bite into his ribs. He grunted in pain but the Pict wasn't done with him yet. A hand gripped his shield-rim and pulled hard, not to rip it from his grip but simply to tug it down, and this time the blade came scything towards his head. Gawain ducked it just in time and felt his heart lurch as wind ruffled his hair. He shoved the fear away and drove his shield forward with all his strength, gaining precious distance from his maddened attacker.

The slender Pict staggered back and Gawain realised she must be a woman. She was tall for one, and strong to boot, but her screams had been high-pitched and she'd not been heavy when he'd pushed her back. For a ridiculous moment he almost felt guilty for fighting her, then common sense reasserted itself and he readied himself for another charge.

But before that charge could come, hard-eyed Picts on either side of him began to close in. One swiped an axe at him while his comrade lunged with his spear, and Gawain had to step back awkwardly and duck behind his shield. The spear missed him entirely but the axe landed hard on the shield and hacked off a great chunk of wood. Something came at him from his right and Gawain swung his sword that way, but he struck only air as the attacking Pict dodged back.

Looking around Gawain realised he was all but surrounded, and what little safety lay in the shieldwall was disappearing as more Venicones were cut down. He couldn't see Halwen but he knew she would be back there, and he prayed that she'd find some way to escape this, knowing full well that she couldn't. He bellowed in rage and frustration, and started hacking wildly at anything that moved. They might be doomed but damn it all, the Picts would pay a toll for his death. His side burned but he ground his teeth against the pain, determined to make the bastards bleed before he fell.

But then a noise cut through the clashing steel and roaring war-cries; a strong sound but sweet as well, one that made Gawain think of hunts and festivals. A heartbeat later he recognised the war-horn for what it was, and he grinned even as the Picts around him backed off. When they began to run Gawain looked down the slope and almost laughed when saw the source of the sound.

It was impossible, but a score of horsemen were cantering between the houses with a band of spearmen following close behind. A banner fluttered over them showing the proud Red Fox, and at their head, his hair bright in the sunshine, rode Gaheris. The fairest son of Lot galloped his steed towards the slope, and Gawain almost laughed as he saw the dark skin of the rider behind him. Gaheris and Burian sped towards the milling Picts with swords in their hands and comrades at their back, and what had been a warband mere moments ago became a routed mob. As the Picts scattered voices called out from riders and spearmen alike, and Gawain ignored the pain in his ribs and echoed his people's war-cry.

'Lothian!'

The woman in the ram's-skull helm tried to rush him in a last mad dash, but two of her people caught her arms and started dragging her back down the slope. A wiser man would have let them go; their chances of escape were slim at best, and Gawain was in no shape to be running anywhere. But Ulfric had died saving his life, and that bitch was the one who'd killed him. He put a hand to his side and gingerly touched the place where her sword had broken the mail. Blood oozed from the wound but not at any great pace, and Gawain's limited knowledge of healing told him he was unlikely to die of it. At least, not yet. He could make no use of a shield and he let it slide from his arm to thud dully on the grass. His leg had started to burn in earnest again but he forced himself to ignore the pain and took a quick glance about him.

Only a few feet away was the body of the flat-faced man, and Gawain hobbled towards it, cursing under his breath. He wiped the sword on the dead man's trews, vowed to take back Drustan's scale coat when this was done, and then sheathed his blade before making a last attempt to free his axe from the dead Pict's abdomen. He resolved that if he couldn't do it in three heaves he would abandon the weapon and chase the Pict with sword alone, but, either by God's grace or by Huntsman's luck, the axe came free on his second attempt. It made a horrible sound when it came out, and the stench that followed was enough to make him gag, but Gawain held down the bile and hefted the axe to his shoulder.

He turned, grinding his teeth against the pain in his side, and looked down the hill. The woman in the helm had apparently seen sense and was now running north with three of her comrades. For a moment Gawain despaired of catching up with them, but then the Picts were forced to change direction as Gaheris' spearmen moved to cut them off. There was no way they could get through or around them to reach the causeway, and the Picts started making for the north-east ramparts instead. It would hurt like hellfire to reach them before they climbed it, but Gawain had no choice; he had to try.

He half-ran, half-staggered down the slope, ignoring Gaheris' riders and spearmen as they cut down fleeing Picts. At some point he was sure heard his name called, probably by Gaheris or Burian, but there was no time to stop and greet them. There would be time enough to thank his brother and hear Burian's story later; if he slowed down now he might lose Ulfric's killer forever. Battle-lust began burning away the pain wracking his body and somehow Gawain managed to pour on more speed, and it was mere seconds before he'd crossed the open space and was sprinting between the houses. He could see the Picts ahead had almost topped the ramparts and he hit the slope without slowing down, his legs powering him forward with rage-maddened strength.

The rearmost man saw him too late, and the axe bit through his calf as he scrambled up the slope. The Pict cried out and Gawain didn't stop running as he cracked the weapon's haft across his face. The man fell and started rolling downhill but Gawain was already charging at the next doomed Pict. He met him as the earthen bank flattened out, and the fool tried to come at him with only a long dagger in his hand. The war-axe crashed through his cheek long before he reached stabbing range. The Pict's head snapped sideways so fast Gawain was sure his neck had broken, and he spun around a full turn before crumpling in a boneless heap. *Only one more, and then it's her!*

Both remaining Picts must have realised there was no point trying to run; if they tried to edge down the outer slope Gawain would catch them with ease, and would have the high ground when they came to blows. Instead they turned to fight, and Gawain bellowed as he closed the last few feet between them.

'Lothian!'

They shouted something back that he didn't understand, and both Picts tried to come at him at once. Gawain feigned a heavy swing at the woman in the helm, and when she dodged out of range he reversed the movement and slammed the axe-head into her comrade. It caught him in the chest, smacking hard into the bone, and the force of the blow sent him flying out over the rampart's edge. The outer slope was even steeper than the inner, and the Pict began to tumble uncontrollably down to the ditch. If the axe-blow hadn't killed him, chances were good that he'd crack his skull before reaching the bottom. Not that it mattered right now.

The woman in the helm didn't pause after her comrade was downed. She screamed at Gawain and came at him with blistering speed, her sword dancing in front of her like a silvery serpent. For all his righteous anger Gawain was forced to step back, blocking the many cuts as best he could. The Pict clearly knew that the advantage of the axe was in range and strength, and she was robbing him of them by driving him back and keeping close. Gawain batted aside stroke after stroke but it was only a matter of time before one of them got through, and he took a foolish risk that would either save him or get him killed. Leaping back a pace, he tossed the axe in the air just as the Pict pressed forward. She was too good to be struck by the flying haft and swayed away with ease, but the pause in her attacks gained Gawain a vital second, and he drew his sword and charged her with a roar.

His first strikes were parried but he kept driving forward before she could counter, and now *he* was the one forcing his opponent back. Their weapons now had near equal range, and his free hand meant she would hesitate to move too close; if he managed to catch hold of her, Gawain could simply drag her to the ground and crush her. But for all the change in her fortunes the Pict did not panic, and though the ram's skull hid it Gawain he knew that beneath the helm her face would be calm. *She knows her trade.* A moment later, he learned just how well she knew it.

Gawain hadn't realised he'd been favouring one leg, the battle-lust was blocking out nearly all his pain, but something in his gait must have given him away because the Pictish woman spotted the weakness in seconds. After a few backwards steps she quickly ducked in close, and before Gawain could grab her she slammed a shin into his thigh. Pain exploded from the arrow-wound and Gawain cried out as the leg buckled under him. He kept his sword up and deflected the Pict's next cut, but then her knee came up and struck him full in the face, and for a moment Gawain thought he'd gone blind. He felt his back hit the earth and tried to swipe at her as he fell, but a heavy boot crunched into his wounded side and he gasped and doubled up in pain. His nose was gushing blood and he felt so dizzy he was sure he would vomit. Another kick sent his sword flying from his fingers, but he barely had the strength to notice, much less try to reach for it.

His vision was blurry as he looked at up at his skull-faced enemy, and when she spoke her voice echoed in his head.

'Be grateful that your death is quick.'

The Pict was breathing hard, though whether through emotion or exertion Gawain couldn't tell. She nodded towards the settlement.

'When next I see them, every soul down there will burn alive for this.'

The blurred shape above him raised her sword, and a second later it was plunging down towards Gawain's throat.

Whether the strength came from Christ or Cernunnos Gawain never knew, but in that moment the pain of his wounds became insignificant, and as the blade came down he shuffled in and kicked out hard at his enemy's legs. He felt his boot strike bone, heard a shocked intake of breath, and with an agonised shout he scrambled to his feet, grabbed the Pict by one shoulder, and swung his other fist at her head with all the strength he had. He felt his hand explode with pain, but also heard the ram's skull crack under the blow, and the Pictish woman's feet came off the ground. For a mad moment she seemed to hover in mid-air, then she disappeared over the rampart, and Gawain heard crashing as her armoured body tumbled to the ditch.

Standing up had made him dizzy again and he dropped to his knees on the grass. He knew he ought to go to the rampart's edge and look down; that woman had killed Ulfric, and no matter how dangerous the fall might be, he *had* to make sure she had died for that. But trying to stand up again got him nowhere, and when he tried to crawl forward his whole body screamed in agony. Gawain collapsed to the dirt with his head pounding like a Beltane drum, and the last thing he felt was cool grass on his cheek.

Chapter Twenty-Five

He couldn't have been unconscious for long, but when he came to his senses Gawain dearly wished he could have stayed asleep. His entire body was hurting in one way or another, and his skull felt like a drunken blacksmith had set an anvil behind his eyes. He'd have loved to keep lying there and drift into painless sleep, but he knew he had to get up. Gaheris and his men had probably driven the last of the Picts from Tahrnax already, but he couldn't be sure until he went down there, and rescued or not there was still the chance that Halwen or Gareth had been hurt in the fighting.

It was hard work, but Gawain managed to crawl a few paces to where his axe lay. He used it as a staff to heave himself first to his knees and then to his feet, biting his lip and squeezing his eyes shut against the pain. He found his sword after a quick look around and, after spitting curses as he bent to lift it, sheathed it at his hip with a grunt. Both it and the axe seemed to have doubled in weight, and just the effort of moving them was exhausting. He grimaced at the prospect of the walk back to the hall, but he fixed Gareth and Halwen's faces in his mind and made himself start hobbling down the slope.

He'd travelled less than a quarter of the way when a man came rushing up the grassy bank. He looked to be somewhere near thirty, with pitch-black hair and a shield slung over his back; a man of Lothian, then. He smiled and held out a hand as he approached.

'Are you hurt, lord?'

Gawain tried to shrug nonchalantly but the effort made him wince, and the man came and put an arm under his shoulder. Gawain found he wasn't too proud to accept the help.

'Thank you…?'

He left a pause and the older man answered.

'Iestyn, lord.'

Gawain nodded at his human crutch.

'Thank you, Iestyn.'

Iestyn smiled again.

'Glad to be of help, lord.'

Gawain was so tired it took him a moment to realise what the Lothian man was calling him. He went on before Gawain could comment.

'That was quite some brawl you were having here, lord.'

Gawain nodded as they shuffled down the slope.

'I'm grateful to you for coming when you did; you saved us all.'

Surprisingly, Iestyn scoffed at that.

'You boys seemed to be doing well enough before we got here.' He jerked his head back towards the rampart. 'A couple of us saw you taking their chief up there. We even started up that way to aid you, but you knocked the bastard down before we reached the bank.'

Iestyn looked at him with something like admiration.

'It's no mean feat to face a Pictish chief alone, lord. They breed them savage up here.'

It had been hard work, true enough, but Gawain wasn't sure how to respond to the compliment. With one arm around

Iestyn's shoulders and the other leaning on the axe Gawain couldn't wave the words away, but he tried to sound casual as he answered.

'I had strong gods with me, and my blood was up. Any other maddened dog would do the same.'

The words made him think of Mabb, and he hoped that he too was unharmed after the fighting. The big hound had probably taken a Pictish hand or two but he had no defence against a spear thrust, and some bastard northerner might have stabbed the loyal beast. Gawain would have upped his pace if he could, but advancing at a hobble was painful enough, and he forced himself to be patient as Iestyn helped him along.

After a tortuous walk they got down the slope and past the houses, and into the open space before the hill. Bodies littered the grass, growing thicker as they went up the slope, and Gawain tried to take comfort that though many a local man had fallen, most of the dead were fur-clad Picts. Men with the Red Fox on their shields were wandering among them and spearing any who still lived, while others tried to help the wounded Venicones as best they could. Gawain remembered that poor Cethin was still lying dead beneath the causeway, and took bitter comfort that the steward must have died well; one of the Picts there had been wounded after all, and for a man who'd never fought in his life, Cethin had not disgraced himself. *Who will watch over this place now?* Even if Berlak came back from his sulking, Cethin had said that he and Luned spent almost no time here. Gawain pushed the thought away for now. He had more immediate concerns.

As they slowly clambered up the hill, Gawain started scanning the bodies for any sign of Ulfric's straw-coloured hair. The Saxon gods insisted that warriors be buried with their swords, and Gaheris' men might bury him in the Christian fashion without thinking. And Gawain would need to thank his friend's shade for saving his life. He was still looking among the dead when Gareth came hurrying up, and Gawain felt cold dread fill his gut. Questions came flooding out before his brother could open his mouth.

'Gareth, are you alright? Is Halwen hurt? Are *you* hurt? Is Gaheris…?'

But Iestyn put a friendly hand on his chest, and Gawain made himself take a breath and let Gareth speak.

'I'm alright, but you have to come quickly.'

The boy's face was wet with tears and Gawain ground his teeth and began hurrying up the slope. Iestyn and Gareth kept pace with him, and a few moments later his heart almost burst with relief. Halwen, alive and beautiful, came rushing at him from a knot of people at the hall door, and without a word she flung her arms around him. Gawain let go of the axe and squeezed her back. It hurt his wounded side horribly, but it was the warmest, most wonderful feeling in the world and he ignored the pain and held her close. He could feel she was shaking and he pressed her to his chest and stroked a hand over her hair. Gareth was loitering anxiously, and after a few seconds the pair broke the embrace. Like Gareth, Halwen's face was marred with tears, and when they walked a few more paces Gawain felt his own eyes burn.

On the hall step, surrounded by the little group, Father Iain lay with his priestly robe drenched in blood. A single glance was enough to tell Gawain the wound was fatal, and he covered the distance between them in the space of a heartbeat. He collapsed to his knees beside the priest and took his hand in his. It felt so small. Iain's face was bone white and his kindly eyes were unfocused and staring. He was still breathing, albeit shallowly, and Gawain felt the old man's fingers feebly try to squeeze his hand. He squeezed back gently.

'Father?'

It came out as a hoarse whisper that even he could barely hear, but Iain's head turned a little at the sound.

'Gawain?'

Iain's voice was even softer than Gawain's was, and it sounded weak and thin. Tears were flooding down Gawain's face, but for all his frailty Iain was composed.

'The village is made safe?'

Gawain nodded.

'It is, father.'

Iain shifted his head a bare fraction.

'You are unhurt? And the others too?'

There was no need to burden him with talk of Ulfric.

'We are well, father.'

The old man managed a very small smile.

'Good. That is good.' He let out a slow sigh and closed his eyes. 'God be praised.'

Gawain squeezed his hand tighter.

'Father, you have to stay awake.'

He knew it was pointless but he didn't care. Ulfric and Drustan were already dead because of him, Iain could not die too. He found himself babbling, his voice becoming something foolish and desperate.

'Father you have to stay with me, please. Please, just sit up and say, "Gawain my boy, you're a fool to be worried". *Please*, father!'

But Iain didn't open his eyes. His slender fingers squeezed back with what little strength they had and when he spoke, his words were calm.

'You're not a boy, Gawain.'

Gawain had no answer for him. He just knelt in silence, held the old man's hand, and wept as Iain left for his heaven.

The journey home took longer than the journey north, but even on horseback Gawain had been in no shape to maintain much of a pace. Neither Berlak nor Luned had appeared to see them off from Tahrnax, and Gawain hoped quietly that someone wise could be found to replace Cethin. His death, more than the absence of their lord and lady, had hit the village hard. When all was said and done, Gawain struggled not to feel angry with Berlak. However noble his motivations, and whatever his grand plan for Britain involved, this elaborate testing could surely have been achieved in some easier way? Gawain supposed that were it not for the Green Man's challenge he and the others wouldn't have been at Tahrnax to help the locals when the Picts arrived, but Berlak could not have known that. *And when his town was threatened, he ignored it for the sake of his damned schemes.* Yet for all his disapproval of what Berlak had done, Gawain had to admit he was curious about what his plans for him had been. *Well, you're not likely to find out now.*

Gawain put it from his mind and did his best to concentrate on what the bishop was saying. Dun Edin's longhall was full of people who were only half-listening to his waffle, but dull though it was Gawain felt he ought to do his best to stay attentive; for Iain's sake. Bishop Dyfan, almost sober for a change, had been extolling Iain's virtues for some considerable time now, and every soul in the hall had grown weary of his droning voice. The old man, white-haired, fat, and with none of Iain's wisdom or eloquence, had spent most of the feast staring open-mouthed at anything with breasts, and now that he was finally doing something sincere, he did it in the most boring way imaginable. For all his efforts, Gawain struggled not to yawn.

The eulogy seemed to last for days on end, and when it was finally over and the hall cheered and raised their cups, Gawain suspected it was mostly born of gratitude that the old bore had stopped talking. Dyfan sat down, narrowly avoided slipping from the bench, and fixed his eyes on the chest of the nearest serving girl. Just as the hall was about to relax into easy chatter, Druid Elgan stood up and raised a hand. No-one actually groaned, Elgan was at least a better speaker than Dyfan, but neither did the hall seem to relish the prospect of another grey-beard's droning. Fortunately, the druid kept things brief.

'My good friend the bishop has said near all that can be said.' He nodded towards Dyfan, who was too busy quaffing wine to notice, then went on. 'Father Iain was a man of great wisdom and kindness, and was a man for whom we all had only the highest admiration and respect. He was a credit to the God of Rome, and when his soul finds the next world may Christ greet him as a friend.'

The druid raised his cup and the hall drank, though he remained standing when they were done.

'We also mourn for the noble Peleus and his warriors, who died as heroes in an ambush set by cowards.'

There was a rumble of consent. The bodies had been discovered by the Venicones only days ago, and it was said that the the head of Peleus had been left impaled on a spear. Gawain stifled a growl; another of Lot's finest warlords, dead at the hands of the Picts.

Druid Elgan continued.

'And we mourn for two other fine men; one who was our champion of many years and whose deeds go beyond all counting, and one who was taken from us young, but who made his ancestors proud in the manner of his passing.'

The druid bowed his head first towards Burian and then to Ekbert, both of whom nodded back respectfully. Elgan raised his cup again.

'To Drustan ab Hywel, and Ulfric ab Ekbert.'

Once again the hall drank, and the familiar jolt of guilt went through Gawain's stomach. He knew that Iain would say that God had taken them north for a purpose and that Tahrnax had been saved by their efforts, but all the same Gawain couldn't forget that Iain, Ulfric and Drustan had all come north because of him. And now they were dead. He'd spoken to Ekbert and Elswid, and to Burian and his family, and no-one seemed to hold a grudge against Gawain for the deaths of their loved ones, but all the same it was no easy thing to let go of. Mabb, who had apparently adopted Gawain as his new master, nuzzled his leg beneath the table, and Gawain slipped the hound one of Una's sausages.

The next man to stand was Lot himself, and like Dyfan he knew the hall's mood well enough to keep his speech brief.

'With Drustan gone to his rest, I shall be naming a new champion on Midsummer's Day. I put forward the name of my son, Gaheris ab Lot.'

There was a round of cheering, a joyful one this time, and Gawain added his voice to it eagerly. Gaheris had not only saved them all at Tahrnax but he had long forgotten all his anger at Gawain, and when he'd found them after the battle he had embraced him and Gareth like they were his long-lost sons. He was a fine man, a cunning warrior, and had more than earned the respect of every man in that hall. The king went on after the cheer died away.

'Any man who seeks to challenge him must name himself by Midsummer's Eve, and may God favour the boldest.'

Lot would almost certainly be hoping the Huntsman gave his favour to the champion as well, but he could be politic when he wanted to and the bishop was still present, if not entirely attentive. Gawain had every faith that Gaheris would be champion, whether or not anybody decided to challenge him; either Christ or Cernunnos or both had taken an interest in his brother. Gawain wasn't sure which god it had been, but he was certain that Gaheris' arrival in Tahrnax had been the work of one of them. Burian surviving his arrow-wound and swimming the river had been a wonder all of its own, but for him to then find Gaheris had been an undeniable miracle. The eldest Lothian had only taken a minor detour from his route, and Burian had only become slightly lost as he tried to reach aid, yet the two had stumbled across each other in the space of a day, and Gaheris' trackers had scoured both sides of the Avon Du in the hopes of finding Gawain and his companions. Miracle had followed miracle, and it had ended with Gaheris' victory over the Picts. *Drustan would be proud of him.*

Thinking of the former champion drew Gawain's eyes to Burian, who was sitting beside Anna at the very end of the high table. It had been a gracious gesture of King Lot to allow him there, and though the two leaned into each other and smiled, they were respectful enough not to flaunt how close they truly were. Not that they were fooling anyone. A glance at Morgause told Gawain that she hardly approved of the pairing, but the queen was a realist and would know that forbidding Anna from seeing Burian would only encourage her to do it anyway. *A wise woman, my mother.* Gawain only hoped she maintained the same stoic attitude to him and Halwen. The queen surely still intended for him to marry Leanor of Bernicia, but that could, and *would*, have to wait.

He reached across to Halwen and squeezed her hand as the king sat down and talk resumed. Like Burian, she'd been permitted to sit at the high table purely because one of Lot's children had asked nicely, and like Burian and Anna she and Gawain took care to be modest. But they had kissed again each night on their journey south, and this time Gawain had been bright enough not to press his luck and ruin things. Halwen smiled at him.

'So, will *you* be challenging Gaheris at Midsummer?'

It was clearly a jest and Gawain smiled at the idea.

'I think I have had enough fighting for a while. Besides, do you not remember what he did to my face the last time we fought?'

Halwen's brows drew together and she tilted her head, scrutinising him.

'I suppose it's possible he *might* make you look worse, but...'

She twitched and bit back a giggle as Gawain prodded her in the ribs. She shuffled closer to him on the bench and, just about remaining in the bounds of propriety, gave him a gentle kiss on one cheek. It made Gawain feel warm down to his toes.

'You are right, of course. Best not to risk that face of yours. Besides,' she nodded over to Gaheris, 'if you damaged *his* face every girl in Dun Edin would be after your blood.'

Gawain gave her hand another squeeze and smiled.

'Every girl but you, of course?'

Halwen gave him a shocked look.

'*I* would be busy defending you from them.'

Gawain laughed. For all the pain of loss he still felt, at this moment he was undeniably happy. He was still battered and bruised from head to foot, and there'd been no glorious battle with the Green Man to brag about, but he'd surprised himself by how little he cared about that. He had done his share of fighting and come out alive without disgracing himself, and now he was home with a wonderful woman who cared for him the same way he did for her; what he had with Halwen couldn't last, they both knew that, but while it did he would cherish it. *For now at least, life is good.*

He was so busy gazing at Halwen and marvelling at his good fortune, that when Gaheris stood up he didn't even notice. It was only when the hall fell silent that he looked up at his brother. Gaheris raised his voice to the hall.

'Before I leave you all to your feasting, I will ask that once again you raise your cups.'

He held out his own and a serving man filled it to the brim. The whole hall, including Gawain and Halwen, reached for their ale.

'We have lost heroes these last few days, and we have celebrated the victory of Lothian warriors against the Picts. But this,' he indicated his overfull cup, 'is to the man who made that victory possible; a young man with heart of oak, who held a shieldwall of farmers and fisher-folk against the warband of a Pictish lord.' He looked straight at Gawain and grinned. 'A man whose courage is rivalled only by his stupidity.'

Gawain felt himself wanting to tremble with excitement, and he felt Halwen's hand on his arm as Gaheris went on.

'Even if I am to be Lothian's new champion, I have decided that Drustan's armour shall be given to Gawain in recognition of his great valour.'

For a moment Gawain almost laughed; the scale coat would need some re-working if it was going to fit him, and a moment later Halwen whispered in his ear.

'I'll have my father look at it.'

He could hear her smile, and all around the hall men and women were doing the same. He saw Burian and Gareth, Anna and Morgause, Dyfan and Elgan and even King Lot himself, all looking at him and smiling. Gawain almost felt himself redden. Gaheris deserved the glory of this victory; after all, without him it would have been a slaughter. Gawain had done little but delay the inevitable. True enough he'd killed the man who dishonoured Drustan, but the woman who'd slain Ulfric had not been found and his friend's death remained unavenged. Gawain had done no more than any other man would have, yet here Gaheris was, calling his foolish little brother a hero in front of everyone in Dun Edin. It was almost more than he could bear to hear, and when Gaheris raised his cup Gawain felt he might burst with pride.

'To my brother!'

But King Lot stood before Gaheris could drink, and he called out in a voice that echoed from the rafters.

'To my son! To Gawain, the Hero of Tahrnax!'

This time men didn't just sit to drink but *stood*. Chairs and benches scraped on the hall floor as scores of people rose to their feet and lifted their cups in the air. A cheer went up from every throat, and Gawain struggled not to grin as the hall of Dun Edin rang with a single voice.

'Gawain! Gawain! Gawain!'

Epilogue

The morning sun was pleasingly warm, though Gawain wouldn't have cared if they'd been lying in a blizzard. All the same, he supposed the fine weather had turned a wonderful morning into a perfect one, even if the sun wasn't the most vital feature of his day. He and Halwen lay on the grass outside the eastern rampart, their arms around each other and their lips meeting and parting in gentle kisses. Halwen's lips were as soft and welcoming as ever and here, out of sight of the rest of Dun Edin, it was pleasant not to have to be hurried or furtive. Here they could take their time, enjoying the sun's warmth and the contentment that came only from the arms of a loved one.

After a while they took a pause to simply lie there, and Halwen began twisting her fingers through his hair. Carefully, she removed one of the bronze rings from her red-gold locks and began braiding it into Gawain's hair instead. There was no need for words. Like Gawain she knew that what they had was on borrowed time, but there was nothing sad in the gesture. This was something of hers that would always be with him, whatever the future held. When she was done Gawain took her hand in his and kissed it, then took in a breath ready to tell Halwen that he loved her.

'Forgive me the interruption, but I must speak with you.'

The voice had come from above and behind them, and the lovers almost jumped with shock. Gawain was halfway to his feet, his heart hammering, when he realised why he knew that voice. Berlak of Tahrnax was standing only a few paces away, dressed in neither his lordly garb nor in the wild raiment of the Green Man. Today he wore the grey-white robe of a druid and carried an oaken staff in his right hand. His hair and beard were still brown streaked with silver, but something about his eyes made him seem much older than he had done a few days ago. He wore a very small smile on his face, as did the woman standing next to him.

It took Gawain a moment to recognise her as Luned. Her face was as fair as ever but her luscious dark locks were gone, replaced by red tresses that would have made Gaheris envious. Like Berlak she too wore a druid's long robe, though the staff she carried was shorter and seemed to be willow instead of oak. Gawain came to his feet, feeling awkward, embarrassed, and angry all at once, and he felt Halwen stand up just beside him. He opened his mouth but Berlak held up a hand before he could speak.

'I know that you have questions, and you have my word they shall be answered. But first I would have you both accept my thanks, and my gifts.'

He reached behind his long robes and by some magic or trickery produced an iron-rimmed shield. It looked well-made and was painted holly green, with a red Solomon's Star emblazoned across it and the Red Fox of Lothian prowling in the star's hollow centre.

Berlak handed it to Gawain, who took it somewhat awkwardly.

'My thanks, lord, I…'

But Berlak was not finished. From behind his back he somehow also produced a long-handled war-axe, and Gawain knew it as the one Berlak had once carried as the Green Man. It was a beautiful weapon, and when Berlak passed it to him Gawain could feel that the balance of the heavy axe was perfect. He felt lost for words, and had just opened his mouth to mumble another clumsy thanks when Luned cut across him.

'And for you, my child.'

She stepped towards Halwen, and Gawain saw that she was holding the green-and-gold girdle he had left behind at Maes Gwyr. For a moment Gawain felt his cheeks redden; he'd been very vague when telling Halwen of Luned's attempts to seduce him, but a glance at the robed woman told him he had nothing to fear. There was no hint of desire or jealousy about her, and Gawain suspected she had all but forgotten what passed between them in the chambers at Tahrnax's hall. *It was all just part of Berlak's damned test.* Gawain couldn't decide if he was angry or relived. Luned placed the girdle in Halwen's hands with a friendly smile.

'I gave this to Gawain before he faced his challenge at Maes Gwyr. I give it to you, as a companion worthy of his heart.'

Once again Gawain felt a flush of embarrassment but Halwen gave no sign of discomfort.

'My thanks, lady.'

Gawain decided he'd had enough of this. They weren't at Tahrnax now, this was *his* home and he would not be made to feel foolish by these people anymore. He kept courteous but made his voice firm.

'We are most grateful to you both, but now I would have my questions answered, Lord Berlak.'

The old lord smiled again.

'Berlak is not my name, my friend. Or rather, it is but one of my names.'

He straightened his back, and for some reason Gawain couldn't help but feel a little awed by him. His voice became deeper, until it was something almost sombre.

'I am Merlyn, Lord of the Stones,' he gestured towards Luned, 'this is Nimue, Lady of the Lake.'

The two druids fixed their eyes on him with an almost unnerving intensity.

'Gawain, there is much that we must speak of.'

Also by the same author

The Caledon Saga:

Wildcat

Leaping Wolf

Lion Cub

Proud Fox

About the Author

JP Harker is the pen-name of James Thomas, a mild-mannered hospital clerk and martial arts instructor from Glamorgan, South Wales. Having studied archaeology at university, specializing in Roman Britain, James first tried his hand at writing historical and fantasy fiction as a student. His first efforts were not impressive! A few years later he tried again and managed to improve, then got a little better a few years after that. Finally, in 2014 he started taking writing seriously and began work on a fantasy world, which led to the creation of the Caledon Saga. Gawain is the first book of his new series, following the early lives of Arthur's knights and the eventual formation of Camelot.

www.jpharker.co.uk

Printed in Great Britain
by Amazon

63892093R00210